THE BEAT COLLECTION

Also by Barry Miles in Virgin Books

CHARLES BUKOWSKI
JACK KEROUAC: KING OF THE BEATS
GINSBERG: A BIOGRAPHY
WILLIAM BURROUGHS: EL HOMBRE INVISIBLE

THE BEAT COLLECTION

Edited by Barry Miles

First published in Great Britain in 2005 by Virgin Books
Virgin Books Ltd
Thames Wharf Studios
Rainville Road
London
W6 9HA

A catalogue record for this book is available
from the British Library.

ISBN 1 85227 264 3

The paper used in this book is a natural, recyclable product
made from wood grown in sustainable forests. The manufacturing
process conforms to the regulations of the country of origin.

Typeset by Phoenix Photosetting, Chatham, Kent

Printed and bound in Great Britain by Creative Print & Design

CONTENTS

INTRODUCTION

The Beats used to call Times Square 'The Big Room'. Not for them the quiet tree-lined streets of Greenwich Village – that came later – but in 1944–5, it had to be Times Square: the centre of the universe, a 24-hour meeting place where servicemen and prostitutes, tourists and hustlers, cops and reporters gathered in the glaring neon for the latest news of the war. It was the energy centre of New York with its all-night cafeterias, late-night bars, cigar stores, newsstands, honking traffic and the endlessly flashing, moving neon, brighter than day.

The core Beats – Jack Kerouac, William Burroughs and Allen Ginsberg – and their close friends, Lucien Carr, Joan Vollmer and Edie Parker, first met in the two months after Christmas 1943. All but Burroughs were attending or had just left Columbia University and they lived near the campus on the edge of West Harlem. Burroughs was older, born in 1914, and had studied at Harvard and at medical school in Vienna before the war. It was through him that they met Herbert Huncke, a Times Square junkie, male prostitute and thief, with whom Burroughs shared an interest in crime and morphine. Burroughs had studied anthropology at Harvard, and he applied this to his approach to Times Square, leading his friends on a systematic study of the bars and 24-hour cafeterias on Broadway and 7th Avenue, noting the differences in clientele, intrigued by the low-life. The Beats were young, middle-class kids, torn by the petty restrictive rules of Columbia, the mindless anarchy of war, and the puritan values of the country at large. They felt alienated from the establishment and spent much of their time in the West End Bar, across from the main gate to Columbia, or in the Angle Bar on Times Square, trying to formulate a 'New Vision', as they called it, to make sense of the world as they found it.

They might have been any group of disaffected students, confused by the uncertainties of wartime and its challenge to established values, but of the core group, all three became well-known writers, known collectively as The Beat Generation. The ending of the war increased their belief that a new set of values was needed: how could life continue as before after the horrific revelations of the concentration camps and the complicity of ordinary German people, and the dropping of the atomic bomb, callously annihilating the innocent civilian population of two large Japanese cities? Clearly madness reigned under the cover of bourgeois respectability. To them, the denizens of Times Square – the junkies and prostitutes, the hustlers and thieves, the con-men, homosexuals, transvestites and outcasts engaged in their daily struggle for survival – were more real, closer to real human values, more in touch with human emotions and feelings than the uptight citizens behind their white picket fences and in the corridors of power.

The group expanded and changed; Neal Cassady, a young car thief from Denver who burned with an intense energy and enthusiasm for life and experience, was added to the circle, bringing with him wives and girlfriends and a connection to Colorado. Ginsberg met the young poet Gregory Corso shortly after he was released from jail in 1950 and he became another core member, featuring in Kerouac's books and Ginsberg's poetry. John Clellon Holmes, then trying to make it as a writer in New York, joined in their activities and later wrote about it. But they were not yet a group, they had no label.

In the end the defining word came from Herbert Huncke: 'When I said I was *beat* I was *beat*, man, I was tired, exhausted, worn out. That's what I meant.' It was Times Square hipster slang, probably originating with black musicians. The others took it up from him. In 1948, Jack Kerouac and John Clellon Holmes were sitting, talking about Gertrude Stein, Hemingway and the Lost Generation, and Holmes asked Kerouac how he thought their generation might be classified in the future. What word might characterise the young people of their circle; their wariness, their suspicion of authority, their sense of helplessness in the face of the hydrogen bomb and the heated rhetoric of the warmongers, their interest in jazz and willingness to experiment? Kerouac was particularly drawn to the young hipsters of the Times Square area whom he thought best expressed their collective attitude: 'Being right down to it, to ourselves, because we *really* know where we are – and a weariness with all the forms, all the conventions of the world . . . it's something like that.

So I guess you might say we're a *beat* generation.' Holmes caught it immediately, 'That's it!' he said. He later defined it much as Huncke had done, to mean dead beat, worn out, the view from the bottom where everything is etched with a sharp clarity; what Holmes later called being 'at the bottom of your personality, looking up.'

Holmes used the term in a 1952 piece in the *New York Times* headlined 'This is the Beat Generation' and the phrase caught on; journalists are always looking for shorthand labels and this was a good angle, rather like Juvenile Delinquents. In 1958, after the Russians had launched the world's first artificial satellite, *Sputnik*, the phrase was further refined in an article about the bohemian community living in the North Beach area of San Francisco by *San Francisco Chronicle* columnist Herb Caen who combined the two threats to American society and called them Beatniks. (A decade later he was also credited with coining the term Hippie.)

Kerouac saw it as having a more saintly meaning, defining it as 'beatitude', something stemming from his Catholicism, but he also identified a belief in spontaneity, of being right here in the present and acting on the impulse, unconstrained by conventions and morality. In one of the best known quotes from *On The Road*, Kerouac wrote: 'The only people for me are the mad ones, the ones who are mad to live, mad to talk, mad to be saved, desirous of everything at the same time, the ones who never yawn or say a commonplace thing but burn, burn, burn like fabulous yellow Roman candles exploding like spiders across the stars and in the middle you see the blue centrelight pop and everybody goes "Awww!" ' As far as society was concerned Kerouac and his friends really *were* mad, and certifiably so.

Of the core group of Kerouac, Burroughs and Ginsberg, Burroughs was the first to be deemed crazy. After attempts to join the navy and the fledgling CIA, Burroughs found himself in 1940 living in the Hotel Taft in New York City, playing out the endgame of an unhappy love affair with a part-time prostitute named Jack Anderson. After being evicted when hotel security found them in bed together, Burroughs moved to Anderson's Greenwich Village rooming house, but the walls were thin and through them he could hear Anderson entertaining male clients and partying with women friends. Engulfed by loneliness, distracted by lacklove and Anderson's indifference, Burroughs bought a pair of poultry shears and, mirroring Van Gogh's desperate plea for attention, he cut off the last joint of the little finger of his left hand. Whereas Van Gogh presented his ear to a horror-struck prostitute, Burroughs took his severed finger to his psychoanalyst and found himself, a few hours later, in Bellevue where he was diagnosed as a paranoid-schizophrenic. His father flew in from St. Louis and transferred him to the private Payne-Whitney clinic where he remained for a month before being taken to St. Louis and the care of his worried parents.

Jack Kerouac had hoped to join the war as a pilot in the Navy Air Force V-12 programme but when he took the examination in March 1943 he failed, and was sent instead to undergo basic training at boot camp in Newport, Rhode Island. Kerouac's eagerness for experience and action did not mix well with the regimentation and regulations of military life. One rule he found particularly objectionable was the prohibition on smoking before breakfast. He had only been in the navy three weeks when he appeared at morning parade with a cigarette dangling defiantly between his lips. The sergeant major inspecting the troops smacked it out of his mouth. Jack's reaction was to haul off and punch him. He lay down his rifle and made his way to the library where the military police arrested him. Jack later summed up the event: 'I was in the navy, but I was discharged after two months. Schizoid personality. They gave me a rifle and they sent me marching out on the drill field, right turn, left turn, and I said, "Aw, I don't want to do this," and I went to the library and I started to read.'

The military psychiatrist asked about his emotional life and paid close attention when he said that he was more attached to his male friends, both spiritually and emotionally, than to his girlfriends. Asked if he was the centre of attention in any group, Jack unhesitatingly said yes and explained that he dedicated his life to having experiences in order to write about them, 'sacrificing myself on the altar of art.' It came as no surprise when they diagnosed him as schizophrenic; suffering from *dementia praecox* as it was called in those days. In May 1943 he was given an honourable discharge for having an 'indifferent character'. He was not a coward – as a merchant marine he was soon to brave the German submarines waiting in the cold waters of the North Atlantic – it was the military discipline that he could not accept.

Allen Ginsberg, the youngest of the group, was not pronounced mad until 1949. Of all the Beats, it was Ginsberg in particular who romanticised Herbert Huncke as some sort of saintly fallen angel, even though Huncke had stolen $200-worth of valuable books when Allen had allowed him to stay in an apartment he was flat-sitting for a friend. At 8 a.m. one snowy morning, Huncke appeared once more at Allen's door having been released from Riker's Island ten days before and having lived on the streets for ten days on a diet of Benzedrine and coffee. He was semi-delirious and suicidal, his shoes were soaking wet, his feet bloody: 'Who walked all night with their shoes filled with blood on the snowbank docks waiting for a door in the East River to open . . .' as Ginsberg later wrote in 'Howl'. Allen invited him in, bathed his feet, and slowly coaxed him back to life. Taking advantage of Ginsberg's passivity, Huncke began to take over the apartment, rearranging the furniture, installing two of his underworld friends, Jack Melody and Vicki Russell, as room-mates and filling the rooms with stolen goods, so that eventually Allen had to sleep on the couch and keep his clothes and possessions in his desk as Huncke had appropriated his dresser.

Dimly realising that this could only end badly, Ginsberg decided to remove all incriminating papers from the flat and on April 22, 1949 he asked to be driven to his brother's house in Queens to store them. But it was a stolen car and filled with stolen clothes. When Jack Melody made a wrong way turn into a one-way street in Queens, a police prowl car signalled for him to stop. Instead he floored the accelerator and Ginsberg found himself in a high-speed car chase. After six blocks the car hit the curb and turned over twice coming to rest upside down with Allen inside, his glasses broken, clutching his journals. 'I had a complete, final, and awful sense of what I might call Divine Wrath,' he wrote.

While Huncke was returned to Riker's Island, two of Ginsberg's Columbia University professors, Lionel Trilling and Mark Van Doren, pulled enough strings for him to be sent to the Columbia Presbyterian Psychiatric Institute where he spent eight months being taught how to be normal, heterosexual, and to fit into American consumer society. While there he met fellow patient Carl Solomon, to whom 'Howl' is dedicated. To Allen, it was Carl, Neal Cassady and his other friends, 'the best minds of my generation' who had all been driven mad by American society which was then at its most complacent, conformist and regimented.

Though America had the world's highest standard of living, the actual quality of life was poor. Millions of Americans had moved to the soulless suburbs where they lived in virtually identical stucco boxes with sexless twin beds and picture windows to show off their spotless lives. The men commuted each day and wore their hair in crew cuts like convicts, Prussian Military Academy style, while their bored wives devoted their time to home-making. Wife swapping parties and alcoholism were rife. These were the days of rabid anti-communism, of the House of un-American Activities and the McCarthy witch-hunts, when large numbers of Americans were brainwashed into believing that it was somehow patriotic to buy a new model car each year; 'What's good for General Motors is good for America' the slogan went. It was a society based on runaway consumerism, where people thought what *Time-Life* and the church told them to think; a society based on fear, where people built bomb shelters and worried that the Russian hordes would invade at any moment. It was a society based on lies.

The Beats identified the sickness in society, the refusal to see reality. *Naked Lunch*, according to Burroughs, was when you finally saw what was *really* on the end of the fork. Ginsberg showed how the authoritarian system ground down the individual, distorting their emotions and psyches to fit into conformist, consuming society. He identified 'the madman bum and angel' who escaped, injured, flawed, but still mentally alive, and proclaimed their sainthood. Kerouac reinvigorated the reader, showing what freedom could mean, should mean, proposing challenges, excitement, kicks! He was the biggest threat of all.

Naturally the Beats were not the only ones to challenge the appalling state America had arrived at but they proved to be the most visible targets. Their rejection of the American Dream provoked intemperate fury from both church and state; the former because the Beats were opposed to censorship, rejected traditional puritan American family values, and believed instead in free love and free-ranging eroticism. For the latter, J. Edgar Hoover over at the FBI, saw them as a direct threat to society, classifying them along with 'eggheads' and 'commies' as one of the three main threats to the American way of life.

The original trio of madmen fanned out to spread the word and by the mid-fifties all of the original group had dispersed: Burroughs first to Mexico City, then to Tangier; Neal Cassady and Allen Ginsberg to San Francisco, where Ginsberg energised an existing poetry scene into what became known as the San Francisco Poetry Renaissance. Here he encountered Lawrence Ferlinghetti, whose

City Lights Bookshop provided a centre for the local poets and whose company was to publish Ginsberg's first book, *Howl and Other Poems*. Ginsberg met poets Gary Snyder, Lew Welch and Philip Whalen who had all been room-mates at Reed College, and introduced them to Jack Kerouac who, as usual, was flitting between his friends. Together with Michael McClure, another key member of the group who wrote memorably about the scene in his book *Scratching the Beat Surface*, this group of poets introduced ecological issues into the Beat consciousness which had previously been essentially urban in character. McClure, along with Snyder and Whalen, read at the legendary Six Gallery when Ginsberg performed 'Howl' in public for the first time. A community developed in North Beach, traces of which exist even today; a certain atmosphere in the old Italian coffee shops, old Beat characters still propping up the bar at Vesuvio's next door to City Lights Bookshop or at Specs across the street.

After the success of 'Howl', Ginsberg, accompanied by his new lover Peter Orlovsky, returned to New York where a home-grown poetry scene had also emerged, parallel to, rather than part of, the Beat Generation. Known as the New York School, it centred on John Ashbery and Kenneth Koch but also included Frank O'Hara, who spanned the two groups. This was a brief stop-off for Ginsberg who was on his way to join Burroughs in Tangier. Jack Kerouac got there first and had already typed part of Burroughs' *The Naked Lunch* before Ginsberg and Orlovsky arrived. By 1958, Ginsberg, Gregory Corso and William Burroughs were all living in the Beat Hotel in Paris, the last great communal activity by this group of writers. It was here that Burroughs finished *The Naked Lunch*, Ginsberg began 'Kaddish' and Corso wrote 'Bomb' and most of his other poems included here.

The Beats not only questioned society's norms, but challenged existing literary forms: they were advocates of free verse at a time when even this was seen as a daring departure; they wrote about subject matter that few people had dared to describe before, and were the subjects of numerous obscenity cases because of it; they experimented with the very nature of fiction and of literature, including tape-recording transcriptions, bits of ad copy, strange words not in the dictionary, slang and obscenities never before seen in poetry or prose. Back in New York, Greenwich Village, always a centre of bohemian and artistic activity, was now filled with

Beatniks; both genuine and weekend. The old Italian coffee shops around Bleecker and MacDougal began to feature poetry readings and the bars were filled with abstract expressionist painters and poets and with writers working on the newly started *Village Voice* newspaper. For every poet like Diane DiPrima and LeRoi Jones there was a weekender who donned a beret, sandals and a French Breton fisherman's sweater, picked up a pair of bongos and headed off to the cafes off Bleecker and MacDougal. Many were students at New York University, which has its campus in the middle of the Village, and others were simply getting in on the act. Beatniks became good copy for the newspapers and tourists began to visit the area to look at them. Photographer Fred McDarrah and poet Ted Joans took advantage of the media interest to launch a tongue-in-cheek organisation called Rent-a-Beatnik, where impoverished poets would show up at society parties and read their poetry or play bongos. There were books of cartoons, spoofs in *Mad* magazine, and a lot of young people who arrived in the Village simply because they aspired to the free lifestyle that was promised, much as hippies arrived in San Francisco a decade later. The Beats of course continued right on through the sixties and seventies and many of the younger ones are still living; however we have concentrated here on the first energetic flowering, the youthful good humour and fresh insight of these remarkable writers.

Barry Miles 2005

THE ORIGINAL BEATS: NEW YORK 1944–53

JACK KEROUAC
1922–1969

HOME AT CHRISTMAS

I<small>T'S A</small> S<small>UNDAY AFTERNOON</small> in New England just three days before Christmas—Ma's making the roast in the kitchen range, also tapioca pudding so when Sister Nin comes in from outdoors with the shovel she's been wielding in the blizzard there are cold waves of snowy air mixing with the heat steams of tapioca over the stove and in my mouth I can taste whipped cream cold from the icebox on the hot pudding tonight.

While Ma cooks she also sits at the round kitchen table reading the *Boston American*—Pa's in the parlor playing the Gospel Singers of Sunday cigar-smoke funnies time—I'm getting ready to take my big blizzard walk into the Massachusetts Shroud begins just down the end of dirt road Phebe Avenue, I'm rummaging in the closet for my hockey stick which will be my walking-stick and feeling-stick to find where puddles and creeklets have disappeared under two feet of snow this day.

"Where you goin'?"

"Take my walk."

"Be careful don't fall in the ice—You're goin' to your Pine Brook?—Oh you're crazy you!" (exasperation)

I start out, down the porch steps, overshoes, woolcap, coat, corduroy pants, mittens—There are Christmas wreaths in all the windows of sweet Phebe—No sign of G.J. or Billy with the kids sliding on the park slope, no sign of them on their porch except

G.J.'s sister in her coat all wrapped communing with the plicking fall of vast snows in a silence of her own, girl-like, watching it pile on the porch rail, the little rills, sadnesses, mysteries—She waves—I plod down off our Sisshoveled walk into Mrs. Quinn's unshoveled walk where the going is deep, profound, happy—No shoveled walks all the way to Billy's where bigbrother sixfoot Jack has worked, in muffler with pink cheeks and white teeth, laughing— Black birds in the black cherry tree, and in the new snow breadcrumbs, bird tweak tracks, a little dot of kitty yellow, a star blob of plopsnow ball against Old MacArthur's wreathy front door—O the clean porches of New England in the holy dry snow that's drifting across new painted planks to pile in corners over rubber doormats, sleds, overshoes—The steam in the windows, the frost, the faces looking out—And over the sandbank now and down on semi-snow-plowed Phebe comes the great fwoosh of hard stormwind from the river cracking leafless shrubs in stick-unison, throwing swirls of coldsifted power, pure, the freezing freshness everywhere, the sand frozen solid underneath—

Down at the end of Phebe I'm in the middle of the road now preparing my big Arab strides for the real business of crossing miles of field and forest to my wanted Brook which in summer's a rendezvous of swimmers crossing gold and greenleaf day, bees of bugs, hay, haze, but now the gigantic Snow King has laid his drape upon the world, locked it in new silence, all you hear is the profound higher-than-human-ear screaming of snow radios bedazzling and electrifying the air like orgones and spermatazoas in a Universe Dance—They start black specks from heaven, swirl to avoid my gaze, fall white and ploppy on my nose—I turn my face up to the sweet soft kiss of Heaven—My feet are getting cold, I hurry on—Always with a smile of my numb cheeks and pinked lips I think (remembering movies) how really comfortable it would be to lie down and go to sleep in the soft thick snow, head rested—I plod, the hockey stick trails after—I go through the sandbank draw and rise to survey the sand field bordered on the other side by a cut of earth with saplings and boulders—I cluck up my horse and off we gallop in a snowbound Westerner to the scene, deep, the sand field is all milky creamy waves of smooth level snow, my blasphemous impertinence tracks make a sad plod in the smoothness—I jump up the cut, stand to survey further vast fields stretching a mile to the wall of pines, the forest of Pine

Brook in the unbelievable riot murk beyond, the momentous swing of other swirlstorms.

One last look at Phebe, turning, I see the sweet rooftops of life, of man, of mother and father and children, my heart aches to go back home, I see the dear smokewhip of chimneys, the innocent fall of snow from roofs, the bedangled icicles, the little piteous fences outlined in all that numb null white, the tracks of people, the gleeful steplets of humans twinkling and twittering across the snow and already again over the sandbank ridge a great pall of wind and snow sweeping to fill holes with soft new outline—The mystery—Tears in my eyes from cold and wonder I turn and strike across the plain— The grief of birch that's bent and wintering, the strange mist—Far off the white story frame house in the pine woods stands proud, families are in there furying, living—

The left field of our baseball field is lost—Where the spring bubbles from short right I can see just snow and just one hint of blackening snow where waters below have formed a slush and darking ice—Behind me now I can see my footsteps in silence and sadness of white distance filling, forming, growing vaguer, returning to the macrocosmos of even snow from the microcosmos of my striving—and far back of that and now by distance seeable where before by nearness not, the vague unbelievable hardly-discernible caped gray smoke stacks of the mills across the river and the dim smoke urging to rise from their warm Dickensian interiors of grime, labor, personal involvements among dye vats to the universe of the blizzard oversweeping all—

I reach the end of the plain, go up the wagon path past the backstop homeplate pines, the rocks, past the Greek farm on the left now stilled from Cretan ripple olive peace of summers to frost squat Winter—The top of the hill, the view of the woods, the descent into the woods—The pond at the bottom of the hill, the star beneath the ice in the bottom of the pond, the ice skaters thronging by, an old La Salle with a mattress in the back clonking by and sloshing in the snowplow's flat—I circle the pond, the houses, the French Canadian *paisans* are stomping their feet on still-screened porches, Christmas trees on their backs—Merry Christmas zings in the air—It darkens, dusk's about to come, I've got to hurry, the first heartbreaking Christmas light comes on red and blue in a little farm window across the locked pond—My nose snuffles, my hands the back of em are like thronged red leather—Off the road and into the country path, the fear of shrouded woods ahead—No more houses now, just bushes and pines and boulders and occasional clearings, occasional woodpiles beautifully wreathed with a snow crown—The jump over the little property wire fence, the old tree base where black rocks of Indian Summer kid fires show stark dark through iced snowtops, remnant pieces of charred wood, the pine fronds gray as dead birds—Somewhere above, the coalblack crow is yawking, cr-a-a-a-ck, c-r-a-a-ck, I see the flop of raven twit limbs battering onward through treetop twigs of aerial white to a hole in the heart of the forest, to the central pine and pain of my aching desire, the real Christmas is hiding somewhere from me and it is still, it is holy, it is dark, it is insane, the crow broods there, some Nativity darker than Christianity, with Wise Men from underground, a Virgin Mary of the ice and snow, a Joseph of the trees, a Jesus like a star—a Bethlehem of pinecones, rocks, snakes—Stonewalls, eyes—

But dark gray is the nightfall reality now, I plow my hockey stick in front of me, sometimes it sinks three feet in culverts, holes—I jump and stagger and grind—Now a solid wall of pine is overhead, through the dark skinny limbs I can see loured gloomy night is over-shadowing the blizzard's white shadow—Darker, deeper, the forest densens like a room—Numbbuzzing silences ring my ears, I pause to listen, I hear stars—I hear one dog, one farmer-door slam a mile away—I hear a hoot of sledders, a keen shrill of littlegirl—I hear the tick of snowflake on snow, on limb—Ice is forming on my eyebrows—I come haunting, emerging from the forest, go down the hill to the brook, the stonewall has crystal icing in the heavy winter dim—Black bleak lines in the sky—my mouth is awed open, vapors puff out, it's stopped snowing and I've begun to sense a blue scene in the new night—Soon I see one star above—I reach the brook, it flows under jagged ice caps black as ink, gurgly, silver at the ice rim, cold steaming between blanketwhite banks to its destinations and rivers down—I follow in the gloom—Our diving board's all white, alone, unsupple, stiffwooded in wintertime—Our trapeze hangs looping, dull, iceroped—

"Aaooo!" I yell in the one-room world—My stick penetrates no bottom, I've found a traphole, I walk around cautiously, follow the river bank—Suddenly there's an orange feeling in the air, the sun somewhere has pirouetted protruding limbs into the mass of brass and iron blizzards, silver's being rouged by the blast-works of the real hidden tropic sky—An Arabian Nights blue spreads blue-icing in the West, the Evestar sparks and shivers in the blanket, one lank icicle suddenly stabs from its center to the earth, dissolves—Cold. No more snowfalls, now the faint howl winds of the New England bring Alaskan shivers from the other hill, down my collar—

I leave the black brook, see the first and last touch of orange on the deepwaters, I know it's beautiful now and everything is good, I hurry back to my city—The path follows the brook, turns off in tangled tragic brushwood, goes deep across a cornfield—I hurry in a semi circling road back across my pond jumping path to the top of Moody Street where again the snowplow's work is piled in double rumps each side, my liberated feet moving in snowshoe flopping jingling gladness—There stands the white Colonial house, on the iron lawn the Christmas-glittering spruce, the noble snowy porch, fresh beginnings of a cocktail party inside—I've reached the top of the hill overlooking all Lowell.

And there she is in the keen blue winternight, be-starred above, the round brown sadface of the City Hall clock in her granite tower a mile and a half away, the speechless throat of throbbing red neons against distant redbrick of bowling alleys, business, Squares, Chinese restaurants—the giant river scything white and black around, from wilderness of hoar to wilderness of hoar and sea—The thunder and the rumble everywhere in the roundandround horizon phantom night, the distant snake of a hundred-car freight (Boston & Maine), the clean snow smoke in the new snow plain, the red glow of the locomotive's boilers, the distant two-long-one-short-one-long howl at a countryroad crossing, the lone wee caboose at the rear drawn to other worlds, to deeper night—The blue mill eternity windows, sighing froth of falls, reflections of the city actual sad in river's ice—And the one long thoroughfare Moody Street from my feet ribboning clear down Pawtucketville suburb and over the river and down the dense fantastic humaned Little Canada to the downtown thrill—Clear. Cold. Immortal.

I start home down the middle of the plowed street, joyous cries on all sides of sliding kids, the run, the thap of feet, the slap of the sled down, the crumpy ride of the runners over nostalgic snow, rock scrapes, sparks like stars—The scarved bundled gleechildren of New England screeching, the black and white fantasy of their turmoil—Sister Marie is yelling irritably at her brother Ray down the level ice wood of the tenement "Yes, I'm going, yes I'm going. I told you a hundred times!" The wash hangs stiff and frozen, long underwear stands by itself hanged, brown porchlights are on where the mother is packing the frozen wash in fragrant piles—Little tiny nameless infant bundled-to-the-ears sits brooding in the snow like Shakespeare's bird, the wreathed window's golden with Christmas behind him, he's looking and wondering: "Where was I born and what is my name? Roland Lambert? Roland Lambert? Who is that, Roland Lambert? Who are you Roland? Hello Mister that passes—" I wave my hand, my footsteps squeak and squidge in the tightpacked snow—I come down deeper in the joy of people.

Past Mr. Vernon, the white houses, the spruce, the lost parochial white yard of night, the concrete wall, the first grocery store— Screams, snow slush, traffic ahead of me—Oilstove heat rushes down dim hallways, out the raw door—There's Al Roberts throwing a snowball at Joe Plouffe, another one, crazy crisscrossing snowballs, hoots, whoopees—The boys are ducking into the brown scarred door of the club for a brew—There's Jim with his Christmas tree, his rubbers are too low, the snow spills into his shoes, against his silk socks, he yells: "Last damn time I'm gonna buy a Christmas tree!" Mrs. T. is yelling to Mrs. H. across the wash rope of the court: "What time ya goin?"—Doors slam, buses ball by, cars race motors in drifts sending blue exhaust in the blue purity—Keen. That same star shudders exploding on the roof of the church where candles flicker—There go the old ladies of the parish to their evening vespers, bundled in black coats, white faced, gray brushed-back hair, their poor little fragile hands hidden in muffs of indoor prayer—Golden light spills from Blezan's store onto the scuffled sidewalk where the gang stands wrangling, I go in to buy my Old Nick and Clark's, browse at my usual comic books and pulp magazines—The wood stove is red hot in the back, there's the smell of heated overshoes, snow wet floors, infolded night, smoke—I hurry down Gershom, past the snowball fights, the yoo-hoos, the proud adults in big coats bundling off to social evenings, adjusting scarves, opening garage doors, guffawing—The rosy faced girls are hurrying to the bus, the show, the dance—Sad is the long fence of the long yard and the great high white frozen tree where the sick boy lives— I see him in the window, watching—Little narrow Sarah Avenue hasn't got a window that's not red or green or blue, not one sidewalk unmusical with shovels—Wearily I come to the corner, turn up Phebe, my three mile circle's complete, come to my house on slow wet sodden feet, glad—

Everything is saved. There's heat and warm joy in my house. I linger at the window looking in. My heart breaks to see they're moving so slowly, with such dear innocence within, they don't realize time and death will catch them—not now. Ma moves to lift the pot with such a bemused and serious hardly-knowing goodness and sadness—My father's huge still presence, his thighs in the chair, the absent-minded darkin-thought face, so wordless, unexplainable, sad—My sister bending over her adolescent fingernails so preoccupied, ravenously attentive in the dream—When I open the door they look up blandly, with blue eyes—I stand facing them all red-faced and frozen—

"Well—it's about time! You missed your supper!—The roast is in the oven, it's not as hot any more—Your mashed potatoes are almost cold—Sit down, crazy!"

I sit at the sparking table in the bright warm light, ready. She brings me a big helping, glass of milk, bread, butter, tapioca pudding with whipped cream.

"When you're finished eating we're going to go get the Christmas tree and put it up, ah?"

"Yes!"

"Eat, honey, after your big walk you must be hungry."

That night in bed I can still see the great bulging star white as ice beating in the dark field of heaven among the lesser glittering arrays, I can see its reflection in an icicle that depends from an eave above my window, I can hear my winter apple tree cracking black limbs in frost, see the Milky Way all far and cold and cragdeep in Time—I smell the softcoal heat of the furnace in the cellar—Soon dawn, the rosy spread over pure snowfields, the witless winter bird with his muffly feathers inward—My sleep is deep in New England wintertime night.

JAZZ OF THE BEAT GENERATION

OUT WE JUMPED in the warm mad night hearing a wild tenorman's bawling horn across the way going "EE-YAH! EE-YAH!" and hands clapping to the beat and folks yelling "Go, go, go!" Far from escorting the girls into the place, Dean was already racing across the street with his huge bandaged thumb in the air yelling "Blow, man, blow!" A bunch of colored men in

Saturday night suits were whooping it up in front. It was a sawdust saloon, all wood, with a small bandstand near the john on which the fellows huddled with their hats on blowing over people's heads, a crazy place, not far from Market Street, in the dingy skid-row rear of it, near Harrison and the big bridge causeway; crazy floppy women wandered around sometimes in their bathrobes, bottles clanked in alleys. In back of the joint in a dark corridor beyond the splattered toilets, scores of men and women stood against the wall drinking wine-spodi-odi and spitting at the stars . . . wine, whiskey and beer. The behatted tenorman was blowing at the peak of a wonderfully satisfactory free idea, a rising and falling riff that went from "EE-yah!" to a crazier "EE-de-lee-yah!" and blasted along to the rolling crash of butt-scarred drums hammered by a big brutal-looking curl-sconced Negro with a bullneck who didn't give a damn about anything but punishing his tubs, crash, rattle-ti-boom crash. Uproars of music and the tenorman *had it* and everybody knew he had it. Dean was clutching his head in the crowd and it was a mad crowd. They were all urging that tenorman to hold it and keep it with cries and wild eyes; he was raising himself from a crouch and going down again with his horn, looping it up in a clear cry above the furor. A six-foot skinny Negro woman was rolling her bones at the man's hornbell, and he just jabbed it at her, "Ee! ee! ee!" He had a foghorn tone; his horn was taped; he was a shipyard worker and he didn't care. Everybody was rocking and roaring; Galatea and Alice with beers in their hands were standing on their chairs shaking and jumping. Groups of colored studs stumbled in from the street falling over one another to get there. "Stay with it man!" roared a man with a foghorn voice, and let out a big groan that must have been heard clear to Sacramento, "Ah-haa!"—"Whoo!" said Dean. He was rubbing his chest, his belly, his T-shirt was out, the sweat splashed from his face. Boom, kick, that drummer was kicking his drums down the cellar and rolling the beat upstairs with his murderous sticks, rattlety-boom! A big fat man was jumping on the platform making it sag and creak. "Yoo!" The pianist was only pounding the keys with spread-eagled fingers, chords only, at intervals when the great tenorman was drawing breath for another blast of phrase, Chinese chords, they shuddered the piano in every timber, chink and wire, *boing!* The tenorman jumped down from the platform and just stood buried in the crowd blowing around; his hat was over his eyes; somebody pushed it back for him. He just hauled back and stamped his foot and blew down a hoarse baughing blast, and drew breath, and raised the horn and blew high wide and screaming in the air. Dean was directly in front of him with his face glued to the bell of the horn, clapping his hands, pouring sweat on the man's keys; and the man noticed and laughed in his horn a long quivering crazy mule's hee-haw and everybody else laughed and they rocked and rocked; and finally the tenorman decided to blow his top and crouched down and held a note in high C for a long time as everything else crashed along skittely-boom and the cries increased and I thought the cops would come swarming from the nearest precinct.

It was just a usual Saturday night goodtime, nothing else; the bebop winos were wailing away, the workingman tenors, the cats who worked and got their horns out of hock and blew and had their women troubles, and came on in their horns with a will, saying things, a lot to say, talkative horns, you could almost hear the words and better than that the harmony, made you hear the way to fill up blank spaces of time with the tune and very consequence of your hands and breath and dead soul; summer, August 1949, and Frisco blowing mad, the dew on the muscat in the interior fields of Joaquin and down in Watsonville the lettuce blowing, the money flowing for Frisco so seasonal and mad, the railroads rolling, extraboards roaring, crates of melons on sidewalks, bananas coming off elevators, tarantulas suffocating in the new crazy air, chipped ice and the cool interior smells of grape tanks, cool bop hepcats standing slumped with horn and no lapels and blowing like Wardell, like Brew Moore softly . . . all of it insane, sad, sweeter than the love of mothers yet harsher than the murder of fathers. The clock on the wall quivered and shook; nobody cared about that thing. Dean was in a trance. The tenorman's eyes were fixed straight on him; he had found a madman who not only understood but cared and wanted to understand more and much more than there was, and they began duelling for this; everything came out of the horn, no more phrases, just cries, cries, "Baugh" and down to "Beep!" and up to "EEEEE!" and down to clinkers and over to sideways echoing horn-sounds and horse-laughs and he tried everything, up, down, sideways, upside down, dog fashion, horizontal, thirty degrees, forty degrees and finally he fell back in somebody's arms and gave up and everybody pushed around and yelled "Yes, yes, he done blowed that one!" Dean wiped himself with his handkerchief.

Up steps Freddy on the bandstand and asks for a slow beat and looks sadly out the open door over people's heads and begins singing "Close Your Eyes." Things quiet down for a minute. Freddy's wearing a tattered suède jacket, a purple shirt with white buttons, cracked shoes and zoot pants without press; he didn't care. He looked like a pimp in Mecca, where there are no pimps; a barren woman's child, which is a dream; he looked like he was beat to his socks; he was down, and bent, and he played us some blues with his vocals. His big brown eyes were concerned with sadness, and the singing of songs slowly and with long thoughtful pauses. But in the second chorus he got excited and embraced the mike and jumped down from the bandstand and bent to it and to sing a note he had to touch his shoe tops and pull it all up to blow, and he blew so much he staggered from the effect, he only recovered himself in time for the next long slow note. "Mu-u-u-u-sic pla-a-a-a-a-a-a-ay!" He leaned back with his face to the ceiling, mike held at his fly. He shook his shoulders, he gave the hip sneer, he swayed. Then he leaned in almost falling with his pained face against the mike. "Ma-a-a-ke it dream-y for dan-cing"—and he looked at the street outside, Folsom, with his lips curled in scorn—"while we go ro-man-n-n-cing"—he staggered sideways—"Lo-o-o-ove's holi-da-a-a-ay"—he shook his head with disgust and weariness at the whole world—"Will make it seem"— what would it make it seem?—everybody waited, he mourned—"O—kay." The piano hit a chord. "So baby come on and just clo-o-o-o-se your pretty little ey-y-y-es"—his mouth quivered, offered; he looked at us, Dean and me, with an expression that seemed to say "Hey now, what's this thing we're all putting down in this sad brown world"—and then he came to the end of his song and for this there had to be elaborate preparations during which time you could send all the messages to Garcia around the world twelve times and what difference did it make to anybody because here we were dealing with the pit and prune juice of poor beat life itself and the pathos of people in the Godawful streets, so he said and sang it, "Close—your—" and blew it way up to the ceiling with a big voice that came not from training but feeling and that much better, and blew it through to the stars and on up—"Ey-y-y-y-y-y-es" and in arpeggios of applause staggered off the platform ruefully, broodingly, nonsatisfied, artistic, arrogant. He sat in the corner with a bunch of boys and paid no attention to them. They gave him beers. He looked down and wept. He was the greatest.

Dean and I went over to talk to him. We invited him out to the car. In the car he suddenly yelled "Yes! ain't nothing I like better than good kicks! Where do we go?" Dean jumped up and down in the seat giggling maniacally. "Later! later!" said Freddy. "I'll get my boy to drive us down to Jamson's Nook, I got to sing. Man I *live* to sing. Been singing 'Close Your Eyes' for a month—I don't want to sing nothing else. What are you two boys up to?"

We told him we were going to New York tomorrow. "Lord, I ain't never been there and they tell me it's a real jumping town but I ain't got no cause complaining where I am. I'm married you know." "Oh yes?" said Dean lighting up. "And where is the little darling tonight and I bet she's got a lots of nice friends . . . man . . ." "What do you mean?" said Freddy looking at him half-smiling out of the corner. "I tole you I was married to her, didn't I?"—"Oh yes, Oh yes," blushed Dean. "I was just asking. Maybe she's got a couple of friends downtown, or somethin', you know man, a ball, I'm only lookin for a ball, a gang ball, man."—"Yah, what's the good of balls, life's too sad to be ballin all the time, Jim," said Freddy lowering his eye to the street. "Shee-it," he said, "I ain't got no money and I don't care tonight."

We went back in for more. The girls were so disgusted with Dean and I for jumping around with everybody else that they had left by now, gone to Jamson's Nook on foot; the car we'd come in, and had to push from down Mission, wouldn't run anyway. We saw a horrible sight in the bar; a white hipster fairy of some kind had come in wearing a Hawaiian shirt and was asking the big bull-necked drummer if he could sit in. The musicians looked at him suspiciously. He sat at the tubs and they started the beat of a blues number and he began stroking the snares with soft goofy bop brushes, swaying his neck with that complacent Reich-analyzed ecstasy that doesn't mean anything but too much T and soft foods and goofy kicks in cafeterias and pads at dawn and on the cool order. But he didn't care. The musicians looked at him and said, "Yeah, yeah, that's what the man does, shh-ee-eet." He smiled joyously into space and kept the beat with butterfly brushes, softly, with bop subtleties, a giggling rippling background for big solid foghorn blues. The big Negro bull-neck drummer sat waiting for his turn to come back. "What that man doing?" he said. "Play the music," he said. "What in hell!" he said. "Shh-ee-eet!" and looked away red-eyed. Freddy's boy showed up at this moment; he was a little taut Negro with a great big Cadillac. We all jumped in. He hunched over the wheel and blew the car clear across San Francisco without stopping once, seventy miles per hour; he was fulfilling his mission with a fixed smile, his destiny we'd expected of the rumors and songs of him. Right through traffic and nobody even noticed he was so good. Dean was in ecstasies. "Dig *this* guy, man—dig the way he sits right in that seat with the feel of the car under his both haunches, a little bit forward, to the left, against the gut of the car and he don't make any outward indication and just balls that jack and can talk all night while doing it, only thing is he doesn't bother with life, listen to them, O man the things, the things, he lets Freddy do that, and Freddy's his boy, and tells him about life, listen to them, O man the things ... the things I could—I wish—let's not stop, man, we've got to keep going now!" And Freddy's boy wound around a corner and bowled us right in front of Jamson's Nook and was parked. "Yes!" yelled Dean. A cab squeaked to a stop in the street; out of it jumped a skinny seventy-year-old withered little Negro preacherman who threw a dollar bill at the cabby and yelled "Blow!" and ran into the club pulling on his coat (just come out of work) and dashed right through the downstairs bar yelling "Go, go, go!" and stumbled upstairs almost falling on his face and blew the door open and fell into the jazz session room with his hands out to support him against anything he might fall on, and he fell right on Lampshade who was reduced to working as a waiter in Jamson's Nook that summer (the great Lampshade whom I'd seen shout the blues with veins helling in his neck and his overcoat on), and the music was there blasting and blasting and the preacherman stood transfixed in the open door screaming "Blowblow-blow!" And the man was a little short Negro with an alto horn that Dean said obviously lived with his grandmother, "Just like my boy Jim!", slept all day and blew all night and blew a hundred choruses before he was ready to jump for fair, and that's what he was doing. "It's Carlo Marx!" screamed Dean above the fury. And it was. This little grandmother's boy with the scrapped up alto had beady glittering eyes, small crooked feet, spindly legs in formal black pants, like our friend Carlo, and he hopped and flopped with his horn and threw his feet around and kept his eyes transfixed on the audience (which was just people laughing at a dozen tables, the room thirty by thirty feet and low ceiling) and he never stopped. He was very simple in his ideas. Ideas meant nothing to him. What he liked was the surprise of a new simple variation of chorus. He'd go from "ta-potato-rup, ta-potato-rup" repeating and hopping to it and kissing and smiling into his horn—and then to "ta-potatola-dee-rup, ta-pota-tola-DEE-rup!" and it was all great moments of laughter and understanding for him and everyone else who heard. His tone was clear as a bell, high, pure, and blew straight in our faces from two feet away. Dean stood in front of him, oblivious to everything else in the world, with his head bowed, his hands socking in together, his whole body jumping on his heels and the sweat, always the sweat pouring and splashing down his tormented neck to literally lie in a pool at his feet. Galatea and Alice were there and it took us five minutes to realize it. Whoo, Frisco nights, the end of the continent and the end of the road and the end of all dull doubt. Lampshade was roaring around with trays of beer: everything he did was in rhythm: he yelled at the waitress with the beat: "Hey now, baby-baby, make a way, make a way, it's Lampshade coming your way!" and he hurled by her with the beers in the air and roared through the swinging doors in the kitchen and danced with the cooks and came sweating back. Ronnie Morgan, who'd earlier in the evening performed at the Hey Now Club screaming and kicking over the mike, now sat absolutely motionless at a corner table with an untouched drink in front of him, staring gook-eyed into space, his hands hanging at his sides till they almost touched the floor, his feet outspread like lolling tongues, his body shriveled into absolute weariness and entranced sorrow and what-all was on his mind: a man who knocked himself out every night and let the others put the quietus to him at dawn. Everything swirled around him like a cloud. And that little grandmother's alto, that little Carlo Marx hopped and monkey-danced with his magic horn and blew two hundred choruses of blues, each one more frantic than the other and no signs of failing energy or willingness to call anything a day. The whole room shivered. It has since been closed down, naturally.

Dean and I raced on to the East Coast. At one point we drove a 1947 Cadillac limousine across the state of Nebraska at 110 miles an hour, beating hotshot passenger trains and steel wheel freights in one nervous shuddering snapup of the gas. We told stories and zoomed East. There were hoboes by the tracks, wino bottles, the moon shining on woodfires. There were white-faced cows out in the plains, dim as nuns. There was dawn, Iowa; the Mississippi River at Davenport, and Chicago by nightfall. "Oh man" said Dean to me as we stood in front of a bar on North Clark Street in the hot summer night, "dig these old Chinamen that cut by Chicago. What a weird town—whee! And that woman in that window up there, just looking down with her big breasts hanging from her old nightgown. Just big wide eyes waiting. Wow! Sal we gotta go and never stop going till we get there."—"Where we going man?" —"Obvious question say Charley Chan. But we gotta go, we gotta GO." Then here came a gang of young bop musicians carrying their instruments out of cars. They piled right into a saloon and we followed them. They set themselves up and started blowing. There we were. The leader was a slender drooping curly-haired pursy-mouth tenorman, thin of shoulder, twenty-one, lean, loose, blowing modern and soft, cool in his sports shirt without undershirt, self-indulgent, sneering. Dean and I were like car thieves and juvenile heroes on a mad—with our T-shirts and beards and torn pants—but the bop, the combo! How that cool leader picked up his horn and frowned in it and blew cool and complex and was dainty stamping his foot to catch ideas and ducked to miss others—saying "Wail" very quietly when the other boys took solos. He was the leader, the encourager, the school-maker, the Teshmaker, the Bix, the Louis in the great formal school of new underground subterranean American music that would someday be studied all over the universities of Europe and the world. Then there was Pres, a husky handsome blond like a freckled boxer, like Jackie Cooper, meticulously molded in his sharkskin plaid suit with the long drape and the collar falling back and the tie undone for exact sharpness and casualness, sweating and hitching up his horn and writhing into it, and a tone just like Pres Lester Young himself, blowing round and Lester-like as they all leaned and jammed together, the heroes of the hip generation. "You see man Pres has the technical anxieties of a money-making musician, he's the only one who's expensively dressed, obvious big band employee, see him grow worried when he blows a clinker, but the leader, that cool cat, tells him not to worry and just blow truth." They roll into a tune —"Idaho." The Negro alto high-school broad-gash-mouth Yardbird tall kid blows over their heads in a thing of his own, move-less on the horn, fingering, erect, an idealist who reads Homer and Bird, cool, contemplative, grave—raises his horn and blows into it quietly and thoughtfully and elicits birdlike phrases and architec-tural Miles Davis logics. The children of the great bop innovators. Once there was Louis Armstrong blowing his beautiful bop in the muds of New Orleans; even before him the mad tuba-players and trombone kings who'd paraded on official days and broke up their Sousa marches into ragtime, on Bourbon, Dauphine and South Rampart and Perdido Street too. After which came swing, and Roy Eldridge vigorous and virile blasting the horn for everything it had in waves of power and natural tuneful reason—"I Want a Little Girl," "I Got Rhythm," a thousand choruses of "Wonderful"— leaning to it with glittering eyes and a lovely smile and sending it out broadcast to rock the jazz world. Then had come Charlie Parker, a kid in his mother's woodshed in Kansas City, the dirty snow in late March, smoke from stovepipes, wool hats, pitiful brown mouths breathing vapor, faint noise of music from down the way— blowing his tied-together alto among the logs, practicing on rainy days, coming out to watch the old swinging Basie and Bennie Moten band that had Hot Lips Page and the rest—lost names in swingin' Kaycee—nostalgia of alcohol, human mouths chewing and talking in smoky noisy jazzrooms, yeah, yah, yeah, yah, last Sunday afternoon and the long red sunset, the lost girl, the spilt wine— Charlie Parker leaving home and unhappiness and coming to the Apple, and meeting mad Monk and madder Gillespie ... Charlie Parker in his early days when he was out of his mind and walked in a circle while playing his horn. Younger than Lester, also from K.C., that gloomy saintly goof in whom the history of jazz is wrapped: Lester. Here were the children of the modern jazz night blowing their horns and instruments with belief; it was Lester started it all— his fame and his smoothness as lost as Maurice Chevalier in a stage-door poster—his drape, his drooping melancholy disposition in the sidewalk, in the door, his porkpie hat. ("At sessions all over the country from Kansas City to the Apple and back to L.A. they called him Pork Pie because he'd wear that gone hat and blow in it.") What door-standing influence has Dean gained from this cul-tural master of his generation? What mysteries as well as masteries? What styles, sorrows, collars, the removal of collars, the removal of lapels, the crepesole shoes, the beauty goof—that sneer of Lester's, that compassion for the dead which Billy has too, Lady Day—those poor little musicians in Chicago, their love of Lester, early heroisms in a room, records of Lester, early Count, suits hanging in the closet, tanned evenings in the rosy ballroom, the great tenor solo in the shoeshine jukebox, you can hear Lester blow and he is the greatness of America in a single Negro musician—he is just like the river, the river starts in near Butte, Montana, in frozen snow caps (Three Forks) and meanders on down across states and entire territorial areas of dun bleak land with hawthorn crackling in the sleet, picks up rivers at Bismarck, Omaha, and St. Louis just north, another at Kay-ro, another in Arkansas, Tennessee, comes deluging on New Orleans with muddy news from the land and a roar of subterranean excitement that is like the vibration of the entire land sucked of its gut in mad midnight, fevered, hot, the big mudhole rank clawpole old frogular pawed-soul titanic Mississippi from the North, full of wires, cold wood and horn—Lester, so, holding, his horn high in Doctor Pepper chickenshacks, backstreet. Basie Yaycee wearing greasy smeared corduroy bigpants and in torn flap smoking jacket without straw, scuffle-up shoes all slopey Mother Hubbard, soft, pudding, and key ring, early handkerchiefs, hands up, arms up, horn horizontal, shining dull, in wood-brown whiskeyhouse with ammoniac urine from broken gut bottles around fecal pukey bowl and a gal sprawled in it legs spread in brown cotton stockings, bleeding at belted mouth, moaning "yes" as Lester, horn placed, has started blowing, "blow for me mother blow for me," 1938, later, earlier, Miles is still on his daddy's checkered knee, Louis' only got twenty years behind him, and Lester blows all Kansas City to ecstasy and now Americans from coast to coast go mad, and fall by, and everybody's picking up. Stranger flowers now than ever, for as the Negro alto kid mused over everyone's head with dignity, the slender blond kid from Curtis Street, Denver, jeans and studded belt and red shirt, sucked on his mouthpiece while waiting for the others to finish; and when they did he started, and you had to look around to see where the new solo was coming from, for it came from his angelical smiling lips upon the mouthpiece and it was a soft sweet fairy-tale solo he played. A new kind of sound in the night, sweet, plaintive, cold; like cold jazz. Someone from South Main Street, or Market, or Canal, or Streetcar, he's the sweet new alto blowing the tiny heart-breaking salute in the night which is coming, a beauteous and whistling horn; blown easily but fully in a soft flue of air, out comes the piercing thin lament completely softened, the New Sound, the prettiest. And the bass player: wiry redhead with wild eyes jabbing his hips at the fiddle with every driving slap, at hot moments his mouth hung open; behind him, driving, the sad-looking dissipated drummer, completely goofed, chewing gum, wide-eyed, rocking the neck with that Reich kick, dropping bombs with his foot, urging balloons. The piano—a big husky Italian truck-driving kid with meaty hands and a burly and thoughtful joy; anybody start a fight with the band, he will step down; dropping huge chords like a Wolfean horse turding in the steamy Brooklyn winter morn. They played an hour. Nobody was listening. Old North Clark bums lolled at the bar, whores screeched in anger. Secret Chinamen went by. Noises of hootchy-kootchy interfered. They went right on. Out on the sidewalk came an apparition—a sixteen-year-old kid with a goatee and a trombone case. Thin as rickets, mad-faced, he wanted to join this group and blow with them. They knew him from before and didn't want to be bothered with him. He crept into the bar and meekly undid his trombone case and raised the horn to his lips. No opening. Nobody looked at him. They finished, packed up and left for another bar. The boy had his horn out, all assembled and polished of bell and no one cared. He wanted to jump. He was the Chicago Kid. He slapped on his dark glasses, raised the trombone to his lips alone in the bar, and went "Baugh!" Then he rushed out after them. They just wouldn't let him play with them, like the sandlot baseball gang back of the gas tank. "All these guys live with their grandmothers just like my boy Jim and our Carlo Marx alto!" said Dean and we rushed after the whole gang. They went across the street. We went in.

There is no end to the night. At great roar of Chicago dawn we all staggered out and shuddered in the raggedness. It would start all over tomorrow night. We rushed on to New York. "There ain't nothing left after that," said Dean. "Whee!" he said. We seek to find new phrases; we try hard, we writhe and twist and blow; every now and then a clear harmonic cry gives new suggestions of a tune, a thought, that will someday be the only tune and thought in the world and which will raise men's souls to joy. We find it, we lose, we wrestle for it, we find it again, we laugh, we moan. Go moan for man. It's the pathos of people that gets us down, all the lovers in this dream.

BELIEF & TECHNIQUE FOR MODERN PROSE

List of Essentials

1. Scribbled secret notebooks, and wild typewritten pages, for yr own joy
2. Submissive to everything, open, listening
3. Try never get drunk outside yr own house
4. Be in love with yr life
5. Something that you feel will find its own form
6. Be crazy dumbsaint of the mind
7. Blow as deep as you want to blow
8. Write what you want bottomless from bottom of the mind
9. The unspeakable visions of the individual
10. No time for poetry but exactly what is
11. Visionary tics shivering in the chest
12. In tranced fixation dreaming upon object before you
13. Remove literary, grammatical and syntactical inhibition
14. Like Proust be an old teahead of time
15. Telling the true story of the world in interior monolog
16. The jewel center of interest is the eye within the eye
17. Write in recollection and amazement for yourself
18. Work from pithy middle eye out, swimming in language sea
19. Accept loss forever
20. Believe in the holy contour of life
21. Struggle to sketch the flow that already exists intact in mind
22. Dont think of words when you stop but to see picture better
23. Keep track of every day the date emblazoned in yr morning
24. No fear or shame in the dignity of yr experience, language & knowledge
25. Write for the world to read and see yr exact pictures of it
26. Bookmovie is the movie in words, the visual American form
27. In praise of Character in the Bleak inhuman Loneliness
28. Composing wild, undisciplined, pure, coming in from under, crazier the better
29. You're a Genius all the time
30. Writer-Director of Earthly movies Sponsored & Angeled in Heaven

ESSENTIALS OF SPONTANEOUS PROSE

SET-UP. The object is set before the mind, either in reality, as in sketching (before a landscape or teacup or old face) or is set in the memory wherein it becomes the sketching from memory of a definite image-object.

PROCEDURE. Time being of the essence in the purity of speech, sketching language is undisturbed flow from the mind of personal secret idea-words, *blowing* (as per jazz musician) on subject of image.

METHOD. No periods separating sentence-structures already arbitrarily riddled by false colons and timid usually needless commas—but the vigorous space dash separating rhetorical breathing (as jazz musician drawing breath between outblown phrases)—"measured pauses which are the essentials of our speech"—"divisions of the *sounds* we hear"—"time and how to note it down." (William Carlos Williams)

SCOPING. Not "selectivity" of expression but following free deviation (association) of mind into limitless blow-on-subject seas of thought, swimming in sea of English with no discipline other than rhythms of rhetorical exhalation and expostulated statement, like a fist coming down on a table with each complete utterance, bang! (the space dash)—Blow as deep as you want—write as deeply, fish as far down as you want, satisfy yourself first, then reader cannot fail to receive telepathic shock and meaning-excitement by same laws operating in his own human mind.

LAG IN PROCEDURE. No pause to think of proper word but the infantile pileup of scatalogical buildup words till satisfaction is gained, which will turn out to be a great appending rhythm to a thought and be in accordance with Great Law of timing.

TIMING. Nothing is muddy that *runs in time* and to laws of *time*—Shakespearian stress of dramatic need to speak now in own unalterable way or forever hold tongue—*no revisions* (except obvious rational mistakes, such as names or *calculated* insertions in act of not writing but *inserting*).

CENTER OF INTEREST. Begin not from preconceived idea of what to say about image but from jewel center of interest in subject of image at *moment* of writing, and write outwards swimming in sea of language to peripheral release and exhaustion—Do not afterthink except for poetic or P.S. reasons. Never afterthink to "improve" or defray impressions, as, the best writing is always the most painful personal wrung-out tossed from cradle warm protective mind—tap from yourself the song of yourself, *blow!—now!—your* way is your only way—"good"—or "bad"—always honest, ("ludicrous"), spontaneous, "confessional" interesting, because not "crafted." Craft *is* craft.

STRUCTURE OF WORK. Modern bizarre structures (science fiction, etc.) arise from language being dead, "different" themes give illusion of "new" life. Follow roughly outlines in out-fanning movement over subject, as river rock, so mindflow over jewel-center need (run your mind over it, *once*) arriving at pivot, where what was dim formed "beginning" becomes sharp-necessitating "ending" and language shortens in race to wire of time-race of work, following laws of Deep Form, to conclusion, last words, last trickle—Night is The End.

MENTAL STATE. If possible write "without consciousness" in semi-trance (as Yeats' later "trance writing") allowing subconscious to admit in own uninhibited interesting necessary and so "modern" language what conscious art would censor, and write excitedly, swiftly, with writing-or-typing-cramps, in accordance (as from center to periphery), with laws of orgasm, Reich's "beclouding of consciousness." *Come* from within, out—to relaxed and said.

(from) THE RAILROAD EARTH

THERE WAS A LITTLE ALLEY in San Francisco back of the Southern Pacific station at Third and Townsend in redbrick of drowsy lazy afternoons with everybody at work in offices in the air you feel the impending rush of their commuter frenzy as soon they'll be charging en masse from Market and Sansome buildings on foot and in buses and all well-dressed thru workingman Frisco of Walkup? ? truck drivers and even the poor grime-bemarked Third Street of lost bums even Negroes so hopeless and long left East and meanings of responsibility and *try* that now all they do is stand there spitting in the broken glass sometimes fifty in one afternoon against one wall at Third and Howard and here's all these Millbrae and San Carlos neat-necktied producers and commuters of America and Steel civilization rushing by with San Francisco *Chronicles* and green *Call-Bulletins* not even enough time to be disdainful, they've got to catch 130, 132, 134, 136 all the way up to 146 till the time of evening supper in homes of the railroad earth when high in the sky the magic stars ride above the following hotshot freight trains.—It's all in California, it's all a sea, I swim out of it in afternoons of sun hot meditation in my jeans with head on handkerchief on brakeman's lantern or (if not working) on books, I look up at blue sky of perfect lostpurity and feel the warp of wood of old America beneath me and have insane conversations with Negroes in several-story windows above and everything is pouring in, the switching moves of boxcars in that little alley which is so much like the alleys of Lowell and I hear far off in the sense of coming night that engine calling our mountains.

But it was that beautiful cut of clouds I could always see above the little S.P. alley, puffs floating by from Oakland or the Gate of Marin to the north or San Jose south, the clarity of Cal to break your heart. It was the fantastic drowse and drum hum of lum mum afternoon nathin' to do, ole Frisco with end of land sadness—the people—the alley full of trucks and cars of businesses nearabouts and nobody knew or far from cared who I was all my life three thousand five hundred miles from birth-O opened up and at last belonged to me in Great America.

Now it's night in Third Street the keen little neons and also yellow bulblights of impossible-to-believe flops with dark ruined shadows moving back of torn yellow shades like a degenerate China with no money—the cats in Annie's Alley, the flop comes on, moans, rolls, the street is loaded with darkness. Blue sky above with stars hanging high over old hotel roofs and blowers of hotels moaning out dusts of interior, the grime inside the word in mouths falling out tooth by tooth, the reading rooms tick tock bigclock with creak chair and slantboards and old faces looking up over rimless spectacles bought in some West Virginia or Florida or Liverpool England pawnshop long before I was born and across rains they've come to the end of the land sadness end of the world gladness all you San Franciscos will have to fall eventually and burn again. But I'm walking and one night a bum fell into the hole of the construction job where theyre tearing a sewer by day the husky Pacific & Electric youths in torn jeans who work there often I think of going up to some of em like say blond ones with wild hair and torn shirts and say "You oughta apply for the railroad its much easier work you dont stand around the street all day and you get much more pay" but this bum fell in the hole you saw his foot stick out, a British MG also driven by some eccentric once backed into the hole and as I came home from a long Saturday afternoon local to Hollister out of San Jose miles away across verdurous fields of prune and juice joy here's this British MG backed and legs up wheels up into a pit and bums and cops standing around right outside the coffee shop—it was the way they fenced it but he never had the nerve to do it due to the fact that he had no money and nowhere to go and O his father was dead and O his mother was dead and O his sister was dead and O his where-about was dead was dead.—But and then at that time also I lay in my room on long Saturday afternoons listening to Jumpin' George with my fifth of tokay no tea and just under the sheets laughed to hear the crazy music "Mama, he treats your daughter mean," Mama, Papa, and dont you come in here I'll kill you etc. getting high by myself in room glooms and all wondrous knowing about the Negro the essential American out there always finding his solace his meaning in the fellaheen street and not in abstract morality and even when he has a church you see the pastor out front bowing to the ladies on the make you hear his great vibrant voice on the sunny Sunday afternoon sidewalk full of sexual vibratos saying "Why yes Mam but de gospel do say that man was born of woman's womb—" and no and so by that time I come crawling out of my warmsack and hit the street when I see the railroad ain't gonna call me till 5 AM Sunday morn probably for a local out of Bayshore in fact always for a local out of Bayshore and I go to the wailbar of all the wildbars in the world the one and only Third-and-Howard and there I go in and drink with the madmen and if I get drunk I git.

The whore who come up to me in there the night I was there with Al Buckle and said to me "You wanta play with me tonight Jim, and?" and I didnt think I had enough money and later told this to Charley Low and he laughed and said "How do you know she wanted money always take the chance that she might be out just for love or just out for love you know what I mean man dont be a sucker." She was a goodlooking doll and said "How would you like to oolyakoo with me mon?" and I stood there like a jerk and in fact bought drink got drink drunk that night and in the 299 Club I was hit by the proprietor the band breaking up the fight before I had a chance to decide to hit him back which I didnt do and out on the street I tried to rush back in but they had locked the door and were looking at me thru the forbidden glass in the door with faces like undersea—I should have played with her shurro-uruuruuruuruuru-uruurkdiei.

Despite the fact I was a brakeman making 600 a month I kept going to the Public restaurant on Howard Street which was three eggs for 26 cents 2 eggs for 21 this with toast (hardly no butter) coffee (hardly no coffee and sugar rationed) oatmeal with dash of milk and sugar the smell of soured old shirts lingering above the cookpot steams as if they were making skidrow lumberjack stews out of San Francisco ancient Chinese mildewed laundries with poker games in the back among the barrels and the rats of the earthquake days, but actually the food somewhat on the level of an oldtime 1890 or 1910 section-gang cook of lumber camps far in the North with an oldtime pigtail Chinaman cooking it and cussing out those who didnt like it. The prices were incredible but one time I had the beefstew and it was absolutely the worst beefstew I ever et, it was incredible I tell you—and as they often did that to me it was with the most intensest regret that I tried to convey to the geek back of counter what I wanted but he was a tough sonofabitch, ech, titi, I thought the counterman was kind of queer especially he handled gruffly the hopeless drooldrunks, "What now you doing you think you can come in here and cut like that for God's sake act like a man won't you and eat or get out-t-t-t-"—I always did wonder what a guy like that was doing working in a place like that because, but why some sympathy in his horny heart for the busted wrecks, all up and down the street were restaurants like the Public catering exclusively to bums of the black, winos with no money, who found 21 cents left over from wine panhandlings and so stumbled in for their third or fourth touch of food in a week, as sometimes they didnt eat at all and so you'd see them in the corner puking white liquid which was a couple quarts of rancid sauterne rotgut or sweet white sherry and they had nothing on their stomachs, most of them had one leg or were on crutches and had bandages around their feet, from nicotine and alcohol poisoning together, and one time finally on my up Third near Market across the street from Breens, when in early 1952 I lived on Russian Hill and didnt quite dig the complete horror and humor of railroad's Third Street, a bum a thin sickly littlebum like Anton Abraham lay face down on the pavement with crutch aside and some old remnant newspaper sticking out and it seemed to me he was dead. I looked closely to see if he was breathing and he was not, another man with me was looking down and we agreed he was dead, and soon a cop came over and took and agreed and called the wagon, the little wretch weighed about 50 pounds in his bleeding count and was stone mackerel snotnose cold dead as a bleeding doornail—ah I tell you—and who could notice but other half dead deadbums bums bums bums dead dead times X times X times all dead bums forever dead with nothing and all finished and out—there.—And this was the clientele in the Public Hair restaurant where I ate many's the morn a 3-egg breakfast with almost dry toast and oatmeal a little saucer of, and thin sickly dishwater coffee, all to save 14 cents so in my little book proudly I could make a notation and of the day and prove that I could live comfortably in America while working seven days a week and earning 600 a month I could live on less than 17 a week which with my rent of 4.20 was okay as I had also to spend money to eat and sleep sometimes on the other end of my Watsonville chaingang run but preferred most times to sleep free of charge and uncomfortable in cabooses of the crummy rack—my 26-cent breakfast, my pride.—And that incredible semi-queer counterman who dished out the food, threw it at you, slammed it, had a languid frank expression straight in your eyes like a 1930s lunchcart heroine in Steinbeck and at the steam-table itself labored coolly a junkey-looking Chinese with an actual stocking in his hair as if they'd just Shanghai'd him off the foot of Commercial Street before the Ferry Building was up but forgot it was 1952, dreamed it was 1860 goldrush Frisco—and on rainy days you felt they had ships in the back room.

I'd take walks up Harrison and the boomcrash of truck traffic towards the glorious girders of the Oakland Bay Bridge that you could see after climbing Harrison Hill a little like radar machine of eternity in the sky, huge, in the blue, by pure clouds crossed, gulls, idiot cars streaking to destinations on its undinal boom across shmoshwaters flocked up by winds and news of San Rafael storms

and flash boats.—There O I always came and walked and negoti-
ated whole Friscos in one afternoon from the overlooking hills of
the high Fillmore where Orient-bound vessels you can see on
drowsy Sunday mornings of poolhall goof like after a whole night
playing drums in a jam session and a morn in the hall of cuesticks I
went by the rich homes of old ladies supported by daughters or
female secretaries with immense ugly gargoyle Frisco millions fronts
of other days and way below is the blue passage of the Gate, the
Alcatraz mad rock, the mouths of Tamalpais, San Pablo Bay,
Sausalito sleepy hemming the rock and bush over yonder, and the
sweet white ships cleanly cutting a path to Sasebo.—Over Harrison
and down to the Embarcadero and around Telegraph Hill and up
the back of Russian Hill and down to the play streets of Chinatown
and down Kearney back across Market to Third and my wild-night
neon twinkle fate there, ah, and then finally at dawn of a Sunday
and they did call me, the immense girders of Oakland Bay still
haunting me and all that eternity too much to swallow and not
knowing who I am at all but like a big plumb longhaired baby
waking up in the dark trying to wonder who I am the door knocks
and it's the desk keeper of the flop hotel with silver rims and white
hair and clean clothes and sickly potbelly said he was from Rocky
Mount and looked like yes, he had been desk clerk of the Nash
Buncome Association hotel down there in 50 successive heatwave
summers without the sun and only palmos of the lobby with cigar
crutches in the albums of the South and him with his dear mother
waiting in a buried log cabin of graves with all that mashed past his-
toried underground afoot with the stain of the bear the blood of the
tree and cornfields long plowed under and Negroes whose voices
long faded from the middle of the wood and the dog barked his last,
this man had voyageured to the West Coast too like all the other
loose American elements and was pale and sixty and complaining of
sickness, might at one time been a handsome squire to women with
money but now a forgotten clerk and maybe spent a little time in jail
for a few forgeries or harmless cons and might also have been a railroad clerk and might have wept and might have never made it, and
that day I'd say he saw the bridgegirders up over the hill of traffic of
Harrison like me and woke up mornings with same lost, is now
beckoning on my door and breaking in the world on me and he is
standing on the frayed carpet of the hall all worn down by black
steps of sunken old men for last 40 years since earthquake and the

toilet stained, beyond the last toilet bowl and the last stink and stain I guess yes is the end of the world the bloody end of the world, so now knocks on my door and I wake up, saying "How what howp howelk howel of the knavery they've meaking, ek and wont let me slepit? Whey they dool? Whand out wisis thing that comes flarming-ing around my dooring in the mouth of the night and there everything knows that I have no mother, and no sister, and no father and no bot sosstle, but not crib" I get up and sit up and says "Howowow?" and he says "Telephone?" and I have to put on my jeans heavy with knife, wallet, I look closely at my railroad watch hanging on little door flicker of closet door face to me ticking silent the time, it says 4:30 AM of a Sunday morn, I go down the carpet of the skidrow hall in jeans and with no shirt and yes with shirt tails hanging gray workshirt and pick up phone and ticky sleepy night desk with cage and spittoons and keys hanging and old towels piled clean ones but frayed at edges and bearing names of every hotel of the moving prime, on the phone is the Crew Clerk, "Kerroway?" "Yeah." "Kerroway it's gonna be the Sherman Local at 7 AM this morning." "Sherman Local right." "Out of Bayshore, you know the way?" "Yeah." "You had that same job last Sunday—Okay Keroway-y-y-y-y." And we mutually hang up and I say to myself okay it's the Bayshore bloody old dirty hagglous old coveted old madman Sherman who hates me so much especially when we were at Redwood Junction kicking boxcars and he always insists I work the rear end tho as one-year man it would be easier for me to follow pot but I work rear and he wants me to be right there with a block of wood when a car or cut of cars kicked stops, so they wont roll down that incline and start catastrophes, O well anyway I'll be learning eventually to like the railroad and Sherman will like me some day, and anyway another day another dollar.

And there's my room, small, gray in the Sunday morning, now all the franticness of the street and night before is done with, bums sleep, maybe one or two sprawled on sidewalk with empty poorboy on a sill—my mind whirls with life.

So there I am in dawn in my dim cell—2½ hours to go till the time I have to stick my railroad watch in my jean watchpocket and cut out allowing myself exactly 8 minutes to the station and the 7:15 train No. 112 I have to catch for the ride five miles to Bayshore through four tunnels, emerging from the sad Rath scene of Frisco gloom gleak in the rainymouth fogmorning to a sudden valley with grim hills rising to the sea, bay on left, the fog rolling in like demented in the draws that have little white cottages disposed real-estatically for come-Christmas blue sad lights—my whole soul and concomitant eyes looking out on this reality of living and working in San Francisco with that pleased semiloin-located shudder, energy for sex changing to pain at the portals of work and culture and natural foggy fear.—There I am in my little room wondering how I'll really manage to fool myself into feeling that these next 2½ hours will be well filled, fed, with work and pleasure thoughts.—It's so thrilling to feel the coldness of the morning wrap around my thick quilt blankets as I lay there, watch facing and ticking me, legs spread in comfy skidrow soft sheets with soft tears or sew lines in 'em, huddled in my own skin and rich and not spending a cent on—I look at my littlebook—and I stare at the words of the Bible.—On the floor I find last red afternoon Saturday's *Chronicle* sports page with news of football games in Great America the end of which I bleakly see in the gray light entering.—The fact that Frisco is built of wood satisfies me in my peace, I know nobody'll disturb me for 2½ hours and all bums are asleep in their own bed of eternity awake or not, bottle or not—it's the joy I feel that counts for me.—On the floor's my shoes, big lumberboot flopjack workshoes to colomp over rockbed with and not turn the ankle—solidity shoes that when you put them on, yokewise, you know you're working now and so for same reason shoes not be worn for any reason like joys of restaurant and shows.—Night-before shoes are on the floor beside the clunkershoes a pair of blue canvas shoes à la 1952 style, in them I'd trod soft as ghost the indented hill sidewalks of Ah Me Frisco all in the glitter night, from the top of Russian Hill I'd looked down at one point on all roofs of North Beach and the Mexican nightclub neons, I'd descended to them on the old steps of Broadway under which they were newly laboring a mountain tunnel—shoes fit for watersides, embarcaderos, hill and plot lawns of park and tiptop vista.—Workshoes covered with dust and some oil of engines—the crumpled jeans nearby, belt, blue railroad hank, knife, comb, keys, switch keys and caboose coach key, the knees white from Pajaro Riverbottom finedusts, the ass black from slick sandboxes in yardgoat after yardgoat—the gray workshorts, the dirty undershirt, sad shorts, tortured socks of my life.—And the Bible on my desk next to the peanut butter, the lettuce, the raisin bread, the crack in the plaster, the stiff-with-old-dust lace drape now no longer laceable but hard as—after all those years of hard dust eternity in that Cameo skid inn with red eyes of rheumy oldmen dying there staring without hope out on the dead wall you can hardlysee thru window-dusts and all you heard lately in the shaft of the rooftop middle way was the cries of a Chinese child whose father and mother were always telling him to shu shand then screaming at him, he was a pest and his tears from China were most persistent and worldwide and represented all our feelings in broken-down Cameo tho this was not admitted by bum one except for an occasional harsh clearing of throat in the halls or moan of nightmarer—by things like this and neglect of a hard-eyed alcoholic oldtime chorusgirl maid the cur-tains had now absorbed all the iron they could take and hung stiff and even the dust in them was iron, if you shook them they'd crack and fall in tatters to the floor and spatter like wings of iron on the bong and the dust would fly into your nose like filings of steel and choke you to death, so I never touched them. My little room at 6 in the comfy dawn (at 4:30) and before me all that time, that fresh-eyed time for a little coffee to boil water on my hot plate, throw some coffee in, stir it, French style, slowly carefully pour it in my white tin cup, throw sugar in (not California beet sugar like I should have been using but New Orleans cane sugar, because beet racks I carried from Oakland out to Watsonville many's the time, a 80-car freight train with nothing but gondolas loaded with sad beets looking like the heads of decapitated women).—Ah me how but it was a hell and now I had the whole thing to myself, and make my raisin toast by sitting it on a little wire I'd especially bent to place over the hotplate, the toast crackled up, there, I spread the mar-garine on the still red hot toast and it too would crackle and sink in golden, among burnt raisins and this was my toast.—Then two eggs gently slowly fried in soft margarine in my little skidrow frying pan about half as thick as a dime in fact less, a little piece of tiny tin you could bring on a camp trip—the eggs slowly fluffled in there and swelled from butter steams and I threw garlic salt on them, and when they were ready the yellow of them had been slightly filmed with a cooked white at the top from the tin cover I'd put over the frying pan, so now they were ready, and out they came, I spread them out on top of my already prepared potatoes which had been boiled in small pieces and then mixed with the bacon I'd already fried in small pieces, kind of raggely mashed bacon potatoes, with eggs on top steaming, and on the side lettuce, with peanut butter dab nearby on side.—I had heard that peanut butter and lettuce contained all the vitamins you should want, this after I had originally started to eat this combination because of the deliciousness and nostalgia of the taste—my breakfast ready at about 6:45 and as I eat already I'm dressing to go piece by piece and by the time the last dish is washed in the little sink at the boiling hot-water tap and I'm taking my lastquick slug of coffee and quickly rinsing the cup in the hot water spout and rushing to dry it and plop it in its place by the hot plate and the brown carton in which all the groceries sit tightly wrapped in brown paper, I'm already picking up my brakeman's lantern from where it's been hanging on the door handle and my tattered timetable's long been in my backpocket folded and ready to go, everything tight, keys, timetable, lantern, knife, handkerchief, wallet, comb, railroad keys, change and myself. I put the light out on the sad dab mad grub little diving room and hustle out into the fog of the flow, descending the creak hall steps where the old men are not yet sitting with Sunday morn papers because still asleep or some of them I can now as I leave hear beginning to disfawdle to wake in their rooms with their moans and yorks and scrapings and horror sounds, I'm going down the steps to work, glance to check time of watch with clerk cage clock.—A hardy two or three oldtimers sitting already in the dark brown lobby under the tockboom clock, toothless, or grim, or elegantly mustached—what thought in the world swirling in them as they see the young eager brakeman bum hurrying to his thirty dollars of the Sunday—what memories of old homesteads, built without sympathy, hornyhanded fate dealt them the loss of wives, childs, moons—libraries collapsed in their time—oldtimers of the telegraph wired wood Frisco in the fog gray top time sitting in their brown sunk sea and will be there when this afternoon my face flushed from the sun, which at eight'll flame out and make sunbaths for us at Redwood, they'll still be here the color of paste in the green underworld and still reading the same editorial over again and wont understand where I've been or what for or what.—I have to get out of there or suffocate, out of Third Street or become a worm, it's alright to live and bed-wine in and play the radio and cook little breakfasts and rest in but O my I've got to go now to work, I hurry down Third to Townsend for my 7:15 train—it's 3 minutes to go, I start in a panic to jog, goddam it I didn't give myself enough time this morning, I hurry down under the Harrison ramp to the Oakland-Bay Bridge, down past Schweibacker-Frey the great dim red neon printshop always spectrally my father the dead executive I see there, I run and hurry past the beat Negro grocery stores where I buy all my peanut butter and raisin bread, past the redbrick railroad alley now mist and wet, across Townsend, the train is leaving!

Fatuous railroad men, the conductor old John J. Coppertwang 35 years pure service on ye olde S.P. is there in the gray Sunday morning with his gold watch out peering at it, he's standing by the engine yelling up pleasantries at old hoghead Jones and young fireman Smith with the baseball cap is at the fireman's seat munching sandwich—"We'll how'd ye like old Johnny O yestiddy, I guess he didnt score so many touch-downs like we thought." "Smith bet six dollars on the pool down in Watsonville and said he's rakin' in thirty four." "I've been in that Watsonville pool—." They've been in the pool of life fleartiming with one another, all the long pokerplaying nights in brownwood railroad places, you can smell the mashed cigar in the wood, the spittoon's been there for more than 750,099 years and the dog's been in and out and these old boys by old shaded brown light have bent and muttered and young boys too with their new brakeman passenger uniform the tie undone the coat thrown back the flashing youth smile of happy fatuous well-fed goodjobbed careered futured pensioned hospitalized taken-care-of railroad men.—35, 40 years of it and then they get to be conductors and in the middle of the night they've been for years called by the Crew Clerk yelling "Cassady? It's the Maximush localized week do you for the right lead" but now as old men all they have is a regular job, a regular train, conductor of the 112 with goldwatch is helling up his pleasantries at all fire dog crazy Satan hoghead Willis why the wildest man this side of France and Frankincense, he was known once to take his engine up that steep grade . . . 7:15, time to pull, as I'm running thru the station hearing the bell jangling and the steam chuff they're pulling out, O I come flying out on the platform and forget momentarily or that is never did know what track it was and whirl in confusion a while wondering what track and cant see no train and this is the time I lose there, 5, 6, 7 seconds when the train tho underway is only slowly unchugging to go and a man a fat executive could easily run up and grab it but when I yell to Assistant Stationmaster "Where's 112?" and he tells me the last track which is the track I never dreamed I run to it fast as I can go and dodge people à la Columbia halfback and cut into track fast as off-tackle where you carry the ball with you to the left and feint with neck and head and push of ball as tho you're gonna throw yourself all out to fly around that left end and everybody psychologically chuffs with you that way and suddenly you contract and you like whiff of smoke are buried in the hole in tackle, cutback play, you're flying into the hole almost before you yourself know it, flying into the track I am and there's the train about 30 yards away even as I look picking up tremendously momentum the kind of momentum I would have been able to catch if I'd a looked a second earlier—but I run, I know I can catch it. Standing on the back platform are the rear brakeman and an old deadheading conductor ole Charley W. Jones, why he had seven wives and six kids and one time out at Lick no I guess it was Coyote he couldnt see on account of the steam and out he come and found his lantern in the igloo regular anglecock of my herald and they gave him fifteen benefits so now there he is in the Sunday har har owlala morning and he and young rear man watch incredulously his student brakeman running like a crazy trackman after their departing train. I feel like yelling "Make your airtest now make your airtest now!" knowing that when a passenger pulls out just about at the first crossing east of the station they pull the air a little bit to test the brakes, on signal from the engine, and this momentarily slows up the train and I could manage it, and could catch it, but they're not making no airtest the bastards, and I hek knowing I'm going to have to run like a sonofabitch. But suddenly I get embarrassed thinking what are all the people of the world gonna say to see a man running so devilishly fast with all his might sprinting thru life like Jesse Owens just to just to catch a goddam train and all of them with their hysteria wondering if I'll get killed when I catch the back platform and Blam, I fall down and go boom and lay supine across the crossing, so the old flagman when the train has flowed by will see that everything lies on the earth in the same stew, all of us angels will die and we dont ever know how or our own diamond, O heaven will enlighten us and open our eyes—open our eyes, open our eyes.—I know I wont get hurt, I trust my shoes, hand grip, feet, solidity of yipe and cripe of gripe and grip and strength and need no mystic strength to measure the musculature in my rib back—but damn it all it's a social embarrassment to be caught sprinting like a maniac after a train especially with two men gaping at me from rear of train and shaking their heads and yelling I cant make it even as I half-heartedly sprint after them with open eyes trying to communicate that I can and not for them to get hysterical or laugh, but I realize it's all too much for me, not the run, not the speed of the train which anyway two seconds after I gave up the complicated chase did indeed slow down at the crossing in the airtest before chugging up again for good and Bayshore. So I was late for work, and old Sherman hated me and was about to hate me more.

The ground I would have eaten in solitude, cronch—the railroad earth, the flat stretches of long Bayshore that I have to negotiate to get to Sherman's bloody caboose on track 17 ready to go with pot pointed to Redwood and the morning's 3-hour work.—I get off the bus at Bayshore Highway and rush down the little street and turn in—boys riding the pot of a switcheroo in the yardgoat day come yelling by at me from the headboards and footboards "Come on down ride with us" otherwise I would have been about 3 minutes even later to my work but now I hop on the little engine that momentarily slows up to pick me up and it's alone not pulling any-thing but tender, the guys have been up to the other end of the yard to get back on some track of necessity.—That boy will have to learn to flag himself without nobody helping him as many's the time I've seen some of these young goats think they have everything but the plan is late, the word will have to wait, the massive arboreal thief with the crime of the kind, and air and all kinds of ghouls—ZONKed! made tremendous by the flare of the whole crime and encrudalatures of all kinds—San Franciscos and shroudband Bayshores the last and the last furbelow of the eek plot pall prime tit top work oil twicks and wouldn't you?—the railroad earth I would have eaten alone, cronch, on foot head bent to get to Sherman who ticking watch observes with finicky eyes the time to go to give the hiball sign get on going it's Sunday no time to waste the only day of his long seven-day-a-week worklife he gets a chance to rest a little bit at home when "Eee Christ" when "Tell that sonofabitch student this is no party picnic damn this shit and throb tit you tell them something and how do you what the hell expect to underdries out tit all you bright tremendous trouble anyway, we's LATE" and this is the way I come rushing up late. Old Sherman is sitting in the crummy over his switch lists, when he sees me with cold blue eyes he says "You know you're supposed to be here 7:30 dont you so what the hell you doing gettin' in here at 7:50 you're twenty goddam minutes late, what the fuck you think this your birthday?" and he gets up and leans off the rear bleak platform and gives the high sign to the enginemen up front we have a cut of about 12 cars and they say it easy and off we go slowly at first, picking up momentum to the work, "Light that goddam fire" says Sherman he's wearing brand-new workshoes just about bought yestiddy and I notice his clean coveralls that his wife washed and set on his chair just that morning probably and I rush up and throw coal in the potbelly flop and take a fusee and two fusses and light them crack em. Ah fourth of the July when the angels would smile on the horizon and all the racks where the mad are lost are returned to us forever from Lowell of my soul prime and single meditated longsong hope to heaven of prayers and angels and of course the sleep and interested eye of images and but now we detect the missing buffoon there's the poor goodman rear man aint even in the train yet and Sherman looks out sulkily the back door and sees his rear man waving from fifteen yards aways to stop and wait for him and being an old railroad man he certainly isnt going to run or even walk fast, it's well understood, conductor Sherman's got to get up off his switchlist desk chair and pull the air and stop the goddam train for rear man Arkansaw Charley, who sees this done and just come up lopin' in his flop overalls without no care, so he was late too, or at least had gone gossiping in the yard office while waiting for the stupid head brakeman, the tagman's up in front on the presumably pot. "First thing we do is pick up a car in front at Redwood so all's you do get off at the crossing and stand back to flag, not too far." "Dont I work the head end?" "You work the hind end we got not much to do and I wanna get it done fast," snarls the conductor. "Just take it easy and do what we say and watch and flag." So it's peaceful Sunday morning in California and off we go, tack-a-tick, lao-tichi-couch, out of the Bayshore yards, pause momentarily at the main line for the green, ole 71 or ole whatever been by and now we get out and go swamming up the tree valleys and town vale hollows and main street crossing parking-lot last-night attendant plots and Stanford lots of the world—to our destination in the Pooh which I can see, and, so to while the time I'm up in the cupolo and with my newspaper dig the latest news on the front page and also consider and make notations of the money I spent already for this day Sunday absolutely not jot spend a nothing—California rushes by and with sad eyes we watch it reel the whole bay and the discourse falling off to gradual gils that ease and graduate to Santa Clara Valley then and the fig and behind is the fog immemoriate while the mist closes and we come running out to the bright sun of the Sabbath Californiay—

At Redwood I get off and standing on sad oily ties of the brakie railroad earth with red flag and torpedoes attached and fusees in back-pocket with timetable crushed against and I leave my hot jacket in crummy standing there then with sleeves rolled up and there's the porch of a Negro home, the brothers are sitting in shirt-sleeves talking with cigarettes and laughing and little daughter standing amongst the weeds of the garden with her playpail and pig-tails and we the railroad men with soft signs and no sound pick up our flower, according to same goodman train order that for the last entire lifetime of attentions ole conductor industrial worker har-lotized Sherman has been reading carefully son so's not to make a mistake:

"Sunday morning October 15 pick up flower car at Redwood, Dispatcher M.M.S."

(from) OLD ANGEL MIDNIGHT

1 FRIDAY AFTERNOON IN THE UNIVERSE, in all directions in & out you got your men women dogs children horses pones tics perts parts pans pools palls pails parturiences and petty Thieveries that turn into heavenly Buddha — I know boy what's I talkin about case I made the world & when I made it I no lie & had Old Angel Midnight for my name and concocted up a world so *nothing* you had forever thereafter make believe it's real — but that's alright because now everything'll be alright & we'll soothe the forever boys & girls & before we're thru we'll find a name for this Goddam Golden Eternity & tell a story too — and but d y aver read a story as vast as this that begins Friday Afternoon with workinmen on scaffolds painting white paint & ants merlying in lil black dens & microbes warring in yr kidney & mesaroolies microbing in the innards of mercery & microbe microbes dreaming of the ultimate microbehood which then ultimates outward to the endless vast empty atom which is this imaginary universe, ending nowhere &

ne'er e'en born as Bankei well poled when he ferried his mother over the rocks to Twat You Tee and people visit his hut to enquire "What other planet features this?" & he answers "What other planet?" tho the sounds of the entire world are now swimming thru this window from Mrs McCartiola's twandow & Ole Poke's home dronk again & acourse you hear the cats wailing in the wailbar wildbar wartfence moonlight midnight Angel Dolophine immensity Visions of the Tathagata's Seat of Purity & Womb so that here is all this infinite immaterial meadowlike golden ash swimswarming in our enlighten brains & the silence Shh shefallying in our endless ear & still we refuse naked & blank to hear What the Who? the Who? Too What You? will say the diamond boat & Persepine, Recipine, Mill town, Heroine, & Fack matches the silver ages everlasting swarmswallying in a simple broom — and at night ya raise the square white light from your ghost beneath a rootdrinkin tree & Coyote wont hear ya but you'll ward off the inexistency devils just to pass the time away & meanwhile it's timeless to the ends of the last lightyear it might as well be gettin late Friday afternoon where we start so's old Sound can come home when worksa done & drink his beer & tweak his children's eyes —

2 and what talents it takes to bail boats out you'd never flank till flail pipe throwed howdy who was it out the bar of the seven seas and all the Italians of 7th Street in Sausaleety slit sleet with paring knives that were used in the ream kitchens to cut the innards of gizzards out on a board, wa, twa, wow, why, shit, Ow, man, I'm tellin you — Wait — We bait the rat and forget to mark the place and soon Cita comes and eat it and puke out grit — fa yen pas d cas, fa yen pas d case, chanson d idiot, imbecile, vas malade — la sonora de madrigal — but as soon as someone wants to start then the world takes on these new propensities:

1. Bardoush
   (the way the craydon bi fa shta ma j en vack)
2. Flaki — arrete — interrupted chain saw sting eucalyptus words inside the outside void that good God we cant believe is anything so arsaphallawy any the pranaraja of madore with his bloody arse kegs, shit — go to three.

3 Finally just about the time they put wood to the poets of France & fires broke out recapitulating the capitulation of the continent of

Mu located just south of Patch, Part, with his hair askew and wearing goldring ears & Vaseline Hair Oil in his arse ass hole flaunted all the old queers and lecherous cardinals who wrote (write) pious manuals & announced that henceforth he was to be the sole provender provider this side of Kissthat.

Insteada which hey marabuda you son of a betch you cucksucker you hey hang dat board down here I'll go cot you on the Yewneon ya bum ya — lick, lock, lick, lock, mix it for pa-tit a a lamana lacasta reda va da Poo moo koo — la — swinging Friday afternoon in eternity here comes Kee pardawac with long golden robe flowing through the Greek Islands with a Bardic (forgot) with a lard (?) with a marde manual onder his Portugee Tot Sherry Rotgut, singing "Kee ya."

Tried to warn all of you, essence of stuff wont do — God why did you make the world?

Answer: — Because I gwt pokla renamash ta va in ming the atss are you forever with it?

I like the bliss of mind.

Awright I'll call up all the fuckin Gods, right now! Parya! Arrive! Ya damn hogfuckin lick lip twillerin fishmonger! Kiss my purple royal ass baboon! Poota! Whore! You and yr retinues of chariots & fucks! Devadatta! Angel of Mercy! Prick! Lover! Mush! Run on ya dog eared kiss willying nilly Dexter Michigan ass-warlerin ratpole! The rat in my cellar's an old canuck who wasnt fooled by rebirth but b God gotta admit I was born for the same reason I bring this glass to my lip —?

Rut! Old God whore, the key to ecstasy is forevermore furthermore blind! Potanyaka! God of Mercy! Boron O Mon Boron! All of ye! Rush! Ghosts & evil spirits, if you appear I'm saved. How can you fool an old man with a stove & wine drippin down his chin? The flowers are my little sisters and I love them with a dear heart. Ashcans turn to snow and milk when I look. I know sinister alleys. I had a vision of Han Shan a darkened by sun bum in odd rags standing short in the gloom scarey to see. Poetry, all these vicious writers and bores & Scriptural Apocraphylizers fucking their own dear mothers because they want ears to sell —

And the axe haiku.

All the little fine angels amercyin and this weary prose hand handling dumb pencils like in school long ago the first redsun special. Henry Millers everywhere Fridaying the world — Rexroths.

Rexroths not a bad egg. Creeley. Creeley. Real magination realizing rock roll rip snortipatin oyster stew of Onatona Scotiat Shores where six birds week the nest and part wasted his twill till I.

Mush. Wish. Wish I could sing ya songs of a perty nova spotia patonapeein pack wallower wop snot polly — but caint — cause I'll get sick & die anyway & you too, born to die, little flowers. Fiorella. Look around. The burlap's buried in the wood on an angle, axe haiku. La religion c'est d la marde! Pa! d la marde! J m en dor. —

God's asleep dreaming, we've got to wake him up! Then all of a sudden when we're asleep dreaming, he comes and wakes us up — how gentle! How are you Mrs Jones? Fine Mrs Smith! Tit within Tat — Eye within Tooth — Bone within Light, like — Drop some little beads of sweetness in that stew (O Phoney Poetry!) — the heart of the onion — That stew's too good for me to eat, you! —

People, shmeople

4 Boy, says Old Angel, this amazing nonsensical rave of yours wherein I spose you'd think you'd in some lighter time find hand be-almin ya for the likes of what ya davote yaself to, pah — bum with a tail only means one thing, — They know that in sauerkraut bars, god the chew chew & the wall lips — And not only that but all them in describable paradises — aye ah — Old Angel m boy — Jack, the born with a tail bit is a deal that you never dream'd to redeem — verify — try to see as straight — you wont believe even in God but the devil worries you — you & Mrs Tourian — great gaz-zuz & I'd as lief be scoured with a leaf rust as hear this poetizin horseshit everywhere I want to hear the sounds thru the window you promised me when the Midnight bell on 7th St did toll bing bong & Burroughs and Ginsberg were asleep & you lay on the couch in that timeless moment in the little red bulblight bus & saw drapes of eternity parting for your hand to begin & so's you could affect — & *ee*ffect — the total turningabout & deep revival of world robeflowing literature till it shd be something a man'd put his eyes on & continually read for the sake of reading & for the sake of the Tongue & not just these insipid stories writ in insipid aridities & paranoias bloomin & why yet the image — let's hear the Sound of the Universe, son, & no more part twaddle — And dont expect nothing from me, my middle name is Opprobrium, Old Angel Midnight Opprobrium, boy, O.A.M.O. —

Pirilee pirilee, tzwé tzwi tzwa, — tack tick — birds & firewood. The dream is already ended and we're already awake in the golden eternity.

5 Then when rat tooth come ravin and fradilaboodala back-ala backed up, trip tripped himself and fell falling on top of Old Smokey because *his pipe* was not right, had no molasses in it, tho it looked like a morasses brarrel, but then the cunts came. She had a long cunt that sitick out of her craw a mile long like Mexican Drawings showing hungry drinkers reaching Surrealistic Thirsts with lips like Aztec — Akron Lehman the Hart Crane Hero of Drunken Records came full in her cunt spoffing & overflowing white enlightened seminal savior juice out of his canal-hole into her hungry river bed and that made the old nannies gab and kiss that.

6 O he was quite racy — real estate queen — Europe & Niles — for pleasure — stom stomp absolute raze making noise — I can write them but I cant puctuate them — then he said comma comma comma — That skinny guy with black hair — Atlean Rage — in India in the last year he's getting even ignoring all common publications & getting Urdu Nothing Sanskrit by Sir Yak Yak Yak forty page thing Norfolk — let's all get drunk I wanta take pictures — dont miss with Mrs. lately in trust picture pitcher pithy lisp — that's an artistic kit for sex — Trying to think of a rule in Sankrit Mamma Sanskrit Sounding obviously twins coming in here Milltown Equinell Miopa Parte Watacha Peemana Kowava you get sticky ring weekends & wash the tub, Bub — I'll be gentle like a lamb in the Bible — Beautiful color yr lipstick thanx honey — Got a match Max? — Taxi crabs & murdercycles — Let's go to Trilling & ask him — I gotta wash my conduct — Dont worry about nothin — I love Allen Ginsberg — Let that be recorded in heaven's unchange-able heart — Either bway — Rapples — Call up Allen Price Jones — Who is that? — They re having fun on the bed there — Soo de ya bee la — And there came the picture of Ang Bong de Beela — Fuck it or get it in or wait something for the bee slime — Then the ants'll crawl over bee land — Ants in bands wailing neath my bloody ow pants, owler pants — Ta da ba dee — He thinlis I'm competive in a long pleasant souse of Wishing all of ye bleed stay meditation every-body martini destroy my black — Allen ye better voice the stare, this beer these room sandwiches — Where did you get these? Big

greasy socialists — Are you gonna konk, Allen? Mighty tall in the saddle — Anybody got a ceegiboo? — The moon is a piece of tea — (Under the empty blue sky, vertebrate zoology.)

7 And make the most malign detractor eat from the love of the lamb — and the pot that's for everybody not diminish when somebody comes — Tathagata, give me that —

Visions of Al

Women are so variously beautiful it's such a pleasure

Think happy thoughts of the Buddha who abides throughout detestable phenomena like lizards and man eating ogres, with perfect compassion and blight, caring not one way or the other the outcome of our term of time because celestial birds are singing in the golden heaven. In the golden hall of the Buddha, think, I am already ensconced on a tray of gold, invisible and radiant with singing, by the side of my beloved hand, which has done its work and exists no more to tone up the troubles of this birth-and-death imaginary world — And that's because the Old Angel Midnight is a Fike — that's because the Old Angle Midnight never was. And the story of love is a long sad tale ending in graves, many heads bend beneath the light, arguments are raving avid lipt and silly in silly secular rooms silly seconsular rooms full of height agee — Swam! reacht the other shore, folded, in magnificence, shouldered the wheel of iron light, and shuddered no more, and rowed the fieldstar across her bed of ashen samsara sorrow towards in here, the bliss evermore.

So.

Saw sight saver & fixt him. — Love you all, children, happy days and happy dreams and happy thoughts forevermore —

Dont forget to put a dime in the coin box by dipping your finger in ancid inkl the holy old forevermore holy water & bleep blap bloop the sign a the cross, when facing the altar down the aisle when you're waltzing — Ding! Up you go, smoke

8 The Mill Valley trees, the pines with green mint look and there's a tangled eucalyptus hulk stick fallen thru the late sunlight tangle of those needles, hanging from it like a live wire connecting it to the ground — just below, the notches where little Fred sought to fell sad pine — not bleeding much — just a lot of crystal sap the ants are mining in, motionless like cows on the grass & so they must be

aphyds percolatin up a steam to store provender in their bottomless bellies that for all I know are bigger than bellies of the Universe beyond — The little tragic windy cottages on the high last city-ward hill and today roosting in sun hot dream above the tree head of seas and meadowpatch whilst tee-kee-kee-pearl the birdies & mommans mark & ululate moodily in this valley of peaceful firewood in stacks that make you think of Oregon in the morning in 1928 when Back was home on the range lake and his hunting knife threw away and went to sit among the Ponderosa Pines to think about love his girl's bare bodice like a fennel seed the navel in her milk bun — Shorty McGonigle and Roger Nulty held up the Boston Bank and murdered a girl in these old woods and next you saw the steely green iron photograph in True Detective showing black blotches in the black blotch running culvert by the dirty roadside not Oregon at all, or Jim Back so happy with his mouth a black of grass depending —

> Hummingbird hums
> hello — bugs
> Race and swoop

> Two ants hurry
> to catch up
> With lonely Joe

> The tree above
> me is like
> A woman's thigh
> Smooth Eucalyptus bumps
> and muscle swells

> I would I were a weed
> a week, would leave.
> Why was the rat
> mixed up
> in the sun?

Because Buddhidharma came from the West with dark eyebrows, and China had a mountain wall, and mists get lost above the Yangtze Gorge and this is a mysterious yak the bird makes, yick, — wowf wow wot sings the dog blud blut blup below the Homestead

Deer — red robins with saffron scarlet or orange rud breasts make a racket in the dry dead car crash tree Neal mentioned "He went off the road into a eucalyptus" and "it's all busting out," indicating the prune blossoms and Bodhidharma came from the India West to seek converts to his wall-gazing and ended up with Zen magic monks mopping each and one and all and other in mud koan puddles to prove the crystal void.

Wow

9 Lookin over der sports page I see assorted perms written in langosten field hand that wd make the 2 silhouetted movie champeens change their quiet dull dialog to something fog — ah, Old Angel Midnight, it will be all over in a year.

Dying is ecstasy.

I'm not a teacher, not a sage, not a Roshi, not a writer or master or even a giggling dharma bum I'm my mother's son & my mother is the universe —

What is this universe
but a lot of waves
And a craving desire
is a wave
Belonging to a wave

WILLIAM BURROUGHS
1914–1997

TWILIGHT'S LAST GLEAMINGS
[with Kells Elvins]

PLEASE IMAGINE AN EXPLOSION ON A SHIP

A paretic named Perkins sat askew on his broken wheelchair. He arranged his lips.

"You pithyathed thon of a bidth!" he shouted.

Barbara Cannon, a second-class passenger, lay naked in a first-class bridal suite with Stewart Lindy Adams. Lindy got out of bed and walked over to a window and looked out.

"Put on your clothes, honey," he said. "There's been an accident."

A first-class passenger named Mrs. Norris was thrown out of bed by the explosion. She lay there shrieking until her maid came and helped her up.

"Bring me my wig and my kimono," she told the maid. "I'm going to see the captain."

Dr. Benway, ship's doctor, drunkenly added two inches to a four-inch incision with one stroke of his scalpel.

"There was a little scar, Doctor," said the nurse, who was peering over his shoulder. "Perhaps the appendix is already out."

"The appendix *out*!" the doctor shouted. "*I'm* taking the appendix out! What do you think I'm doing here?"

"Perhaps the appendix is on the left side," said the nurse. "That happens sometimes, you know."

"Can't you be quiet?" said the doctor. "I'm coming to that!" He threw back his elbows in a movement of exasperation. "Stop breathing down my neck!" he yelled. He thrust a red fist at her. "And get me another scalpel. This one has no edge to it."

He lifted the abdominal wall and searched along the incision. "I know where an appendix is. I studied appendectomy in 1904 at Harvard."

The floor tilted from the force of the explosion. The doctor reeled back and hit the wall.

"Sew her up!" he said, peeling off his gloves. "I can't be expected to work under such conditions!"

At a table in the bar sat Christopher Hitch, a rich liberal; Colonel Merrick, retired; Billy Hines of Newport; and Joe Bane, writer.

"In all my experience as a traveler," the Colonel was saying, "I have never encountered such service."

Billy Hines twisted his glass, watching ice cubes. "Frightful service," he said, his face contorted by a suppressed yawn.

"Do you think the captain controls this ship?" said the Colonel, fixing Christopher Hitch with a bloodshot blue eye. "Unions!" shouted the Colonel. "Unions control this ship!"

Hitch gave out with a laugh that was supposed to be placating but ended up oily. "Things aren't so bad, really," he said, patting at the Colonel's arm. He didn't land the pat, because the Colonel drew his arm out of reach. "Things will adjust themselves."

Joe Bane looked up from his drink of straight rye. "It's like I say, Colonel," he said. "A man—"

The table left the floor and the glasses crashed. Billy Hines remained seated, looking blankly at the spot where his glass had been. Christopher Hitch rose uncertainly. Joe Bane jumped up and ran away.

"By God!" said the Colonel. "I'm not surprised!"

Also at a table in the bar sat Philip Bradshinkel, investment banker; his wife, Joan Bradshinkel; Branch Morton, a St. Louis politician; and Morton's wife, Mary Morton. The explosion knocked their table over.

Joan raised her eyebrows in an expression of sour annoyance. She looked at her husband and sighed.

"I'm sorry this happened, dear," said her husband. "Whatever it is, I mean."

Mary Morton said, "Well, I declare!"

Branch Morton stood up, pushing back his chair with a large red hand. "Wait here," he said. "I'll find out."

Mrs. Norris pushed through a crowd on C Deck. She rang the elevator bell and waited. She rang again and waited. After five minutes she walked up to A Deck.

The Negro orchestra, high on marijuana, remained seated after the explosion. Branch Morton walked over to the orchestra leader.

"Play 'The Star-Spangled Banner,' " he ordered.

The orchestra leader looked at him.

"What you say?" he asked.

"You black baboon, play 'The Star-Spangled Banner' on your horn!"

"Contract don't say nothing 'bout no Star-Spangled Banner," said a thin Negro in spectacles.

"This old boat am swinging on down!" someone in the orchestra yelled, and the musicians jumped down off the platform and scattered among the passengers.

Branch Morton walked over to a jukebox in a corner of the saloon. He saw "The Star-Spangled Banner" by Fats Waller. He put in a handful of quarters. The machine clicked and buzzed and began to play:

"OH SAY CAN YOU? YES YES"

Joe Bane fell against the door of his stateroom and plunged in. He threw himself on the bed and drew his knees up to his chin. He began to sob.

His wife sat on the bed and talked to him in a gentle hypnotic voice. "You can't stay here, Joey. This bed is going underwater. You can't stay here."

Gradually the sobbing stopped and Bane sat up. She helped him put on a life belt. "Come along," she said.

"Yes, honey face," he said, and followed her out the door.

"AND THE HOME OF THE BRAVE"

*   *   *

Mrs. Norris found the door to the captain's cabin ajar. She pushed it open and stepped in, knocking on the open door. A tall, thin, red-haired man with horn-rimmed glasses was sitting at a desk littered with maps. He glanced up without speaking.

"Oh Captain, is the ship sinking? Someone set off a bomb, they said. I'm Mrs. Norris—you know, Mr. Norris, shipping business. Oh the ship *is* sinking! I know, or you'd say something. Captain, you will take care of us? My maid and me?" She put out a hand to touch the captain's arm. The ship listed suddenly, throwing her heavily against the desk. Her wig slipped.

The captain stood up. He snatched the wig off her head and put it on.

"Give me that kimono!" he ordered.

Mrs. Norris screamed. She started for the door. The captain took three long, springy strides and blocked her way. Mrs. Norris rushed for a window, screaming. The captain took a revolver from his side pocket. He aimed at her bald pate outlined in the window, and fired.

"You Goddamned old fool," he said. "Give me that kimono!"

Philip Bradshinkel walked up to a sailor with his affable smile.

"Room for the ladies on this one?" he asked, indicating a lifeboat.

The sailor looked at him sourly.

"No!" said the sailor. He turned away and went on working on the launching davit.

"Now wait a minute," said Bradshinkel. "You can't mean that. Women and children first, you know."

"Nobody goes on this lifeboat but the crew," said the sailor.

"Oh, I understand," said Bradshinkel, pulling out a wad of bills.

The sailor snatched the money.

"I thought so," said Bradshinkel. He took his wife by the arm and started to help her into the lifeboat.

"Get that old meat outa here!" screamed the sailor.

"But you made a bargain! You took my money!"

"Oh, for Chrissakes," said the sailor. "I just took your dough so it wouldn't get wet!"

"But my wife is a woman!"

Suddenly the sailor became very gentle.

"All my life," he said, "all my life I been a sucker for a classy dame. I seen 'em in the Sunday papers laying on the beach. Soft messy tits. They just lay there and smile dirty. Jesus they heat my pants!"

Bradshinkel nudged his wife. "Smile at him." He winked at the sailor. "What do you say?"

"Naw," said the sailor, "I ain't got time to lay her now."

"Later," said Bradshinkel.

"Later's no good. Besides she's special built for you. She can't give me no kids and she drinks alla time. Like I say, I just seen her in the Sunday papers and wanted her like a dog wants rotten meat."

"Let me talk to this man," said Branch Morton. He worked his fingers over the fleshy shoulder of his wife and pulled her under his armpit.

"This little woman is a mother," he said. The sailor blew his nose on the deck. Morton grabbed the sailor by the biceps.

"In Clayton, Missouri, seven kids whisper her name through their thumbs before they go to sleep."

The sailor pulled his arm free. Morton dropped both hands to his sides, palms facing forward.

"As man to man," he was pleading. "As man to man."

Two Negro musicians, their eyes gleaming, came up behind the two wives. One took Mrs. Morton by the arm, the other took Mrs. Bradshinkel.

"Can we have dis dance witchu?"

"THAT OUR FLAG WAS STILL THERE"

Captain Kramer, wearing Mrs. Norris's kimono and wig, his face heavily smeared with cold cream, and carrying a small suitcase, walked down to C Deck, the kimono billowing out behind him. He opened the side door to the purser's office with a pass key. A thin-shouldered man in a purser's uniform was stuffing currency and jewels into a suitcase in front of an open safe.

The captain's revolver swung free of his brassiere and he fired twice.

"SO GALLANTLY STREAMING"

Finch, the radio operator, washed down bicarbonate of soda and belched into his hand. He put the glass down and went on tapping out S.O.S.

"S.O.S. . . . S.S. *America* . . . S.O.S. . . . off Jersey coast . . . S.O.S. . . . son-of-a-bitching set . . . S.O.S. . . . might smell us . . . S.O.S. . . .

son-of-a-bitching crew . . . S.O.S. . . . *Comrade* Finch . . . comrade in
a pig's ass . . . S.O.S. . . . Goddamned captain's a brown artist . . .
S.O.S. . . . S.S. *America* . . . S.O.S. . . . S.S. Crapbox. . ."

Lifting his kimono with his left hand, the captain stepped in
behind the radio operator. He fired one shot into the back of Finch's
head. He shoved the small body aside and smashed the radio with a
chair.

"O'ER THE RAMPARTS WE WATCH"

Dr. Benway, carrying his satchel, pushed through the passengers
crowded around Lifeboat No. 1.

"Are you all right?" he shouted, seating himself among the
women. "I'm the doctor."

"BY THE ROCKETS' RED GLARE"

When the captain reached Lifeboat No. I there were two seats left.
Some of the passengers were blocking each other as they tried to
force their way in, others were pushing forward a wife, a mother, or
a child. The captain shoved them all out of his way, leapt into the
boat and sat down. A boy pushed through the crowd in the
captain's wake.

"Please," he said. "I'm only thirteen."

"Yes yes," said the captain, "you can sit by me."

The boat started jerkily toward the water, lowered by four male
passengers. A woman handed her baby to the captain.

"Take care of my baby, for God's sake!"

Joe Bane landed in the boat and slithered noisily under a thwart.
Dr. Benway cast off the ropes. The doctor and the boy started to
row. The captain looked back at the ship.

"OH SAY CAN YOU SEE."

A third-year divinity student named Titman heard Perkins in his
stateroom, yelling for his attendant. He opened the door and looked
in.

"What do you want, thicken thit?" said Perkins.

"I want to help you," said Titman.

"Thtick it up and thwitht it!" said Perkins.

"Easy does it," said Titman, walking over toward the broken
wheelchair. "Everything is going to be okey-dokey."

"Thneaked off!" Perkins put a hand on one hip and jerked the elbow forward in a grotesque indication of dancing. "Danthing with floothies!"

"We'll find him," said Titman, lifting Perkins out of the wheel-chair. He carried the withered body in his arms like a child. As Titman walked out of the stateroom, Perkins snatched up a butcher knife used by his attendant to make sandwiches.

"Danthing with floothies!"

"BY THE DAWN'S EARLY LIGHT!"

A crowd of passengers was fighting around Lifeboat No. 7. It was the last boat that could be launched. They were using bottles, broken deck chairs and fire axes. Titman, carrying Perkins in his arms, made his way through the fighting unnoticed. He placed Perkins in a seat at the stern.

"There you are," said Titman. "All set."

Perkins said nothing. He sat there, chin drawn back, eyes shining, the butcher knife clutched rigidly in one hand.

A hysterical crowd from second class began pushing from behind. A big-faced shoe clerk with long yellow teeth grabbed Mrs. Bane and shoved her forward. "Ladies first!" he yelled.

A wedge of men formed behind him and pushed. A shot sounded and Mrs. Bane fell forward, hitting the lifeboat. The wedge broke, rolling and scrambling. A man in an ROTC uniform with a .45 automatic in his hand stood by the lifeboat. He covered the sailor at the launching davit.

"Let this thing down!" he ordered.

As the lifeboat slid down toward the water, a cry went up from the passengers on deck. Some of them jumped into the water, others were pushed by the people behind.

"Let 'er go, God damn it, let 'er go!" yelled Perkins.

"Throw him out!"

A hand rose out of the water and closed on the side of the boat. Springlike, Perkins brought the knife down. The fingers fell into the boat and the bloody stump of hand slipped back into the water.

The man with the gun was standing in the stern. "Get going!" he ordered. The sailors pulled hard on the oars.

Perkins worked feverishly, chopping on all sides. "Bathtardth, thonthabitheth!" The swimmers screamed and fell away from the boat.

"That a boy."

"Don't let 'em swamp us."

"Atta boy, Comrade."

"Bathtardth, thonthabitheth! Bathtardth, thonthabitheth!"

"OH SAY DO DAT STAR-SPANGLED BANNER YET WAVE"

The Evening News

Barbara Cannon showed your reporter her souvenirs of the disaster: a life belt autographed by the crew, and a severed human finger.

"I don't know," said Miss Cannon. "I feel sorta bad about this old finger."

"O'ER THE LAND OF THE FREE"

(1935)

from JUNKY (DEFINITIVE EDITION)

My first experience with junk was during the War, about 1944 or 1945. I had made the acquaintance of a man named Norton who was working in a shipyard at the time. Norton, whose real name was Morelli or something like that, had been discharged from the peacetime Army for forging a pay check, and was classified 4-F for reasons of bad character. He looked like George Raft, but was taller. Norton was trying to improve his English and achieve a smooth, affable manner. Affability, however, did not come natural to him. In repose, his expression was sullen and mean, and you knew he always had that mean look when you turned your back.

Norton was a hard-working thief and he did not feel right unless he stole something every day from the shipyard where he worked. A tool, some canned goods, a pair of overalls, anything at all. One day he called me up and said he had stolen a Tommy gun. Could I find someone to buy it? I said, "Maybe. Bring it over."

The housing shortage was getting under way. I paid fifteen dollars per week for a dirty apartment that opened onto a companionway and never got any sunlight. The wallpaper was flaking off because the radiator leaked steam when there was any steam in it to leak. I had the windows sealed shut against the cold with a caulking of newspapers. The place was full of roaches and occasionally I killed a bedbug.

I was sitting by the radiator, a little damp from the steam, when I heard Norton's knock. I opened the door, and there he was standing in the dark hall with a big parcel wrapped in brown paper under his arm. He smiled and said, "Hello."

I said, "Come in, Norton, and take off your coat."

He unwrapped the Tommy gun and we assembled it and snapped the firing pin.

I said I would find someone to buy it.

Norton said, "Oh, here's something else I picked up."

It was a flat yellow box with five one-half grain syrettes of morphine tartrate.

"This is just a sample," he said, indicating the morphine. "I've got fifteen of these boxes at home and I can get more if you get rid of these."

I said, "I'll see what I can do."

At that time I had never used any junk and it did not occur to me to try it. I began looking for someone to buy the two items and that is how I ran into Roy and Herman.

I knew a young hoodlum from upstate New York who was working as a short-order cook in Riker's, "cooling off," as he explained. I called him and said I had something to get rid of, and made an appointment to meet him in the Angle Bar on Eighth Avenue near 42nd Street.

This bar was a meeting place for 42nd Street hustlers, a peculiar breed of four-flushing, would-be criminals. They are always looking for a "set-up man," someone to plan jobs and tell them exactly what to do. Since no "set-up man" would have anything to do with people so obviously inept, unlucky, and unsuccessful, they go on looking, fabricating preposterous lies about their big scores, cooling off as dishwashers, soda jerks, waiters, occasionally rolling a drunk or a timid queer, looking, always looking, for the "set-up man" with a big job who will say, "I've been watching you. You're the man I need for this set-up. Now listen. . ."

Jack—through whom I met Roy and Herman—was not one of these lost sheep looking for the shepherd with a diamond ring and a gun in the shoulder holster and the hard, confident voice with overtones of connections, fixes, set-ups that would make a stickup sound easy and sure of success. Jack was very successful from time to time and would turn up in new clothes and even new cars. He was also an inveterate liar who seemed to lie more for himself than for any visible audience. He had a clean-cut, healthy country face, but there was something curiously diseased about him. He was subject to sudden fluctuations in weight, like a diabetic or a sufferer from liver trouble. These changes in weight were often accompanied by an uncontrollable fit of restlessness, so that he would disappear for some days.

The effect was uncanny. You would see him one time a fresh-faced kid. A week or so later he would turn up so thin, sallow and old-looking, you would have to look twice to recognize him. His face was lined with suffering in which his eyes did not participate. It was a suffering of his cells alone. He himself—the conscious ego that looked out of the glazed, alert-calm hoodlum eyes—would have nothing to do with this suffering of his rejected other self, a suffering of the nervous system, of flesh and viscera and cells.

He slid into the booth where I was sitting and ordered a shot of whisky. He tossed it off, put the glass down and looked at me with his head tilted a little to one side and back.

"What's this guy got?" he said.

"A Tommy gun and about thirty-five grains of morphine."

"The morphine I can get rid of right away, but the Tommy gun may take a little time."

Two detectives walked in and leaned on the bar talking to the bartender. Jack jerked his head in their direction. "The law. Let's take a walk."

I followed him out of the bar. He walked through the door sliding sideways. "I'm taking you to someone who will want the morphine," he said. "You want to forget this address."

We went down to the bottom level of the Independent Subway. Jack's voice, talking to his invisible audience, went on and on. He had a knack of throwing his voice directly into your consciousness. No external noise drowned him out. "Give me a thirty-eight every time. Just flick back the hammer and let her go. I'll drop anyone at five hundred feet. Don't care what you say. My brother has two 30-caliber machine guns stashed in Iowa."

We got off the subway and began to walk on snow-covered sidewalks between tenements.

"The guy owed me for a long time, see? I knew he had it but he wouldn't pay, so I waited for him when he finished work. I had a roll of nickels. No one can hang anything on you for carrying U.S. currency. Told me he was broke. I cracked his jaw and took my money off him. Two of his friends standing there, but they kept out of it. I'd've switched a blade on them."

We were walking up tenement stairs. The stairs were made of worn black metal. We stopped in front of a narrow, metal-covered door, and Jack gave an elaborate knock inclining his head to the floor like a safecracker. The door was opened by a large, flabby, middle-aged queer, with tattooing on his forearms and even on the backs of his hands.

"This is Joey," Jack said, and Joey said, "Hello there."

Jack pulled a five-dollar bill from his pocket and gave it to Joey. "Get us a quart of Schenley's, will you, Joey?"

Joey put on an overcoat and went out.

In many tenement apartments the front door opens directly into the kitchen. This was such an apartment and we were in the kitchen.

After Joey went out I noticed another man who was standing there looking at me. Waves of hostility and suspicion flowed out from his large brown eyes like some sort of television broadcast. The effect was almost like a physical impact. The man was small and very thin, his neck loose in the collar of his shirt. His complexion was fading from brown to a mottled yellow, and pancake make-up had been heavily applied in an attempt to conceal a skin eruption. His mouth was drawn down at the corners in a grimace of petulant annoyance.

"Who's this?" he said. His name, I learned later, was Herman.

"Friend of mine. He's got some morphine he wants to get rid of."

Herman shrugged and turned out his hands. "I don't think I want to bother, really."

"Okay," Jack said, "we'll sell it to someone else. Come on, Bill."

We went into the front room. There was a small radio, a china Buddha with a votive candle in front of it, pieces of bric-a-brac. A man was lying on a studio couch. He sat up as we entered the room and said hello and smiled pleasantly, showing discolored, brownish teeth. It was a Southern voice with the accent of East Texas.

Jack said, "Roy, this is a friend of mine. He has some morphine he wants to sell."

The man sat up straighter and swung his legs off the couch. His jaw fell slackly, giving his face a vacant look. The skin of his face was smooth and brown. The cheek-bones were high and he looked Oriental. His ears stuck out at right angles from his asymmetrical skull. The eyes were brown and they had a peculiar brilliance, as though points of light were shining behind them. The light in the room glinted on the points of light in his eyes like an opal.

"How much do you have?" he asked me.

"Seventy-five half grain syrettes."

"The regular price is two dollars a grain," he said, "but syrettes go for a little less. People want tablets. Those syrettes have too much water and you have to squeeze the stuff out and cook it down." He paused and his face went blank: "I could go about one-fifty a grain," he said finally.

"I guess that will be okay," I said.

He asked how we could make contact and I gave him my phone number.

Joey came back with the whisky and we all had a drink. Herman stuck his head in from the kitchen and said to Jack, "Could I talk to you for a minute?"

I could hear them arguing about something. Then Jack came back and Herman stayed in the kitchen. We all had a few drinks and Jack began telling a story.

"My partner was going through the joint. The guy was sleeping, and I was standing over him with a three-foot length of pipe I found in the bathroom. The pipe had a faucet on the end of it, see? All of a sudden he comes up and jumps straight out of bed, running. I let him have it with the faucet end, and he goes on running right out into the other room, the blood spurting out of his head ten feet every time his heart beat." He made a pumping motion with his hand. "You could see the brain there and the blood coming out of it." Jack began to laugh uncontrollably. "My girl was waiting out in the car. She called me—ha-ha-ha!—she called me—ha-ha-ha!—a cold-blooded killer."

He laughed until his face was purple.

A few nights after meeting Roy and Herman, I used one of the syrettes, which was my first experience with junk. A syrette is like a toothpaste tube with a needle on the end. You push a pin down through the needle; the pin punctures the seal; and the syrette is ready to shoot.

Morphine hits the backs of the legs first, then the back of the neck, a spreading wave of relaxation slackening the muscles away from the bones so that you seem to float without outlines, like lying in warm salt water. As this relaxing wave spread through my tissues, I experienced a strong feeling of fear. I had the feeling that some horrible image was just beyond the field of vision, moving, as

I turned my head, so that I never quite saw it. I felt nauseous; I lay down and closed my eyes. A series of pictures passed, like watching a movie: A huge, neon-lighted cocktail bar that got larger and larger until streets, traffic, and street repairs were included in it; a waitress carrying a skull on a tray; stars in a clear sky. The physical impact of the fear of death; the shutting off of breath; the stopping of blood.

I dozed off and woke up with a start of fear. Next morning I vomited and felt sick until noon.

Roy called that night.

"About what we were discussing the other night," he said. "I could go about four dollars per box and take five boxes now. Are you busy? I'll come over to your place. We'll come to some kind of agreement."

A few minutes later he knocked at the door. He had on a Glen plaid suit and a dark, coffee-colored shirt. We said hello. He looked around blankly and said, "If you don't mind, I'll take one of those now."

I opened the box. He took out a syrette and injected it into his leg. He pulled up his pants briskly and took out twenty dollars. I put five boxes on the kitchen table.

"I think I'll take them out of the boxes," he said. "Too bulky."

He began putting the syrettes in his coat pockets. "I don't think they'll perforate this way," he said. "Listen, I'll call you again in a day or so after I get rid of these and have some more money." He was adjusting his hat over his asymmetrical skull. "I'll see you."

Next day he was back. He shot another syrette and pulled out forty dollars. I laid out ten boxes and kept two.

"These are for me," I said.

He looked at me, surprised. "You use it?"

"Now and then."

"It's bad stuff," he said, shaking his head. "The worst thing that can happen to a man. We all think we can control it at first. Sometimes we don't want to control it." He laughed. "I'll take all you can get at this price."

Next day he was back. He asked if I didn't want to change my mind about selling the two boxes. I said no. He bought two syrettes for a dollar each, shot them both, and left. He said he had signed on for a two-month trip.

* * *

During the next month I used up the eight syrettes I had not sold. The fear I had experienced after using the first syrette was not noticeable after the third; but still, from time to time, after taking a shot I would wake up with a start of fear. After six weeks or so I gave Roy a ring, not expecting him to be back from his trip, but then I heard his voice on the phone.

I said, "Say, do you have any to sell? Of the material I sold you before?"

There was a pause.

"Ye-es," he said, "I can let you have six, but the price will have to be three dollars per. You understand I don't have many."

"Okay," I said. "You know the way. Bring it on over."

It was twelve one-half grain tablets in a thin glass tube. I paid him eighteen dollars and he apologized again for the retail rate.

Next day he bought two grains back.

"It's mighty hard to get now at any price," he said, looking for a vein in his leg. He finally hit a vein and shot the liquid in with an air bubble. "If air bubbles could kill you, there wouldn't be a junkie alive," he said, pulling up his pants.

Later that day Roy pointed out to me a drugstore where they sold needles without any questions—very few drugstores will sell them without a prescription. He showed me how to make a collar out of paper to fit the needle to an eyedropper. An eyedropper is easier to use than a regular hypo, especially for giving yourself vein shots.

Several days later Roy sent me to see a doctor with a story about kidney stones, to hit him for a morphine prescription. The doctor's wife slammed the door in my face, but Roy finally got past her and made the doctor for a ten-grain script.

The doctor's office was in junk territory on 102nd, off Broadway. He was a doddering old man and could not resist the junkies who filled his office and were, in fact, his only patients. It seemed to give him a feeling of importance to look out and see an office full of people. I guess he had reached a point where he could change the appearance of things to suit his needs and when he looked out there he saw a distinguished and diversified clientele, probably well-dressed in 1910 style, instead of a bunch of ratty-looking junkies come to hit him for a morphine script.

Roy shipped out at two- or three-week intervals. His trips were Army Transport and generally short. When he was in town we generally split a few scripts. The old croaker on 102nd finally lost his mind altogether and no drugstore would fill his scripts, but Roy located an Italian doctor out in the Bronx who would write.

I was taking a shot from time to time, but I was a long way from having a habit. At this time I moved into an apartment on the Lower East Side. It was a tenement apartment with the front door opening into the kitchen.

I began dropping into the Angle Bar every night and saw quite a bit of Herman. I managed to overcome his original bad impression of me, and soon I was buying his drinks and meals, and he was hitting me for "smash" (change) at regular intervals. Herman did not have a habit at this time. In fact, he seldom got a habit unless someone else paid for it. But he was always high on something—weed, benzedrine, or knocked out of his mind on "goof balls." He showed up at the Angle every night with a big slob of a Polack called Whitey. There were four Whities in the Angle set, which made for confusion. This Whitey combined the sensitivity of a neurotic with a psychopath's readiness for violence. He was convinced that nobody liked him, a fact that seemed to cause him a great deal of worry.

One Tuesday night Roy and I were standing at the end of the Angle bar. Subway Mike was there, and Frankie Dolan. Dolan was an Irish boy with a cast in one eye. He specialized in crummy scores, beating up defenseless drunks, and holding out on his confederates. "I got no honor," he would say. "I'm a rat." And he would giggle.

Subway Mike had a large, pale face and long teeth. He looked like some specialized kind of underground animal that preys on the animals of the surface. He was a skillful lush-worker, but he had no front. Any cop would do a double-take at sight of him, and he was well known to the subway squad. So Mike spent at least half of his time on the Island doing the five-twenty-nine for jostling.

This night Herman was knocked out on "nembies" and his head kept falling down onto the bar. Whitey was stomping up and down the length of the bar trying to promote some free drinks. The boys at the bar sat rigid and tense, clutching their drinks, quickly pocketing their change. I heard Whitey say to the bartender, "Keep this for me, will you?" and he passed his large clasp knife across the bar. The boys sat there silent and gloomy under the fluorescent lights. They were all afraid of Whitey, all except Roy. Roy sipped his beer grimly. His eyes shone with their peculiar phosphorescence. His long asymmetrical body was draped against the bar. He didn't look at Whitey, but at the opposite wall where the booths were located. Once he said to me, "He's no more drunk than I am. He's just thirsty."

Whitey was standing in the middle of the bar, his fists doubled up, tears streaming down his face. "I'm no good," he said. "I'm no good. Can't anyone understand I don't know what I'm doing?"

The boys tried to get as far away from him as possible without attracting his attention.

Subway Slim, Mike's occasional partner, came in and ordered a beer. He was tall and bony, and his ugly face had a curiously inanimate look, as if made out of wood. Whitey slapped him on the back and I heard Slim say, "For Christ's sake, Whitey." There was more interchange I didn't hear. Somewhere along the line Whitey must have got his knife back from the bartender. He got behind Slim and suddenly pushed his hand against Slim's back. Slim fell forward against the bar, groaning. I saw Whitey walk to the front of the bar and look around. He closed his knife and slipped it into his pocket.

Roy said, "Let's go."

Whitey had disappeared and the bar was empty except for Mike, who was holding Slim up on one side. Frankie Dolan was on the other.

I heard next day from Frankie that Slim was okay. "The croaker at the hospital said the knife just missed a kidney."

Roy said, "The big slob. I can see a real muscle man, but a guy like that going around picking up dimes and quarters off the bar. I was ready for him. I was going to kick him in the belly first, then get one of those quart beer bottles from the case on the floor and break it over his sconce. With a big villain like that you've got to use strategy."

We were all barred from the Angle, which shortly afterwards changed its name to the Roxy Grill.

One night I went to the Henry Street address to look up Jack. A tall, red-haired girl met me at the door.

"I'm Mary," she said. "Come in."

It seemed that Jack was in Washington on business.

"Come on into the front room," she said, pushing aside a red corduroy curtain. "I talk to landlords and bill collectors in the kitchen. We *live* in here."

I looked around. The bric-a-brac had gone. The place looked like a chop suey joint. There were black and red lacquered tables scattered around, black curtains covered the window. A colored wheel had been painted on the ceiling with little squares and triangles of different colors giving a mosaic effect.

"Jack did that," Mary said, pointing to the wheel. "You should have seen him. He stretched a board between two ladders and lay down on it. Paint kept dripping into his face. He gets a kick out of doing things like that. We get some frantic kicks out of that wheel when we're high. We lay on our backs and dig the wheel and pretty soon it begins to spin. The longer you watch it, the faster it spins."

This wheel had the nightmarish vulgarity of Aztec mosaics, the bloody, vulgar nightmare, the heart throbbing in the morning sun, the garish pinks and blues of souvenir ashtrays, postcards and calendars. The walls were painted black and there was a Chinese character in red lacquer on one wall.

"We don't know what it means," she said.

"Shirts thirty-one cents," I suggested.

She turned on me her blank, cold smile. She began talking about Jack. "I'm queer for Jack," she said. "He works at being a thief just like any job. Used to come home nights and hand me his gun. 'Stash that!' He likes to work around the house, painting and making furniture."

As she talked she moved around the room, throwing herself from one chair to another, crossing and uncrossing her legs, adjusting her slip, so as to give me a view of her anatomy in installments.

She went on to tell me how her days were numbered by a rare disease. "Only twenty-six cases on record. In a few years I won't be able to get around at all. You see, my system can't absorb calcium and the bones are slowly dissolving. My legs will have to be amputated eventually, then the arms."

There was something boneless about her, like a deep-sea creature. Her eyes were cold fish eyes that looked at you through a viscous medium she carried about with her. I could see those eyes in a shapeless, protoplasmic mass undulating over the dark sea floor.

"Benzedrine is a good kick," she said. "Three strips of the paper or about ten tablets. Or take two strips of benny and two goof balls. They get down there and have a fight. It's a good drive."

Three young hoodlums from Brooklyn drifted in, woodenfaced, hands-in-pockets, stylized as a ballet. They were looking for Jack.

He had given them a short count in some deal. At least, that was the general idea. They conveyed their meaning less by words than by significant jerks of the head and by stalking around the apartment and leaning against the walls. At length, one of them walked to the door and jerked his head. They filed out.

"Would you like to get high?" Mary asked. "There may be a roach around here somewhere." She began rummaging around in drawers and ashtrays. "No, I guess not. Why don't we go uptown? I know several good connections we can probably catch about now."

A young man lurched in with some object wrapped in brown paper under one arm. "Ditch this on your way out," he said, putting it down on the table. He staggered into the bedroom on the other side of the kitchen. When we got outside I let the wrapping paper fall loose revealing the coin box of a pay toilet crudely jimmied open.

In Times Square we got in a taxi and began cruising up and down the side streets, Mary giving directions. Every now and then she would yell "Stop!" and jump out, her red hair streaming, and I would see her overhaul some character and start talking. "The connection was here about ten minutes ago. This character's holding, but he won't turn loose of any." Later: "The regular connection is gone for the night. He lives in the Bronx. But just stop here for a minute. I may find someone in Kellogg's." Finally: "No one seems to be anywhere. It's a bit late to score. Let's buy some benny tubes and go over to Ronnie's. They have some gone numbers on the box. We can order coffee and get high on benny."

Ronnie's was a spot near 52nd and Sixth where musicians came for fried chicken and coffee after one p.m. We sat down in a booth and ordered coffee. Mary cracked a benzedrine tube expertly, extracting the folded paper, and handed me three strips. "Roll it up into a pill and wash it down with coffee."

The paper gave off a sickening odor of menthol. Several people nearby sniffed and smiled. I nearly gagged on the wad of paper, but finally got it down. Mary selected some gone numbers and beat on the table with the expression of a masturbating idiot.

I began talking very fast. My mouth was dry and my spit came out in round white balls—spitting cotton, it's called. We were walking around Times Square. Mary wanted to locate someone with a "piccolo" (victrola). I was full of expansive, benevolent feelings, and suddenly wanted to call on people I hadn't seen in months or even years, people I did not like and who did not like me. We made a number of unsuccessful attempts to locate the ideal piccolo-owning host. Somewhere along the line we picked up Peter and finally decided to go back to the Henry Street apartment where there was at least a radio.

Peter and Mary and I spent the next thirty hours in the apartment. From time to time we would make coffee and swallow more benzedrine. Mary was describing the techniques she used to get money from the "Johns" who formed her principal source of revenue.

"Always build a John up. If he has any sort of body at all say, 'Oh, don't ever hurt me.' A John is different from a sucker. When you're with a sucker you're on the alert all the time. You give him nothing. A sucker is just to be taken. But a John is different. You give him what he pays for. When you're with him you enjoy yourself and you want him to enjoy himself, too.

"If you want to really bring a man down, light a cigarette in the middle of intercourse. Of course, I really don't like men at all sexually. What I really dig is chicks. I get a kick out of taking a proud chick and breaking her spirit, making her see she is just an animal. A chick is never as beautiful after she's been broken. Say, this is sort of a fireside kick," she said, pointing to the radio which was the only light in the room.

Her face contorted into an expression of monkey-like rage as she talked about men who accosted her on the street. "Sonofabitch!" she snarled. "They can tell when a woman isn't looking for a pickup. I used to cruise around with brass knuckles on under my gloves just waiting for one of those peasants to crack at me."

TO ALLEN GINSBURG, 23 MAY 1953
(LIMA, PERU)

Dear Al,

Enclose a routine I dreamed up. The idea did come to me in a dream from which I woke up laughing—

Rolled for $200 in traveller's checks. No loss really as American Express refunds. Recovering from a bout of Pisco neuritis, and Doc has taken a lung X-ray. First Caqueta malaria, then Esmeraldas grippe, now Pisco neuritis—(Pisco is local liquor. Seems to be poison)—can't leave Lima until neuritis clears up.

May 24 (1953)

Ho hum dept. Rolled again. My glasses and a pocket knife. Losing all my fucking valuables in the service.

This is nation of kleptomaniacs. In all my experience as a homosexual I have never been the victim of such idiotic pilferings of articles of no conceivable use to anyone else. Glasses and traveller's checks yet.

Trouble is I share with the late Father Flangan—he of Boy's Town—the deep conviction that there is no such thing as a bad boy.

Got to lay off the juice. Hand shaking so I can hardly write. Must cut short.

Love,
Bill

ROOSEVELT AFTER INAUGURATION

Immediately after the Inauguration Roosevelt appeared on the White House balcony dressed in the purple robes of a Roman Emperor and, leading a blind toothless lion on a gold chain, hog-called his constituents to come and get their appointments. The constituents rushed up grunting and squealing like the hogs they were.

An old queen known to the Brooklyn Police as "Jerk Off Annie," was named to the Joint Chiefs of Staff, so that the younger staff officers were subject to unspeakable indignities in the lavatories of the Pentagon, to avoid which many set up field latrines in their offices.

To a transvestite lizzie went the post of Congressional Librarian. She immediately barred the male sex from the premises—a world-famous professor of philology suffered a broken jaw at the hands of a bull dyke when he attempted to enter the Library. The Library was given over to Lesbian orgies, which she termed the Rites of the Vested Virgins.

A veteran panhandler was appointed Secretary of State, and disregarding the dignity of his office, solicited nickels and dimes in the corridors of the State Department.

"Subway Slim" the lush worker assumed the office of Under Secretary of State and Chief of Protocol, and occasioned diplomatic rupture with England when the English Ambassador "came up on him"—lush worker term for a lush waking up when you are going through his pockets—at a banquet in the Swedish Embassy.

Lonny the Pimp became Ambassador-at-Large, and went on tour with fifty "secretaries," exercising his despicable trade.

A female impersonator, known as "Eddie the Lady," headed the Atomic Energy Commission, and enrolled the physicists into a male chorus which was booked as "The Atomic Kids."

In short, men who had gone grey and toothless in the faithful service of their country were summarily dismissed in the grossest terms—like "You're fired you old fuck. Get your piles outa here."— and in many cases thrown bodily out of their offices. Hoodlums and riffraff of the vilest caliber filled the highest offices of the land. To mention only a few of his scandalous appointments:

Secretary of the Treasury: "Pantopon Mike," an old-time schmecker.

Head of the FBI: A Turkish Bath attendant and specialist in unethical massage.

Attorney General: A character known as "The Mink," a peddler of used condoms and a short-con artist.

Secretary of Agriculture: "Catfish Luke," the wastrel of Cuntville, Alabama, who had been drunk twenty years on paregoric and lemon extract.

Ambassador to the Court of St. James's: "Blubber Wilson," who hustled his goofball money shaking down fetishists in shoe stores.

Postmaster General: "The Yen Pox Kid," an old-time junky and con man on the skids. Currently working a routine known as "Taking It Off the Eye"— you plant a fake cataract in the savage's eye (savage is con man for sucker)—cheapest trick in the industry.

When the Supreme Court overruled some of the legislation perpetrated by this vile rout, Roosevelt forced that august body, one after the other, on threat of immediate reduction to the rank of Congressional Lavatory Attendants, to submit to intercourse with a purple-assed baboon; so that venerable, honored men surrendered themselves to the embraces of a lecherous snarling simian, while Roosevelt and his strumpet wife and the veteran brown-nose Harry Hopkins, smoking a communal hookah of hashish, watched the lamentable sight with cackles of obscene laughter. Justice Blackstrap succumbed to a rectal hemorrhage on the spot, but Roosevelt only laughed and said coarsely, "Plenty more where that came from."

Hopkins, unable to control himself, rolled on the floor in sycophantic convulsions, saying over and over "You're killin' me, Chief. You're killin' me."

Justice Hockactonsvol had both ears bitten off by the simian, and when Chief Justice Howard P. Herringbone asked to be excused, pleading his piles, Roosevelt told him brutally, "Best thing for piles is a baboon's prick up the ass. Right Harry?"

"Right Chief. I use no other. You heard what the man said. Drop your moth-eaten ass over that chair and show the visiting simian some Southern hospitality."

Roosevelt then appointed the baboon to replace Justice Blackstrap, "diseased."

"I'll have to remember that one boss," said Hopkins, breaking into loud guffaws.

So henceforth the proceedings of the Court were carried on with a screeching simian shitting and pissing and masturbating on the table and not infrequently leaping on one of the Justices and tearing him to shreds.

"He is entering a vote of dissent," Roosevelt would say with an evil chuckle. The vacancies so created were invariably filled by simians, so that, in the course of time, the Supreme Court came to consist of nine purple-assed baboons; and Roosevelt, claiming to be the only one able to interpret their decisions, thus gained control of the highest tribunal in the land.

He then set himself to throw off the restraints imposed by Congress and the Senate. He loosed innumerable crabs and other vermin in both houses. He had a corps of trained idiots who would rush in at a given signal and shit on the floor, and hecklers equipped with a brass band and fire hoses. He instituted continuous repairs. An army of workmen trooped through the Houses, slapping the solons in the face with boards, spilling hot tar down their necks, dropping tools on their feet, undermining them with air hammers; and finally he caused a steam shovel to be set up on the floors, so that the recalcitrant solons were either buried alive or drowned when the Houses flooded from broken water mains. The survivors attempted to carry on in the street, but were arrested for loitering and were sent to the workhouse like common bums. After release they were barred from office on the grounds of their police records.

Then Roosevelt gave himself over to such vile and unrestrained conduct as is shameful to speak of. He instituted a series of contests designed to promulgate the lowest acts and instincts of which the human species is capable. There was a Most Unsavory Act Contest, a Cheapest Trick Contest, Molest a Child Week, Turn In Your Best

Friend Week—professional stool pigeons disqualified—and the coveted title of All-Around Vilest Man of the Year. Sample entries: The junky who stole an opium suppository out of his grandmother's ass; the ship captain who put on women's clothes and rushed into the first lifeboat; the vice-squad cop who framed people, planting an artificial prick in their fly.

Roosevelt was convulsed with such hate for the species as it is, that he wished to degrade it beyond recognition. He could endure only the extremes of human behavior. The average, the middle-aged (he viewed middle age as a condition with no relation to chronological age), the middle-class, the bureaucrat filled him with loathing. One of his first acts was to burn every record in Washington; thousands of bureaucrats threw themselves into the flames.

"I'll make the cocksuckers glad to mutate," he would say, looking off into space as if seeking new frontiers of depravity.

(1953)

(from INTERZONE)
INTERNATIONAL ZONE

A miasma of suspicion and snobbery hangs over the European Quarter of Tangier. Everyone looks you over for the price tag, appraising you like merchandise in terms of immediate practical or prestige advantage. The Boulevard Pasteur is the Fifth Avenue of Tangier. The store clerks tend to be discourteous unless you buy something immediately. Inquiries without purchase are coldly and grudgingly answered.

My first night in town I went to a fashionable bar, one of the few places that continues prosperous in the present slump: dim light, well-dressed androgynous clientele, reminiscent of many bars on New York's Upper East Side.

I started conversation with a man on my right. He was wearing one of those brown sackcloth jackets, the inexpensive creation of an ultra-chic Worth Avenue shop. Evidently it is the final touch of smartness to appear in a twelve-dollar jacket, the costume jewelry pattern—I happened to know just where the jacket came from and how much it cost because I had one like it in my suitcase. (A few days later I gave it to a shoeshine boy.)

The man's face was grey, puffy, set in a mold of sour discontent, *rich* discontent. It's an expression you see more often on women, and if a woman sits there long enough with that expression of rich discontent and sourness, a Cadillac simply builds itself around her. A man would probably accrete a Jaguar. Come to think, I had seen a Jaguar parked outside the bar.

The man answered my questions in cautious, short sentences, carefully deleting any tinge of warmth or friendliness.

"Did you come here direct from the States?" I persisted.

"No. From Brazil."

He's warming up, I thought. I expected it would take two sentences to elicit that much information.

"So? And how did you come?"

"By yacht, *of course*."

I felt that anything would be an anticlimax after that, and allowed my shaky option on his notice to lapse.

The European Quarter of Tangier contains a surprising number of firstclass French and international restaurants, where excellent food is served at very reasonable prices. Sample menu at The Alhambra, one of the best French restaurants: Snails *à la bourgogne*, one half partridge with peas and potatoes, a frozen chocolate mousse, a selection of French cheeses, and fruit. Price: one dollar. This price and menu can be duplicated in ten or twelve other restaurants.

Walking downhill from the European Quarter, we come, by inexorable process of suction, to the Socco Chico—Little Market— which is no longer a market at all but simply a paved rectangle about a block long, lined on both sides with shops and cafés. The Café Central, by reason of a location that allows the best view of the most people passing through the Socco, is the official meeting place of the Socco Chico set. Cars are barred from the Socco between eight A.M. and twelve midnight. Often groups without money to order coffee will stand for hours in the Socco, talking. During the day they can sit in front of the cafés without ordering, but from five to eight P.M. they must relinquish their seats to paying clients, unless they can strike up a conversation with a group of payers.

The Socco Chico is the meeting place, the nerve center, the switchboard of Tangier. Practically everyone in town shows there once a day at least. Many residents of Tangier spend most of their waking hours in the Socco. On all sides you see men washed up here in hopeless, dead-end situations, waiting for job offers, acceptance checks, visas, permits that will never come. All their lives they have drifted with an unlucky current, always taking the wrong turn. Here they are. This is it. Last stop: the Socco Chico of Tangier.

The market of psychic exchange is as glutted as the shops. A nightmare feeling of stasis permeates the Socco, like nothing can happen, nothing can change. Conversations disintegrate in cosmic inanity. People sit at café tables, silent and separate as stones. No other relation than physical closeness is possible. Economic laws, untouched by any human factor, evolve equations of ultimate stasis. Someday the young Spaniards in gabardine trench coats talking about soccer, the Arab guides and hustlers pitching pennies and smoking their *kief* pipes, the perverts sitting in front of the cafés looking over the boys, the boys parading past, the mooches and pimps and smugglers and money changers, will be frozen forever in a final, meaningless posture.

Futility seems to have gained a new dimension in the Socco. Sitting at a café table, listening to some "proposition," I would suddenly realize that the other was telling a fairy story to a child, the child inside himself: pathetic fantasies of smuggling, of trafficking in diamonds, drugs, guns, of starting nightclubs, bowling alleys, travel agencies. Or sometimes there was nothing wrong with the idea, except it would never be put into practice—the crisp, confident voice, the decisive gestures, in shocking contrast to the dead, hopeless eyes, drooping shoulders, clothes beyond mending, now allowed to disintegrate undisturbed.

Some of these men have ability and intelligence, like Brinton, who writes unpublishably obscene novels and exists on a small income. He undoubtedly has talent, but his work is hopelessly unsalable. He has intelligence, the rare ability to see relations between disparate factors, to coordinate data, but he moves through life like a phantom, never able to find the time, place and person to put anything into effect, to realize any project in terms of three-dimensional reality. He could have been a successful business executive, anthropologist, explorer, criminal, but the conjuncture of circumstances was never there. He is always too late or too early. His abilities remain larval, discarnate. He is the last of an archaic line, or the first here from another space-time way—in any case a man without context, of no place and no time.

Chris, the English Public School man, is the type who gets involved in fur farming, projects to raise ramie, frogs, cultured pearls. He had, in fact, lost all his savings in a bee-raising venture in the West Indies. He had observed that all the honey was imported and expensive. It looked like a sure thing, and he invested all he had. He did not know about a certain moth preying on the bees in that area, so that bee-raising is impossible.

"The sort of thing that could only happen to Chris," his friends say, for this is one chapter in a fantastic saga of misfortune. Who but Chris would be caught short at the beginning of the war, in a total shortage of drugs, and have a molar extracted without anesthetic? On another occasion he had collapsed with peritonitis and been shanghaied into a Syrian hospital, where they never heard of penicillin. He was rescued, on the verge of death, by the English consul. During the Spanish occupation of Tangier, he had been mistaken for a Spanish Communist and held for three weeks incommunicado in a detention camp.

Now he is broke and jobless in the Socco Chico, an intelligent man, willing to work, speaking several languages fluently, yet bearing the indelible brand of bad luck and failure. He is carefully shunned by the Jaguar-driving set, who fear contagion from the mysterious frequency that makes, of men like Chris, lifelong failures. He manages to stay alive teaching English and selling whiskey on commission.

Robbins is about fifty, with the face of a Cockney informer, the archetypal "Copper's Nark." He has a knack of pitching his whiny voice directly into your consciousness. No external noise drowns him out. Robbins looks like some unsuccessful species of *Homo non sapiens*, blackmailing the human race with his existence.

"Remember me? I'm the boy you left back there with the lemurs and the baboons. I'm not equipped for survival like *some* people." He holds out his deformed hands, hideously infantile, unfinished, his greedy blue eyes searching for a spot of guilt or uncertainty, on which he will fasten like a lamprey.

Robbins had all his money in his wife's name to evade income tax, and his wife ran away with a perfidious Australian. ("And I thought he was my friend.") This is one story. Robbins has a series, all involving his fall from wealth, betrayed and cheated by dishonest associates. He fixes his eyes on you probingly, accusingly: are you another betrayer who would refuse a man a few pesetas when he is down?

Robbins also comes on with the "I can't go home" routine, hinting at dark crimes committed in his native land. Many of the

Socco Chico regulars say they can't go home, trying to mitigate the dead grey of prosaic failure with a touch of borrowed color.

As a matter of fact, if anyone was wanted for a serious crime, the authorities could get him out of Tangier in ten minutes. As for these stories of disappearing into the Native Quarter, living there only makes a foreigner that much more conspicuous. Any guide or shoeshine boy would lead the cops to your door for five pesetas or a few cigarettes. So when someone gets confidential over the third drink you have bought him and tells you he can't go home, you are hearing the classic prelude to a touch.

A Danish boy is stranded here waiting for a friend to come with money and "the rest of his luggage." Every day he meets the ferry from Gibraltar and the ferry from Algeciras. A Spanish boy is waiting for a permit to enter the French Zone (for some reason persistently denied), where his uncle will give him a job. An English boy was robbed of all his money and valuables by a girlfriend.

I have never seen so many people in one place without money, or any prospects of money. This is partly due to the fact that anyone can enter Tangier. You don't have to prove solvency. So people come here hoping to get a job, or become smugglers. But there are no jobs in Tangier, and smuggling is as overcrowded as any other line. So they end up on the burn in the Socco Chico.

All of them curse Tangier, and hope for some miracle that will deliver them from the Socco Chico. They will get a job on a yacht, they will write a best-seller, they will smuggle a thousand cases of Scotch into Spain, they will find someone to finance their roulette system. It is typical of these people that they all believe in some gambling system, usually a variation on the old routine of doubling up when you lose, which is the pattern of their lives. They always back up their mistakes with more of themselves.

Some of the Socco Chico regulars, like Chris, make a real effort to support themselves. Others are full-time professional spongers. Antonio the Portuguese is mooch to the bone. He won't work. In a sense, he can't work. He is a mutilated fragment of the human potential, specialized to the point where he cannot exist without a host. His mere presence is an irritation. Phantom tendrils reach out from him, feeling for a point of weakness on which to fasten.

Jimmy the Dane is another full-time mooch. He has a gift for showing precisely when you don't want to see him, and saying exactly what you don't want to hear. His technique is to make you dislike him more than his actual behavior, a bit obnoxious to be sure, warrants. This makes you feel guilty toward him, so you buy him off with a drink or a few pesetas.

Some mooches specialize in tourists and transients, making no attempt to establish themselves on terms of social equality with the long-term residents. They use some variation of the short con, strictly one-time touches.

There is a Jewish mooch who looks vaguely like a detective or some form of authority. He approaches a tourist in a somewhat peremptory manner. The tourist anticipates an inspection of his passport or some other annoyance. When he finds out it is merely a question of a small "loan," he often gives the money in relief.

A young Norwegian has a routine of approaching visitors without his glass eye, a really unnerving sight. He needs money to buy a glass eye, or he will lose a job he is going to apply for in the morning. "How can I work as a waiter looking so as this?" he says, turning his empty socket on the victim. "I would frighten the customers, is it not?"

Many of the Socco Chico regulars are left over from the Boom. A few years ago the town was full of operators and spenders. There was a boom of money changing and transfer, smuggling and borderline enterprise. Restaurants and hotels turned customers away. Bars served a full house around the clock.

What happened? What gave out? What corresponds to the gold, the oil, the construction projects? Largely, inequalities in prices and exchange rates. Tangier is a clearinghouse, from which currency and merchandise move in any direction towards higher prices. Under this constant flow of goods, shortages created by the war are supplied, prices and currency approach standard rates, and Tangier is running down like the dying universe, where no movement is possible because all energy is equally distributed.

Tangier is a vast overstocked market, everything for sale and no buyers. A glut of obscure brands of Scotch, inferior German cameras and Swiss watches, second-run factory-reject nylons, typewriters unknown anywhere else, is displayed in shop after shop. There is quite simply too much of everything, too much merchandise, housing, labor, too many guides, pimps, prostitutes and smugglers. A classic, archetypical depression.

The guides of Tangier are in a class by themselves, and I have never seen their equal for insolence, persistence and all-around obnoxiousness. It is not surprising that the very word "guide" carries, in Tangier, the strongest opprobrium.

The Navy issues a bulletin on what to do if you find yourself in shark-infested waters: "Above all, avoid making uncoordinated, flailing movements that might be interpreted by a shark as the struggles of a disabled fish." The same advice might apply to keeping off guides. They are infallibly attracted by the uncoordinated movements of the tourist in a strange medium. The least show of uncertainty, of not knowing exactly where you are going, and they rush on you from their lurking places in side streets and Arab cafés.

"Want nice girl, mister?"

"See Kasbah? Sultan's Palace?"

"Want *kief*? Watch me fuck my sister?"

"Caves of Hercules? Nice boy?"

Their persistence is amazing, their impertinence unlimited. They will follow one for blocks, finally demanding a tip for the time they have wasted.

Female prostitution is largely confined to licensed houses. On the other hand, male prostitutes are everywhere. They assume that all visitors are homosexual, and solicit openly in the streets. I have been approached by boys who could not have been over twelve.

A casino would certainly bring in more tourists, and do much to alleviate the economic condition of Tangier. But despite the concerted efforts of merchants and hotel owners, all attempts to build a casino have been blocked by the Spanish on religious grounds.

Tangier has a dubious climate. The winters are cold and wet. In summer the temperature is pleasant, neither too hot nor too cool, but a constant wind creates a sandstorm on the beach, and people who sit there all day get sand in their ears and hair and eyes. Owing to a current, the water is shock-cold in mid-August, so even the hardiest swimmers can only stay in a few minutes. The beach is not much of an attraction.

All in all, Tangier does not have much to offer the visitor except low prices and a buyer's market. I have mentioned the unusually large number of good restaurants (a restaurant guide put out by the American and Foreign Bank lists eighteen first-class eating places where the price for a complete meal ranges from eighty cents to two dollars and a half). You have your choice of apartments and houses. Sample price for one large room with bath and balcony overlooking the harbor, comfortably furnished, utilities and maid service included: $25 per month. And there are comfortable rooms for $10. A tailor-made suit of imported English material that would cost $150 in the U.S. is $50 in Tangier. Name brands of Scotch run $2 to $2.50 a fifth.

Americans are exempt from the usual annoyances of registering with the police, renewing visas and so forth, that one encounters in Europe and South America. No visa is required for Tangier. You can stay as long as you want, work, if you can find a job, or go into business, without any formalities or permits. And Americans have extraterritorial rights in Tangier. Cases civil or criminal involving an American citizen are tried in consular court, under District of Columbia law.

The legal system of Tangier is rather complex. Criminal cases are tried by a mixed tribunal of three judges. Sentences are comparatively mild. Two years is usual for burglary, even if the criminal has a long record. A sentence of more than five years is extremely rare. Tangier does have capital punishment. The method is a firing squad of ten gendarmes. I know of only one case in recent years in which a death sentence was carried out.

In the Native Quarter one feels definite currents of hostility, which, however, are generally confined to muttering in Arabic as you pass. Occasionally I have been openly insulted by drunken Arabs, but this is rare. You can walk in the Native Quarter of Tangier with less danger than on Third Avenue of New York City on a Saturday night.

Violent crime is rare. I have walked the streets at all hours, and never was any attempt made to rob me. The infrequency of armed robbery is due less, I think, to the pacific nature of the Arabs than to the certainty of detection in a town where everybody knows everybody else, and where the penalties for violent crime, especially if committed by a Moslem, are relatively severe.

The Native Quarter of Tangier is all you expect it to be: a maze of narrow, sunless streets, twisting and meandering like footpaths, many of them blind alleys. After four months, I still find my way in the Medina by a system of moving from one landmark to another. The smell is almost incredible, and it is difficult to identify all the ingredients. Hashish, seared meat and sewage are well represented. You see filth, poverty, disease, all endured with a curiously apathetic indifference.

People carry huge loads of charcoal down from the mountains on their backs—that is, the women carry loads of charcoal. The men ride on donkeys. No mistaking the position of women in this society. I noticed a large percentage of these charcoal carriers had their noses eaten away by disease, but was not able to determine whether there is any occupational correlation. It seems more likely that they all come from the same heavily infected district.

Hashish is the drug of Islam, as alcohol is ours, opium the drug of the Far East, and cocaine that of South America. No effort is made to control its sale or use in Tangier, and every native café reeks of the smoke. They chop up the leaves on a wooden block, mix it with tobacco, and smoke it in little clay pipes with a long wooden stem.

Europeans occasion no surprise or overt resentment in Arab cafés. The usual drink is mint tea served very hot in a tall glass. If you hold the glass by top and bottom, avoiding the sides, it doesn't burn the hand. You can buy hashish, or *kief*, as they call it here, in any native café. It can also be purchased in sweet, resinous cakes to eat with hot tea. This resinous substance, a gum extracted from the cannabis plant, is the real hashish, and much more powerful than the leaves and flowers of the plant. The gum is called *majoun*, and the leaves *kief*. Good *majoun* is hard to find in Tangier.

Kief is identical with our marijuana, and we have here an opportunity to observe the effects of constant use on a whole population. I asked a European physician if he had noted any definite ill effects. He said: "In general, no. Occasionally there is drug psychosis, but it rarely reaches an acute stage where hospitalization is necessary." I asked if Arabs suffering from this psychosis are dangerous. He said: "I have never heard of any violence directly and definitely traceable to *kief*. To answer your question, they are usually not dangerous."

The typical Arab café is one room, a few tables and chairs, a huge copper or brass samovar for making tea and coffee. A raised platform covered with mats extends across one end of the room. Here the patrons loll about with their shoes off, smoking *kief* and playing cards. The game is Redondo, played with a pack of forty-two cards—rather an elementary card game. Fights start, stop, people walk around, play cards, smoke *kief*, all in a vast, timeless dream.

There is usually a radio turned on full volume. Arab music has neither beginning nor end. It is timeless. Heard for the first time, it may appear meaningless to a Westerner, because he is listening for a time structure that isn't there.

I talked with an American psychoanalyst who is practicing in Casablanca. He says you can never complete analysis with an Arab. Their superego structure is basically different. Perhaps you can't complete analysis with an Arab because he has no sense of time. He never completes anything. It is interesting that the drug of Islam is hashish, which affects the sense of time so that events, instead of appearing in an orderly structure of past, present and future, take on a simultaneous quality, the past and future contained in the present moment.

Tangier seems to exist on several dimensions. You are always finding streets, squares, parks you never saw before. Here fact merges into dream, and dreams erupt into the real world. Unfinished buildings fall into ruin and decay, Arabs move in silently like weeds and vines. A catatonic youth moves through the market-place, bumping into people and stalls like a sleepwalker. A man, barefooted, in rags, his face eaten and tumescent with a horrible skin disease, begs with his eyes alone. He does not have the will left to hold out his hand. An old Arab passionately kisses the sidewalk. People stop to watch for a few moments with bestial curiosity, then move on.

Nobody in Tangier is exactly what he seems to be. Along with the bogus fugitives of the Socco Chico are genuine political exiles from Europe: Jewish refugees from Nazi Germany, Republican Spaniards, a selection of Vichy French and other collaborators, fugitive Nazis. The town is full of vaguely disreputable Europeans who do not have adequate documents to go anywhere else. So many people are here who cannot leave, lacking funds or papers or both. Tangier is a vast penal colony.

The special attraction of Tangier can be put in one word: exemption. Exemption from interference, legal or otherwise. Your private life is your own, to act exactly as you please. You will be talked about, of course. Tangier is a gossipy town, and everyone in the foreign colony knows everyone else. But that is all. No legal pressure or pressure of public opinion will curtail your behavior. The cop stands here with his hands behind his back, reduced to his basic function of keeping order. That is all he does. He is the other extreme from the thought police of police states, or our own vice squad.

Tangier is one of the few places left in the world where, so long as you don't proceed to robbery, violence, or some form of crude, anti-social behavior, you can do exactly what you want. It is a sanctuary of noninterference.

(from THE NAKED LUNCH)
THE BLACK MEAT

"We friends, yes?"

The shoe shine boy put on his hustling smile and looked up into the Sailor's dead, cold, undersea eyes, eyes without a trace of warmth or lust or hate or any feeling the boy had ever experienced in himself or seen in another, at once cold and intense, impersonal and predatory.

The Sailor leaned forward and put a finger on the boy's inner arm at the elbow. He spoke in his dead, junky whisper.

"With veins like that, Kid, I'd have myself a time."

He laughed, black insect laughter that seemed to serve some obscure function of orientation like a bat's squeak. The Sailor laughed three times. He stopped laughing and hung there motion-less listening down into himself. He had picked up the silent frequency of junk. His face smoothed out like yellow wax over the high cheekbones. He waited half a cigarette. The Sailor knew how to wait. But his eyes burned in a hideous dry hunger. He turned his face of controlled emergency in a slow half pivot to case the man who had just come in. "Fats" Terminal sat there sweeping the café with blank, periscope eyes. When his eyes passed the Sailor he nodded minutely. Only the peeled nerves of junk sickness would have registered a movement.

The Sailor handed the boy a coin. He drifted over to Fats' table with his floating walk and sat down. They sat a long time in silence. The café was built into one side of a stone ramp at the bottom of a high white canyon of masonry. Faces of The City poured through silent as fish, stained with vile addictions and insect lusts. The lighted café was a diving bell, cable broken, settling into black depths.

The Sailor was polishing his nails on the lapels of his glen plaid suit. He whistled a little tune through his shiny, yellow teeth.

When he moved an effluvium of mold drifted out of his clothes, a musty smell of deserted locker rooms. He studied his nails with phosphorescent intensity.

"Good thing here, Fats. I can deliver twenty. Need an advance of course."

"On spec?"

"So I don't have the twenty eggs in my pocket. I tell you it's jellied consommé. One little whoops and a push." The Sailor looked at his nails as if he were studying a chart. "You know I always deliver."

"Make it thirty. And a ten tube advance. This time tomorrow."

"Need a tube now, Fats."

"Take a walk, you'll get one."

The Sailor drifted down into the Plaza. A street boy was shoving a newspaper in the Sailor's face to cover his hand on the Sailor's pen. The Sailor walked on. He pulled the pen out and broke it like a nut in his thick, fibrous, pink fingers. He pulled out a lead tube. He cut one end of the tube with a little curved knife. A black mist poured out and hung in the air like boiling fur. The Sailor's face dissolved. His mouth undulated forward on a long tube and sucked in the black fuzz, vibrating in supersonic peristalsis, disappeared in a silent, pink explosion. His face came back into focus unbearably sharp and clear, burning yellow brand of junk searing the grey haunch of a million screaming junkies.

"This will last a month," he decided, consulting an invisible mirror.

All streets of the City slope down between deepening canyons to a vast, kidney-shaped plaza full of darkness. Walls of street and plaza are perforated by dwelling cubicles and cafés, some a few feet deep, others extending out of sight in a network of rooms and corridors.

At all levels criss-cross of bridges, cat walks, cable cars. Catatonic youths dressed as women in gowns of burlap and rotten rags, faces heavily and crudely painted in bright colors over a stratum of beatings, arabesques of broken, suppurating scars to the pearly bone, push against the passer-by in silent clinging insistence.

Traffickers in the Black Meat, flesh of the giant aquatic black centipede—sometimes attaining a length of six feet—found in a lane of black rocks and iridescent, brown lagoons, exhibit paralyzed crustaceans in camouflaged pockets of the Plaza visible only to the Meat Eaters.

Followers of obsolete unthinkable trades, doodling in Etruscan, addicts of drugs not yet synthesized, black marketeers of World War III, excisors of telepathic sensitivity, osteopaths of the spirit, investigators of infractions denounced by bland paranoid chess players, servers of fragmentary warrants taken down in hebephrenic short-hand charging unspeakable mutilations of the spirit, officials of unconstituted police states, brokers of exquisite dreams and nostalgias tested on the sensitized cells of junk sickness and bartered for raw materials of the will, drinkers of the Heavy Fluid sealed in translucent amber of dreams.

The Meet Café occupies one side of the Plaza, a maze of kitchens, restaurants, sleeping cubicles, perilous iron balconies and basements opening into the underground baths.

On stools covered in white satin sit naked Mugwumps sucking translucent, colored syrups through alabaster straws. Mugwumps have no liver and nourish themselves exclusively on sweets. Thin, purple-blue lips cover a razor-sharp beak of black bone with which they frequently tear each other to shreds in fights over clients. These creatures secrete an addicting fluid from their erect penises which prolongs life by slowing metabolism. (In fact all longevity agents have proved addicting in exact ratio to their effectiveness in prolonging life.) Addicts of Mugwump fluid are known as Reptiles. A number of these flow over chairs with their flexible bones and black-pink flesh. A fan of green cartilage covered with hollow, erectile hairs through which the Reptiles absorb the fluid sprouts from behind each ear. The fans, which move from time to time touched by invisible currents, serve also some form of communication known only to Reptiles.

During the biennial Panics when the raw, peeled Dream Police storm the City the Mugwumps take refuge in the deepest crevices of the wall, sealing themselves in clay cubicles, and remain for weeks in biostasis. In those days of grey terror the Reptiles dart about faster and faster, scream past each other at supersonic speed, their flexible skulls flapping in black winds of insect agony.

The Dream Police disintegrate in globs of rotten ectoplasm swept away by an old junky, coughing and spitting in the sick morning. The Mugwump Man comes with alabaster jars of fluid and the Reptiles get smoothed out.

The air is once again still and clear as glycerine.

The Sailor spotted his Reptile. He drifted over and ordered a green syrup. The Reptile had a little, round disk mouth of brown gristle, expressionless green eyes almost covered by a thin membrane of eyelid. The Sailor waited an hour before the creature picked up his presence.

"Any eggs for Fats?" he asked, his words stirring through the Reptile's fan hairs.

It took two hours for the Reptile to raise three pink transparent fingers covered with black fuzz.

Several Meat Eaters lay in vomit, too weak to move. (The Black Meat is like a tainted cheese, overpoweringly delicious and nauseating so that the eaters eat and vomit and eat again until they fall exhausted.)

A painted youth slithered in and seized one of the great black claws sending the sweet, sick smell curling through the café.

(From THE NAKED LUNCH)
HOSPITAL (BENWAY)

The lavatory has been locked for three hours solid . . . I think they are using it for an operating room. . .

NURSE: "I can't find her pulse, doctor."

DR. BENWAY: "Maybe she got it up her snatch in a finger stall."

NURSE: "Adrenalin, doctor?"

DR. BENWAY: "The night porter shot it all up for kicks." He looks around and picks up one of those rubber vacuum cups at the end of a stick they use to unstop toilets . . . He advances on the patient . . . "Make an incision, Doctor Limpf," he says to his appalled assistant . . . "I'm going to massage the heart."

Doctor Limpf shrugs and begins the incision. Doctor Benway washes the suction cup by swishing it around in the toilet bowl. . .

NURSE: "Shouldn't it be sterilized, doctor?"

DR. BENWAY: "Very likely but there's no time." He sits on the suction cup like a cane seat watching his assistant make the incision . . . "You young squirts couldn't lance a pimple without an electric vibrating scalpel with automatic drain and suture . . . Soon we'll be operating by remote control on patients we never see . . . We'll be nothing but button pushers. All the skill is going out of surgery . . . All the know-how and make-do . . . Did I ever tell you about the time I performed an appendectomy with a rusty sardine can? And once I was caught short without instrument one and removed a uterine tumor with my teeth. That was in the Upper Effendi, and besides. . ."

DR. LIMPF: "The incision is ready, doctor."

DR. BENWAY forces the cup into the incision and works it up and down. Blood spurts all over the doctors, the nurse and the wall . . . The cup makes a horrible sucking sound.

NURSE: "I think she's gone, doctor."

DR. BENWAY: "Well, it's all in the day's work." He walks across the room to a medicine cabinet . . . "Some fucking drug addict has cut my cocaine with Saniflush! Nurse! Send the boy out to fill this Rx on the double!"

Doctor Benway is operating in an auditorium filled with students: "Now, boys, you won't see this operation performed very often and there's a reason for that . . . You see it has absolutely no medical value. No one knows what the purpose of it originally was or if it had a purpose at all. Personally I think it was a pure artistic creation from the beginning. Just as a bull fighter with his skill and knowledge extricates himself from danger he has himself invoked, so in this operation the surgeon deliberately endangers his patient, and then, with incredible speed and celerity, rescues him from death at the last possible split second. . .

"Did any of you ever see Doctor Tetrazzini perform? I say perform advisedly because his operations were performances. He would start by throwing a scalpel across the room into the patient and then make his entrance like a ballet dancer. His speed was incredible: 'I don't give them time to die,' he would say. Tumors put him in a frenzy of rage. 'Fucking undisciplined cells!' he would snarl, advancing on the tumor like a knife-fighter."

A young man leaps down into the operating theater and, whipping out a scalpel, advances on the patient.

DR. BENWAY: "An *espontáneo*! Stop him before he guts my patient!"

(*Espontáneo* is a bull-fighting term for a member of the audience who leaps down into the ring, pulls out a concealed cape and attempts a few passes with the bull before he is dragged out of the ring.)

The orderlies scuffle with the *espontáneo*, who is finally ejected from the hall. The anesthetist takes advantage of the confusion to pry a large gold filling from the patient's mouth. . .

I am passing room 10 they moved me out of yesterday . . . Maternity case I assume . . . Bedpans full of blood and Kotex and nameless female substances, enough to pollute a continent . . . If someone comes to visit me in my old room he will think I gave birth to a monster and the State Department is trying to hush it up. . .

Music from *I Am an American* . . . An elderly man in the striped pants and cutaway of a diplomat stands on a platform draped with the American flag. A decayed, corseted tenor—bursting out of a Daniel Boone costume—is singing "The Star-Spangled Banner," accompanied by a full orchestra. He sings with a slight lisp. . .

THE DIPLOMAT (reading from a great scroll of ticker tape that keeps growing and tangling around his feet): "And we categorically deny that any male citizen of the United States of America. . ."

TENOR: "Oh thay can you thee . . ." His voice breaks and shoots up to a high falsetto.

In the control room the Technician mixes a bicarbonate of soda and belches into his hand: "God damned tenor's a brown artist!" he mutters sourly. "Mike! rumph," the shout ends in a belch. "Cut that swish fart off the air and give him his purple slip. He's through as of right now . . . Put in that sex-changed Liz athlete . . . She's a full-time tenor at least . . . *Costume?* How in the fuck should I know? I'm no dress designer swish from the costume department! *What's that?* The entire costume department occluded as a security risk? What am I, an octopus? Let's see . . . How about an Indian routine? Pocahontas or Hiawatha? . . . No, that's not right. Some citizen cracks wise about giving it back to the Indians . . . A Civil War uniform, the coat North and the pants South like it show they got together again? She can come on like Buffalo Bill or Paul Revere or that citizen wouldn't give up the shit, I mean the ship, or a GI or a Doughboy or the Unknown Soldier . . . That's the best deal . . .Cover her with a monument, that way nobody has to look at her. . ."

The Lesbian, concealed in a papier-mâché Arc de Triomphe, fills her great lungs and looses a tremendous bellow.

"Oh say do that Star-Spangled Banner yet wave. . ."

A great rent rips the Arc de Triomphe from top to bottom. The Diplomat puts a hand to his forehead. . .

THE DIPLOMAT: "That any male citizen of the United States has given birth in Interzone or at any other place. . ."

"O'er the land of the FREEEEEEEEEEE. . ."

The Diplomat's mouth is moving but no one can hear him. The Technician clasps his hands over his ears: "Mother of God!" he screams. His plate begins to vibrate like a Jew's harp, suddenly flies out of his mouth ... He snaps at it irritably, misses and covers his mouth with one hand.

The Arc de Triomphe falls with a ripping, splintering crash, reveals the Lesbian standing on a pedestal clad only in a leopard-skin jockstrap with enormous falsie basket ... She stands there smiling stupidly and flexing her huge muscles ... The Technician is crawling around on the control room floor looking for his plate and shouting unintelligible orders: "Thess thupper thonic!! Thut ur oth thu thair!"

THE DIPLOMAT (wiping sweat from his brow): "To any creature of any type or description. . ."

"And the home of the brave."

The Diplomat's face is grey. He staggers, trips in the scroll, sags against the rail, blood pouring from eyes, nose and mouth, dying of cerebral hemorrhage.

THE DIPLOMAT (barely audible): "The Department denies ... un-American ... It's been destroyed ... I mean it never was ... Categor ..." *Dies.*

In the Control Room instrument panels are blowing out ... Great streamers of electricity crackle through the room ... The Technician, naked, his body burned black, staggers about like a figure in *Götterdämmerung*, screaming: "Thubber thonic!! Oth thu thair!!!" A final blast reduces the Technician to a cinder.

> *"Gave proof through the night*
> *That our flag was still there. . ."*

(from THE NAKED LUNCH)
ORDINARY MEN AND WOMEN (The Talking Asshole Routine)

BENWAY: "Don't take it so hard, kid ... *Jedermann macht eine kleine Dummheit.*" (Everyone makes a little dumbness.)

SCHAFER: "I tell you I can't escape a feeling ... well, of *evil* about this."

BENWAY: "Balderdash, my boy ... We're scientists ... Pure scientists. Disinterested research and damned be him who cries 'Hold, *too much*!' Such people are no better than party poops."

SCHAFER: "Yes, yes, of course ... and yet ... I can't get that stench out of my lungs. . ."

BENWAY (irritably): "None of us can ... Never smelled anything remotely like it . . . Where was I? Oh yes, what would be the result of administering curare plus iron lung during acute mania? Possibly the subject, unable to discharge his tensions in motor activity, would succumb on the spot like a jungle rat. Interesting cause of death, what?"

Schafer is not listening. "You know," he says impulsively, "I think I'll go back to plain old-fashioned surgery. The human body is scandalously inefficient. Instead of a mouth and an anus to get out of order why not have one all-purpose hole to eat *and* eliminate? We could seal up nose and mouth, fill in the stomach, make an air hole direct into the lungs where it should have been in the first place. . ."

BENWAY: "Why not one all-purpose blob? Did I ever tell you about the man who taught his asshole to talk? His whole abdomen would move up and down you dig farting out the words. It was unlike anything I ever heard.

"This ass talk had a sort of gut frequency. It hit you right down there like you gotta go. You know when the old colon gives you the elbow and it feels sorta cold inside, and you know all you have to do is turn loose? Well this talking hit you right down there, a bubbly, thick stagnant sound, a sound you could *smell*.

"This man worked for a carnival you dig, and to start with it was like a novelty ventriloquist act. Real funny, too, at first. He had a number he called 'The Better 'Ole' that was a scream, I tell you. I forget most of it but it was clever. Like, 'Oh I say, are you still down there, old thing?'

" 'Nah! I had to go relieve myself.'

"After a while the ass started talking on its own. He would go in without anything prepared and his ass would ad-lib and toss the gags back at him every time.

"Then it developed sort of teeth-like little raspy incurving hooks and started eating. He thought this was cute at first and built an act around it, but the asshole would eat its way through his pants and start talking on the street, shouting out it wanted equal rights. It would get drunk, too, and have crying jags nobody loved it and it wanted to be kissed same as any other mouth. Finally it talked all the time day and night, you could hear him for blocks screaming at it to shut up, and beating it with his fist, and sticking candles up it, but nothing did any good and the asshole said to him: 'It's you who will shut up in the end. Not me. Because we don't need you around here any more. I can talk and eat *and* shit.'

"After that he began waking up in the morning with a transparent jelly like a tadpole's tail all over his mouth. This jelly was what the scientists call un-D.T., Undifferentiated Tissue, which can grow into any kind of flesh on the human body. He would tear it off his mouth and the pieces would stick to his hands like burning gasoline jelly and grow there, grow anywhere on him a glob of it fell. So finally his mouth sealed over, and the whole head would have amputated spontaneous—(did you know there is a condition occurs in parts of Africa and only among Negroes where the little toe amputates spontaneously?)—except for the *eyes*, you dig. That's one thing the asshole *couldn't* do was see. It needed the eyes. But nerve connections were blocked and infiltrated and atrophied so the brain couldn't give orders any more. It was trapped in the skull, sealed off. For a while you could see the silent, helpless suffering of the brain behind the eyes, then finally the brain must have died, because the eyes *went out*, and there was no more feeling in them than a crab's eye on the end of a stalk.

"That's the sex that passes the censor, squeezes through between bureaus, because there's always a space *between*, in popular songs and Grade B movies, giving away the basic American rottenness, spurting out like breaking boils, throwing out globs of that un-D.T. to fall anywhere and grow into some degenerate cancerous life-form, reproducing a hideous random image. Some would be entirely made of penis-like erectile tissue, others viscera barely covered over with skin, clusters of three and four eyes together, crisscross of mouth and assholes, human parts shaken around and poured out any way they fell.

"The end result of complete cellular representation is cancer. Democracy is cancerous, and bureaus are its cancer. A bureau takes root anywhere in the state, turns malignant like the Narcotic Bureau, and grows and grows, always reproducing more of its own kind, until it chokes the host if not controlled or excised. Bureaus cannot live without a host, being true parasitic organisms. (A cooperative on the other hand *can* live without the state. That is the road to follow. The building up of independent units to meet needs of the people who participate in the functioning of the unit. A bureau operates on opposite principle of *inventing needs* to justify its existence.) Bureaucracy is wrong as a cancer, a turning away from the human evolutionary direction of infinite potentials and differentiation and independent spontaneous action to the complete parasitism of a virus.

"(It is thought that the virus is a degeneration from more complex life-form. It may at one time have been capable of independent life. Now has fallen to the borderline between living and dead matter. It can exhibit living qualities only in a host, by using the life of another—the renunciation of life itself, a *falling* towards inorganic, inflexible machine, towards dead matter.)

"Bureaus die when the structure of the state collapses. They are as helpless and unfit for independent existences as a displaced tapeworm, or a virus that has killed the host.

"In Timbuktu I once saw an Arab boy who could play a flute with his ass, and the fairies told me he was really an individual in bed. He could play a tune up and down the organ hitting the most erogenously sensitive spots, which are different on everyone, of course. Every lover had his special theme song which was perfect for him and rose to his climax. The boy was a great artist when it came to improvising new combines and special climaxes, some of them notes in the unknown, tie-ups of seeming discords that would suddenly break through each other and crash together with a stunning, hot sweet impact."

ALLEN GINSBERG

1926–1997

PULL MY DAISY [with Jack Kerouac and Neal Cassady]

Pull my daisy
tip my cup
all my doors are open
Cut my thoughts
for coconuts
all my eggs are broken
Jack my Arden
gate my shades
woe my road is spoken
Silk my garden
rose my days
now my prayers awaken

Bone my shadow
dove my dream
start my halo bleeding
Milk my mind &
make me cream
drink me when you're ready
Hop my heart on
harp my height
seraphs hold me steady
Hip my angel
hype my light
lay it on the needy

Heal the raindrop
sow the eye
bust my dust again
Woe the worm
work the wise
dig my spade the same
Stop the hoax
what's the hex
where's the wake
how's the hicks
take my golden beam

Rob my locker
lick my rocks
leap my cock in school
Rack my lacks
lark my looks
jump right up my hole
Whore my door
beat my boor
eat my snake of fool
Craze my hair
bare my poor
asshole shorn of wool

Say my oops
ope my shell
bite my naked nut
Roll my bones
ring my bell
call my worm to sup
Pope my parts
pop my pot
raise my daisy up
Poke my pap
pit my plum
let my gap be shut

New York, Spring—Fall 1949

HOWL
For Carl Solomon

I

I saw the best minds of my generation destroyed by madness, starving hysterical naked,
dragging themselves through the negro streets at dawn looking for
an angry fix,
angelheaded hipsters burning for the ancient heavenly connection to
the starry dynamo in the machinery of night,
who poverty and tatters and hollow-eyed and high sat up smoking
in the supernatural darkness of cold-water flats floating
across the tops of cities contemplating jazz,
who bared their brains to Heaven under the El and saw
Mohammedan angels staggering on tenement roofs illumi-
nated,
who passed through universities with radiant cool eyes hallucinating Arkansas and Blake-light tragedy among the scholars of
war,
who were expelled from the academies for crazy & publishing
obscene odes on the windows of the skull,
who cowered in unshaven rooms in underwear, burning their
money in wastebaskets and listening to the Terror through
the wall,
who got busted in their pubic beards returning through Laredo with
a belt of marijuana for New York,
who ate fire in paint hotels or drank turpentine in Paradise Alley,
death, or purgatoried their torsos night after night
with dreams, with drugs, with waking nightmares, alcohol and cock
and endless balls,
incomparable blind streets of shuddering cloud and lightning in the
mind leaping toward poles of Canada & Paterson, illuminat-
ing all the motionless world of Time between,
Peyote solidities of halls, backyard green tree cemetery dawns, wine
drunkenness over the rooftops, storefront boroughs of
teahead joyride neon blinking traffic light, sun and moon
and tree vibrations in the roaring winter dusks of Brooklyn,
ashcan rantings and kind king light of mind,
who chained themselves to subways for the endless ride from
Battery to holy Bronx on benzedrine until the noise of wheels

and children brought them down shuddering mouth-
wracked and battered bleak of brain all drained of brilliance
in the drear light of Zoo,

who sank all night in submarine light of Bickford's floated out and
sat through the stale beer afternoon in desolate Fugazzi's, listening to the crack of doom on the hydrogen jukebox,

who talked continuously seventy hours from park to pad to bar to
Bellevue to museum to the Brooklyn Bridge,

a lost battalion of platonic conversationalists jumping down the
stoops off fire escapes off windowsills off Empire State out of
the moon,

yacketayakking screaming vomiting whispering facts and memories
and anecdotes and eyeball kicks and shocks of hospitals and
jails and wars,

whole intellects disgorged in total recall for seven days and nights
with brilliant eyes, meat for the Synagogue cast on the pavement,

who vanished into nowhere Zen New Jersey leaving a trail of
ambiguous picture postcards of Atlantic City Hall,

suffering Eastern sweats and Tangerian bone-grindings and
migraines of China under junk-withdrawal in Newark's
bleak furnished room,

who wandered around and around at midnight in the railroad
yard wondering where to go, and went, leaving no broken
hearts,

who lit cigarettes in boxcars boxcars boxcars racketing through
snow toward lonesome farms in grandfather night,

who studied Plotinus Poe St. John of the Cross telepathy and bop
kabbalah because the cosmos instinctively vibrated at their
feet in Kansas,

who loned it through the streets of Idaho seeking visionary indian
angels who were visionary indian angels,

who thought they were only mad when Baltimore gleamed in supernatural ecstasy,

who jumped in limousines with the Chinaman of Oklahoma on the
impulse of winter midnight streetlight smalltown rain,

who lounged hungry and lonesome through Houston seeking jazz
or sex or soup, and followed the brilliant Spaniard to con-
verse about America and Eternity, a hopeless task, and so
took ship to Africa,

who disappeared into the volcanoes of Mexico leaving behind
    nothing but the shadow of dungarees and the lava and ash of
    poetry scattered in fireplace Chicago,

who reappeared on the West Coast investigating the FBI in beards
    and shorts with big pacifist eyes sexy in their dark skin
    passing out incomprehensible leaflets,

who burned cigarette holes in their arms protesting the narcotic
    tobacco haze of Capitalism,

who distributed Supercommunist pamphlets in Union Square
    weeping and undressing while the sirens of Los Alamos
    wailed them down, and wailed down Wall, and the Staten
    Island ferry also wailed,

who broke down crying in white gymnasiums naked and trembling
    before the machinery of other skeletons,

who bit detectives in the neck and shrieked with delight in police-
    cars for committing no crime but their own wild cooking
    pederasty and intoxication,

who howled on their knees in the subway and were dragged off the
    roof waving genitals and manuscripts,

who let themselves be fucked in the ass by saintly motorcyclists, and
    screamed with joy,

who blew and were blown by those human seraphim, the sailors,
    caresses of Atlantic and Caribbean love,

who balled in the morning in the evenings in rosegardens and the
    grass of public parks and cemeteries scattering their semen
    freely to whomever come who may,

who hiccuped endlessly trying to giggle but wound up with a sob
    behind a partition in a Turkish Bath when the blond &
    naked angel came to pierce them with a sword,

who lost their loveboys to the three old shrews of fate the one eyed
    shrew of the heterosexual dollar the one eyed shrew that
    winks out of the womb and the one eyed shrew that does
    nothing but sit on her ass and snip the intellectual golden
    threads of the craftsman's loom,

who copulated ecstatic and insatiate with a bottle of beer a sweet-
    heart a package of cigarettes a candle and fell off the bed,
    and continued along the floor and down the hall and ended
    fainting on the wall with a vision of ultimate cunt and come
    eluding the last gyzym of consciousness,

who sweetened the snatches of a million girls trembling in the sunset, and were red eyed in the morning but prepared to sweeten the snatch of the sunrise, flashing buttocks under barns and naked in the lake,

who went out whoring through Colorado in myriad stolen night-cars, N.C., secret hero of these poems, cocksman and Adonis of Denver—joy to the memory of his innumerable lays of girls in empty lots & diner backyards, moviehouses' rickety rows, on mountaintops in caves or with gaunt waitresses in familiar roadside lonely petticoat upliftings & especially secret gas-station solipsisms of johns, & hometown alleys too,

who faded out in vast sordid movies, were shifted in dreams, woke on a sudden Manhattan, and picked themselves up out of basements hung-over with heartless Tokay and horrors of Third Avenue iron dreams & stumbled to unemployment offices,

who walked all night with their shoes full of blood on the snowbank docks waiting for a door in the East River to open to a room full of steamheat and opium,

who created great suicidal dramas on the apartment cliff-banks of the Hudson under the wartime blue floodlight of the moon & their heads shall be crowned with laurel in oblivion,

who ate the lamb stew of the imagination or digested the crab at the muddy bottom of the rivers of Bowery,

who wept at the romance of the streets with their pushcarts full of onions and bad music,

who sat in boxes breathing in the darkness under the bridge, and rose up to build harpsichords in their lofts,

who coughed on the sixth floor of Harlem crowned with flame under the tubercular sky surrounded by orange crates of theology,

who scribbled all night rocking and rolling over lofty incantations which in the yellow morning were stanzas of gibberish,

who cooked rotten animals lung heart feet tail borsht & tortillas dreaming of the pure vegetable kingdom,

who plunged themselves under meat trucks looking for an egg,

who threw their watches off the roof to cast their ballot for Eternity outside of Time, & alarm clocks fell on their heads every day for the next decade,

who cut their wrists three times successively unsuccessfully, gave up and were forced to open antique stores where they thought they were growing old and cried,

who were burned alive in their innocent flannel suits on Madison
    Avenue amid blasts of leaden verse & the tanked-up clatter
    of the iron regiments of fashion & the nitroglycerine shrieks
    of the fairies of advertising & the mustard gas of sinister
    intelligent editors, or were run down by the drunken taxi-
    cabs of Absolute Reality,
who jumped off the Brooklyn Bridge this actually happened and
    walked away unknown and forgotten into the ghostly daze
    of Chinatown soup alleyways & firetrucks, not even one free
    beer,
who sang out of their windows in despair, fell out of the subway
    window, jumped in the filthy Passaic, leaped on negroes,
    cried all over the street, danced on broken wineglasses bare-
    foot smashed phonograph records of nostalgic European
    1930s German jazz finished the whiskey and threw up
    groaning into the bloody toilet, moans in their ears and the
    blast of colossal steamwhistles,
who barreled down the highways of the past journeying to each
    other's hotrod-Golgotha jail-solitude watch or Birmingham
    jazz incarnation,
who drove crosscountry seventytwo hours to find out if I had a vision
    or you had a vision or he had a vision to find out Eternity,
who journeyed to Denver, who died in Denver, who came back to
    Denver & waited in vain, who watched over Denver &
    brooded & loned in Denver and finally went away to find
    out the Time, & now Denver is lonesome for her heroes,
who fell on their knees in hopeless cathedrals praying for each
    other's salvation and light and breasts, until the soul illumi-
    nated its hair for a second,
who crashed through their minds in jail waiting for impossible crim-
    inals with golden heads and the charm of reality in their
    hearts who sang sweet blues to Alcatraz,
who retired to Mexico to cultivate a habit, or Rocky Mount to
    tender Buddha or Tangiers to boys or Southern Pacific to the
    black locomotive or Harvard to Narcissus to Woodlawn to
    the daisychain or grave,
who demanded sanity trials accusing the radio of hypnotism &
    were left with their insanity & their hands & a hung jury,
who threw potato salad at CCNY lecturers on Dadaism and subse-
    quently presented themselves on the granite steps of the

madhouse with shaven heads and harlequin speech of
  suicide, demanding instantaneous lobotomy,
and who were given instead the concrete void of insulin Metrazol
  electricity hydrotherapy psychotherapy occupational therapy
  pingpong & amnesia,
who in humorless protest overturned only one symbolic pingpong
  table, resting briefly in catatonia,
returning years later truly bald except for a wig of blood, and tears
  and fingers, to the visible madman doom of the wards of the
  madtowns of the East,
Pilgrim State's Rockland's and Greystone's foetid halls, bickering
  with the echoes of the soul, rocking and rolling in the midnight solitude-bench dolmen-realms of love, dream of life a
  nightmare, bodies turned to stone as heavy as the moon,
with mother finally ******, and the last fantastic book flung out of
  the tenement window, and the last door closed at 4 A.M. and
  the last telephone slammed at the wall in reply and the last
  furnished room emptied down to the last piece of mental furniture, a yellow paper rose twisted on a wire hanger in the
  closet, and even that imaginary, nothing but a hopeful little
  bit of hallucination—
ah, Carl, while you are not safe I am not safe, and now you're really
  in the total animal soup of time—
and who therefore ran through the icy streets obsessed with a
  sudden flash of the alchemy of the use of the ellipsis catalog a
  variable measure and the vibrating plane,
who dreamt and made incarnate gaps in Time & Space through
  images juxtaposed, and trapped the archangel of the soul
  between 2 visual images and joined the elemental verbs and
  set the noun and dash of consciousness together jumping
  with sensation of Pater Omnipotens Aeterna Deus
to recreate the syntax and measure of poor human prose and stand
  before you speechless and intelligent and shaking with
  shame, rejected yet confessing out the soul to conform to the
  rhythm of thought in his naked and endless head,
the madman bum and angel beat in Time, unknown, yet putting
  down here what might be left to say in time come after
  death,
and rose reincarnate in the ghostly clothes of jazz in the goldhorn
  shadow of the band and blew the suffering of America's

naked mind for love into an eli eli lamma lamma sabacthani saxophone cry that shivered the cities down to the last radio
with the absolute heart of the poem of life butchered out of their own bodies good to eat a thousand years.

II

What sphinx of cement and aluminum bashed open their skulls and ate up their brains and imagination?

Moloch! Solitude! Filth! Ugliness! Ashcans and unobtainable dollars! Children screaming under the stairways! Boys sobbing in armies! Old men weeping in the parks!

Moloch! Moloch! Nightmare of Moloch! Moloch the loveless! Mental Moloch! Moloch the heavy judger of men!

Moloch the incomprehensible prison! Moloch the crossbone soulless jailhouse and Congress of sorrows! Moloch whose buildings are judgment! Moloch the vast stone of war! Moloch the stunned governments!

Moloch whose mind is pure machinery! Moloch whose blood is running money! Moloch whose fingers are ten armies! Moloch whose breast is a cannibal dynamo! Moloch whose ear is a smoking tomb!

Moloch whose eyes are a thousand blind windows! Moloch whose skyscrapers stand in the long streets like endless Jehovahs! Moloch whose factories dream and croak in the fog! Moloch whose smokestacks and antennae crown the cities!

Moloch whose love is endless oil and stone! Moloch whose soul is electricity and banks! Moloch whose poverty is the specter of genius! Moloch whose fate is a cloud of sexless hydrogen! Moloch whose name is the Mind!

Moloch in whom I sit lonely! Moloch in whom I dream Angels! Crazy in Moloch! Cocksucker in Moloch! Lacklove and manless in Moloch!

Moloch who entered my soul early! Moloch in whom I am a consciousness without a body! Moloch who frightened me out of my natural ecstasy! Moloch whom I abandon! Wake up in Moloch! Light streaming out of the sky!

Moloch! Moloch! Robot apartments! invisible suburbs! skeleton treasuries! blind capitals! demonic industries! spectral nations! invincible madhouses! granite cocks! monstrous bombs!

They broke their backs lifting Moloch to Heaven! Pavements, trees, radios, tons! lifting the city to Heaven which exists and is everywhere about us!

Visions! omens! hallucinations! miracles! ecstasies! gone down the American river!

Dreams! adorations! illuminations! religions! the whole boatload of sensitive bullshit!

Breakthroughs! over the river! flips and crucifixions! gone down the flood! Highs! Epiphanies! Despairs! Ten years' animal screams and suicides! Minds! New loves! Mad generation! down on the rocks of Time!

Real holy laughter in the river! They saw it all! the wild eyes! the holy yells! They bade farewell! They jumped off the roof! to solitude! waving! carrying flowers! Down to the river! into the street!

III

Carl Solomon! I'm with you in Rockland
　　where you're madder than I am
I'm with you in Rockland
　　where you must feel very strange
I'm with you in Rockland
　　where you imitate the shade of my mother
I'm with you in Rockland
　　where you've murdered your twelve secretaries
I'm with you in Rockland
　　where you laugh at this invisible humor
I'm with you in Rockland
　　where we are great writers on the same dreadful typewriter
I'm with you in Rockland
　　where your condition has become serious and is reported on
　　the radio
I'm with you in Rockland
　　where the faculties of the skull no longer admit the worms of
　　the senses
I'm with you in Rockland
　　where you drink the tea of the breasts of the spinsters of Utica
I'm with you in Rockland
　　where you pun on the bodies of your nurses the harpies of
　　the Bronx

I'm with you in Rockland
> where you scream in a straightjacket that you're losing the
> game of the actual pingpong of the abyss

I'm with you in Rockland
> where you bang on the catatonic piano the soul is innocent
> and immortal it should never die ungodly in an armed mad-
> house

I'm with you in Rockland
> where fifty more shocks will never return your soul to its
> body again from its pilgrimage to a cross in the void

I'm with you in Rockland
> where you accuse your doctors of insanity and plot the
> Hebrew socialist revolution against the fascist national
> Golgotha

I'm with you in Rockland
> where you will split the heavens of Long Island and resurrect
> your living human Jesus from the superhuman tomb

I'm with you in Rockland
> where there are twentyfive thousand mad comrades all
> together singing the final stanzas of the Internationale

I'm with you in Rockland
> where we hug and kiss the United States under our bedsheets
> the United States that coughs all night and won't let us sleep

I'm with you in Rockland
> where we wake up electrified out of the coma by our own
> souls' airplanes roaring over the roof they've come to drop
> angelic bombs the hospital illuminates itself imaginary walls
> collapse O skinny legions run outside O starry-spangled
> shock of mercy the eternal war is here O victory forget your
> underwear we're free

I'm with you in Rockland
> in my dreams you walk dripping from a sea-journey on the
> highway across America in tears to the door of my cottage in
> the Western night

San Francisco, 1955–1956

FOOTNOTE TO HOWL

Holy! Holy! Holy! Holy! Holy! Holy! Holy! Holy! Holy! Holy!
Holy! Holy! Holy! Holy! Holy!

The world is holy! The soul is holy! The skin is holy! The nose is
holy! The tongue and cock and hand and asshole holy!
Everything is holy! everybody's holy! everywhere is holy! everyday
is in eternity! Everyman's an angel!
The bum's as holy as the seraphim! the madman is holy as you my
soul are holy!
The typewriter is holy the poem is holy the voice is holy the hearers
are holy the ecstasy is holy!
Holy Peter holy Allen holy Solomon holy Lucien holy Kerouac holy
Huncke holy Burroughs holy Cassady holy the unknown
buggered and suffering beggars holy the hideous human
angels!
Holy my mother in the insane asylum! Holy the cocks of the grand-
fathers of Kansas!
Holy the groaning saxophone! Holy the bop apocalypse! Holy the
jazzbands marijuana hipsters peace peyote pipes & drums!
Holy the solitudes of skyscrapers and pavements! Holy the cafete-
rias filled with the millions! Holy the mysterious rivers of
tears under the streets!
Holy the lone juggernaut! Holy the vast lamb of the middleclass!
Holy the crazy shepherds of rebellion! Who digs Los Angeles
IS Los Angeles!
Holy New York Holy San Francisco Holy Peoria & Seattle Holy
Paris Holy Tangiers Holy Moscow Holy Istanbul!
Holy time in eternity holy eternity in time holy the clocks in space
holy the fourth dimension holy the fifth International holy
the Angel in Moloch!
Holy the sea holy the desert holy the railroad holy the locomotive
holy the visions holy the hallucinations holy the miracles
holy the eyeball holy the abyss!
Holy forgiveness! mercy! charity! faith! Holy! Ours! bodies! suffer-
ing! magnanimity!
Holy the supernatural extra brilliant intelligent kindness of the soul!

Berkeley, 1955

A SUPERMARKET IN CALIFORNIA

What thoughts I have of you tonight, Walt Whitman, for I
walked down the sidestreets under the trees with a headache self-
conscious looking at the full moon.

In my hungry fatigue, and shopping for images, I went into the neon fruit supermarket, dreaming of your enumerations!

What peaches and what penumbras! Whole families shopping at night! Aisles full of husbands! Wives in the avocados, babies in the tomatoes! —and you, García Lorca, what were you doing down by the watermelons?

I saw you, Walt Whitman, childless, lonely old grubber, poking among the meats in the refrigerator and eyeing the grocery boys.

I heard you asking questions of each: Who killed the pork chops? What price bananas? Are you my Angel?

I wandered in and out of the brilliant stacks of cans following you, and followed in my imagination by the store detective.

We strode down the open corridors together in our solitary fancy tasting artichokes, possessing every frozen delicacy, and never passing the cashier.

Where are we going, Walt Whitman? The doors close in an hour. Which way does your beard point tonight?

(I touch your book and dream of our odyssey in the supermarket and feel absurd.)

Will we walk all night through solitary streets? The trees add shade to shade, lights out in the houses, we'll both be lonely.

Will we stroll dreaming of the lost America of love past blue automobiles in driveways, home to our silent cottage?

Ah, dear father, graybeard, lonely old courage-teacher, what America did you have when Charon quit poling his ferry and you got out on a smoking bank and stood watching the boat disappear on the black waters of Lethe?

Berkeley, 1955

SUNFLOWER SUTRA

I walked on the banks of the tincan banana dock and sat down
  under the huge shade of a Southern Pacific locomotive to
  look at the sunset over the box house hills and cry.
Jack Kerouac sat beside me on a busted rusty iron pole, companion,
  we thought the same thoughts of the soul, bleak and blue

and sad-eyed, surrounded by the gnarled steel roots of trees of machinery.

The oily water on the river mirrored the red sky, sun sank on top of final Frisco peaks, no fish in that stream, no hermit in those mounts, just ourselves rheumy-eyed and hung-over like old bums on the river-bank, tired and wily.

Look at the Sunflower, he said, there was a dead gray shadow against the sky, big as a man, sitting dry on top of a pile of ancient sawdust—

—I rushed up enchanted—it was my first sunflower, memories of Blake—my visions—Harlem

and Hells of the Eastern rivers, bridges clanking Joes Greasy Sandwiches, dead baby carriages, black treadless tires forgotten and unretreaded, the poem of the riverbank, condoms & pots, steel knives, nothing stainless, only the dank muck and the razor-sharp artifacts passing into the past—

and the gray Sunflower poised against the sunset, crackly bleak and dusty with the smut and smog and smoke of olden locomotives in its eye—

corolla of bleary spikes pushed down and broken like a battered crown, seeds fallen out of its face, soon-to-be-toothless mouth of sunny air, sunrays obliterated on its hairy head like a dried wire spiderweb,

leaves stuck out like arms out of the stem, gestures from the sawdust root, broke pieces of plaster fallen out of the black twigs, a dead fly in its ear,

Unholy battered old thing you were, my sunflower O my soul, I loved you then!

The grime was no man's grime but death and human locomotives,

all that dress of dust, that veil of darkened railroad skin, that smog of cheek, that eyelid of black mis'ry, that sooty hand or phallus or protuberance of artificial worse-than-dirt—industrial—modern—all that civilization spotting your crazy golden crown—

and those blear thoughts of death and dusty loveless eyes and ends and withered roots below, in the home-pile of sand and sawdust, rubber dollar bills, skin of machinery, the guts and innards of the weeping coughing car, the empty lonely tincans with their rusty tongues alack, what more could I name, the smoked ashes of some cock cigar, the cunts of

wheelbarrows and the milky breasts of cars, wornout asses
out of chairs & sphincters of dynamos—all these
entangled in your mummied roots—and you there standing before
me in the sunset, all your glory in your form!
A perfect beauty of a sunflower! a perfect excellent lovely sunflower
existence! a sweet natural eye to the new hip moon, woke up
alive and excited grasping in the sunset shadow sunrise
golden monthly breeze!
How many flies buzzed round you innocent of your grime, while you
cursed the heavens of the railroad and your flower soul?
Poor dead flower? when did you forget you were a flower? when did
you look at your skin and decide you were an impotent dirty
old locomotive? the ghost of a locomotive? the specter and
shade of a once powerful mad American locomotive?
You were never no locomotive, Sunflower, you were a sunflower!
And you Locomotive, you are a locomotive, forget me not!
So I grabbed up the skeleton thick sunflower and stuck it at my side
like a scepter,
and deliver my sermon to my soul, and Jack's soul too, and anyone
who'll listen,
—We're not our skin of grime, we're not our dread bleak dusty
imageless locomotive, we're all golden sunflowers inside,
blessed by our own seed & hairy naked accomplishment-
bodies growing into mad black formal sunflowers in the
sunset, spied on by our eyes under the shadow of the mad
locomotive riverbank sunset Frisco hilly tincan evening
sitdown vision.

Berkeley, 1955

AMERICA

America I've given you all and now I'm nothing.
America two dollars and twentyseven cents January 17, 1956.
I can't stand my own mind.
America when will we end the human war?
Go fuck yourself with your atom bomb.
I don't feel good don't bother me.
I won't write my poem till I'm in my right mind.
America when will you be angelic?

When will you take off your clothes?
When will you look at yourself through the grave?
When will you be worthy of your million Trotskyites?
America why are your libraries full of tears?
America when will you send your eggs to India?
I'm sick of your insane demands.
When can I go into the supermarket and buy what I need with my
    good looks?
America after all it is you and I who are perfect not the next world.
Your machinery is too much for me.
You made me want to be a saint.
There must be some other way to settle this argument.
Burroughs is in Tangiers I don't think he'll come back it's sinister.
Are you being sinister or is this some form of practical joke?
I'm trying to come to the point.
I refuse to give up my obsession.
America stop pushing I know what I'm doing.
America the plum blossoms are falling.
I haven't read the newspapers for months, everyday somebody goes
    on trial for murder.
America I feel sentimental about the Wobblies.
America I used to be a communist when I was a kid I'm not sorry.
I smoke marijuana every chance I get.
I sit in my house for days on end and stare at the roses in the closet.
When I go to Chinatown I get drunk and never get laid.
My mind is made up there's going to be trouble.
You should have seen me reading Marx.
My psychoanalyst thinks I'm perfectly right.
I won't say the Lord's Prayer.
I have mystical visions and cosmic vibrations.
America I still haven't told you what you did to Uncle Max after he
    came over from Russia.
I'm addressing you.
Are you going to let your emotional life be run by Time Magazine?
I'm obsessed by Time Magazine.
I read it every week.
Its cover stares at me every time I slink past the corner candystore.
I read it in the basement of the Berkeley Public Library.
It's always telling me about responsibility. Businessmen are serious.
    Movie producers are serious. Everybody's serious but me.

It occurs to me that I am America.
I am talking to myself again.

Asia is rising against me.
I haven't got a chinaman's chance.
I'd better consider my national resources.
My national resources consist of two joints of marijuana millions of
     genitals an unpublishable private literature that jetplanes
     1400 miles an hour and twentyfive-thousand mental institu-
     tions.
I say nothing about my prisons nor the millions of underprivileged
     who live in my flowerpots under the light of five hundred
     suns.
I have abolished the whorehouses of France, Tangiers is the next to
     go.
My ambition is to be President despite the fact that I'm a
     Catholic.

America how can I write a holy litany in your silly mood?
I will continue like Henry Ford my strophes are as individual as his
     automobiles more so they're all different sexes.
America I will sell you strophes $2500 apiece $500 down on your
     old strophe
America free Tom Mooney
America save the Spanish Loyalists
America Sacco & Vanzetti must not die
America I am the Scottsboro boys.
America when I was seven momma took me to Communist Cell
     meetings they sold us garbanzos a handful per ticket a ticket
     costs a nickel and the speeches were free everybody was
     angelic and sentimental about the workers it was all so
     sincere you have no idea what a good thing the party was in
     1835 Scott Nearing was a grand old man a real mensch
     Mother Bloor the Silk-strikers' Ewig-Weibliche made me cry
     I once saw the Yiddish orator Israel Amter plain. Everybody
     must have been a spy.
America you don't really want to go to war.
America it's them bad Russians.
Them Russians them Russians and them Chinamen. And them
     Russians.

The Russia wants to eat us alive. The Russia's power mad. She
     wants to take our cars from out our garages.
Her wants to grab Chicago. Her needs a Red *Reader's Digest*. Her
     wants our auto plants in Siberia. Him big bureaucracy
     running our fillingstations.
That no good. Ugh. Him make Indians learn read. Him need big
     black niggers. Hah. Her make us all work sixteen hours a
     day. Help.
America this is quite serious.
America this is the impression I get from looking in the television
     set.
America is this correct?
I'd better get right down to the job.
It's true I don't want to join the Army or turn lathes in precision
     parts factories, I'm nearsighted and psychopathic anyway.
America I'm putting my queer shoulder to the wheel.

Berkeley, 17 January 1956

MANY LOVES

> *"Resolved to sing no songs henceforth but those of manly*
> *attachment"*
> —*Walt Whitman*

Neal Cassady was my animal: he brought me to my knees
and taught me the love of his cock and the secrets of his mind
And we met and conversed, went walking in the evening by the park
Up to Harlem, recollecting Denver, and Dan Budd, a hero
And we made shift to sack out in Harlem, after a long evening,
Jack and host in a large double bed, I volunteered for the cot, and
     Neal
Volunteered for the cot with me, we stripped and lay down.
I wore my underwear, my shorts, and he his briefs—
lights out on the narrow bed I turned to my side, with my back to
     his Irish boy's torso,
and huddled and balanced on the edge, and kept distance—
and hung my head over and kept my arm over the side, withdrawn
And he seeing my fear stretched out his arm, and put it around my
     breast

Saying "Draw near me" and gathered me in upon him:
I lay there trembling, and felt his great arm like a king's
And his breasts, his heart slow thudding against my back,
and his middle torso, narrow and made of iron, soft at my back,
his fiery firm belly warming me while I trembled—
His belly of fists and starvation, his belly a thousand girls kissed in
      Colorado
his belly of rocks thrown over Denver roofs, prowess of jumping
      and fists, his stomach of solitudes,
His belly of burning iron and jails affectionate to my side:
I began to tremble, he pulled me in closer with his arm, and hugged
      me long and close
my soul melted, secrecy departed, I became
Thenceforth open to his nature as a flower in the shining sun.
And below his belly, in white underwear, tight between my but-
      tocks,
His own loins against me soft, nestling in comradeship, put forth &
      pressed into me, open to my awareness,
slowly began to grow, signal me further and deeper affection, sexual
      tenderness.
So gentle the man, so sweet the moment, so kind the thighs that
      nuzzled against me smooth-skinned powerful, warm by my
      legs
That my body shudders and trembles with happiness, remember-
      ing—
His hand opened up on my belly, his palms and fingers flat against
      my skin
I fell to him, and turned, shifting, put my face on his arm resting,
my chest against his, he helped me to turn, and held me closer
his arm at my back beneath my head, and arm at my buttocks
      tender holding me in,
our bellies together nestling, loins touched together, pressing and
      knowledgeable each other's hardness, and mine stuck out of
      my underwear.
Then I pressed in closer and drew my leg up between his, and he lay
      half on me with his thighs and bedded me down close,
      caressing
and moved together pressing his cock to my thigh and mine to his
slowly, and slowly began a love match that continues in my imagi-
      nation to this day a full decade.

Thus I met Neal & thus we felt each other's flesh and owned each
    other bodies and souls.
So then as I lay on his breast with my arms clasped around his neck
    and his cheek against mine,
I put my hand down to feel his great back for the first time, jaws and
    pectorals of steel at my fingers,
closer and stiller, down the silken iron back to his waist, the whole
    of his torso now open
my hand at his waist trembling, waited delaying and under the
    elastic of his briefs,
I first touched the smooth mount of his rock buttocks, silken in
    power, rounded in animal fucking and bodily nights over
    nurses and schoolgirls,
O ass of long solitudes in stolen cars, and solitudes on curbs, musing
    fist in cheek,
Ass of a thousand farewells, ass of youth, youth's lovers,
Ass of a thousand lonely craps in gas stations ass of great painful
    secrecies of the years
O ass of mystery and night! ass of gymnasiums and muscular
    pants
ass of high schools and masturbation ass of lone delight, ass of
    mankind, so beautiful and hollow, dowry of Mind and
    Angels,
Ass of hero, Neal Cassady, I had at my hand: my fingers traced the
    curve to the bottom of his thighs.
I raised my thighs and stripped down my shorts to my knees, and
    bent to push them off
and he raised me up from his chest, and pulled down his pants the
    same,
humble and meek and obedient to his mood our silence,
and naked at long last with angel & greek & athlete & hero and
    brother and boy of my dreams
I lay with my hair intermixed with his, he asking me "What shall we
    do now?"
—And confessed, years later, he thinking I was not a queer at first to
    please me & serve me, to blow me and make me come,
    maybe or if I were queer, that's what I'd likely want of a
    dumb bastard like him.
But I made my first mistake, and made him then and there my
    master, and bowed my head, and holding his buttock

Took up his hard-on and held it, feeling it throb and pressing my
       own at his knee & breathing showed him I needed him, cock,
       for my dreams of insatiety & lone love.

—And I lie here naked in the dark, dreaming

Arctic, 10 August 1956

TO AUNT ROSE

Aunt Rose—now—might I see you
with your thin face and buck tooth smile and pain
        of rheumatism—and a long black heavy shoe
          for your bony left leg
   limping down the long hall in Newark on the running carpet
        past the black grand piano
          in the day room
            where the parties were
    and I sang Spanish loyalist songs
       in a high squeaky voice
          (hysterical) the committee listening
      while you limped around the room
        collected the money—
Aunt Honey, Uncle Sam, a stranger with a cloth arm
       in his pocket
         and huge young bald head
           of Abraham Lincoln Brigade

—your long sad face
        your tears of sexual frustration
          (what smothered sobs and bony hips
             under the pillows of Osborne Terrace)
    —the time I stood on the toilet seat naked
        and you powdered my thighs with calamine
          against the poison ivy—my tender
             and shamed first black curled hairs
   what were you thinking in secret heart then
         knowing me a man already—
and I an ignorant girl of family silence on the thin pedestal
        of my legs in the bathroom—Museum of Newark.

Aunt Rose
Hitler is dead, Hitler is in Eternity; Hitler is with
Tamburlane and Emily Brontë

Though I see you walking still, a ghost on Osborne Terrace
down the long dark hall to the front door
limping a little with a pinched smile
in what must have been a silken
flower dress
welcoming my father, the Poet, on his visit to Newark
—see you arriving in the living room
dancing on your crippled leg
and clapping hands his book
had been accepted by Liveright

Hitler is dead and Liveright's gone out of business
The Attic of the Past and *Everlasting Minute* are out of print
Uncle Harry sold his last silk stocking
Claire quit interpretive dancing school
Buba sits a wrinkled monument in Old
Ladies Home blinking at new babies

last time I saw you was the hospital
pale skull protruding under ashen skin
blue veined unconscious girl
in an oxygen tent
the war in Spain has ended long ago
Aunt Rose

Paris, June 1958

KADDISH

For Naomi Ginsberg, 1894–1956

I

Strange now to think of you, gone without corsets & eyes, while I
walk on the sunny pavement of Greenwich Village.

downtown Manhattan, clear winter noon, and I've been up all
   night, talking, talking, reading the Kaddish aloud, listening
   to Ray Charles blues shout blind on the phonograph

the rhythm the rhythm—and your memory in my head three years
   after—And read Adonais' last triumphant stanzas aloud—
   wept, realizing how we suffer—

And how Death is that remedy all singers dream of, sing, remember,
   prophesy as in the Hebrew Anthem, or the Buddhist Book of
   Answers—and my own imagination of a withered leaf—at
   dawn—

Dreaming back thru life, Your time—and mine accelerating toward
   Apocalypse,

the final moment—the flower burning in the Day—and what comes
   after,

looking back on the mind itself that saw an American city

a flash away, and the great dream of Me or China, or you and a
   phantom Russia, or a crumpled bed that never existed—

like a poem in the dark—escaped back to Oblivion—

No more to say, and nothing to weep for but the Beings in the
   Dream, trapped in its disappearance,

sighing, screaming with it, buying and selling pieces of phantom,
   worshipping each other,

worshipping the God included in it all—longing or inevitability?—
   while it lasts, a Vision—anything more?

It leaps about me, as I go out and walk the street, look back over my
   shoulder, Seventh Avenue, the battlements of window office
   buildings shouldering each other high, under a cloud, tall as
   the sky an instant—and the sky above—an old blue place.

or down the Avenue to the south, to—as I walk toward the Lower
   East Side—where you walked 50 years ago, little girl—from
   Russia, eating the first poisonous tomatoes of America—
   frightened on the dock—

then struggling in the crowds of Orchard Street toward what?—
   toward Newark—

toward candy store, first home-made sodas of the century, hand-
   churned ice cream in backroom on musty brownfloor
   boards—

Toward education marriage nervous breakdown, operation, teaching school, and learning to be mad, in a dream—what is this
   life?

Toward the Key in the window—and the great Key lays its head of
     light on top of Manhattan, and over the floor, and lays down
     on the sidewalk—in a single vast beam, moving, as I walk
     down First toward the Yiddish Theater—and the place of
     poverty
you knew, and I know, but without caring now—Strange to have
     moved thru Paterson, and the West, and Europe and here
     again,
with the cries of Spaniards now in the doorstoops doors and dark
     boys on the street, fire escapes old as you
—Tho you're not old now, that's left here with me—
Myself, anyhow, maybe as old as the universe—and I guess that dies
     with us—enough to cancel all that comes—What came is
     gone forever every time—
That's good! That leaves it open for no regret—no fear radiators,
     lacklove, torture even toothache in the end—
Though while it comes it is a lion that eats the soul—and the lamb,
     the soul, in us, alas, offering itself in sacrifice to change's
     fierce hunger—hair and teeth—and the roar of bonepain,
     skull bare, break rib, rot-skin, braintricked Implacability.
Ai! ai! we do worse! We are in a fix! And you're out, Death let you
     out, Death had the Mercy, you're done with your century,
     done with God, done with the path thru it—Done with your-
     self at last—Pure—Back to the Babe dark before your Father,
     before us all—before the world—
There, rest. No more suffering for you. I know where you've gone,
     it's good.
No more flowers in the summer fields of New York, no joy now, no
     more fear of Louis,
and no more of his sweetness and glasses, his high school decades,
     debts, loves, frightened telephone calls, conception beds, rel-
     atives, hands—
No more of sister Elanor,—she gone before you—we kept it secret—
     you killed her—or she killed herself to bear with you—an
     arthritic heart—But Death's killed you both—No matter—
Nor your memory of your mother, 1915 tears in silent movies weeks
     and weeks—forgetting, agrieve watching Marie Dressler
     address humanity, Chaplin dance in youth,
or Boris Godunov, Chaliapin's at the Met, halling his voice of a
     weeping Czar—by standing room with Elanor & Max—

watching also the Capitalists take seats in Orchestra, white furs, diamonds,

with the YPSL's hitch-hiking thru Pennsylvania, in black baggy gym skirts pants, photograph of 4 girls holding each other round the waste, and laughing eye, too coy, virginal solitude of 1920

all girls grown old, or dead, now, and that long hair in the grave—lucky to have husbands later—

You made it—I came too—Eugene my brother before (still grieving now and will gream on to his last stiff hand, as he goes thru his cancer—or kill—later perhaps—soon he will think—)

And it's the last moment I remember, which I see them all, thru myself, now—tho not you

I didn't foresee what you felt—what more hideous gape of bad mouth came first—to you—and were you prepared?

To go where? In that Dark—that—in that God? a radiance? A Lord in the Void? Like an eye in the black cloud in a dream? Adonoi at last, with you?

Beyond my remembrance! Incapable to guess! Not merely the yellow skull in the grave, or a box of worm dust, and a stained ribbon—Deaths-head with Halo? can you believe it?

Is it only the sun that shines once for the mind, only the flash of existence, than none ever was?

Nothing beyond what we have—what you had—that so pitiful—yet Triumph,

to have been here, and changed, like a tree, broken, or flower—fed to the ground—but mad, with its petals, colored, thinking Great Universe, shaken, cut in the head, leaf stript, hid in an egg crate hospital, cloth wrapped, sore—freaked in the moon brain, Naughtless.

No flower like that flower, which knew itself in the garden, and fought the knife—lost

Cut down by an idiot Snowman's icy—even in the Spring—strange ghost thought—some Death—Sharp icicle in his hand—crowned with old roses—a dog for his eyes—cock of a sweatshop—heart of electric irons.

All the accumulations of life, that wear us out—clocks, bodies, consciousness, shoes, breasts—begotten sons—your Communism—'Paranoia' into hospitals.

You once kicked Elanor in the leg, she died of heart failure later.
    You of stroke. Asleep? within a year, the two of you, sisters
    in death. Is Elanor happy?
Max grieves alive in an office on Lower Broadway, lone large mus-
    tache over midnight Accountings, not sure. His life
    passes—as he sees—and what does he doubt now? Still
    dream of making money, or that might have made money,
    hired nurse, had children, found even your Immortality,
    Naomi?
I'll see him soon. Now I've got to cut through—to talk to you—as I
    didn't when you had a mouth.
Forever. And we're bound for that, Forever—like Emily Dickinson's
    horses—headed to the End.
They know the way—These Steeds—run faster than we think—it's
    our own life they cross—and take with them.

Magnificent, mourned no more, marred of heart, mind
behind, married dreamed, mortal changed—Ass and face done with
murder.
    In the world, given, flower maddened, made no Utopia, shut
under pine, almed in Earth, balmed in Lone, Jehovah, accept.
    Nameless, One Faced, Forever beyond me, beginningless,
endless, Father in death. Tho I am not there for this Prophecy, I am
unmarried, I'm hymnless, I'm Heavenless, headless in blisshood I
would still adore
    Thee, Heaven, after Death, only One blessed in Nothingness,
not light or darkness, Dayless Eternity—
    Take this, this Psalm, from me, burst from my hand in a day,
some of my Time, now given to Nothing—to praise Thee—But
Death
    This is the end, the redemption from Wilderness, way for the
Wonderer, House sought for All, black handkerchief washed clean
by weeping—page beyond Psalm—Last change of mine and
Naomi—to God's perfect Darkness—Death, stay thy phantoms!

II

    Over and over—refrain—of the Hospitals—still haven't
written your history—leave it abstract—a few images
    run thru the mind—like the saxophone chorus of houses and
years—remembrance of electrical shocks.

By long nites as a child in Paterson apartment, watching over your nervousness—you were fat—your next move—

By that afternoon I stayed home from school to take care of you—once and for all—when I vowed forever that once man disagreed with my opinion of the cosmos, I was lost—

By my later burden—vow to illuminate mankind—this is release of particulars—(mad as you)—(sanity a trick of agreement)—

But you stared out the window on the Broadway Church corner, and spied a mystical assassin from Newark,

So phoned the Doctor—'OK go way for a rest'—so I put on my coat and walked you downstreet—On the way a grammarschool boy screamed, unaccountably—'Where you goin Lady to Death'? I shuddered—

and you covered your nose with motheaten fur collar, gas mask against poison sneaked into downtown atmosphere, sprayed by Grandma—

And was the driver of the cheesebox Public Service bus a member of the gang? You shuddered at his face, I could hardly get you on—to New York, very Times Square, to grab another Greyhound—

where we hung around 2 hours fighting invisible bugs and jewish sickness—breeze poisoned by Roosevelt—

out to get you—and me tagging along, hoping it would end in a quiet room in a Victorian house by a lake.

Ride 3 hours thru tunnels past all American industry, Bayonne preparing for World War II, tanks, gas fields, soda factories, diners, locomotive roundhouse fortress—into piney woods New Jersey Indians—calm towns—long roads thru sandy tree fields—

Bridges by deerless creeks, old wampum loading the streambed—down there a tomahawk or Pocahontas bone—and a million old ladies voting for Roosevelt in brown small houses, roads off the Madness highway—

perhaps a hawk in a tree, or a hermit looking for an owl-filled branch—

All the time arguing—afraid of strangers in the forward double seat, snoring regardless—what busride they snore on now?

'Allen, you don't understand—it's—ever since those 3 big

sticks up my back—they did something to me in Hospital, they poisoned me, they want to see me dead—3 big sticks, 3 big sticks—

'The Bitch! Old Grandma! Last week I saw her, dressed in pants like an old man, with a sack on her back, climbing up the brick side of the apartment

'On the fire escape, with poison germs, to throw on me—at night—maybe Louis is helping her—he's under her power—

'I'm your mother, take me to Lakewood' (near where Graf Zeppelin had crashed before, all Hitler in Explosion) 'where I can hide.'

We got there—Dr. Whatzis rest home—she hid behind a closet—demanded a blood transfusion.

We were kicked out—tramping with Valise to unknown shady lawn houses—dusk, pine trees after dark—long dead street filled with crickets and poison ivy—

I shut her up by now—big house REST HOME ROOMS— gave the landlady her money for the week—carried up the iron valise—sat on bed waiting to escape—

Neat room in attic with friendly bedcover—lace curtains— spinning wheel rug—Stained wallpaper old as Naomi. We were home.

I left on the next bus to New York—laid my head back in the last seat, depressed—the worst yet to come?—abandoning her, rode in torpor—I was only 12.

Would she hide in her room and come out cheerful for breakfast? Or lock her door and stare thru the window for sidestreet spies? Listen at keyholes for Hitlerian invisible gas? Dream in a chair—or mock me, by—in front of a mirror, alone?

12 riding the bus at nite thru New Jersey, have left Naomi to Parcae in Lakewood's haunted house—left to my own fate bus— sunk in a seat—all violins broken—my heart sore in my ribs—mind was empty—Would she were safe in her coffin—

Or back at Normal School in Newark, studying up on America in a black skirt—winter on the street without lunch—a penny a pickle—home at night to take care of Elanor in the bedroom—

First nervous breakdown was 1919—she stayed home from school and lay in a dark room for three weeks—something bad— never said what—every noise hurt—dreams of the creaks of Wall Street—

Before the gray Depression—went upstate New York—recovered—Lou took photo of her sitting crossleg on the grass—her long hair wound with flowers—smiling—playing lullabies on mandolin—poison ivy smoke in left-wing summer camps and me in infancy saw trees—

or back teaching school, laughing with idiots, the backward classes—her Russian specialty—morons with dreamy lips, great eyes, thin feet & sicky fingers, swaybacked, rachitic—

great heads pendulous over Alice in Wonderland, a blackboard full of C A T.

Naomi reading patiently, story out of a Communist fairy book—Tale of the Sudden Sweetness of the Dictator—Forgiveness of Warlocks—Armies Kissing—

Deathsheads Around the Green Table—The King & the Workers—Paterson Press printed them up in the '30s till she went mad, or they folded, both.

O Paterson! I got home late that nite. Louis was worried. How could I be so—didn't I think? I shouldn't have left her. Mad in Lakewood. Call the Doctor. Phone the home in the pines. Too late.

Went to bed exhausted, wanting to leave the world (probably that year newly in love with R——my high school mind hero, jewish boy who came a doctor later—then silent neat kid—

I later laying down life for him, moved to Manhattan—followed him to college—Prayed on ferry to help mankind if admitted—vowed, the day I journeyed to Entrance Exam—

by being honest revolutionary labor lawyer—would train for that—inspired by Sacco Vanzetti, Norman Thomas, Debs, Altgeld, Sandburg, Poe—Little Blue Books. I wanted to be President, or Senator.

ignorant woe—later dreams of kneeling by R's shocked knees declaring my love of 1941—What sweetness he'd have shown me, tho, that I'd wished him & despaired—first love—a crush—

Later a mortal avalanche, whole mountains of homosexuality, Matterhorns of cock, Grand Canyons of asshole—weight on my melancholy head—

meanwhile I walked on Broadway imagining Infinity like a rubber ball without space beyond—what's outside?—coming home to Graham Avenue still melancholy passing the lone green hedges across the street, dreaming after the movies—)

The telephone rang at 2 A.M.—Emergency—she'd gone mad—Naomi hiding under the bed screaming bugs of Mussolini—Help! Louis! Buba! Fascists! Death!—the landlady frightened—old fag attendant screaming back at her—

Terror, that woke the neighbors—old ladies on the second floor recovering from menopause—all those rags between thighs, clean sheets, sorry over lost babies—husbands ashen—children sneering at Yale, or putting oil in hair at CCNY—or trembling in Montclair State Teachers College like Eugene—

Her big leg crouched to her breast, hand outstretched Keep Away, wool dress on her thighs, fur coat dragged under the bed—she barricaded herself under bedspring with suitcases.

Louis in pajamas listening to phone, frightened—do now?—Who could know?—my fault, delivering her to solitude?—sitting in the dark room on the sofa, trembling, to figure out—

He took the morning train to Lakewood, Naomi still under bed—thought he brought poison Cops—Naomi screaming—Louis what happened to your heart then? Have you been killed by Naomi's ecstasy?

Dragged her out, around the corner, a cab, forced her in with valise, but the driver left them off at drugstore. Bus stop, two hours' wait.

I lay in bed nervous in the 4-room apartment, the big bed in living room, next to Louis' desk—shaking—he came home that nite, late, told me what happened.

Naomi at the prescription counter defending herself from the enemy—racks of children's books, douche bags, aspirins, pots, blood—'Don't come near me—murderers! Keep away! Promise not to kill me!'

Louis in horror at the soda fountain—with Lakewood girlscouts—Coke addicts—nurses—busmen hung on schedule—Police from country precinct, dumbed—and a priest dreaming of pigs on an ancient cliff?

Smelling the air—Louis pointing to emptiness?—Customers vomiting their Cokes—or staring—Louis humiliated—Naomi triumphant—The Announcement of the Plot. Bus arrives, the drivers won't have them on trip to New York.

Phonecalls to Dr. Whatzis, 'She needs a rest,' The mental hospital—State Greystone Doctors—'Bring her here, Mr. Ginsberg.'

Naomi, Naomi—sweating, bulge-eyed, fat, the dress unbuttoned at one side—hair over brow, her stocking hanging evilly on her legs—screaming for a blood transfusion—one righteous hand upraised—a shoe in it—barefoot in the Pharmacy—

The enemies approach—what poisons? Tape recorders? FBI? Zhdanov hiding behind the counter? Trotsky mixing rat bacteria in the back of the store? Uncle Sam in Newark, plotting deathly perfumes in the Negro district? Uncle Ephraim, drunk with murder in the politician's bar, scheming of Hague? Aunt Rose passing water thru the needles of the Spanish Civil War?

till the hired $35 ambulance came from Red Bank—Grabbed her arms—strapped her on the stretcher—moaning, poisoned by imaginaries, vomiting chemicals thru Jersey, begging mercy from Essex County to Morristown—

And back to Greystone where she lay three years—that was the last breakthrough, delivered her to Madhouse again—

On what wards—I walked there later, oft—old catatonic ladies, gray as cloud or ash or walls—sit crooning over floorspace— Chairs—and the wrinkled hags acreep, accusing—begging my 13-year-old mercy—

'Take me home'—I went alone sometimes looking for the lost Naomi, taking Shock—and I'd say, 'No, you're crazy Mama,— Trust the Drs.'—

And Eugene, my brother, her elder son, away studying Law in a furnished room in Newark—

came Peterson-ward next day—and he sat on the brokendown couch in the living room—'We had to send her back to Greystone'—

—his face perplexed, so young, then eyes with tears—then crept weeping all over his face—'What for?' wail vibrating in his cheekbones, eyes closed up, high voice—Eugene's face of pain.

Him faraway, escaped to an Elevator in the Newark Library, his bottle daily milk on windowsill of $5 week furn room downtown at trolley tracks—

He worked 8 hrs. a day for $20/wk—thru Law School years—stayed by himself innocent near negro whorehouses.

Unlaid, poor virgin—writing poems about Ideals and politics letters to the editor Pat Eve News—(we both wrote, denouncing Senator Borah and Isolationists—and felt mysterious toward Paterson City Hall—

I sneaked inside it once—local Moloch tower with phallus spire & cap o' ornament, strange gothic Poetry that stood on Market Street—replica Lyons' Hotel de Ville—

wings, balcony & scrollwork portals, gateway to the giant city clock, secret map room full of Hawthorne—dark Debs in the Board of Tax—Rembrandt smoking in the gloom—

Silent polished desks in the great committee room—Aldermen? Bd of Finance? Mosca the hairdresser aplot—Crapp the gangster issuing orders from the john—The madmen struggling over Zone, Fire, Cops & Backroom Metaphysics—we're all dead—outside by the bus stop Eugene stared thru childhood—

where the Evangelist preached madly for 3 decades, hard-haired, cracked & true to his mean Bible—chalked Prepare to Meet Thy God on civic pave—

or God is Love on the railroad overpass concrete—he raved like I would rave, the lone Evangelist—Death on City Hall—)

But Gene, young,—been Montclair Teachers College 4 years—taught half year & quit to go ahead in life—afraid of Discipline Problems—dark sex Italian students, raw girls getting laid, no English, sonnets disregarded—and he did not know much—just that he lost—

so broke his life in two and paid for Law—read huge blue books and rode the ancient elevator 13 miles away in Newark & studied up hard for the future

just found the Scream of Naomi on his failure doorstep, for the final time, Naomi gone, us lonely—home—him sitting there—

Then have some chicken soup, Eugene. The Man of Evangel wails in front of City Hall. And this year Lou has poetic loves of suburb middle age—in secret—music from his 1937 book—Sincere—he longs for beauty—

No love since Naomi screamed—since 1923?—now lost in Greystone ward—new shock for her—Electricity, following the 40 Insulin.

And Metrazol had made her fat.

So that a few years later she came home again—we'd much advanced and planned—I waited for that day—my Mother again to cook &—play the piano—sing at mandolin—Lung Stew, & Stenka Razin, & the communist line on the war with Finland—and Louis in debt—suspected to be poisoned money—mysterious capitalisms

—& walked down the long front hall & looked at the furniture. She never remembered it all. Some amnesia. Examined the doilies—and the dining room set was sold—

the Mahogany table—20 years love—gone to the junk man—we still had the piano—and the book of Poe—and the Mandolin, tho needed some string, dusty—

She went to the backroom to lie down in bed and ruminate, or nap, hide—I went in with her, not leave her by herself—lay in bed next to her—shades pulled, dusky, late afternoon—Louis in front room at desk, waiting—perhaps boiling chicken for supper—

'Don't be afraid of me because I'm just coming back home from the mental hospital—I'm your mother—'

Poor love, lost—a fear—I lay there—Said, 'I love you Naomi,'—stiff, next to her arm. I would have cried, was this the comfortless lone union?—Nervous, and she got up soon.

Was she ever satisfied? And—by herself sat on the new couch by the front windows, uneasy—cheek leaning on her hand—narrowing eye—at what fate that day—

Picking her tooth with her nail, lips formed an O, suspicion—thought's old worn vagina—absent sideglance of eye—some evil debt written in the wall, unpaid—& the aged breasts of Newark come near—

May have heard radio gossip thru the wires in her head, controlled by 3 big sticks left in her back by gangsters in amnesia, thru the hospital—caused pain between her shoulders—

Into her head—Roosevelt should know her case, she told me—Afraid to kill her, now, that the government knew their names—traced back to Hitler—wanted to leave Louis' house forever.

One night, sudden attack—her noise in the bathroom—like croaking up her soul—convulsions and red vomit coming out of her mouth—diarrhea water exploding from her behind—on all fours in front of the toilet—urine running between her legs—left retching on the tile floor smeared with her black feces—unfainted—

At forty, varicosed, nude, fat, doomed, hiding outside the apartment door near the elevator calling Police, yelling for her girl-friend Rose to help—

Once locked herself in with razor or iodine—could hear her cough in tears at sink—Lou broke through glass green-painted door, we pulled her out to the bedroom.

Then quiet for months that winter—walks, alone, nearby on Broadway, read Daily Worker—Broke her arm, fell on icy street—

Began to scheme escape from cosmic financial murder plots—later she ran away to the Bronx to her sister Elanor. And there's another saga of late Naomi in New York.

Or thru Elanor or the Workmen's Circle, where she worked, addressing envelopes, she made out—went shopping for Campbell's tomato soup—saved money Louis mailed her—

Later she found a boyfriend, and he was a doctor—Dr. Isaac worked for National Maritime Union—now Italian bald and pudgy old doll—who was himself an orphan—but they kicked him out—Old cruelties—

Sloppier, sat around on bed or chair, in corset dreaming to herself—'I'm hot—I'm getting fat—I used to have such a beautiful figure before I went to the hospital—You should have seen me in Woodbine—' This in a furnished room around the NMU hall, 1943.

Looking at naked baby pictures in the magazine—baby powder advertisements, strained lamb carrots—'I will think nothing but beautiful thoughts.'

Revolving her head round and round on her neck at window light in summertime, in hypnotize, in doven-dream recall—

'I touch his cheek, I touch his cheek, he touches my lips with his hand, I think beautiful thoughts, the baby has a beautiful hand.'—

Or a No-shake of her body, disgust—some thought of Buchenwald —some insulin passes thru her head—a grimace nerve shudder at Involuntary (as shudder when I piss)—bad chemical in her cortex—'No don't think of that. He's a rat.'

Naomi: 'And when we die we become an onion, a cabbage, a carrot, or a squash, a vegetable.' I come downtown from Columbia and agree. She reads the Bible, thinks beautiful thoughts all day.

'Yesterday I saw God. What did he look like? Well, in the afternoon I climbed up a ladder—he has a cheap cabin in the country, like Monroe, N.Y. the chicken farms in the wood. He was a lonely old man with a white beard.

'I cooked supper for him. I made him a nice supper—lentil soup, vegetables, bread & butter—miltz—he sat down at the table and ate, he was sad.

'I told him, Look at all those fightings and killings down there, What's the matter? Why don't you put a stop to it?

'I try, he said—That's all he could do, he looked tired. He's a bachelor so long, and he likes lentil soup.'

Serving me meanwhile, a plate of cold fish—chopped raw cabbage dript with tapwater—smelly tomatoes—week-old health food—grated beets & carrots with leaky juice, warm—more and more disconsolate food—I can't eat it for nausea sometimes—the Charity of her hands stinking with Manhattan, madness, desire to please me, cold undercooked fish—pale red near the bones. Her smells—and oft naked in the room, so that I stare ahead, or turn a book ignoring her.

One time I thought she was trying to make me come lay her—flirting to herself at sink—lay back on huge bed that filled most of the room, dress up round her hips, big slash of hair, scars of operations, pancreas, belly wounds, abortions, appendix, stitching of incisions pulling down in the fat like hideous thick zippers— ragged long lips between her legs—What, even, smell of asshole? I was cold—later revolted a little, not much—seemed perhaps a good idea to try—know the Monster of the Beginning Womb—Perhaps— that way. Would she care? She needs a lover.

Yisborach, v'yistabach, v'yispoar, v'yisroman, v'yisnaseh, v'yishador, v'yishalleh, v'yishallol, sh'meh d'kudsho, b'rich hu.

And Louis reestablishing himself in Paterson grimy apart- ment in negro district—living in dark rooms—but found himself a girl he later married, falling in love again—tho sere & shy—hurt with 20 years Naomi's mad idealism.

Once I came home, after longtime in N.Y., he's lonely— sitting in the bedroom, he at desk chair turned round to face me—weeps, tears in red eyes under his glasses—

That we'd left him—Gene gone strangely into army—she out on her own in N.Y., almost childish in her furnished room. So Louis walked down-town to postoffice to get mail, taught in highschool— stayed at poetry desk, forlorn—ate grief at Bickford's all these years—are gone.

Eugene got out of the Army, came home changed and lone— cut off his nose in jewish operation—for years stopped girls on Broadway for cups of coffee to get laid—Went to NYU, serious there, to finish Law.—

And Gene lived with her, ate naked fishcakes, cheap, while

she got crazier—He got thin, or felt helpless, Naomi striking 1920 poses at the moon, half-naked in the next bed.

bit his nails and studied—was the weird nurse-son—Next year he moved to a room near Columbia—though she wanted to live with her children—

'Listen to your mother's plea, I beg you'—Louis still sending her checks—I was in bughouse that year 8 months—my own visions unmentioned in this here Lament—

But then went half mad—Hitler in her room, she saw his mustache in the sink—afraid of Dr. Isaac now, suspecting that he was in on the Newark plot—went up to Bronx to live near Elanor's Rheumatic Heart—

And Uncle Max never got up before noon, tho Naomi at 6 A.M. was listening to the radio for spies—or searching the windowsill,

for in the empty lot downstairs, an old man creeps with his bag stuffing packages of garbage in his hanging black overcoat.

Max's sister Edie works—17 years bookkeeper at Gimbels— lived downstairs in apartment house, divorced—so Edie took in Naomi on Rochambeau Ave—

Woodlawn Cemetery across the street, vast dale of graves where Poe once—Last stop on Bronx subway—lots of communists in that area.

Who enrolled for painting classes at night in Bronx Adult High School—walked alone under Van Cortlandt Elevated line to class—paints Naomiisms—

Humans sitting on the grass in some Camp No-Worry summers yore —saints with droopy faces and long-ill-fitting pants, from hospital—

Brides in front of Lower East Side with short grooms—lost El trains running over the Babylonian apartment rooftops in the Bronx—

Sad paintings—but she expressed herself. Her mandolin gone, all strings broke in her head, she tried. Toward Beauty? or some old life Message?

But started kicking Elanor, and Elanor had heart trouble— came upstairs and asked her about Spydom for hours,—Elanor frazzled. Max away at office, accounting for cigar stores till at night.

'I am a great woman—am truly a beautiful soul—and because of that they (Hitler, Grandma, Hearst, the Capitalists,

Franco, Daily News, the '20s, Mussolini, the living dead) want to shut me up—Buba's the head of a spider network—'

Kicking the girls, Edie & Elanor—Woke Edie at midnite to tell her she was a spy and Elanor a rat. Edie worked all day and couldn't take it—She was organizing the union.—And Elanor began dying, upstairs in bed.

The relatives call me up, she's getting worse—I was the only one left —Went on the subway with Eugene to see her, ate stale fish—

'My sister whispers in the radio—Louis must be in the apartment—his mother tells him what to say—LIARS!—I cooked for my two children —I played the mandolin—'

Last night the nightingale woke me / Last night when all was still / it sang in the golden moonlight / from on the wintry hill. She did.

I pushed her against the door and shouted 'DONT KICK ELANOR!'—she stared at me—Contempt—die—disbelief her sons are so naive, so dumb—'Elanor is the worst spy! She's taking orders!'

'—No wires in the room!'—I'm yelling at her—last ditch, Eugene listening on the bed—what can he do to escape that fatal Mama—'You've been away from Louis years already—Grandma's too old to walk—'

We're all alive at once then—even me & Gene & Naomi in one mythological Cousinesque room—screaming at each other in the Forever—I in Columbia jacket, she half undressed.

I banging against her head which saw Radios, Sticks, Hitlers—the gamut of Hallucinations—for real—her own universe—no road that goes elsewhere—to my own—No America, not even a world—

That you go as all men, as Van Gogh, as mad Hannah, all the same —to the last doom—Thunder, Spirits, Lightning!

I've seen your grave! O strange Naomi! My own—cracked grave! Shema Y'Israel—I am Svul Avrum—you—in death?

Your last night in the darkness of the Bronx—I phonecalled—thru hospital to secret police

that came, when you and I were alone, shrieking at Elanor in my ear —who breathed hard in her own bed, got thin—

Nor will forget, the doorknock, at your fright of spies,—Law advancing, on my honor—Eternity entering the room—you running to the bathroom undressed, hiding in protest from the last heroic fate—

staring at my eyes, betrayed—the final cops of madness rescuing me —from your foot against the broken heart of Elanor,

your voice at Edie weary of Gimbels coming home to broken radio —and Louis needing a poor divorce, he wants to get married soon—Eugene dreaming, hiding at 125 St., suing negroes for money on crud furniture, defending black girls—

Protests from the bathroom—Said you were sane—dressing in a cotton robe, your shoes, then new, your purse and newspaper clippings—no—your honesty—

as you vainly made your lips more real with lipstick, looking in the mirror to see if the Insanity was Me or a carful of police.

or Grandma spying at 78—Your vision—Her climbing over the walls of the cemetery with political kidnapper's bag—or what you saw on the walls of the Bronx, in pink nightgown at midnight, staring out the window on the empty lot—

Ah Rochambeau Ave.—Playground of Phantoms—last apartment in the Bronx for spies—last home for Elanor or Naomi, here these communist sisters lost their revolution—

'All right—put on your coat Mrs.—let's go—We have the wagon downstairs—you want to come with her to the station?'

The ride then—held Naomi's hand, and held her head to my breast, I'm taller—kissed her and said I did it for the best—Elanor sick—and Max with heart condition—Needs—

To me—'Why did you do this?'—'Yes Mrs., your son will have to leave you in an hour'—The Ambulance

came in a few hours—drove off at 4 A.M. to some Bellevue in the night downtown—gone to the hospital forever. I saw her led away—she waved, tears in her eyes.

Two years, after a trip to Mexico—bleak in the flat plain near Brentwood, scrub brush and grass around the unused RR train track to the crazyhouse—

new brick 20 story central building—lost on the vast lawns of mad-town on Long Island—huge cities of the moon.

Asylum spreads out giant wings above the path to a minute black hole —the door—entrance thru crotch—

I went in—smelt funny—the halls again—up elevator—to a glass door on a Women's Ward—to Naomi—Two nurses buxom white—They led her out, Naomi stared—and I gaspt—She'd had a stroke—

Too thin, shrunk on her bones—age come to Naomi—now broken into white hair—loose dress on her skeleton—face sunk, old! withered—cheek of crone—

One hand stiff—heaviness of forties & menopause reduced by one heart stroke, lame now—wrinkles—a scar on her head, the lobotomy—ruin, the hand dipping downwards to death—

O Russian faced, woman on the grass, your long black hair is crowned with flowers, the mandolin is on your knees—

Communist beauty, sit here married in the summer among daisies, promised happiness at hand—

holy mother, now you smile on your love, your world is born anew, children run naked in the field spotted with dandelions,

they eat in the plum tree grove at the end of the meadow and find a cabin where a white-haired negro teaches the mystery of his rainbarrel—

blessed daughter come to America, I long to hear your voice again, remembering your mother's music, in the Song of the Natural Front—

O glorious muse that bore me from the womb, gave suck first mystic life & taught me talk and music, from whose pained head I first took Vision—

Tortured and beaten in the skull—What mad hallucinations of the damned that drive me out of my own skull to seek Eternity till I find Peace for Thee, O Poetry—and for all humankind call on the Origin

Death which is the mother of the universe!—Now wear your nakedness forever, white flowers in your hair, your marriage sealed behind the sky —no revolution might destroy that maidenhood—

O beautiful Garbo of my Karma—all photographs from 1920 in Camp Nicht-Gedeiget here unchanged—with all the teachers from Newark —Nor Elanor be gone, nor Max await his specter—nor Louis retire from this High School—

Back! You! Naomi! Skull on you! Gaunt immortality and revolution come—small broken woman—the ashen indoor eyes of hospitals, ward grayness on skin—

'Are you a spy?' I sat at the sour table, eyes filling with tears—'Who are you? Did Louis send you?—The wires—'

in her hair, as she beat on her head—'I'm not a bad girl—don't murder me!—I hear the ceiling—I raised two children—'

Two years since I'd been there—I started to cry—She stared—nurse broke up the meeting a moment—I went into the bathroom to hide, against the toilet white walls

'The Horror' I weeping—to see her again—'The Horror'—as if she were dead thru funeral rot in—'The Horror!'

I came back she yelled more—they led her away—'You're not Allen—' I watched her face—but she passed by me, not looking—

Opened the door to the ward,—she went thru without a glance back, quiet suddenly—I stared out—she looked old—the verge of the grave—'All the Horror!'

Another year, I left N.Y.—on West Coast in Berkeley cottage dreamed of her soul—that, thru life, in what form it stood in that body, ashen or manic, gone beyond joy—

near its death—with eyes—was my own love in its form, the Naomi, my mother on earth still—sent her long letter—& wrote hymns to the mad —Work of the merciful Lord of Poetry.

that causes the broken grass to be green, or the rock to break in grass —or the Sun to be constant to earth—Sun of all sunflowers and days on bright iron bridges—what shines on old hospitals—as on my yard—

Returning from San Francisco one night, Orlovsky in my room—Whalen in his peaceful chair—a telegram from Gene, Naomi dead—

Outside I bent my head to the ground under the bushes near the garage—knew she was better—

at last—not left to look on Earth alone—2 years of solitude—no one, at age nearing 60—old woman of skulls—once long-tressed Naomi of Bible—

or Ruth who wept in America—Rebecca aged in Newark—David remembering his Harp, now lawyer at Yale

or Svul Avrum—Israel Abraham—myself—to sing in the wilderness toward God—O Elohim!—so to the end—2 days after her death I got her letter—

Strange Prophecies anew! She wrote—'The key is in the window, the key is in the sunlight at the window—I have the key— Get married Allen don't take drugs—the key is in the bars, in the sunlight in the window.

Love,
your mother'

which is Naomi—

Hymmnn

In the world which He has created according to his will Blessed
    Praised

Magnified Lauded Exalted the Name of the Holy One Blessed is
    He!

In the house in Newark Blessed is He! In the madhouse Blessed is
    He! In the house of Death Blessed is He!

Blessed be He in homosexuality! Blessed be He in Paranoia! Blessed
    be He in the city! Blessed be He in the Book!

Blessed be He who dwells in the shadow! Blessed be He! Blessed be
    He!

Blessed be you Naomi in tears! Blessed be you Naomi in fears!
    Blessed Blessed Blessed in sickness!

Blessed be you Naomi in Hospitals! Blessed be you Naomi in soli-
    tude! Blest be your triumph! Blest be your bars! Blest be your
    last years' loneliness!

Blest be your failure! Blest be your stroke! Blest be the close of your
    eye!

Blest be the gaunt of your cheek! Blest be your withered thighs!

Blessed be Thee Naomi in Death! Blessed be Death! Blessed be
    Death!

Blessed be He Who leads all sorrow to Heaven! Blessed be He in the
    end!

Blessed be He who builds Heaven in Darkness! Blessed Blessed
    Blessed be He! Blessed be He! Blessed be Death on us All!

III

Only to have not forgotten the beginning in which she drank cheap
    sodas in the morgues of Newark,

only to have seen her weeping on gray tables in long wards of her
    universe

only to have known the weird ideas of Hitler at the door, the wires
     in her head, the three big sticks
rammed down her back, the voices in the ceiling shrieking out her
     ugly early lays for 30 years,
only to have seen the time-jumps, memory lapse, the crash of wars,
     the roar and silence of a vast electric shock,
only to have seen her painting crude pictures of Elevateds running
     over the rooftops of the Bronx
her brothers dead in Riverside or Russia, her lone in Long Island
     writing a last letter—and her image in the sunlight at the
     window
'The key is in the sunlight at the window in the bars the key is in the
     sunlight,'
only to have come to that dark night on iron bed by stroke when the
     sun gone down on Long Island
and the vast Atlantic roars outside the great call of Being to its own
to come back out of the Nightmare—divided creation—with her
     head lain on a pillow of the hospital to die
—in one last glimpse—all Earth one everlasting Light in the familiar
     black-out—no tears for this vision—
But that the key should be left behind—at the window—the key in
     the sunlight—to the living—that can take
that slice of light in hand—and turn the door—and look back see
Creation glistening backwards to the same grave, size of universe,
size of the tick of the hospital's clock on the archway over the white
     door—

IV

O mother
what have I left out
O mother
what have I forgotten
O mother
farewell
with a long black shoe
farewell
with Communist Party and a broken stocking
farewell
with six dark hairs on the wen of your breast
farewell

with your old dress and a long black beard around the vagina
farewell
with your sagging belly
with your fear of Hitler
with your mouth of bad short stories
with your fingers of rotten mandolins
with your arms of fat Paterson porches
with your belly of strikes and smokestacks
with your chin of Trotsky and the Spanish War
with your voice singing for the decaying overbroken workers
with your nose of bad lay with your nose of the smell of the pickles
    of Newark
with your eyes
with your eyes of Russia
with your eyes of no money
with your eyes of false China
with your eyes of Aunt Elanor
with your eyes of starving India
with your eyes pissing in the park
with your eyes of America taking a fall
with your eyes of your failure at the piano
with your eyes of your relatives in California
with your eyes of Ma Rainey dying in an aumbulance
with your eyes of Czechoslovakia attacked by robots
with your eyes going to painting class at night in the Bronx
with your eyes of the killer Grandma you see on the horizon from
    the Fire-Escape
with your eyes running naked out of the apartment screaming into
    the hall
with your eyes being led away by policemen to an ambulance
with your eyes strapped down on the operating table
with your eyes with the pancreas removed
with your eyes of appendix operation
with your eyes of abortion
with your eyes of ovaries removed
with your eyes of shock
with your eyes of lobotomy
with your eyes of divorce
with your eyes of stroke
with your eyes alone

with your eyes
with your eyes
with your Death full of Flowers

V

Caw caw caw crows shriek in the white sun over grave stones in
Long Island
Lord Lord Lord Naomi underneath this grass my halflife and my
own as hers
caw caw my eye be buried in the same Ground where I stand in
Angel
Lord Lord great Eye that stares on All and moves in a black cloud
caw caw strange cry of Beings flung up into sky over the waving
trees
Lord Lord O Grinder of giant Beyonds my voice in a boundless field
in Sheol
Caw caw the call of Time rent out of foot and wing an instant in the
universe
Lord Lord an echo in the sky the wind through ragged leaves the
roar of memory
caw caw all years my birth a dream caw caw New York the bus the
broken shoe the vast highschool caw caw all Visions of the
Lord
Lord Lord Lord caw caw caw Lord Lord Lord caw caw caw Lord

Paris, December 1957–New York, 1959

HERBERT HUNCKE

1915–1996

ELSIE JOHN

SOMETIMES I REMEMBER CHICAGO AND MY EXPERIENCES WHILE GROW-
ing up and as a youth. I remember in particular the people I knew
and—as frequently happens—I think, with people, I associate whole
periods of time as indicative of certain changes within myself. But
mostly I think about the people and I recall one person rather
vividly, not only because he was out of the ordinary, but because I
recognize now what a truly beautiful creature he was.

He was a giant—well over six and one half feet tall with a large
egg-shaped head. His eyes were enormous and a very deep sea-blue
with a hidden expression of sadness as though contemplating the
tragedy of his life as irrevocable. Also there were times when they
appeared gay and sparkling and full of great understanding. They
were alive eyes always—and had seen much and were ever questing.
His hair was an exquisite shade of henna red which he wore quite
long like a woman's. He gave it special care and I can see it reflecting the light from an overhead bulb which hung shadeless in the
center of his room while he sat crosslegged in the center of a big
brass bed fondling his three toy pekes who were his constant companions and received greatly of his love. His body was huge with
long arms which ended with thin hands and long tapering fingers
whose nails were sometimes silver or green or scarlet. His mouth
was large and held at all times a slightly idiot smile and was always
painted bright red. He shaded his eyelids green or blue and beaded

the lashes with mascara until they were a good three quarters of an inch long. He exhibited himself among freaks in sideshows as the only true hermaphrodite in human life and called himself Elsie John. When I met him he was in his early thirties.

He came originally from somewhere in Germany and before coming to this country had traveled—travailed if you prefer—much of Europe and could talk for hours of strange experiences he'd had. He was a user of drugs, and although he liked cocaine best he would shoot up huge amounts of heroin, afterward sitting still like a big brooding idol.

When I first knew him he was living in a little theatrical hotel on North State Street. It was an old hotel and in all probability is no longer in existence. Apparently at one time it had been a sort of hangout for vaudeville actors. It was shabby and run down and the rooms were small and in need of fresh paint. He lived in one of these rooms with his three dogs and a big wardrobe trunk. One of the things I remember distinctly was his standing in front of a long thin mirror which hung on the wall opposite his bed—applying makeup—carefully working in the powder bases and various cosmetics creating the mask which he was seldom without.

When I met him he was coming out of a lesbian joint with a couple of friends and upon seeing him for the first time I was sort of struck dumb. He was so big and strange. It happened that one of the girls knew him and he invited us all up to his room to smoke pot—tea as it was called in those days. His voice was rather low and pleasant with a slight accent which gave everything he said a meaning of its own. When we were leaving he suggested I come back, and it was not much time until I became a constant visitor and something of a friend.

He liked being called Elsie and later when I introduced him it was always as Elsie.

We began using junk together and sometimes I would lie around his place for two or three days. A friend of mine called John who was later shot to death by narcotics bulls while making a junk delivery—they grabbed him as he was handing the stuff over and he broke free and ran down the hall and they shot him—joined us and we became a sort of threesome.

Elsie was working an arcade show on West Madison Street, and though junk was much cheaper then than now he wasn't really making enough to support his habit as he wanted to and decided to begin pushing. As a pusher he wasn't much of a success. Everybody soon got wise he wouldn't let you go sick and per result much more was going out than coming in. Eventually one of the cats he'd befriended got caught shooting up and when asked where he scored turned in Elsie's name. I will never forget the shock and the terror of the moment the door was thrust open and a big red-faced cop kind of shouting "Police" shoved into the room followed by two more— one who sort of gasped upon seeing Elsie and then turned to one of the others saying, "Get a load of this degenerate bastard—we sure hit the jackpot this time. This is a queer sonofabitch if I ever saw one. What the hell are these?"—as he became aware of the dogs who had gathered around Elsie and who were barking and yipping. "Goddamned lap dogs—what do they lap on you?" he said as he sort of thrust himself toward Elsie.

Elsie had drawn himself up to his full height and then suddenly began saying, "I'm a hermaphrodite and I've got papers to prove it"—and he tried to shove a couple of pamphlets which he used in his sideshow gimmick toward the cop. Meanwhile one of the others had already found our works and the stash of junk—about half an ounce—and was busy tearing Elsie's trunk apart, pulling out the drawers and dumping their contents in the center of the bed. It was when one of the cops stepped on a dog that Elsie began crying.

They took us all down to the city jail on South State Street and since Johnnie and I were minors they let us go the next morning.

The last time I saw Elsie was in the bullpen—sort of cowering in the corner surrounded by a group of young Westside hoods who had been picked up the same night we were—who were exposing themselves to him and yelling all sorts of obscenities.

BILL BURROUGHS

THE FIRST YEAR OF MY ACQUAINTANCE WITH BILL REMAINED ORDINARY in the sense of what is usual in the early stages of any friendship between two people. We gradually began to relax—or at least I did—and a degree of respect for one another evolved. I believe Bill found me interesting and someone he could use as a sort of show-piece to exhibit before his more conservative associates—as an example of an underworld type—and someone he could rely upon to be amusing and colorful. My story-telling ability had always stood me in good stead, and even then my experience had been varied and considerably out of the ordinary as far as Bill's friends were concerned. Frankly, I derived a certain pleasure in being candid and open about myself, and nothing pleased me more than an appreciative group of listeners.

Allen was very young at the time and still rather confused about his future and what he wanted or exactly what he would do once school was over. As usual he was filled with love and deep-felt desire to communicate with his fellow men. Then—as now—he was ready to believe in the best in those he met, and we became very good friends. Allen has never failed me and had always been quick to offer a helping hand. He held Bill in admiration and had seen only goodness and kindness in him. Frequently we haven't seen eye-to-eye regarding Bill. Still, I firmly believe that Allen's awareness of what lies below the surface of Bill's personality has always been closer to the truth than my own. But then Allen sees the world with a less jaundiced eye than I.

And then there was Jack Kerouac—who regarded everyone with suspicion but looked up to Bill and dreamed of becoming a writer.

We were a strange group, although there were many others, and along with Joan, we were the people who formed the inner circle. As closely as I am able to recall, we were the most constant companions of Bill's life.

Prior to the time I am speaking of, Bill had spent much of his life in various schools. He had traveled and done much that most people live an entire lifetime without experiencing. He was then and is now one of the most erudite men I've ever known.

Time passed and about two years after making his acquaintance, through a series of unexpected happenings—drug addiction, his and Joan's relationship, departure from New York, and a desire to experiment with the possibilities of growing marijuana and Oriental poppies, maybe manufacturing opium—Joan, her daughter Julie (four years of age), Bill and myself lived together in Texas. I look back to it as one of my greatest experiences—and also as the time I finally learned to understand Bill to a great extent—and to at last respect him as I have few people in my life.

Following a general breaking-up of the close group—or better, a spreading-out: with Allen and Kerouac going their respective ways—Allen to sea as a merchant seaman and Jack going into seclusion at home where apparently he continued working at becoming a writer—others drifting homeward to other states and cities—Bill and Joan and Julie began looking for a place somewhere in the Southwest they could settle in a while, and finally located the beautiful little cabin we lived in through the last of the winter of 1946 and up until September or almost October of 1947. It was situated on the edge of a piece of property consisting of some ninety-seven acres in the midst of a pinewoods which began at the top of a gentle incline with the cabin in an enclosed yard or fenced-in area at the top and several sheds and an old collapsing barn—and then rolled downward into a bayou, twisting and turning its way thru the country—a place of tropical vines and Spanish-moss-draped trees—where sunlight filtered through the heavy lush green-growing vegetation and one felt one could get lost—or have strange adventures—and that it had always been there since the beginning of time and had barely felt the intrusion of man. It was wild and beautiful and mysterious, and I always imagined I was entering a great steaming jungle each time I would go down to explore its shadowed depths.

The preceding year had been hectic and discouraging for me and I was extremely anxious to depart New York. All through the month of December and immediately following the first of the year I had spent much time following up the possibility of obtaining a berth aboard a tanker and of going back to sea. I had been given a lead on a tanker company that had sold a number of their ships to the Chinese and were supposedly anxious to sail their ships to Shanghai where the crew was to be discharged, given plane tickets back to the States, and then rehired in order to staff another ship bound for China to once again follow the same procedure of disembarking—flying back to the States—and making the same voyage—or perhaps become a member of another crew sailing elsewhere. It sounded made to order for me, and the afternoon I received word from Bill and Joan—plus fare and expenses for joining them in Texas—I had been given notice to report the following day at one of the piers in Brooklyn, to board a ship ready for sailing to Shanghai. I had been hired as a second cook at a salary of $350 per month with an additional bonus of $500 payable upon my return to New York. I am unable to recall what the bonus was supposedly for or what risk or inconvenience it justified but it sounded attractive—and besides just the mere thought of leaving NYC was stimulating. One can easily see my dilemma when Joan and Bill's message arrived and it became my problem to immediately reach a decision of whether it be Texas with Joan and Bill—or China and a quick return to NYC plus a good supply of money, and that had long been a desperate need. Let it suffice that curiosity and love for Joan tipped the scale in favor of joining Burroughs and helping him with his plans for experimenting with the soilless growth of marijuana and Oriental poppies. The idea was, if successful, I might become his partner in developing an American opium outlet, and perhaps corner a small part of the already thriving and fantastically lucrative junk business. I immediately wired Texas announcing my date and hour of arrival.

In the most recent of Joan's letters she had spoken of the remoteness of their location, and therefore when they sent my ticket it was for as far as Houston where I would be met by Bill and driven in his Jeep by him the last fifty miles to the little town of New Waverly, which was exactly twelve miles from where Bill had settled and was the nearest town or community of any size to his place.

Until then my dealings with Bill had been mostly brief and usually of a business nature. He had been much more closely involved with Phil White. He had met Phil the same night he had met me about two years previously. We met a very short time after my return from a great trip along with Phil down through the Caribbean Sea, the Panama Canal and into the Pacific to Hawaii and back. Phil and myself became crew members of this old tanker just at the end of the war, and although we had not been overly anxious to make any trip at the time, we were nonetheless rather concerned with cutting down our narcotics habits and this trip seemed ready-made for the purpose when we first set sail. It worked out quite the opposite, and although the voyage had been great and exciting it thoroughly failed to fulfill the original purpose. We returned still hooked and perhaps using a shade less junk than at the beginning. Running directly into an old queen and acquaintance who had access to the ship's medical supplies—plus no compunction about stealing the morphine Syrettes from the lifeboat kits—had been the major cause of our continued use of stuff, even while at sea. There was something ludicrous about going to sea ostensibly to stop using junk and completely failing. Just who in hell expects to board a ship out from the mainland and then discover shortly after losing sight of the shore that they have just run into the proverbial one chance in a thousand, the one person—the medical officer excluded—who has a direct line to the medical supplies—and at the same time, immediately becomes enamored with one's partner and friend, and is more than willing to turn over the keys of the ship's stores or do anything at all within his scope to prove his love and willingness to cooperate toward making his loved one happy?

Both Phil and myself had squandered our payoff quickly—it was comparatively small. Both of us had spent a great deal of money in each of the ports we stopped in and had drawn heavily on our salaries. About a week and a half after our return we were sitting talking in the pad we were staying in on Henry Street (Bill describes the place fairly accurately in his first book—*Junky*) and waiting for Bob Brandenberg to get home. Bob was a young cat who worked up near Columbia University as a soda jerk and shared the pad with us. We expected to borrow enough money to pay for the filling of the prescription of morphine we had gotten from one of the Brooklyn doctors we were seeing at the time. We had used the last of our money to pay the doctor and so far we had met nothing but refusal and apologetic explanation from everybody we'd asked to borrow from, and so Bob was our last hope. Neither Phil nor I was sure of what we'd do if Bob failed us, and therefore we were in rather depressed moods when Bob finally arrived bringing Bill Burroughs—Wm. S. Burroughs, and later alias Bull Lee—with him.

Bozo, who owned the apartment, was cleaning and washing after dinner in the kitchen. Phil and I were sitting talking at the kitchen table and gossiping with Bozo.

Bob introduced Bill and we asked him to join us at the table. He looked around as he was taking his coat off and finally, handing both his hat and coat to Bob, sat down. Bob had gone on through the bedroom and was preparing to settle down for the evening, busily moving from one room to another, constantly talking and asking questions. Phil and Bill were becoming acquainted and Bozo was offering everyone tea or coffee and half-apologizing because of his surroundings and the general slum nature of the neighborhood. I had observed Bill only a moment or two but decided I didn't feel friendly toward him—sizing him up in my mind as dull appearing and a bit smug and self-opinionated and certainly not very hip. Looking at him intently it entered my mind he could conceivably be a policeman or plainclothesman—maybe even FBI—he looks cold-blooded enough to be one. That old chesterfield coat he's wearing went out of style fifteen years ago, and that snap-brim hat: Don't he think he's the rogue. Those glasses—he looks as conservative as they come in them. Glasses without rims must make him feel like he's not wearing glasses at all. I don't like him—and if Bob doesn't ask him to leave, I will. I finally stepped into the other room with Bob—speaking to him of my suspicions and asking him where and how he had met Bill, and most of all why he had brought him home. Bob laughed and reassured me. Bill was trying to pick up a little easy money by selling a sawed-off shotgun. Bob explained he had become acquainted with Bill at the soda fountain of the drugstore where he worked. He said Bill apparently was a steady customer—usually shopping in the store sometime during each afternoon and then stopping at the fountain for a soft drink and a chat. They had become friendly and one afternoon Bill had asked Bob if he had any idea of where he might sell the gun. Bob had been delighted with the question, undoubtedly flattered because of Bill's confidence. Bob wanted nothing quite so much as recognition as an underworld character—preferably in the nature of being thought of in terms of racketeer-gangster and all-around hipster. Bob had spoken of Phil and myself and of the scene in general at the apartment, and had asked Bill to await our return at the apartment and then Bob would escort him downtown and in all probability either Phil or I—or perhaps he himself—would be able to negotiate some kind of deal.

I wasn't completely convinced of Bill's harmlessness and used several arguments in favor of having Bill depart—and had almost reached the point of taking the matter into my own hands when suddenly I heard Phil say, "What's that you just said, Bill? You have morphine? What are they—morphine Syrettes? That sounds very interesting. How many?" Bill and Phil had been hitting it off splendidly and the one thing needed to solidify Phil's interest in his behalf was the mention of having drugs in his possession. Already Bill was telling him how a friend had come into possession of at least a gross of morphine Syrettes and had given them to him to dispose of. He continued, saying, "I am not sure but I think there was a holdup in a drugstore and one of the stick-up men was his friend and had decided after clearing out the cash register to investigate the narcotics cabinet and—seeing this huge package marked morphine—without thinking twice he grabbed it. Later he came to me and asked me if I could get rid of them at a profit. Also he gave me this goddamned shotgun. I don't want the damned thing and want to sell it."

Phil had listened closely, and as Bill finished his little speech Phil called to me, saying, "Hey, Huncke, our friend here has some morphine. He says he wants to sell the stuff and will let it go cheaply." Bill interrupted to say, "Well—as a matter of fact I want to sell all but one or two of these Syrettes. The one or two I keep I'd like to try taking—in order to see what the experience of taking an addictive drug is like. Have either of you any knowledge of this stuff, and if so, do you know how it is taken?"

Phil began laughing and I found myself amused, since we had been using exactly what Bill had to offer, and instinctively I knew Phil was already scheming some way to latch onto the supply and for as little as possible. I knew my desire to lay hold of the stuff was actively developed, and—although I still didn't feel that Bill should be trusted—in thinking about it, I couldn't see where Phil and myself could get into too much trouble since it was Bill who was trying to make some money on the deal—and deciding to sound out Phil in his feelings in the matter, I abruptly departed from Bob and joined Bill and Phil at the kitchen table. Phil needed no prodding and had started to discuss price and the matter of showing Bill how to take off. Bill had brought a few of the Syrettes with him and in no time we three—Bill, Phil, and I—were in the process of shooting up.

Bill was by this time obviously enjoying himself—and I had to admit to myself just possibly he was a nice person trying to experience something a bit more exciting than what he is usually involved with—and he was apparently honest about his interest in drugs.

In attempting to recall the whole scene I find I am unable to do so completely. I can't remember how the gun was finally disposed of— or if it was, for that matter—nor exactly what arrangements were made for the rest of the morphine. Let it suffice Bill took an immediate liking for taking drugs, and soon he and Phil were animatedly discussing the use of stuff—the various forms of drugs—how long Phil had been using—how long I had used—of our serving time for possession—how miserable it was kicking—and everything else either of them could think of in the way of questions and answers.

Bill and Phil arranged to keep in touch with each other, and shortly after coming to terms regarding Phil and myself buying the Syrettes, Bill departed.

It was the beginning of a whole new life for Bill. At that time I saw very little of either of them and was a bit surprised about one week later to run into the two of them about one-thirty in the morning getting ready to take the subway at Seventy-second and Broadway.

Just what it was that caused me to be that far uptown at the time I don't recall, but I can remember wondering a bit what the two of them had in common. They informed me they were making the hole together as partners, with Bill learning to act as a shill and cover-up man for Phil—helping him to pick pockets by standing near, holding a newspaper open, spread wide—Phil standing behind Bill, fingers feeling the inside breast pocket of the mark's suit jacket or perhaps the overcoat pockets searching for the wallet—or poke, as Phil referred to it. Somehow there was something ludicrous about a man of Bill's obvious educational background becoming a business partner with knock-around, knock-down, hard-hustling Phil, who had forgotten more about scuffling for money illegally than most people ever learn. Still, dope or junk has created many a strange relationship, and this was certainly no more unusual than many I'd run across. My feelings were it would undoubtedly be a great experience for Bill—and also I was glad Phil was doing fairly well—and I guessed Bill was at least indirectly responsible for Phil's seeming good luck. The three of us talked together a short while and I learned that they had been in constant touch since the evening of their first meeting, and that already Bill had a habit—not a very big habit, but a habit nonetheless—and that they had been making doctors for scripts. The Syrettes had long been used up and Phil had immediately coached Bill on how to make a doctor. According to Phil, Bill had been a natural. Just before saying good-bye, we all three decided to meet the following day. I would join them on their forage for scripts. Phil had spoken of several doctors he could no longer make but that he felt sure I could. He mentioned their names to Bill and he agreed it was more than likely. Also three people making doctors would, in the end, be able to obtain considerably more stuff than just two people. And so soon we began learning a little about Bill and his life.

My life at the time was in the usual state of chaos with three- or four-day periods of no sleep—making it in a Benzedrine haze—hallucinating—walking along the edge of Central Park peering intently into each clump of bushes, the shadows alive with strange shapes and formations—or of sitting many hours at a stretch in some cafeteria talking with the people of my acquaintance who made up the majority of the Times Square population—a varied and rootless group, frequently homeless and alone, existing from day to day, lonely and oddly frightened, but invariably alert and full of humor and always ready for the big chance—the one break sure to earn them security and realization of the ever-present dream.

Often toward the early dawn hours Bill, Phil and myself would wind up our night consuming cup after cup of coffee—well into the day, so late we were rather early morning—ready to visit our various doctors and pick up as many prescriptions for morphine and Dilaudid as possible. We all three grumbled and complained, swearing we would prefer almost any other method of keeping ourselves straight. Yet in retrospect it was somehow stimulating and cause for amusement—at least conversationally—particularly when Bill would bait Phil about some episode involving one of his doctors' wives who had somehow learned of her husband's enterprising nature and his illegal manner of increasing his income—and had decided to take matters into her own hands. She had started by refusing to allow Phil to see the doctor, using a flimsy excuse and lecturing Phil about vice and corruption and finally backing out of Phil's way when he had barked some foul oath or other at her— telling her to shut the fuck up, that he intended seeing her husband whether she allowed it or not. Bill had found Phil's description of the scene extremely humorous and enjoyed getting Phil wound up.

About then Bill had discovered a small apartment on the same street Bozo's place was—and as the rent was cheap he rented it— presumably intending to move in and set up a sort of studio and working quarters for himself. He was always rather vague about exactly what sort of work he wished to do, and it was some time later I learned of his wish to write.

At the time Bill rented his apartment downtown I was spending most of my time on and around Forty-second Street, hustling, stealing, and simply hanging around—frequenting several of the bars and cafeterias either on Forty-second Street or somewhere else in the Times Square area. It was my third or fourth year on the scene, and not only was I well known, but I had become a figure or character in my own right—and very little had transpired within the immediate vicinity I wasn't aware of. It was about then Kinsey began his investigation or survey of the sex habits of Americans. He had come to New York and intended interviewing as many people as possible, starting at the colleges and finally arriving at Times Square. I was one of the first people he made contact with, and after our interview he suggested my recommending him to as many of my acquaintances as possible. This I was more than willing to do, and in no time we had established a sort of business friendship. I spent much of my time hanging out in a bar on Eighth Avenue and Forty-third Street, and quite often he would stop by and invite me to have dinner with him. One evening Bill joined us and thereafter it was not unusual for Bill, Kinsey and many of Bill's friends and myself to sit in a booth talking, so that we formed a kind of group of seemingly good friends—and although I remained somewhat skeptical of Bill, it was during the time of these gatherings I began to feel friendlier toward him and to respect him.

BILL BURROUGHS, PART II

BILL MOVED UPTOWN NEAR COLUMBIA TO AN APARTMENT OWNED BY Joan Adams. She was studying at Columbia. She was in all probability one of the most charming and intelligent women I've ever met. She and Bill were immediately attracted to each other and from then until her death several years later she and Bill were never separated for very long. She loved Bill ardently and I am quite sure worshiped him in a manner most women seldom attain. He shot her accidentally causing her death.

I of course was an outsider to his environment at the time they met, and when one evening after he and I had been talking and drinking coffee in Bickford's Forty-second Street cafeteria he invited me to visit him uptown and meet his friends, it didn't enter my mind for a moment I would soon be one of the members of his immediate crowd or that from then on our lives would become permanently linked. Yet that is exactly what happened and even now—although we have drifted apart—there is still a very positive bond between us. It was through Bill that I met Allen, who, in a very strange way, has had more influence on my life than anyone I've known.

When I began seeing Bill and his friends constantly—that is, every day—practically living with them—learning to know them more intimately in a way than I had known my own family—my feelings concerning almost all of them, with perhaps one exception—Joan— were those of indifference and, to some degree, hostility. They were all so very, very intellectual—I felt as though at best they were patronizing toward me, and that there was no real feeling of warmth or affection from any of them. Still, they were at the very least interesting, and in a sense—against my will—I found myself becoming involved with them to such an extent it became impossible for me to imagine pulling away. Finally when I was arrested and served my time and returned to find them still friendly and concerned, the die was cast. Since then we have all remained closely connected.

At the time of my arrest Bill was indirectly involved and his family felt it would be an excellent time for him to leave New York.

Following his family's wishes, he and Joan set out for Texas—where they remained for a little longer than a year and where I joined them for a good part of that time.

As I have already mentioned, I corresponded with Joan and Bill—and upon receipt of their invitation to join them in Texas I immediately accepted.

I met Bill in Houston and we began our drive out to the cabin. Bill was looking well and seemed enthusiastic about his plans. He told me he had been using a little paregoric and Pantopon which Bill Garver sent him fairly regularly through the mail. He said that Joan was using Benzedrine and that he was running into difficulty keeping up the supply. He said he had made every town within a radius of fifty miles three or four times already, and he was afraid people were beginning to wonder a little about just what was going on. He said things were in pretty bad shape at the house, and a great deal of work had to be done to make the place livable. He explained that he and Joan were staying at a motel and had been going out to the cabin every day trying to shape things up. He said the bad weather would break soon and then the place would be easier to reach.

He had located in east Texas and we drove fifty miles from Houston over paved highways to the town of New Waverly—a small-sized town about five blocks long: a few stores and a filling station—just off the main highway. We drove on through New Waverly and onto a black macadam road which began twisting and turning as soon as we left the town and continued the same all the way to where we turned off onto a sand and gravel road into the pinewoods. We had covered twelve miles from New Waverly through countryside sparsely dotted with small farms and occasional houses along the road. It was beautiful country and as we drove Bill commented about the people and on the probably near arrival of spring. We finally reached the beginning of the woods on either side and then the turn-off. The weather was gray and damp and Bill said maybe it would be necessary to park the Jeep and walk the last half mile because he was afraid of getting stuck. We remained on the dirt road which had just made a little dip. We drove down on one side of the dip, and just before driving up the opposite side we crossed an old wooden plank bridge. The pinewoods were thick on either side and I couldn't help but wonder just what they hid from view. Every so often there would be a rural mailbox and a roadway leading off the road, but there was no other evidence of people or their houses. We remained on the gravel and dirt road about two miles, and as we came to a pair of car tracks which led into the woods, Bill slowed down and turned the Jeep onto them. We drove a short distance into the woods and I could have touched the trees alongside without difficulty. Suddenly Bill stopped the Jeep. He said we had better walk the rest of the way.

My first impression of the entire scene was that we had found a sort of paradise—and I never changed my feelings. It was a truly beautiful section. The cabin was weather-worn—silver gray—and it appeared to have grown out of the earth instead of having been constructed. It was sturdy and comfortable, and by the time we were finished repairing and straightening everything out, it was a snug little place.

Time flew and spring burst all around us. Then came summer and the heat. And before any of us really realized it, fall was upon us—our crops were picked and we were ready to split back to New York.

Talking or speaking of all that took place during that period of time would fill many pages. Let it suffice—it was an experience I'll perhaps never forget. Bill's son was born in July—and by the time we were ready to leave, Bill had been a father of almost three months' standing.

Bill had thoroughly enjoyed himself. He had played the role of the country squire. He had guns—he even acquired a small hound pup before we left. One thing worth mentioning I think is the occasion on which I saw him in a completely new way. It happened one weekend in Houston and I realized for the first time that he was a handsome man.

I spent many weekends in Houston. I had discovered a drugstore where I was able to purchase as many Benzedrine inhalers and all the barbiturates I wished—and paregoric in half-gallons, if I so desired—and therefore when I'd hit Houston it would be for the purpose of picking up supplies. I'd usually take the bus from New

Waverly and return the following night about eleven-thirty and Bill would meet me, and we'd drive back to the cabin.

On the weekend I referred to I had several other things to do besides pick up drug supplies, and Bill had half-heartedly mentioned the possibility of his falling into Houston sometime Saturday afternoon. I had hit Houston late Friday and wasn't planning on returning until Sunday evening. As soon as I'd arrive in Houston I'd go directly to the Brayos Hotel, which was located alongside Houston's Chinatown. It had been a good hotel at one time, and still gave good service—although it was somewhat removed from the main section of downtown. I had checked in late and all they had left was a two-room suite, which I took. It was late in June and the weather was immensely hot.

I had made friends with several colored cats in the colored section downtown where I'd cop some pot, and one of the cats who owned a record store would let me borrow one of his record players—and I'd hook it up in my room and turn on while listening to some good sounds which my man had either recommended or I had selected.

This weekend had been no different—except when I hit the hotel after picking up the record player I ran into a cat who was a seaman—young, maybe twenty or twenty-one—and after talking with him a while, invited him up to my rooms. He was a beautiful cat and he spent the night with me—smoking and talking and listening to records. He had never actually relaxed and listened to jazz before, and he was very impressed with what he heard. We had enjoyed ourselves and were both a little surprised when there was a knock on the door. And when I asked who was there, Bill replied. I let him in—and after introducing him to my friend, asked him if he was planning on staying overnight and taking me back with him the next day. He replied that he wasn't sure, but that he had come simply to get away from the scene at the cabin and come to Houston. As well as getting reading material and a fresh supply of liquor, he wanted very much to take a bath.

While he had been telling me this the phone rang, and when I answered, it was my pot man and I arranged to meet him. Meanwhile, Bill had seated himself and was busy talking with my friend. I excused myself—explaining I had to keep a meet with the pot man—and after observing the two of them a few minutes to see if they would get along, I split out.

I kept my meet, copped, and sat around talking with the connection and his old lady awhile, and smoked a couple of joints. I was away about two hours, and when I returned, not only had they gotten along, but the two of them were stone-cold drunk.

I had seen Bill slightly intoxicated many times, but this was the first time I'd seen him really drunk. When I came in, Bill was sitting—straddling a straight-back chair—apparently deeply engrossed in what he had been discussing with my friend, who sat facing him in an armchair. Both of them were half-crocked, drunken leers on their faces. They greeted me with real cheery hellos and assured me I should join them in having a drink. Bill reached over toward an almost empty bottle of tequila and said, "Come on, Huncke, have a little snort. It'll make you feel great." He fumbled around looking for his glass and said I could drink from the glass he'd been drinking from. I thanked him and refused, telling him I thought he had had enough also, and wondering what I was going to do about him. It was obvious he could barely sit up, much less stand.

"Bill, come on—no more, please. I think maybe you better stretch out on the bed."

He stood up and rocked back and forth a couple of times and then made straight for the bed and half fell onto it in a big heap. I walked over and helped him stretch out. I removed his glasses, which had fallen askew across his face. He was half laughing and mumbling something I couldn't understand. It was at that moment—as he closed his eyes and then opened them again—looking around, then giving a big sigh—closed them and then fell asleep almost instantly—as I watched him, I began to see his face in a manner I hadn't seen it before—and I was startled as I recognized the beauty of his features—his coloring and his whole being—relaxed and graceful on the bed. His hair had fallen down over one side of his forehead like a cowlick, and he looked like a strange otherworld creature. His eyelids were tinged faintly lavender and belonged with the sharp aquiline nose and the well-shaped mouth now almost closed—the lips red and finely drawn—the corners of his mouth smooth and free of tense lines. He was certainly handsome, and although his entire coloring was delicate and there was nothing harshly masculine about his appearance, there was nothing feminine either. His was a man's face.

I was very touched, and at that instant a certain feeling of love I bear for him to this day sprang into being. I had always known him to be quick with verbal explanation and always logical and practical. He had always seemed complete master of himself, and now—seeing him defenseless and vulnerable—I understood he was lonely and in many ways as bewildered as anyone else.

I have never forgotten those few moments, and recently when I saw him—an older, more self-contained and seemingly satisfied man—every now and then while we talked, the other Bill would come through much the same as then.

We left Texas finally and drove back to New York. We did some business together with the pot, but we began seeing less of each other. Things had changed considerably for everyone. Allen was beginning to take on stature and was doing a lot of writing. Jack had his first book almost completed and Phil had disappeared somewhere with his old lady. New York was different also. The Times Square scene was undergoing rapid change. There was a drive on to clean things up and it was being taken seriously. Most of the old haunts were closed and all-night cafeterias were no longer all-night places. I moved away entirely from the midtown area. Bill and Joan were no longer around Manhattan, having settled in Far Rockaway or some such place. Occasionally we'd meet, but Bill was making plans to return toward the Southwest—New Orleans this time—and then Mexico.

And so it went. That year came to a close and the next few whipped by. Allen began growing up and Jack was ready for the next big break. My life didn't change too radically, but circumstances kept us all more or less separated. I began seeing Allen more often and soon a sort of pattern was established which remains to this day. Allen has always and still does keep me informed concerning Bill.

The first time I ran into him—about five years after our return from Texas—he seemed almost the same. Then, after being in his presence a short while, I recognized an almost imperceptible difference. He seemed more impersonal, with a slight show of interest that was slightly clinical as though one were being observed through a magnifying lens. At first when we met there was an element of snobbishness both intellectually and socially in his dealings with others, and I think, even at this point I am speaking of, it remained, but he had acquired the habit of not showing it openly—covering it beneath a sort of conversational adroitness. He was pleased to renew our friendship, but underneath or inside I don't believe it touched him very deeply.

Joan was dead—and his changes had been many and varied—and I guessed at the time he felt his loneliness intensely, and much of his time was spent attempting to forget at least most of those happenings which might have helped recall her to mind. Their relationship, from what I personally knew, had been of an extremely intimate nature insofar as Joan was concerned, at least. I am quite firmly convinced she barely recognized the existence of others, with—of course—the exception of their children, whom she loved with pride and great tenderness and understanding. She and Bill had something rare—and certainly, from the standpoint of the observer, very fine and beautiful. Unquestionably the adjustments required of Bill to continue seeking meaning and purpose must have placed him under exhausting strain, and I couldn't help but wonder at his self-control.

We saw each other only briefly—about three or four times—and then he departed for South America. From then on until the present time, we have seen very little of each other, and the information I have concerning his private life has reached me by way of Allen.

When he first arrived back in the States after his long sojourn abroad, we met several times for dinner and conversation with the idea of renewing our friendship. I had felt reluctant about meeting him, wondering perhaps if his only reason for seeing me was due to some idea he might have concerning a sense of obligation to someone from the past who was still seeing mutual friends, but had long ago ceased to mean anything in his life. And then of course there was always curiosity as a possible factor. It appeared almost absurd in my mind that he might genuinely be interested in renewing our friendship—and for that matter I am not completely convinced his original association with me was entirely of a friendly nature, although surely there was no enmity involved. At any rate I couldn't help considering myself rather presumptuous—thinking of the famous William Burroughs in the same breath with good old Bill or Bull or even Bill Burroughs. Still, somewhere back along the line he had touched my heart—and besides, my curiosity and desire to make comparison of present and past personality differences—if any—demanded I see him at least once regardless of his reasons for seeing me.

He invited me to have dinner with him and I accepted. It was truly

enjoyable and doubly so because I came away believing he was hon-
estly glad to see me.

We spoke briefly of his stay in Tangiers and of his writing and of
his son. He was amusing concerning Bill Jr.—sounding very much
the typical father—berating the youth of today and their seeming
indifference to the more important aspects of everyday living, their
lack of a sense of responsibility, and his son Bill in particular, who—
according to his father's opinion—is incredibly indifferent. At one
point in the conversation he said, "Why, he didn't even show an
interest in the language. Seemed to prefer hanging around bars."

CARL SOLOMON
1928–1993

SEX AT 20 IN AMERICA

Frivolity 8th Street

Around the time I was 20, I took to wearing my Mother's scarfs and I began to play the role of a tall dark-haired Jewish girl. It was a lot of fun. After studying my Mother in the nude, sneakily, I learned to act very effeminate. Then I started picking up boys. I'd been yearning to do this all my life, ever since I first played the passive role in homosexual intercourse at the age of 4 and learned it wasn't supposed to be done. My two favorite boy friends I now remember. Lee Keene (who had a 9 inch penis) who I picked up in Tony Becino's in New Orleans and Bob Arnold, 14 years old (I was 20 at the time).

I had learned, in the whore-houses of Europe, just what prostitution was and what were the main stimuli in sex through conversation with the young prostitutes who (as a sailor!) it was my function to have intercourse with.

I remember Odette Belmaure, who told me that in spite of her French patriotism, and she was a real French woman, the boys that she preferred were the Germans. Sex is apart from nationality or the BOURGEOIS social role that we are raised in. Her preference seemed logical to me, in spite of my superficial (before I turned gay) City College role of being a dialectical materialist and "anti-fascist". What happens in the headlines is not so important as what really happened behind the scenes and this – away from teachers and professional bullshit artists in class with their medals was what I was beginning to find out about. I too believed in the SUPERMAN. I couldn't understand what they (who drove me into madhouses twice) thought . . . I have never yet seen an attractive psychoanalyst and all their words don't make up for difference nor all their therapies keep me from coquettishly wiggling my shapely Jewish . . . like Bath-Sheba or Rachel in face of the handsome and warlike Philistines . . . her husband was a dentist . . . ass when I see a blond boy of 12 I mean by calling me "Kalmon" and reproaching me for this practice. I much prefer the name of Monique. Bob, a runaway from school 14 years old had an 8 inch penis when erect and I used to enjoy having this forced into my buttocks with the aid of vaseline.

REPORT FROM THE ASYLUM

Afterthoughts of a Shock Patient

A book that is accepted, at the moment, as the definitive work on shock-therapy concludes with the astonishing admission that the curative agent in shock-treatment "REMAINS A MYSTERY SHROUDED WITHIN A MYSTERY."* This confession of ignorance (and it is extended to both insulin and electric shock therapies), by two of the men who actually place the electrodes on the heads of mental patients at one of our psychiatric hospitals, certainly opens this field of inquiry to the sensitive layman as well as to the technician. The testimony that follows is that of an eye-witness, one who has undergone insulin shock treatment and has slept through fifty comas.

One may begin with amusement at the hashish-smokers and their conception of the sublime. They, who at the very most, have been HIGH consider themselves (quite properly) to be persons of EMINENCE and archimandrates of a HIGH Church. A patient emerging from an insulin coma, however, cannot help being a confirmed democrat. There can be no hierarchization of different levels of transcendency when they are induced by an intravenously-injected animal secretion, the very purpose of which is to bombard

* Hoch & Kalinowski, SHOCK THERAPY

insulin-space with neutrons of glucose-time until space vanishes like a frightened child and one awakens terrified to find oneself bound fast by a restraining-sheet (wholly supererogatory to the patient, since, in the waking state, spaceless, mobility seems inconceivable). The ingenuousness of the hashishins is stupendous.

It is as though the Insulin Man were to call his drug by a pet name and spend days thrashing out the differences between GONE POT and NOWHERE POT.

The difference between hashish and insulin is in many ways similar to a difference between surrealism and magic. The one is affective and is administered by the subject himself; the other is violently resisted by the subject (since this substance offers not even the most perverse form of satisfactions); it is forcibly administered in the dead of night by white-clad, impersonal creatures who tear the subject from his bed, carry him screaming into an elevator, strap him to another bed on another floor, and who recall him from his REVERIE (a purely polemic term employed in writing DOWN the hashishin). Thus, insulin come as a succubus, is effective, suggests grace.

In this respect, the paranoid phantasies released by hashish lack substantiality and are of the nature of automatic writing or gratuitous acts. In the case of insulin shock therapy, one finds oneself presented with a complete symbolism of paranoia, beginning with the rude awakening and the enormous hypodermic needle, continuing through the dietary restrictions imposed upon patients receiving shock, and ending with the lapses of memory and the temporary physical disfigurement.

Early in the treatment, which consists of fifty hypoglycemic comas, I reacted in a highly paranoid manner and mocked the doctors by accusing them of AMPUTATING my brain. Of course, my illness was such that I was perpetually joking (having presented myself to the hospital upon reaching my majority, I had requested immediate electrocution since I was now of age – how serious was this request, I have no way of knowing – and was discharged as cured exactly nine months later, the day before Christmas).

Nevertheless, I noted similar paranoid responses on the part of other patients in shock.

For those of us acquainted with Kafka, an identification with K. became inevitable. Slowly, however, the identification with K. and with similar characters came to imply far more than we Kafkians had ever dreamed. We knew it to be true that we had been abducted for the most absurd of reasons: for spending hours at a time in the family shower, for plotting to kill a soldier, for hurling refuse at a lecturer. And, in this particular, the text had been followed quite literally. The need for a revision of the Kafkian perspective arose, however, when the bureaucracy suddenly revealed itself as benevolent. We had not been dragged to a vacant lot and murdered, but had been dragged to a Garden of Earthly Delights and had there been fed (there were exceptions and there is a certain small percentage of fatalities resulting from shock, making the parallel to grace even more obvious.) This impression arose, somehow, from the very nature of the subjective coma.

Upon being strapped into my insulin bed, I would at once break off my usual stream of puns and hysterical chatter. I would stare at the bulge I made beneath the canvas restraining sheet, and my body, insulin-packed, would become to me an enormous concrete pun with infinite levels of association, and thereby, a means of surmounting association with things, much as the verbal puns had surmounted the meaning of words. And beneath this wrathful anticipation of world-destruction lay a vague fear of the consequences.

The coma soon confirms all of the patient's fears. What began as a drugged sleep soon changes organically and becomes one of the millions of psychophysical universes through which he must pass, before being awakened by his dose of glucose. And he cannot become accustomed to these things. Each coma is utterly incomparable to that of the previous day. Lacking a time-sense and inhabiting all of these universes at one and the same time, my condition was one of omnipresence, of being everywhere at no time. Hence, of being nowhere. Hence, of inhabiting that Void of which Antonin Artaud had screamed (I had been conditioned in illness by classical surrealism.)

Invariably, I emerged from the comas bawling like an infant and flapping my arms crazily (after they had been unfastened), screaming, "EAT!" or, "HELP!"

The nurses and doctors would ignore me, letting me flap about until my whole aching body and my aching mind (which felt as if it had been sprained) pulled themselves by their bootstraps out of the void of terror and, suddenly, attained a perfectly disciplined silence. This, of course, won the admiration of the dispensers of grace, who then decided that I was eminently worth saving and promptly brought me my breakfast tray and a glucose apéritif. And in this manner, item by item, the bureaucracy of the hospital presents the insulin MAUDIT with a world of delightful objects all made of sugar – and gradually wins his undying allegiance. If we are not deceived by appearances we will see clearly that it is the entire world of things which imposes itself upon the would-be MAUDIT and eventually becomes the object of his idolatry.

All told, the atmosphere of the insulin-ward was one in which, to the sick, miracles appeared to be occurring constantly. And, most traumatic of all, they were concrete miracles. For example, I am reminded of the day I went into a coma free of crab-lice and emerged thoroughly infested (the sheets are sterilized daily). I had caught the lice in somebody else's coma, since these states of unconsciousness are concrete and are left lying about the universe even after they have been vacated by the original occupant. And this was so credited by one of my fellow patients that he refused to submit to the needle the next day out of fear of venturing into one of my old comas and infesting himself. He believed that I had lied and that I had crabs for some time, having caught them in some previous coma.

Meanwhile, on that following day, I was revived from my coma intravenously by an Egyptian resident psychiatrist, who then, very brusquely, ordered the nurses to wrap the sheets around me a bit tighter lest I should free myself prematurely; I shrieked, "AMEN-HOTIP!"

And there was the day a young patient who had given the impression of being virtually illiterate, receiving his intravenous glucose (one is revived from a deep coma in this manner), and then gave ample evidence that he had become thoroughly acquainted with the works of Jacob Boehme in the course of his coma. Simone de Beauvoir, in her book on her travels in America, expresses her consternation upon finding that a member of the editorial board of PARTISAN REVIEW once openly admitted to being ignorant of the writings of Boehme.

Shortly after my mummification and defiance of Amenhotip, I encountered what appeared to be a new patient, to whom I mumbled amiably, "I'M KIRILOV." He mumbled in reply "I'M MYSHKIN." The cadence of the superreal was never challenged; not one of us would dare assume responsibility for a breach of the unity which each hallucination required.

These collective phantasies in which we dreamed each others' dreams contributed to the terror created by contact with the flat, unpredictable insulin void, which had not yet been rendered entirely felicitous (as it was to be later) by the persistent benevolence of man and glucose, and from which all sorts of incredible horrors might yet spring.

The concomitants of therapeutic purgation were, for me, a rather thoroughly atomized amnesia (produced by an insulin convulsion of a rare type and occurring in not more than 2% of cases) and a burgeoning obesity caused by the heavy consumption of glucose. Much later in my treatment, when intensive psychotherapy had replaced insulin, both of these phenomena came to assume places of great importance in the pattern of my reorientation. As my illness had often been verbalized, the first effect of the amnesia was to create a verbal and ideational aphasia, from which resulted an unspoken panic. I had quite simply forgotten the name of my universe, though it was also true that this name rested on the tip of my tongue throughout the amnesiac period. All ideas and all sense of the object had been lost temporarily, and what remained was a state of conscious ideational absence which can only be defined in clinical terms – as amnesia.* I had been handed, by skilled and provident men, the very concrete void I'd sought. During this period, I had gained sixty pounds, and upon consulting a mirror, I was confronted with the dual inability to recognize myself or to remember what I had looked like prior to treatment, prior to reaching my majority.

When I had recovered from my amnesia sufficiently to find my way about, I was permitted to leave the hospital on Sundays, in the company of a relative of whom I would take immediate leave. My relatives on these occasions seemed entirely oblivious to any change in my behavior or physique. Generally, still rather hazy, I would be escorted by an old neurotic friend to a homosexual bar where, I would be informed, I had formerly passed much time. However, the most appalling situations would arise at this point, since, in my corpulent forgetfulness, I no longer remotely resembled a BUTCH fairy or ROUGH TRADE. I had lost all facility with GAY argot and was

---

* So great was the sense of tangible loss that I later insisted upon an electroencephalographic examination, to reassure myself that no organic damage had resulted from the convulsion.

incapable of producing any erotic response to the objects proffered me.

Almost imperceptibly, however, the process of object-selection began once more in all realms of activity, and gained momentum.

I amazed my friends in a restaurant one Sunday afternoon by insisting that the waiter remove an entrée with which I had been dissatisfied and that he replace it with another. And even greater was their incredulity when they witnessed my abrupt handling of a beggar, this having been the first time that I had ever rejected a request for alms.

> "The yearning infinite recoils
> For terrible is earth"
> –Melville, L'ENVOI

At about this time, I wrote a sort of manifesto, called MANIFEST, which is a most pertinent artifact:

Corsica is an island situated off the coast of Sardinia. Its capital is Ajaccio and it is here that Napoleon Bonaparte was born. Though it is a part of the French Empire, Corsica is not part of the mainland. It is an island. As Capri is an island, and Malta. It is not attached to the European mainland. I am in a position to insist upon this point. There is a body of water separating the two, and it is known as the Mediterranean Sea. This is borne out by the maps now in use. I brook no contradiction. If I am challenged on this point, the world will rush to my assistance in one way or another. What I have just written is a standing challenge to all the forces of evil, of idiocy, of irrelevance, of death, of silence, of vacancy, of transcendency, etc. And I rest secure in the knowledge that my challenge will never be accepted by that SCUM to whom I've addressed it. I've spent considerable time in the clutches of the LOON and I've waited for this opportunity to avenge myself by humiliating the void. Thank you for your kind attention.

—A VEHEMENT ADULT

As the business of selection became increasingly complex, I appeared to develop an unprecedented (for me) suavity in operating within clearly defined limits. Madness had presented itself as an irrelevancy, and I was now busily engaged in assigning values of comparative relevance to all objects within my reach.

My total rejection of psychiatry, which had, after coma, become a final adulation, now passed into a third phase – one of constructive criticism. I became aware of the peripheral obtuseness and the administrative dogmatism of the hospital bureaucracy. My first impulse was to condemn; later, I perfected means of maneuvering freely within the clumsy structure of ward politics. To illustrate, my reading matter had been kept under surveillance for quite some time, and I had at last perfected a means of keeping AU COURANT without unnecessarily alarming the nurses and attendants. I had smuggled several issues of HOUND AND HORN into my ward on the pretext that it was a field-and-stream magazine. I had read Hoch and Kalinowski's SHOCK THERAPY (a top secret manual of arms at the hospital) quite openly, after I had put it in the dust-jacket of Anna Balakian's LITERARY ORIGINS OF SURREALISM. Oddly enough, I hadn't thought it necessary to take such pains with Trotsky's PERMANENT REVOLUTION and had become rudely aware of the entire body politic I had so long neglected when, one evening, I was sharply attacked by the Head Nurse of the ward for "communism". He had slipped behind me on little cat feet and had been reading the book over my shoulder.

The psychiatric ineptitude of the official lower echelons became incredible when, one week before Hallowe'en, it was announced to the patients that a masquerade ball would be held on the appropriate date, that attendance was to be mandatory, and that a prize would be given to the patient wearing the "best" costume. Whereupon, the patients, among whom there was a high spirit of competition, threw themselves precipitously into the work of creating what, for each, promised to be the most striking disguise. The work of sewing, tearing, dyeing, etc., was done in Occupational Therapy, where, at the disposal of all, were an infinite variety of paints, gadgets and fabrics. Supervising all this furious activity was a pedagogic harpy, who had been assigned as Occupational Therapist to see that we didn't destroy any of the implements in the shop (she tried to persuade me to attend the masquerade made up as a dog). Furiously we labored, competing with one another even in regard to speed of accomplishment, fashioning disguised phalluses, swords, spears, scars for our faces, enormous cysts for our heads. When Hallowe'en Night arrived we were led, dazed and semi-amnesiac, into the small gymnasium that served as a dance floor. Insidious tensions intruded themselves as the time for the awarding of the prize approached. Finally, the Social Therapists seated themselves in the center of the polished floor and ordered us to parade past them in a great circle; one of the nurses sat at a piano and played a march; to the strains of the music, we stepped forward to present our respective embodied idealizations to the judges. There were several Hamlets, a Lear, a grotesque Mr. Hyde, a doctor; there were many cases of transvestism; a young man obsessed with the idea that he was an inanimate object had come as an electric-lamp, brightly lit, complete with shade; a boy who had filled his head to the point of bursting with baseball lore had come as a "Brooklyn Bum", in derby and tatters. Suddenly the music stopped; the judges had chosen a winner, rejecting the others; we never learned who the winner had been, so chaotic was the scene that followed. There was a groan of deep torment from the entire group (each feeling that his dream had been condemned). Phantasmal shapes flung themselves about in despair. The nurses and Social Therapists spent the next hour in consoling the losers.

Thus I progressed, after my series of fifty comas had ended, and finally reached my normal weight of 180 lbs. and my true sexual orientation: adult heterosexuality (which became my true sexual orientation only after the basic androgynous death-wish had been re-directed). It is probably true, however, that my case is atypical and that the great majority of such transformations are not quite as thorough-going, and in some cases, fail to materialize at all. There were those patients who were completely unmoved by the experience of the coma, and who found that it did nothing more than to stimulate their appetites. And there were those Kafkians who remained confirmed paranoiacs to the bitter end.

I should like to quote a passage from an article by the French poet, Antonin Artaud, published posthumously in the February, 1949, issue of LES TEMPS MODERNES. Artaud had undergone both electric and insulin shock therapies during his period of confinement which lasted nine years and terminated with his death in March 1948.

"I died at Rodez under electro-shock. I say died. Legally and medically died. Electro-shock coma lasts fifteen minutes. A half an hour or more and then the patient breathes. But one hour after the shock I still had not awakened and had stopped breathing. Surprised at my abnormal rigidity, an attendant had gone to get the physician in charge, who after auscultation found no more signs of life in me.

"I have my personal memories of my death at that moment, but it is not upon them that I base my accusation.

"I limit myself to the details furnished me by Dr. Jean Dequeker, a young intern at the Rodez asylum, who had them from the lips of Dr. Ferdiere himself.

"And the latter asserts that he believed me dead that day, and that he had already summoned two asylum guards to instruct them on the removal of my corpse to the morgue, since an hour and a half after shock I still had not come to.

"And it seems that at the very moment the attendants appeared to remove my body, it quivered slightly, after which I was suddenly wide awake.

"Personally I have a different recollection of the affair.

"But I kept this recollection to myself, and secret, until the day Dr. Jean Dequeker confirmed it to me on the outside.

"And this recollection is that everything Dr. Jean Dequeker told me, I had seen, not this side of the world, but the other. . ."

What he describes above was the experience of us all, but with Artaud and so many others, it stopped short and became the permanent level of existence: the absence of myth represented by the brief "death" was accepted as the culminating, all-embracing myth. Artaud went on to write, in his essay on Van Gogh, that a lunatic

"is a man who has preferred to become what is socially understood as mad rather than forfeit a certain superior idea of human honor"

and to write further that

"a vicious society has invented psychiatry to defend itself from the investigations of certain superior lucid minds whose intuitive powers were disturbing to it"

and that

"every psychiatrist is a low-down son-of-a-bitch."

In Paris, quite outrageously, this heart-rendingly skewed essay written by a grievously ill man was honored with a Prix Sainte-Beuve and was underwritten by several of the most distinguished French critics.

I HAVE A SMALL MIND AND I MEAN TO USE IT.

The sentence above epitomizes the real lesson of insulin, that of tragedy, and it was neither written nor would it have been understood by Artaud, who remains (he wrote that THE DEAD CONTINUE TO REVOLVE AROUND THEIR CORPSES) a sublime comic figure, one who averted his eyes from the specter of reality, one who never admitted to having dimensions or sex, and who was incapable of recognizing his own mortality. (In the list of comic figures of our time we can include the homosexual.)

My release from the hospital was followed by a period of headlong and vindictive commitment to substance, a period which continues, which is full of tactical and syntactical retreats and rapid reversals of opinion. It is obvious by this time, though, that the changes of opinion are becoming less frequent, that the truculent drive toward compulsive readjustment, toward the "acting out" of one's adjustment, has been dissipated. My attitude toward the magic I've witnessed is similar to that of the African student I met a month ago, who told me that his uncle had been a witch-doctor. He had seen his uncle turn into a cat before his eyes. He had simply thrown the uncle-cat a scrap of meat, hadn't been particularly impressed by the magic (though conceding its validity), and had come to America to acquire the political and technological skills with which to modernize his country upon his return.

For the ailing intellect, there can be great danger in the poetizing of the coma-void. Only when it is hopelessly distorted and its concrete nature disguised can it serve as material for myth-making. To confront the coma full-face, one must adhere to factual detail and this procedure need not prove deadening. On the contrary, the real coma administers a fillip to one's debilitated thinking processes. Jarry's debraining-machine was not the surgeon's scalpel but was contained within his own cranium. It was to place the coma thus in context that I undertook this examination of its architectonics.

FURTHER AFTERTHOUGHTS OF A SHOCK PATIENT

At our house, we have frankfurters PEDERASTE.

Frankfurters PEDERASTE consist of corn niblets, pimentos, and frankfurters sliced fine and fried.

Of course, we brook no contradictions.

We eat quietly, discussing the war when we feel impelled to do so. "I think they'll win," says she.

I ignore her remark and go on eating, knowing that if I dispute this point the world will rush to her assistance.

We've accepted the tragic.

Meanwhile, at an Automat table on 42nd Street, a hashishin finishes his coffee and stretches wearily, sighing, "Life's a drag."

The gang of deaf-mutes at the adjacent table, having read his lips and misinterpreted COMME TOUJOURS, elects a delegate to reprimand the boor.

The delegate accosts the hashishin. He is the most articulate of the mutes and speaks, at best, in a spastic manner.

"They – aaaa want you – aaaa to apologize – aaaa!"

His chest swells. He's proud of his little speech.

The hashishin opens an eye and grimaces, "Too much!"

A skeptical instant and the delegate conveys the hashishin's APOLOGIA PRO VITA SUA to his comrades, each deafer than the other. Stealthily, three of them rise and slip out of the cafeteria. They've already conferred. No gestures, but a glance. With dispatch, the delegate strides back to the hashishin's table.

"They – aaaa aren't satisfied – aaaa! Go outside – aaaa and face – aaaa them like a man – aaaa!"

In a subway-car, three hashishins sit eating tarts.

All at once, the door between the car and its neighbor bursts open, spewing forth forty deaf-mutes, all jubilant. They converge on the hashishins. The hashishins cast about, frantically seeking succor. The legitimate passengers in the car ignore them, staring stolidly at the advertisements. A station! Like a herd of bison, the mutes snatch the tarts from the hands of the hashishins and rush through the opening door out onto the platform, laughing silently.

Later in the day, the depredations of the mutes, who desire a senseless society, increase.

Dinner gone, I busy myself with my translations, while she tosses in bed violently, waiting for me to retire. Generally, we're both asleep by eight o'clock.

I am translating Rimbaud. After hissing, "JE SUIS UN NEGRE," he rants on the screech, "JE est UN AUTRE." Refusing to be taken in by an infant of nineteen, I translate. "You're another." She tosses.

No such thing as prophetic humor.

A young hashishin visits the leader of the hashishins at his apartment, seeking more hashish.

The leader of the hashishins tells him, "I don't push no hash no more. I push blossoms now."

The Italian war-cripples riot in Rome, trampling bipeds, plutocrats in space, beneath their crutches, parallelling, in a special way, the riots in England following the adoption of the Gregorian calendar, when the citizenry burned the Pope, plutocrat in time, in effigy, over their eight purloined days. The dogs insist upon having their days and a world in which to roam, to boot.

The dugs of the heroes of Bataan grow longer, requiring bigger and bigger brassières to contain them.

I pause in my translation of Rimbaud to think of my wife, whom I hear tossing in the bed behind me.

With her in mind, I re-peruse a news dispatch which intimates that the heroes of Bataan have, as a result of nutritional disorders suffered at the time, sprouted breasts within the year, breasts which secrete.

I think of Napoleon Bonaparte, who had left Ajaccio a slim and virile youth only to acquire feminine characteristics upon attaining the heights at Austerlitz.

I had rejected heroism the year before; I breathe deeply, eternally grateful.

The mammaries of the heroes of Bataan grow longer and longer.

"DEREGLEMENTS DES SEXES," my text seems to read. I find it exceedingly difficult to get on with the translation.

I'm thinking of her as she continues to rustle in the sheets behind me, trying to lure me into bed.

What can be clearer? Eliot, snickering over his footbath at the dugs of the sissy seer, Tiserias.

I attempt to return to my Rimbaud, both hero and seer, ever over-weening – did HE wear a brassière?

I snicker at the tits of the heroes of Bataan, and get on, at last, with the translation, thankful that I am a man and not a woman.

Meanwhile, the breasts of the heroes of Bataan grow longer and longer, but the nipples remain the same, secreting no more, no less, than ever.

Who wants to be weaned by a hero of Bataan?

Outside in the falling dusk, a falling "transient" wraps his body in an evening newspaper's front page, which is entirely black, but for a tiny headline sacrosanct in white, "YANKS WIN! 7–1". He throws himself to the ground, behind the park benches. He falls asleep easily. Passersby avert their gaze, suspecting or hoping that he is dead.

Time to retire. I put the translation aside, undress and walk to the bed on tip-toe. She awaits me with open arms.

"Has baby finished with his nasty writing?"

I pause on the verge of dream, hesitant.

My dream, too, will be functional, eminently livable. I continue.

NEAL CASSADY
1926–1968

ONE NIGHT IN THE SUMMER OF 1945 ...

First Meeting with Jack Kerouac and Allen Ginsberg at Columbia University

One night in the summer of 1945 I was with a fellow named Hal Chase. We had been drinking and since we were both young and full of the juice of life, we took to speaking of life. Hal, at that time was quite an influence on me, mainly because he had done the things I had not. It follows that what he said to me was more important than might otherwise be the case.

"Another fellow I was most interested in was one Allen Ginsberg."

"Yea? who's he?"

"He's a terribly decadent intellectual whom I roomed with last year at school."

"Tell me about him."

"Well, I don't know of a proper beginning point. However, he's a poet, but, unlike many when he composes rhyme he calls it shit and the like. Also he takes great delight in proving one wrong and even though he knows little of what one is talking about he'll start contradicting, and through sheer perseverance wear one down and make one doubt oneself. In fact, he bothered me so much that near the end of the term I had to take defensive measures."

"Oh yeah? in what way?"

"It's most difficult to explain, but, the main point is –"

Then he described in a rather vague way what he had done to "defend himself" from this wild, terribly brilliant, yet terribly decadent young man. Hal then spoke of his friend's homosexuality and its disasterous effects.

In a short twenty minutes I had an extreme, abstract portrait of a young college Jew, whose amazing mind had the germ of decay in it and whose sterility had produced a blasé, yet fascinating, mask. His soul had dried up into a mind which excreted verbalistic poetry, and his handmade sexlife had created a cynical, symbolic outlook toward all the confusion of life.

This picture, becoming more abstract as time passed, remained firmly with me. Occasionally I wondered about this Allen, but the speculation about him had ceased to be conscious. I had even forgotten he was queer when one evening 18 months later, I met him.

I had gone to New york in the fall of 1946, and having just arrived, I looked up Hal Chase. After supper we went to a rather vapid bar near the campus. We had just ordered our drinks when Hal recognized a voice and said "that's Allen Ginsberg" just as a head popped up from the next booth and looked at me. He had coal-black hair which struck my eye first. It was a bit too long yet not an over-done mass of garish distaste as some more normal poet of an intellectual nature might affect. I was pleased with the manner in which the hair parted and fell into a natural forelock and the swept back sides were perfect for his face, the appearance of its perfectous grooming was belied by the realization that he gave little attention to his crowning glory. Passing from his natural attribute my eyes fastened on his nose. It was plainly a jewish nose, but, more modified than most, in fact, instead of standing out on the face, as is the usual wont of jewish noses, his seemed to blend into a simple statement – "this is a nose, with which to breathe and smell" – his lips were heavy, over-full, almost negroid. At first glance I thought them sensual, yet, looking closer, I somehow felt they lay too peacefully when in repose and disappeared too quickly in a smile to be called sensual or lustful in the accepted sense. Rather, instinctively I felt them there just as the nose was, to be used, not accentuated. If there was any part of his face he was conscious of, it was the eyes. They were large, dark and brooding. I was not quite sure how much of the brooding was there as such; and how much he was putting there for us to read into.

His voice, although I've heard it a thousand times, escapes my memory. I recall it was pleasant, varied and cultured, but the tone qualities are lost to me.

Hal looked up and said "hello Allen." Allen nodded, a bit curt I thought.

"This is Neal Cassady, he just got in from Denver and has never been here before."

"Hello."

"How do you do."

"Neal's looking for a place to stay, any suggestions?"

"Has he tried the Mills Hotel?"

"Hardly, since he's got his wife with him."

"Oh well then, I don't know of any place around here."

We both sat down again in our respective booths. Allen was with someone Hal didn't know and since there were several in our party anyway, there was no attempt made for the two parties to get together.

A few moments later Allen again stuck his head over the top of the booths. "Is your name LuAnne? What a strange name," he said and sat back down. My wife mumbled "yes", looked embarrassed, and suggested we leave. We did.

I didn't see Allen for over a month, then, about January 10, 1947, we met again. A close friend, Jack Kerouac, suggested that we go uptown and he would introduce me to a fabulous woman named Vicki. He had spoken of her many times before and since it suited my mood, I acquiesced.

She lived on 89th St. on the top floor of a large studio apartment building. When we got off the elevator and started down the narrow hall I hear a loud, rapidly talking male voice in eager and earnest oratory. I paused outside the door to listen. He was talking even faster than I had first supposed, so fast, in fact, I half expected the words to blur and run together, but they did not.

"That's Norman. He's a nut on Reichian-Analisis."

"What's that?"

"You'll find out," said Jack and then lightly rapped on the door. The flow of words ceased at once and a girl's voice inquired "Yes, who is it?"

"It's Jack."

"Just a moment."

The door bolts were unlatched and Jack shuffled forward, I followed.

"Hello, greetings and all that, you wonderful boy," slurped Vicki as she gushingly kissed his cheek. Jack quickly looked around the room and mumbled "hello," and then perceiving Allen, "Hi, what you say?"

My first view of the room saw how small it was. I judged it to be about 10 × 14 ft. with a bed and dresser the only furniture. On the bed, which obviously was the seat of all activity that took place in the room, sat Norman and Vicki. Jack and I stood and Allen occupied the small stool by the radio, which was playing...

LETTER TO JACK KEROUAC, 7 MARCH 1947 (KANSAS CITY, MO)

Dear Jack:

I am sitting in a bar on Market St. I'm drunk, well, not quite, but I soon will be. I am here for 2 reasons; I must wait 5 hours for the bus to Denver & lastly but, most importantly, I'm here (drinking) because, of course, because of a woman & *what a woman*! To be chronological about it:

I was sitting on the bus when it took on more passengers at Indianapolis, Indiana – a perfectly proportioned beautiful, intellectual, passionate, personification of Venus De Milo asked me if the seat beside me was taken!!! I gulped, (I'm drunk) gargled & stammered NO! (Paradox of expression, after all, how can one stammer No!!?) She sat – I sweated – She started to speak, I knew it would be generalities, so to tempt her I remained silent.

She (her name Patricia) got on the bus at 8 PM (Dark!) I didn't speak until 10 PM – in the intervening 2 hours I not only of course, determined to make her, but, how to *DO IT*.

I naturally can't quote the conversation verbally, however, I shall attempt to give you the gist of it from 10 PM to 2 AM.

Without the slightest preliminaries of objective remarks (what's your name? where are you going? etc.) I plunged into a completely knowing, completely subjective, personal & so to speak "penetrating her core" way of speech; to be shorter, (since I'm getting unable to write) by 2 AM I had her swearing eternal love, complete subjectivity to me & immediate satisfaction. I, anticipating even more pleasure, wouldn't allow her to blow me on the bus, instead we played, as they say, with each other.

Knowing her supremely perfect being was completely mine (when

I'm more coherent, I'll tell you her complete history & psychological reason for loving me) I could conceive of no obstacle to my satisfaction, well, "the best laid plans of mice & men go astray" and my nemesis was her sister, the bitch.

Pat had told me her reason for going to St. Louis was to see her sister; she had wired her to meet her at the depot. So, to get rid of the sister, we peeked around the depot when we arrived at St. Louis at 4 AM to see if she (her sister) was present. If not, Pat would claim her suitcase, change clothes in the rest room & she and I proceed to a hotel room for a night (years?) of perfect bliss. The sister was not in sight, so She (note the capital) claimed her bag & retired to the toilet to change————long dash————

This next paragraph must, of necessity, be written completely objectively————

Edith (her sister) & Patricia (my love) walked out of the pisshouse hand in hand (I shan't describe my emotions). It seems Edith (bah) arrived at the bus depot early & while waiting for Patricia, feeling sleepy, retired to the head to sleep on a sofa. That's why Pat & I didn't see her.

My desperate efforts to free Pat from Edith failed, even Pat's terror & slave-like feeling toward her rebelled enough to state she must see "someone" & would meet Edith later, *all* failed. Edith was wise; she saw what was happening between Pat & I.

Well, to summarize: Pat & I stood in the depot (in plain sight of the sister) & pushing up to one another, vowed to never love again & then I took the bus for Kansas City & Pat went home, meekly, with her dominating sister. Alas, alas————

In complete (try & share my feeling) dejection, I sat, as the bus progressed toward Kansas City. At Columbia, Mo. a young (19) completely passive (my meat) *virgin* got on & shared my seat . . . In my dejection over losing Pat, the perfect, I decided to sit on the bus (behind the driver) in broad daylight & seduce her, from 10:30 AM to 2:30 PM I talked. When I was done, she (confused, her entire life upset, metaphysically amazed at me, passionate in her immaturity) called her folks in Kansas City, & went with me to a park (it was just getting dark) & I banged her; I screwed as never before; all my pent up emotion finding release in this young virgin (& she was) who is, by the by, a *school teacher*! Imagine, she's had 2 years of Mo. St. Teacher's College & now teaches Jr. High School. (I'm beyond thinking straightly).

I'm going to stop writing. Oh, yes, to free myself for a moment from my emotions, you must read "Dead Souls" parts of it (in which Gogol shows his insight) are quite like you.

I'll elaborate further later (probably?) but at the moment I'm drunk & happy (after all, I'm free of Patricia already, due to the young virgin. I have no name for her. At the happy note of Les Young's "jumping at Mesners" (which I'm hearing) I close till later.

To my Brother

Carry On!

N. L. Cassady

LETTER TO JACK KEROUAC, 3 JULY 1949 (SAN FRANCISCO, CA)

DEAR JACK;

In a way it is too bad you left NY, you see, when Al Hinkle and Jim Holmes left here some weeks ago on their way to Maine, they promised to stop over in NY and give you all the carefully worded apologies I'd prepared.

I hit LuAnne on the forehead on Feb. 2nd and broke my left thumb just above the wrist. The setting of the bones was difficult and took three separate castings, 23 combined hours of sitting on hard benches waiting etc. The final cast had a traction pin stuck thru the tip of my left thumb. In April when they took the cast off the pin infected my bone and I developed osteomyelitis which has become chronic and tomorrow I have another operation which, if it fails (one month in an immobile cast) will result in the amputation of my left thumb.

I took care of the baby, while Carolyn worked, from Feb. to June. Near the end of May I thought my thumb was healed enough for me to work. Carolyn quit her job and on June 1st I went to work for Goodyear as a mold man curing recapped tires. Very hard and hot work but I liked it. Now it seems I will lose my job Tuesday when I show up with my hand in a cast again. This leaves Goodyear in a hell of a hole, since there is no one to take my place. Of course Carolyn has found no other job so there is no income and, when the fifty bucks I've got is gone—

LuAnne has married Ray Murphy who has sharpened a sword and is dashing about town trying to find me so he can cut my throat. I've had two narrow escapes; he got to Liberty Street soon after I moved, and three days ago he finally got my phone number here and called to try and find the address. If the prick does manage to find this house and is foolish enough to attack me I'll kill the bastard.

The general labor situation in Frisco is very bad, however, I'll call various shoe factories and the union to see what chances your mother might have. I'll send on this info soon.

Don't go to China. There is a man at Goodyear who has just come to this country after 25 years there. Everything's tough in China; he really knows. Business, the weather, land, and the whores are terrible.

My terrific, darling, beautiful daughter can now stand alone for 30 seconds at a time. She weighs 22 lbs. and is 29 inches long. I've just figured out she is 31¼ percent English, 27½ percent Irish, 25 percent German, 8¾ percent Dutch, 7½ percent Scotch. 100 percent wonderful.

Try Five-Points in Denver for bop, the Rossonian Hotel; and a couple of places across the street on Welton between 26th and 27th Sts. There may be a spot or two downtown or on the north side where the Dagos live. Other than that I just look for good juke boxes.

Strangely, last nite, big dream about Slim Gaillard. He met me at the hospital. (Spend so much time in Hospitals I dreams of them.) I was sickened by the huge bloated women on the beds with their red meated bellies exposed to the air. There was no skin just raw infected meat like rotten beef. I went across the corridor and made it to a tree outside to puke. The lawn was polluted all about from the green shit I brought up. I didn't want my clothes dirtied and just managed to stagger across a sidewalk to lie down. It was a county hospital and there were poor people standing all around the entrance waiting, and watching me. A group of black men were squatted near where I fell. As I regained my strength I laid there watching them. They were talking in quiet tones. I remember I knew it was Slim only in that his gestures were less animated than the others, and from the wry expression on his face. When I approached him he said that he'd been waiting for me. Perhaps you might know the mixed feelings of admiration and inability to be close to him I felt. I was unable to tell him how dumb I felt not to be coherent about my admiration. That's how the dream ended, with me just sitting there watching his face and wishing I could speak.

Monday, the 4th.

Good news! I saw the doctor this morning and he said I could work while the hand was in the cast.

Sat. midnite, the 16th.

God, just heard that great George Shearing, remember God Shearing, Jack? God Shearing and Devil Gaillard. That's us Jack, a mixture of George and Slim. The images we struck of George, a sightless God; of Slim, an all-seeing being—

My hand stinks. A rotten odor permeates the atmosphere for several feet all about it. The cast weighs heavy. Sweating makes the thumb gooey and it sticks to the plaster-of-P. I do an *impossible* task; my job is so difficult it saps everything from strong, two-fisted men; yet, with one hand I throw the heavy truck tires in a real frenzy of accomplishment. I'm amazed.

Your second letter, a note, a tone of madness consciously expressed; but more, consciously maintained; had the sheet of paper been smaller the sustained note would not have been. Consciously sustained notes may be poor, but, as in music, by far the most diffi-cult, and interesting.

I have a million images, all personal and torn they last but an intense moment, but reoccurring the second time they lead to new ones. And so I rush on from one new discovery to the next, telling myself I'll return and play with this or that. Of course, I never do indulge in this play for when I return the first image is past and with it the power to grasp with enthusiasm. I am a blundering image-seeker who thrives on the ironic tricks my thoughts find on every side. Bless a twisted thing—fuck the blessing, just forgive. Oh, baloney, I'm just sorry I can't write—to you SEE?

All pray for the men of Dingle Island. Soothe the sorry lot. Cast up naked on Dingle; they Dangle. Pushed into playing with themselves; their inner ear feeds only on Female Ells' (or is it Eels?) (yuno, they shock) tonsils. Their eyes are so constructed they see but from the corners. The Order of the Day for this nunnery of the Unsoiled Ulcers is to do Penance for these stricken men of all-flesh. The crea-tures have no bones nor any solid matter excepting the nose's bridge. The better to blow you with little Red Riding. Sit on the pot each night, retch with the rectum, gain the holy Dingle Beery.

Six minnows in the pond, with all around them tadpoles. Who will be selected? Hope it's me, hope it's me, hope it's me; not me; I can't peewee.

Did You Fossilize properly this season? Have your sessions in combat been authentic? I must impress on you all, the extreme urgency of full fossilization. This mission has top priority with the High Command. Pass on these Orders.

Wipe that smile off your face, this is murder, see? We're gonna catch that rat and you're gonna tell us where he is. Sam, bring the girl in here. All right, lady, this the guy?

Classification 3-A, Jazz-hounded C. has a sore butt. His wife gives daily injections of penicillin for his thumb, which produces hives; for he's allergic. He must take 60,000 units of Fleming's juice within a month. He must take one tablet every four hours for this month to combat the allergy produced from this juice. He must take Codeine Aspirin to relieve the pain in the thumb. He must have surgery on his leg for an inflamed cyst. He must rise next Monday at six A.M. to get his teeth cleaned. He must see a foot doctor twice a week for treatment. He must take cough syrup each night. He must blow and snort constantly to clear his nose, which has collapsed just under the bridge where an operation some years ago weakened it. He must lose his thumb on his throwing arm next month.

Carolyn is now five months pregnant with our second child. If it's a boy I shall name it Jack Allen Cassady. If it's a girl I shall name it Carolyn Jean.

Bill on the border, Allen in an institution, Huncke in jail, Jack in Denver, Neal in the land's end. The horizon here is the sea. I lay me down on the brink, the west end. Frantic Frisco, yes, frenzied Frisco, yes, Fateful Frisco. Frisco of frivolous folly; Frisco of fearful fights. Frisco of Fossilization. Frisco: Fully Fashioned Fate.

Your Book sold! I sit here thinking of my elation and how best to let you know. I come up with but one word: Glad, Glad, Glad, oh, so damn Glad, Gee, I feel so Glad. I'm Glad.

Allen; I conjure up things. I wonder; How and why? The details, the details I want. Wot Happened?

Bill I knew would end in Texas, Huncke too, no surprise once he was busted again. But, Allen? How, why, where, etc.

Two things threw reality into sham relief: Your successful sale and Allen's commitment. The whole bugaboo of external forces I've evaded so purposefully for 3 years is brought close once again. This has much bearing to me, not directly, but, as a point of Philosophy, if you will. Your book selling means success you see, or, in competition with the world of big boys, recognition. This bears on the whole idea of constructive involvement and the like. You understand; star on the forehead, etc. Now, Allen's internment means the force that so painfully involved Lucien, and yourself to some degree. This is the force I've evaded with success for three years, almost four. As a preamble to getting to the point, however, I will say I fear you can't feel the deep involvement I have had in this negative fashion. All the struggle for your book, all your constructive involvement has been the prime thing with you. Even thru your period in the nuthouse with Big Slim, your part in Lucien's business, etc. your deep anchor has been this involvement with writing, which, unerringly threw you into the other camp. The camp of involvement had your mother, father, and other factors. To be blunt, you were never in jail so many goddamn times you had nightmares of future arrests. You were never actually obsessed with the year-by-year more-and-more apparent fact that you couldn't escape the law's stranglehold. You, in short, were never where Huncke is now. I was not where H. is now, not for the first few years anyway. I stole over five hundred cars in the period from 1940 to 1944. I was caught but three times for cars. Good average you see, no cause for obsession. My first arrest was for license plates. Wait, forget for a moment the above paragraph, I feel like a remembering of things past. If I don't get back to all the points above etc. forget it. So, here's a brief history of arrests. A case history.

My first job was on a bike delivery around Denver. I met a lad named Ben Gowen with whom I used to steal anything we saw as we cruised in the early A.M. in his 27 Buick. One of the things we did was smash the high school principal's car, another was steal chickens from a man he disliked, another was strip cars and sell the parts. I bought the Buick from him for $20. My first car; it couldn't pass the brake and light inspection, so I decided I needed an out of state license to operate the car without arrest. I went to Wichita, Kansas to get the plates. As I was hitchhiking home with the plates concealed under my coat I passed thru Russell, Kansas. Walking down the main drag I was accosted by a nosey sheriff who must have thought I was pretty young to be hiking. He found the plates and threw me in the two cell jail with a county delinquent who should have been in the home for the old since he couldn't feed himself (The sheriff's wife fed him) and sat thru the day drooling and slobbering. After investigation, which included corny things like a fatherly quiz, then an abrupt turnabout to frighten me with threats, a comparison of my handwriting etc. I was released and hiked back to Denver. As I think back, I can recall much of my crimes and little of my next arrest, but, I believe this was my second arrest. I had been to Indianapolis for the 39 Auto Classic and to South Bend to see Notre Dame and to Calif. to live in L.A. and so all this hitchhiking on my own had made me see the wisdom of hiking in the day and stealing a car when nite fell to make good time. Well, when I returned to Denver this became a habit and every nite I'd sleep in some apt. house bathtub and get up and find some friend's place to eat then steal a car to pick up girls at school when they got out. I might change cars in midafternoon but at any rate I'd get some girl and spend the night in the mountains, returning at day-break to my bathtub. I got tired of this and decided to go back to Calif. I knew a fellow named Bill Smith and he wanted to come along. One day in the spring of 41, I was just 15, we stole a Plymouth on Stout and 16th Sts. We ran out of gas just as we pulled into Colo. Springs. I walked a block or so and saw a 38 Buick at the curb, got in, picked up Bill on the corner and we were off again. Passing thru Pueblo I saw a cop's car behind and suggested we cut and run, but Bill was adamant. Sure enough they stopped us, disbe-lieved our story, and took us down. At the police station I found they had caught us so quickly because it happened I'd picked up the D.A.'s car. An hour later the C. Springs D.A. came to regain his car and take us back to be tried. They wouldn't believe Bill's name was really Bill Smith for it sounded so like an alias. They wouldn't believe he was a hitchhiker too, as I told them. I had some Vaseline for my chapped lips and the desk copper leered and asked if we punked each other. We were confined in the Springs County jail for thirty days, then taken to trial. Smith's father was there and got us off. Again, I returned to Denver.

The next arrest was a year later. During that time I'd returned to my brother's to sleep, but didn't work and kept up the car stealing routine with the girls each nite. I left Jack, lived with one Bill Mackley (I had before). We started to Calif. again. This time Mackley and I had no trouble until we got to Albuquerque. We were washed out in a really disastrous flood (knocked out water supply, etc). We were stranded for two days, getting no rides and finding no cars to steal. We spent the night in a RR roundhouse. Bill wanted to return, me too. I finally saw a doctor park his Buick for a minute in front of the hospital. I dashed up, got in and picked up

Bill and we were off for Denver. After a 100 miles or so we were drunk from the pint we'd found on the floor and Bill wanted to drive. He did, at 80 MPH he skidded in the still raining weather and we hit the ditch. We walked and etc. to get back. I was flirting with Brierly that fall of 41 and living at his Aunt & Uncle's. I was stealing cars with Ben Gowen again and stripping them. One night, we were cruising about and just happened to drive by a lot where I'd parked a hot car some months before, in the summer. I glanced at the spot and, believe it or not, my eyes saw the same car. We couldn't believe it and creep warily up to it. As you know, Jack, a hot car, if left on a lot in the lower downtown section was sure to be found in a few days. (The lot was, since you're in Denver, on Lawrence St. between 19th & 20th.) Well, somehow this car had been sitting there for 5 months and still wasn't found. We were elated. This meant the car was cool by now and we could disguise it and keep it for our own. The local kids had played in it and pulled it apart some, damaged the radio etc. but we got it going, put air in the tires at a station and were—

Just paused to reread the last page—too hastily done, silly: I stop. I've been arrested 10 times and served an aggravated total of 15 months on six convictions.

Sun. P.M.—17th

Sitting on a sore ass in my kitchen with the ball game, gurgling daughter, grass-watering wife, full belly from two dollar steak. A new book, "Escape from Reality" by Norman Taylor is fairly interesting and deals with all forms of junk, stuff, coke, etc. I bought it and gave it to [Jim] Holmes (who is quite a tea-head, now) as a going away present. Glad you and Hal together again; hope he does something tremendous in his field. Suppose Brierly snuck in on the Aspen festival somehow; manager in charge of all underdone men who provide transportation for overdone women. I've always liked the old guy. How's Central City this year? Ed White still in Paris? What else new?

Sat., Mid. 23rd.

I tried to call you by phone last week, but the operator said the phone listed under name Davidson had been disconnected. So guess I'd better mail this. Come to think of it, I've written you 4 letters now since you've left SF. One particularly good one was about St.

Patrick's day and also dealt with the Ides of March. Another one consumed in flames was a travelogue I planned before I broke my hand. The last was bits of paper and like scrap I got together for mailing. After I'd compose a letter I would allow it to lay around for a few days then discard it as outmoded, so, thus you didn't hear from me.

Ain't gonna give nobody my jellyroll, got no jelly in it anyhow. Bass, drums, piano, guitar, tenor, alto, (doubles on good clarinet), trombone.

May as well say it; started a book—again. News is a bit late, I wrote what I've done on it last May. The prologue is wee bit underway—4 pages. Haven't touched it since I started to work June 1. Very dull anyhow: family history, got as far as 1910 when my pop was 17.

You know, you and I've never tossed the ole pigskin around; played catch etc, so I could show you my magnificent arm. 70 yards in football, and an unmeasured distance with a baseball, many times I've awed the opponent with the distance I'd get with a special "hop" I've got when we'd peg rocks and the like. Too bad, like most southpaws, I'm slightly erratic in accuracy.

Tues. 26th.

Just started reading "Dr. Faustus" by T. Mann; despite the reviews I find it the best thing I've ever read by him, except, possibly the "Magic Mountain" (which I read when young and influenced me a lot). Strange to discover his latest work starts much as mine.

Yesterday I had a new cast put on. The thumb looks better and although there'll always be just mush and no bone in its tip, it may be saved; we'll know when this latest (and sixth cast over my folly) cast comes off.

Last night got an illiterate letter from Holmes and Hinkle, who are now in Portland, Maine. They ask about Allen and you. Send them the word, huh? Their address: James T. Holmes, 223 High St., Portland, Maine.

Got to go to work now. Love you; write again please, I'm lonely. Tell your Mother if she really wants to work out here I'll look into it with accurate reporting to you at once. You know how things change and perhaps by now the shoe factory and Union news isn't necessary. I want her to know the speeding ticket in Washington isn't forgotten. God Bless her; honest, Jack, I feel so fond of her when I think of the day I caught her alone and working on that rag rug, waiting for you to come home from Frisco a couple of years ago. Goodbye now, must rush.

NEAL

ADVENTURES IN AUTO-EROTICISM

I stole my first automobile at 14 in 1940; by '47 when swearing off such soul-thrilling pleasures to celebrate advent into manhood, I had had illegally in my possession about 500 cars – whether just for the moment and to be taken back to its owner before he returned (I.E. on Parking lots) or whether taken for the purpose of so altering its appearance as to keep it for several weeks but mostly only for joyriding.

The virgin emotion one builds when first stealing an auto – especially when one can hardly make it function properly, so takes full minutes to get away – is naturally strenuous on the nervous system, and I found it most exciting. I was initiated into this particularly exhilerating pastime (tho undeniably utterly stupid) by a chance meeting with the local bad-boy, whom I had known at school. We came upon a '38 Olds sedan which was parked before the well-light entrance of an apartment house. It so happens this model Olds is a bastardized type – Olds being GM's "experimental" car – and since the ignition, lights, radio etc. are unconventionally set off the dash-board by bull horn-like dials; and because this unfamiliarity heightened his panicky condition, John's efforts to start the car seemed really ludicrous from my tree-trunk vantage point. He turned on the radio, the lights, everything but the key I guess, anyhow, when he finally became so flustered as to honk the horn, he bolted away, failing to even close the door. So it was with a genuine fear, so well-based as to make me think I was pretty brave indeed, that we sneaked back for another try. John, altho belittling his own fright, kept assuring me how easy it was, and this (besides the many minutes of quietude that passed after we had resumed our observation point behind a big tree) finally bolstered my courage enough to run over and drive away in the car.

We left it on the premises of an army post south of town, after stalling the motor on a U turn and even though two soldiers helped hand push us and the engine did sputter a bit we finally had exhausted the battery and had to hitch hike home, arriving so near dawn as to create complications there which, emotional tho they had been, now proved nothing beside my night-long thrill – from which I literally tingled for days until, in fact after serving mass as usual one morning, I left the rectory to find before it a current model Mercury with keys dangling! Naturally, having never driven so powerful an automobile, I burned rubber most of the block, before even realizing how to overcome it. And tho still quite inexperienced a driver I know it took so long to halt the tires' squeel only because each additional release of the accelerator, whether fractional or full-inch, was still not enough to ease the power – hell, come to think of it, I might have even been in high gear!

Anyhow, the erotic nature of the Mercury experience happily included exploring the anatomy of the school girl picked up in it, and therefore has no further, sharper, stronger, more meaningful remembrance than the one of its get-away moments, which included wading thru a three-phase traffic signal in the first block...

LEAVING L.A. BY TRAIN AT NIGHT, HIGH ...

Dark streets, hundreds of silent autos parked almost too close to the rail, mammoth buildings, many still lit, now looming in blacker outline, isolated houses, houses of dirt, of noise, cheery ones, then dark, dark ones; one wonders, the occupation of its owners. Billboards, billboards, drink this, eat that, use all manner of things, EVERYONE, the best, the cheapest, the purest and most satisfying of all their available counterparts. Red lights flicker on every horizon, airplanes beware; cars flash by, more lights. Workers repair the gas main. Signs, signs, lights, lights, streets, streets; it is the dark between that attracts one – what's happening there at this moment? What hidden thing, glorious perhaps, is being passed and lost forever. The congestion slackens, a cone of widening sparcity stretches before the train, now one has left the center and its core is burst past as the interlocking plants terminate grip and entrust us to the automatic block system's meticulous care. The maze of tracks have unwreathed from cross-over webs of railroad intellectuality to become simple main line dignity; these ribbons of accurate gauge so ceaselessly toiled over, respected, feared. Oh, unending high rail of intrigue!

John Clellon Holmes
1926–1988

(from) GO: PART ONE, CHAPTER 3

Three

STOFSKY lived on York Avenue and Seventy-eighth Street in a dreary district of junkshops and saloons. His building was little more than a dilapidated tenement with a watch repair shop downstairs in which a blue bulb burned all night. His apartment was on the fourth floor at the back; and the dingy stairways leading up to it, which smelled perpetually of garbage, were the hideouts of gaunt, fugitive cats from the neighborhood, and an occasional drunk as miserable as they.

Like cold water flats everywhere, Stofsky's place was entered through the kitchen, a small, high-ceilinged room newly painted a violent blue. Its only window gave out on a dirty air-well. To the left of this room was a cubicle not much larger, with a bed (which appeared never to have been made up), a portable clothes closet, and a few paper covered books on an orange crate. Beyond this room was the toilet. To the right of the kitchen, there was another room, more spacious than the others, which had two lofty windows hung with mouldy drapery, once long ago a rich maroon. They gave out on a stunted tree and a network of clotheslines. There was also a bricked up fireplace with a baroque mantel, now chipping and laden with books. Over this, fastened to the wall with leather headed carpet tacks, hung a cheap colored reproduction of

Grünewald's "Crucifixion," which Stofsky had cut out of a magazine. But the pride of the room, and the thing which had most attracted Stofsky to the apartment, was a tremendous map of the world which covered the entire wall opposite the fireplace. It was intricately detailed as to cities, trade routes and prevailing winds, and criss-crossed with countless red meridian lines. Then there were a couple of low coffee tables, too large for the spaces they occupied before a couch and an armchair. These, and the desk against another wall, were always a clutter of ash trays, empty beer bottles, odd volumes of poetry, a few small pieces of tasteless statuary retrieved from the junkshops, and some magazines in which Stofsky's verse had appeared while he was at Columbia.

The story went that he had come into possession of the apartment when a friend of his (an older man whom no one had ever met) suddenly jumped a boat for Europe, leaving the place to him, furniture and all. It cost him fifteen dollars a month, and whenever he could collect enough cash for a bottle of whiskey and some beer he gave parties to show it off.

The party that night was typical. To it, he had invited everyone he could contact and even encouraged these people to ask others, counting on the uninvited guests to bring liquor with which to make themselves more welcome. If Stofsky was introduced to someone in the afternoon, that person was asked to come that night; and everyone, gathered in this haphazard manner, either got along or didn't. The interplay of relationships under the benevolence of alcohol was the main thing, and it was no exaggeration that if nobody else had a good time at his parties, Stofsky at least enjoyed himself immensely.

Now the rooms were thronged with people, many of them unsure just what they were doing there, but intrigued by all the talk, the smoke and laughter, and the ceaseless movement by which people at a party disguise their self-consciousness. The brighter crop of philosophy and literature students from Columbia squatted on the floors, vying for repute in that elaborate game of intellectual snobbery which passes for conversation among the young and intense. They grouped themselves (at a safe distance so as not to appear too interested) around the one or two authentic literary figures that Stofsky had managed to ensnare: a poet of cautious output, a novelist whose work had been appraised as being "not without talent," and a soft-faced critic who spoke in terms of "criteria and intention," and whose articles were fashionably unreadable. Through the rooms, like pale butterflies, flitted a number of young women, girl friends of the students, exchanging the gossip of the sets they traveled in with offhand arrogance, all the time snatching looks over their shoulders so as not to miss anything, and quickly moving on. In the crowded living room where a single light dimly shone, someone was strumming a zither the strings of which had been systematically tuned flat.

Stofsky was everywhere, perhaps the only person acquainted with them all. Like a child giving a tea party for adults, he seemed blissfully unaware that nobody was really at ease. But he found a moment for everyone, and there was something peculiarly charming about his formality and his delighted smiles; something almost winsome in his usually wry mouth as he made graceful chit-chat or expressed interest in trifles: all of which was in bizarre contrast to the discomfort of most of his guests.

As was usual, his close friends, knowing what to expect, clustered together as they arrived and ignored everyone else. This group captured the divan in the living room and refused to budge for the rest of the evening, forming a nucleus around which the party would either coalesce or disintegrate.

There Pasternak sat, his annoyance of the afternoon changing to depression as new hordes of chattering people squeezed in the door. Nearby sat Daniel Verger, his wasted shoulders in their perpetual hunch and his thin lips drawn down in an expression of resignation that gave him the look of a young, sickly sceptic. He was talking with a girl named Bianca, who appeared to be struggling hopelessly to fasten her black, wild eyes upon him. She had a tense, full bosomed body to which she seemed absolutely indifferent at that moment, and every now and again she broke out in a raw, disturbing laugh that bewildered Verger.

The cause of her inattention was the sight of a strikingly handsome young man, who had once been her lover, and who now stood tottering against the wall map, surveying everything with that expression of private irony with which liquor loosens the features. This was Agatson, and Bianca stared at him, not out of personal remembrances (because she saw him almost every day and lived only three blocks from his Twenty-first Street loft), but for the same reason that everyone found it difficult to keep his eyes off him for long.

Agatson was one of those rare people whose reputations are in every way merited. His dissipations, and the exploits accompanying them, were near-legendary among a large group of young people in New York, and his loft was perhaps the only place in the city where a wild, disorderly brawl might be going on at any time. Once, after a week-long binge with him, a noted poet had prophecied that Agatson would be dead in three years or in an asylum, and this had provided the tantalizing aura of doom which was all that was needed to dignify the legend.

Agatson had a spare, muscular body which abuse had hardened. It was the body of a man whose drinking has become a sort of vocation, and who (unlike the run of urban sophisticates) no longer sports his hangovers like so many Purple Hearts earned in the good fight against boredom, but endures them with stoical tenacity and never complains. His dark features had that fleeting, sensual looseness that only the dissolute, just this side of slavery to alcohol, can possess. There was something mocking and remote in his fixed stares and in the curl of lips no longer firm, but not yet lax. Everything about him made even the tipsy onlooker grow alert, as if realizing that this man respected only the prodding of whim and might do anything that came into his head; and yet that all this was somehow the result of a fatal vision of the world. In fact, to many of these young men, Agatson was a symbol of that inability to really believe in anything which they felt stirring within themselves, and the craving for excess which it inspired.

Now, from across the room, his eye caught on the wan face of Verger, and he yelled: "Why if it isn't O. B. Haverton!" Lurching closer, he started to speak with winking, bleary-eyed seriousness, about how they hadn't seen each other since Harvard days, all the time referring to Verger as "ole O. B."

This was plainly foolishness, because Verger was often in the crowd at Agatson's parties and had been trying for months, patiently and vainly, to establish a friendship between them, but some streak of malicious irony had seized Agatson and he went on and on with it.

Verger, who was a theological student and whose bare, drafty flat in Spanish Harlem was filled with abstruse religious books, was, like many bookish people, flustered by a loud voice and never sure he correctly understood what it was saying.

He turned with a tremulous smile to Bianca, and said weakly: "Bill always mispronounces my name."

"You're O. B. Haverton, of course, and you used to write verse to a barmaid on Scullay Square. Do you think I'm drunk or something, O. B.? . . . We used to call him Old Bitch Haverton, you know, behind his back!"

For a moment Verger hesitated. "Well . . . well, I've changed my name," he stumbled out. "To Verger."

"Virgin! . . . Virgin!" Agatson shouted, wheeling on Bianca. "Hey, babe, ole O. B. says he's still virgin! But you used to write all about love, O. B. Didn' you do any research, hey, hey?"

Verger was blushing now for he was not successful with women, and yet often spoke seriously of love as "the one hope." But now he had about convinced himself that Agatson actually was so drunk that he did not recognize him.

Bianca tried to come to the rescue. "Oh, stop it, Bill! Why do you always act like you don't know who he is?"

"What'dya mean, babe," Agatson replied with the easy candor of a man to a woman with whom he is no longer intimate. "He's always masquerading as some guy called Virgin or—"

Verger began to cough convulsively behind his hand, his scrawny chest heaving.

". . . or somebody with tuberculosis out of Thomas Mann!"

This brought a sudden hush for everyone knew that Verger actually had tuberculosis, and knew that Agatson knew it as well.

"Hey, who's this Haverton?" somebody, who had missed this last, yelled gaily from the other room.

Verger had stopped coughing and was trembling with embarrassment which everyone but Agatson shared. "*I am*," he squeeked bravely, looking for the owner of the voice. "Only I changed my name. I didn't want to be recognized, he-he . . . And . . . and if you think I started coughing just now, Bill . . . just *so* you'd recognize me . . . for pity or anything like that . . . if you think I'd do that, or care whether you have your games with me. . ."

But then he broke off, more mortified by his own exclamation and the fact that everyone had heard it, than by Agatson's taunts. Just at that moment, Stofsky came bustling through the crowd.

"What's going on? Games? Games?"

"Aw, everyone's hungup," Pasternak growled. "What did I tell you!"

Agatson, content with himself, had turned toward the drinks with a secretive smile, but said, as he passed an overdressed, wide-eyed blonde girl whom he had never seen before: "He's an impostor, you know, babe. He's just O. B. Haverton in a clean shirt!"

Verger's dry, racking cough had subsided and he muttered apologetically: "The whiskey went down the wrong way ... Oh, don't bother about it, David. Go back to the others! He always pretends he doesn't know me ... And why not? Why should he?" He made an ineffectual flutter with his hand as if to wave Stofsky away, all the time clearing his throat. "Is there any beer left?" And with that he went off quickly, just as Hobbes and Kathryn pushed their way through the groups of people clogging the doorway.

"Why does he take that stuff from Agatson?" Pasternak was complaining to Stofsky. "It's crazy!"

"He believes in Bill," Bianca interjected bitterly. "Don't you know that people who can't believe in anything else always believe in Bill?"

Stofsky gave her a sharply thoughtful look before saying: "But wouldn't he be surprised if he knew he believed in his own pride even more. Poor Verger ..."

At that, Bianca got up as a person gets up who is suddenly giddy, and went up to Hobbes and Kathryn, who had missed this exchange. She and Kathryn got along aloofly, respecting each other's distrust, but now Bianca took her hand and turned to the blonde girl to whom Agatson had spoken.

"This is Christine. She lives down the street from my building."

The girl's pale, heart-shaped face sweetened with a thrilled smile, but she seemed undecided as to whether she should get up or not. Her lips parted wetly.

The three sprawled around her on the floor. She had obviously never been at such a party before and she began to speak to Bianca in a grave, bewildered way. Pasternak had noticed her immediately, if only because her large blue eyes had flashed with panic when Agatson stumbled by.

She was getting everything terribly garbled in her nervousness, and did not seem relaxed having strangers so near her; but still, she was studying them all surreptitiously as if recalling reports about them she had heard. Kathryn took to her instantly because she seemed so helplessly out of place and at the same time eager to make a good impression. After only a few moments, they discovered that their parents had come from the same part of Italy, and they began jabbering away in what Christine called, with a shy, laughing glance at Pasternak, a "gutter dialect."

During this, Bianca leaned toward Hobbes and began whispering hurriedly: "Christine's very unhappy at home, and I felt sorry for her so I brought her along. She doesn't get out very much because Max—that's her husband, a machinist—can't get along with people. They're just simple people, you know; from the neighborhood. But she's got the sweetest little child, Ellie . . . a little elf who is tone-perfect and sings beautifully, but can't even talk yet. So tell Kathryn to be nice to her, will you, and to . . . well, sort of take it easy on her. She's really very conventional, so don't be surprised at anything she says."

Christine was saying to Kathryn in a shocked tone: "Why, that guy spends more time with that old car than he ever does with me! I'm not kidding. I tell you," and this confidingly, "I feel ashamed sometimes because he's so kinda cold, and . . . Well, it makes me feel like a who-er!" She giggled with confusion at her mispronunciation. "I can't get to sleep some nights!"

She looked excitedly about at all the people and the smoke, for an instant forgetting to cover up the fact that it was all different from anything she had ever known before. Agatson was fidgeting with the radio trying to find music, and she observed him with innocent wonder.

"Is he a queer? Doesn't he act like one though! And where did that O.B. Haverton go? . . . But maybe *he*," and she pointed directly at Agatson before she could prevent herself, "was just pie-eyed, eh?"

Kathryn made some off-color joke in Italian that sent Christine into trilling, female laughter.

Soon she was at ease, talking in excited bursts, taking them all into her confidence, and even making quick, refreshing retorts to the things they said. Every once in a while she would sneak a glance at Pasternak, who was staring at her with a preoccupied frown.

Hobbes got him aside, wondering what the trouble was.

"But what a girl!" Pasternak exclaimed, refusing to take his eyes off her. "Look at that hair! Now that's the kind of girl you never find in New York. She's like one of those chicks working in a lunch cart on the highway, a real woman. Right?"

"Well, why don't you speak up then? What's wrong?"

"Oh, you know the way I am!" he snapped back with a twinge of irritation. "I work slow. I'm *looking* at her all the time, and she knows I'm looking. What do you want me to do?"

She was talking openly now, with naive simplicity, about "that gorgon-headed husband of mine! Oh, he doesn't fool me. I know he's out cuckin' around with other women." Her eyes flashed. "It just isn't right to live the way we live, you know. Never getting out. It isn't that I like to be away from him, and be coming here without him. I'm not that way, Paul," and she turned to him earnestly. "But, would you believe it, he doesn't even want me to see anything of Bianca because I seem so happy when I come back. Now what do you think of that?" But she brightened almost immediately.

She never spoke directly to Pasternak, although she sparred warmly with everyone else. But when she glanced at him and found him staring darkly at her, an almost demure glow would soften her delicate features, and she would become distracted. Finally a few people began to dance in the space in the middle of the room, and Pasternak took her from the group without a word. She moved with him gracefully, her long, well-shaped body just a little rigid, her lips quivering, and the abundant blonde hair tumbling down over his arm.

"She's wonderful," Kathryn said. "She was telling me that she's always wanted to sing, and I'll bet she's got a voice too."

"You know, I think she's fallen for Gene."

At this, Bianca intruded with alarm: "But tell him to take it easy. She's really desperate about things, her marriage and everything . . . no matter how she jokes about it. He could hurt her without even trying to. . ."

But as if she thought this warning ultimately futile, after the music faded away Bianca told Christine she had to get home, and Christine, making an unsuccessful effort to disguise her disappointment, went with her. Kathryn struggled with them through the crowds to the door. She took down Christine's phone number, promised to call her soon, and noted the hours during which the husband could be avoided.

"What did you tell her about me?" Pasternak asked as soon as she came back.

"Nothing," Kathryn replied with a smirk. "We didn't talk about any of you. Why? . . . She's had a terrible life, you know. Now don't you go thinking she's just another—"

Pasternak was offended at this. "What do you think I am? I've known girls like that before. Jesus Christ!"

Kathryn laughed. "Don't get excited. I was just joking."

"I could even fall in love with a girl like that," and he went silent.

"Well, she likes you if that's what you want to know . . . My Lord, I told her you'd written this book and she was actually impressed. She thought you were a football player all along."

The radio was turned louder at eleven-thirty to an all night program of wild jazz. Some of the stiffness of the talk disappeared as more liquor was consumed, and somebody, obviously unused to parties of this kind or the protocol connected with them, even passed out in a corner of the kitchen, clutching an empty beer bottle.

Pasternak had gone off morosely into the crowd, Christine's early departure bearing out his forebodings about the night, when Kathryn finally said to Hobbes: "Let's go. I told you it would be terrible. That Christine was all that made me stay *this* long."

"Let's just have one more drink," he implored, jumping up before she could object and heading for the kitchen, where the zither player was sitting on the sink attempting a Bach prelude, with one or two of the students standing unsteadily around him, offering carping criticisms. Hobbes poured out two shots of whiskey, and then noticed that a girl had attached herself to Pasternak in the corner to which he had retired.

Her awkward, boyish figure was bent over toward him, and she thrust her bony face in front of his, speaking with a toothy nasality that indicated she had fled the Midwest. Her lank brown hair was clipped off crudely around her ears, and as she spoke she gesticulated with nervous jerks of her hands. Pasternak nodded every once in a while, but seemed bored by her gibbering. Hobbes approached them.

She was holding forth on the corruption, depravity and general neuroticism of modern life—the favorite topic of the tyro at intellectual parties—, and she turned to Hobbes, absorbing him into her train of thought as though he were just another proof of the contention.

"Nothing's *really* healthy anymore, and, I must confess, I'm just as glad. What a bad sign if it was! I suppose you'll think that I'm morbidly attracted to evil like the Baron du Charlus. But even he was a moralist of this new kind I was speaking about; Gene . . . Well, I don't deny it. I'm afraid I like things that are ... oh, flushed down the drain, if you see what I mean."

Hobbes thought tipsily: "Strictly a case of self-love," and the remark amused him drily, but he said nothing.

"Well then, you oughta meet this thief I know, to see the real thing," Pasternak said. "A real thief and drug addict, none of this intellectual abstraction. Wouldn't she go for Ancke, Paul?"

Hobbes assented and drifted away, taking the drink to Kathryn. Almost as soon as he rejoined her, Stofsky rushed up to them with a shriveled daffodil in one hand.

"Where's Agatson? Have you seen him? He's disappeared somewhere, and I had this monster act all prepared for him. . ."

"Maybe he left with Bianca," Kathryn retorted. "What's the flower for?"

"But it's so early!" Stofsky exclaimed with genuine bewilderment, unable to understand why anyone would willingly leave one of his parties. "Well, you see, I was going to come up to him in front of everybody, and fall on my knees, and plead: 'Be my monster, O Guru!' You know, *really* abjectly ... I even had this flower to present to him. And I'd say: 'I place myself completely in your hands. Be harsh with me, O Nathan!' Can you imagine it? Really grovel so he'd stop needling Verger that way ... Oh, and you know, Verger's gone too. Yes! He was crushed—because of his pride, of course, not Agatson!"

He appeared to be vastly enjoying all this fuss, and all but clapped his forehead dramatically while exclaiming: "Oh, these egoists! You have to be a positive wet-nurse!" And he scurried off.

Pasternak, with the curious girl in tow, had wandered up, and she was still talking. With an intent expression, he held onto her arm, listening to her and yet not listening; and though she seemed aware that he was managing an interest in her physically, she went gushing on about "the purging reality of evil!" just the same.

"You can stay if you want," Kathryn stated tersely after a while. "But I'm going home. It's almost twelve."

"Just a minute, honey. I'll be right with you."

She got up decisively and went away into the mob to search for her coat. Pasternak continued smoking cigarettes and peering at the girl right through her cloud of talk, and she seemed perfectly content to have it that way. When she turned for a moment to fire a remark into someone else's conversation, he leaned toward Hobbes.

"Why the hell did Christine leave so soon? I was just getting along with her."

"She came uptown with Bianca and Bianca had to get home. We'll see her again though. Kathryn got her number."

Pasternak pursed his lips almost primly. "Well, look, this is Verger's cousin. Her name's Georgia. She's all hungup, but what the hell . . . Can I bring her to your place? Will Kathryn mind, do you think?"

"No, of course not. But we'll probably be leaving in a minute. I'll go find her."

The kitchen was stifling and filled with the students who, driven out of the living room by more confident elements, had collected there to sweat, drink and argue insolently among themselves. Kathryn was waiting at the door, glowering down her nose and ignoring them all.

"Are you ready to go now?"

"Yes. Gene's coming along too, with that girl; if that's all right."

"Anything, but let's get out of here. Where are they?"

Pasternak and the skinny Georgia were elbowing through the students toward them, and they almost tripped over the outstretched legs of the person who had passed out.

"We really ought to say goodbye to David," Hobbes suggested. "Otherwise it'll look like a conspiracy."

"Aw, forget about it," Pasternak muttered, all but pushing Georgia out the door. "He's all involved tonight. I told you how he gets. I think something happened with his analyst today, because he was even talking about going back to live with his father out in Hackensack! And you know the trouble he has with his father. He was yelling about 'a crisis' all the way uptown."

They got home and Hobbes and Kathryn went to bed immediately, leaving Pasternak and the girl moving around the living room with the radio playing softly and one warm light burning over the desk.

"What's he going to do, sleep with her?" Kathryn asked, spreading her hair out upon the pillow beside him. He turned onto his back with a sigh.

"I don't know, dear. I guess so."

They lay silent for a moment, letting the bed receive and relax them. Across the ceiling above them, moved the rushing lights of the traffic outside the window, which roared like a mindless turbine in a huge, empty shed.

"God, I'm tired," she breathed. "I drank too much."

"Do you think you can sleep?"

"Yes. I guess so." She listened for a minute, raising her head from the pillow just a bit. "They'd better keep that damn radio down though."

"Goodnight, honey," and he leaned over in the darkness to find her lips. To his surprise, she wound a warm arm about his neck and kissed him back sleepily.

"Goodnight, butch."

* * *

When Hobbes awoke, it was past nine and Kathryn had gone. He found Georgia sleeping on one couch and Pasternak curled up on another. There were a lot of ground-out cigarette butts and one overturned glass of water. The girl was awake and he gave her coffee.

"I hope you and your wife didn't mind," she said. "Did we make a lot of noise?" She gurgled into her cup ridiculously.

Hobbes reassured her and they sat for a while, talking absently. He wondered why she did not come out from underneath the blankets and get dressed, because she had repeated several times that she had an appointment at ten. Her conversation became more affected and obscure, and she finally lay there simply looking at him desperately, her hair disarranged and one bony shoulder peeking out.

He laughed to himself when he realized that she would not get up until he had left the room.

"I guess I'd better go then," she stumbled when he returned to find her hastily clothed. "I hope you didn't mind. It was so nice of you . . . I'll just say goodbye to Gene." She went over to the couch where he lay, tousled and sleeping grimly.

"Well, Gene, I've got to go," she said, but he refused to wake up, although his breathing indicated that he was not actually asleep at all, but merely sulking. "I hope you're not angry with me, Gene. Will you call me?"

He wouldn't say a word, and she tried to smile through her chagrin as she gave it up. "I guess he's still mad at me . . . Well, thanks a lot, Paul. I hope I see you again, you and your wife." She knocked over the wastebasket getting out the door.

Pasternak got up a few minutes later and, over coffee, he said to Hobbes in a disgusted voice. "You know what that dame did to me? She was a virgin all along. A virgin! I argued with her for half an hour, but she wouldn't give in. What do you think of that? . . . Then she got up and danced in just a garter-belt and told me about all the guys she's been 'giving satisfaction to' lately. And she's a virgin! She wouldn't even let me kiss her for an hour! I almost batted her at one point!"

"Well, what happened?"

"Oh, Christ, I let her 'give me satisfaction'! And then you know what she did? Right in the middle of it, she looked up at me and said, 'I don't know what I'm doing this for. I'm not feeling anything at all!' . . . And she laughed, she actually laughed!"

"Maybe it was funny from her position," Hobbes chuckled.

"Hell, I think she's a Lesbian anyway." He was furious just thinking about it. "You know, I'll bet I'm the only guy that's ever been turned down by a whore. Yah, that happened to me once when I was young. A whore! I've got no luck with women at all . . . Look how that girl Christine left last night, just when I was making out. And I really liked her too."

"There's always a next time, Gene."

"Yah."

After a while, Pasternak left to go back home to Long Island City, taking down Christine's address and phone number first. Two days in New York, staying up until odd hours, living an irregular life from one friend's flat to another, usually depressed him, and finally he would slip away and go home for food and sleep and the attempt at work.

Kathryn called at twelve-thirty.

"Did your friends leave, dear?" she asked with a sweet sarcasm that infuriated him because he felt helpless against it. He told her what had happened the night before only after her insistent questioning. She was annoyed and snapped out: "I don't want him to bring any of his girls to the apartment anymore. I hope you understand that. I don't like that kind of thing happening in my house."

GREGORY CORSO
1930–2000

ITALIAN EXTRAVAGANZA

Mrs. Lombardi's month-old son is dead.
I saw it in Rizzo's funeral parlor,
A small purplish wrinkled head.

They've just finished having high mass for it;
They're coming out now
... wow, such a small coffin!
And ten black cadillacs to haul it in.

THE LAST GANGSTER

Waiting by the window
my feet enwrapped with the dead bootleggers of Chicago
I am the last gangster, safe, at last,
waiting by a bullet-proof window.

I look down the street and know
the two torpedoes from St. Louis.
I've watched them grow old
... guns rusting in their arthritic hands.

THE MAD YAK

I am watching them churn the last milk
    they'll ever get from me.
They are waiting for me to die;
They want to make buttons out of my bones.
Where are my sisters and brothers?
That tall monk there, loading my uncle,
    he has a new cap.
And that idiot student of his—
    I never saw that muffler before.
Poor uncle, he lets them load him.
How sad he is, how tired!
I wonder what they'll do with his bones?
And that beautiful tail!
How many shoelaces will they make of that!

FOR MILES

Your sound is faultless
    pure & round
        holy
    almost profound

Your sound is your sound
    true & from within
    a confession
    soulful & lovely

Poet whose sound is played
    lost or recorded
    but heard
    can you recall that 54 night at the Open Door
    when you & bird
    wailed five in the morning some wondrous
    yet unimaginable score?

LAST NIGHT I DROVE A CAR

a dream

Last night I drove a car
    not knowing how to drive
    not owning a car
I drove and knocked down
    people I loved
    ... went 120 through one town.

I stopped at Hedgeville
    and slept in the back seat
    ... excited about my new life.

HAIR

My beautiful hair is dead
Now I am the rawhead
O when I look in the mirror
the bald I see is balder still
When I sleep the sleep I sleep
is not at will
And when I dream I dream children waving goodbye—
It was lovely hair once
it was
Hours before shop windows   gum-machine mirrors   with great
                                                 combs

pockets filled with jars of lanolin
Washed hair I hated
With dirt the waves came easier and stayed
Yet nothing would rid me of dandruff
Vitalis Lucky-Tiger Wildroot Brilliantine nothing—
To lie in bed and be hairless is a blunder only God could allow—
The bumps on my head—I wouldn't mind being bald
if the bumps on my head made people sorry—
Careless God! Now how can old ladies cookie me?
How to stand thunderous on an English cliff

a hectic Heathcliff?
O my lovely stained-glass hair is dry   dark   invisible
not there!
Sun! it is you who are to blame!
And to think I once held my hair to you
like a rich proud silk merhant—
Bald! I'm bald!
Best now I get a pipe
and forget girls.

Subways take me one of your own
seat me anybody
let me off any station anyman
What use my walking up Fifth Ave
or going to theatre for intermission
or standing in front of girls schools
when there is nothing left for me to show—
Wrestlers are bald
And though I'm thin O God give me chance now to wrestle
or even be a Greek wrestler with a bad heart
and make that heart make me sweat
—my head swathed in towels in an old locker room
that I speak good English before I die—
Barbers are murdered in the night!
Razors and scissors are left in rain!
No hairdresser dare scheme a new shampoo!
No premature hair on the babe's pubis!
Wigmaker! help me! my fingernails are knived in your door!
I want a wig of winter's vast network!
A beard of hogs snouting acorns!
Samson bear with me! Just a moustache
and I'd surmount governance over Borneo!
O even a nose hair, an ingrown hair,
and I'd tread beauty a wicked foot, ah victory!
Useless useless
I must move away from sun
Live elsewhere
—a bald body dressed in old lady cloth.
O the fuzzy wuzzy grief!
Mercy, wreathed this coldly lonely head a crowning glory!

I stand in darkness
weeping to angels washing their oceans of hair.
There goes my hair! shackled to a clumping wind!
Come back, hair, come back!
I want to grow sideburns!
I want to wash you, comb you, sun you, love you!
as I ran from you wild before—
I thought surely this nineteen hundred and fifty nine of now
that I need no longer bite my fingernails
but have handsome gray hair
to show how profoundly nervous I am.

Damned be hair!
Hair that must be plucked from soup!
Hair that clogs the bathtub!
Hair that costs a dollar fifty to be murdered!
Disgusting hair! eater of peroxide! dye! sand!
Monks and their bagel heads!
Ancient Egypt and their mops!
Negroes and their stocking caps!
Armies! Universities! Industries! and their branded crews!
Antoinette Du Barry Pompadour and their platinum cakes!
Veronica Lake   Truman Capote   Ishka Bibble   Messiahs
   Paganinis   Bohemians   Hawaiians   poodles

MARRIAGE

Should I get married? Should I be good?
Astound the girl next door with my velvet suit and faustus hood?
Don't take her to movies but to cemeteries
tell all about werewolf bathtubs and forked clarinets
then desire her and kiss her and all the preliminaries
and she going just so far and I understanding why
not getting angry saying You must feel! It's beautiful to feel!
Instead take her in my arms lean against an old crooked tombstone
and woo her the entire night the constellations in the sky—

When she introduces me to her parents
back straightened, hair finally combed, strangled by a tie,

should I sit knees together on their 3rd degree sofa
and not ask Where's the bathroom?
How else to feel other than I am,
often thinking Flash Gordon soap—
O how terrible it must be for a young man
seated before a family and the family thinking
We never saw him before! He wants our Mary Lou!
After tea and homemade cookies they ask What do you do for a
living?

Should I tell them: Would they like me then?
Say All right get married, we're losing a daughter
but we're gaining a son—
And should I then ask Where's the bathroom?

O God, and the wedding! All her family and her friends
and only a handful of mine all scroungy and bearded
just wait to get at the drinks and food—
And the priest! he looking at me as if I masturbated
asking me Do you take this woman for your lawful wedded wife?
And I trembling what to say say Pie Glue!
I kiss the bride all those corny men slapping me on the back
She's all yours, boy! Ha-ha-ha!
And in their eyes you could see some obscene honeymoon going
on—

Then all that absurd rice and clanky cans and shoes
Niagara Falls! Hordes of us! Husbands! Wives! Flowers!
Chocolates!

All streaming into cozy hotels
All going to do the same thing tonight
The indifferent clerk he knowing what was going to happen
The lobby zombies they knowing what
The whistling elevator man he knowing
The winking bellboy knowing
Everybody knowing! I'd be almost inclined not to do anything!
Stay up all night! Stare that hotel clerk in the eye!
Screaming: I deny honeymoon! I deny honeymoon!
running rampant into those almost climactic suites
yelling Radio belly! Cat shovel!
O I'd live in Niagara forever! in a dark cave beneath the Falls
I'd sit there the Mad Honeymooner

devising ways to break marriages, a scourge of bigamy
a saint of divorce—

But I should get married I should be good
How nice it'd be to come home to her
and sit by the fireplace and she in the kitchen
aproned young and lovely wanting my baby
and so happy about me she burns the roast beef
and comes crying to me and I get up from my big papa chair
saying Christmas teeth! Radiant brains! Apple deaf!
God what a husband I'd make! Yes, I should get married!
So much to do! like sneaking into Mr Jones' house late at night
and cover his golf clubs with 1920 Norwegian books
Like hanging a picture of Rimbaud on the lawnmower
like pasting Tannu Tuva postage stamps all over the picket fence
like when Mrs Kindhead comes to collect for the Community Chest
grab her and tell her There are unfavorable omens in the sky!
And when the mayor comes to get my vote tell him
When are you going to stop people killing whales!
And when the milkman comes leave him a note in the bottle
Penguin dust, bring me penguin dust, I want penguin dust—

Yet if I should get married and it's Connecticut and snow
and she gives birth to a child and I am sleepless, worn,
up for nights, head bowed against a quiet window, the past behind
                                                                me,
finding myself in the most common of situations a trembling man
knowledged with responsibility not twig-smear nor Roman coin
                                                          soup—

O what would that be like!
Surely I'd give it for a nipple a rubber Tacitus
For a rattle a bag of broken Bach records
Tack Della Francesca all over its crib
Sew the Greek alphabet on its bib
And build for its playpen a roofless Parthenon

No, I doubt I'd be that kind of father
not rural not snow no quiet window
but hot smelly tight New York City
seven flights up, roaches and rats in the walls

a fat Reichian wife screeching over potatoes Get a job!
And five nose running brats in love with Batman
And the neighbors all toothless and dry haired
like those hag masses of the 18th century
all wanting to come in and watch TV
The landlord wants his rent
Grocery store Blue Cross Gas & Electric Knights of Columbus
Impossible to lie back and dream Telephone snow, ghost parking—
No! I should not get married I should never get married!
But—imagine If I were married to a beautiful sophisticated woman
tall and pale wearing an elegant black dress and long black gloves
holding a cigarette holder in one hand and a highball in the other
and we lived high up in a penthouse with a huge window
from which we could see all of New York and ever farther on
                                        clearer days
No, can't imagine myself married to that pleasant prison dream—

O but what about love? I forget love
not that I am incapable of love
it's just that I see love as odd as wearing shoes—
I never wanted to marry a girl who was like my mother
And Ingrid Bergman was always impossible
And there's maybe a girl now but she's already married
And I don't like men and—
but there's got to be somebody!
Because what if I'm 60 years old and not married,
all alone in a furnished room with pee stains on my underwear
and everybody else is married! All the universe married but me!

Ah, yet well I know that were a woman possible as I am possible
then marriage would be possible—
Like SHE in her lonely alien gaud waiting her Egyptian lover
so I wait—bereft of 2,000 years and the bath of life.

BOMB

Budger of history   Brake of time   You   Bomb
Toy of universe   Grandest of all snatched-sky   I cannot hate you
Do I hate the mischievous thunderbolt   the jawbone of an ass
The bumpy club of One Million B.C.   the mace   the flail   the axe
Catapult Da Vinci   tomahawk Cochise   flintlock Kidd   dagger Rathbone
Ah and the sad desperate gun of Verlaine   Pushkin   Dillinger   Bogart
And hath not St. Michael a burning sword   St. George a lance   David a sling
Bomb   you are as cruel as man makes you   and you're no crueller than cancer
All man hates you   they'd rather die by car-crash   lightning   drowning
Falling off a roof   electric-chair   heart-attack   old age   old age   O Bomb
They'd rather die by anything but you   Death's finger is free-lance
Not up to man whether you boom or not   Death has long since distributed its
categorical blue   I sing thee Bomb   Death's extravagance   Death's jubilee
Gem of Death's supremest blue   The flyer will crash   his death will differ
with the climber who'll fall   To die by cobra is not to die by bad pork
Some die by swamp   some by sea   and some by the bushy-haired man in the night
O there are deaths like witches of Arc   Scarey deaths like Boris Karloff
No-feeling deaths like birth-death   sadless deaths like old pain Bowery
Abandoned deaths   like Capital Punishment   stately deaths like senators
And unthinkable deaths like Harpo Marx   girls on Vogue covers   my own
I do not know just how horrible Bombdeath is   I can only imagine
Yet no other death I know has so laughable a preview   I scope
a city   New York City   streaming   starkeyed   subway shelter
Scores and scores   A fumble of humanity   High heels bend
Hats whelming away   Youth forgetting their combs
Ladies not knowing what to do   with their shopping bags
Unperturbed gum machines   Yet dangerous 3rd rail
Ritz Brothers   from the Bronx   caught in the A train
The smiling Schenley poster will always smile
Impish Death   Satyr Bomb   Bombdeath
Turtles exploding over Istanbul
The jaguar's flying foot
soon to sink in arctic snow
Penguins plunged against the Sphinx
The top of the Empire State
arrowed in a broccoli field in Sicily
Eiffel shaped like a C in Magnolia Gardens
St. Sophia peeling over Sudan
O athletic Death   Sportive Bomb

The temples of ancient times
their grand ruin ceased
Electrons   Protons   Neutrons
gathering Hesperean hair
walking the dolorous golf of Arcady
joining marble helmsmen
entering the final amphitheater
with a hymnody feeling of all Troys
heralding cypressean torches
racing plumes and banners
yet knowing Homer with a step of grace
Lo the visiting team of Present
the home team of Past
Lyre and tuba together joined
Hark the hotdog soda olive grape
gala galaxy robed and uniformed
commissary   O the happy stands
Ethereal root and cheer and boo
The billioned all-time attendance
The Zeusian pandemonium
Hermes racing Owens
the Spitball of Buddha
Christ striking out
Luther stealing third
Planetarium Death   Hosannah Bomb
Gush the final rose   O Spring Bomb
Come with thy gown of dynamite green
unmenace Nature's inviolate eye
Before you the wimpled Past
behind you the hallooing Future   O Bomb
Bound in the grassy clarion air
like the fox of the tally-ho
thy field the universe thy hedge the geo
Leap Bomb   bound Bomb   frolic zig and zag
The stars a swarm of bees in thy binging bag
Stick angels on your jubilee feet
wheels of rainlight on your bunky seat
You are due and behold you are due
and the heavens are with you
hosannah incalescent glorious liaison

BOMB O havoc antiphony molten cleft BOOM
Bomb mark infinity a sudden furnace
spread thy multitudinous encompassed Sweep
set forth awful agenda
Carrion stars   charnel planets   carcass elements
Corpse the universe   tee-hee finger-in-the-mouth hop
over its long long dead Nor
From thy nimbled matted spastic eye
exhaust deluges of celestial ghouls
From thy appellational womb
spew birth-gusts of great worms
Rip open your belly Bomb
from your belly outflock vulturic salutations
Battle forth your spangled hyena finger stumps
along the brink of Paradise
O Bomb   O final Pied Piper
both sun and firefly behind your shock waltz
God abandoned mock-nude
beneath His thin false-talc'd apocalypse
He cannot hear thy flute's
happy-the-day profanations
He is spilled deaf into the Silencer's warty ear
His Kingdom an eternity of crude wax
Clogged clarions untrumpet Him
Sealed angels unsing Him
A thunderless God   A dead God
O Bomb   thy BOOM His tomb
That I lean forward on a desk of science
an astrologer dabbling in dragon prose
half-smart about wars   bombs   especially bombs
That I am unable to hate what is necessary to love
That I can't exist in a world that consents
a child in a park   a man dying in an electric-chair
That I am able to laugh at all things
all that I know and do not know   thus to conceal my pain
That I say I am a poet and therefore love all man
knowing my words to be the acquainted prophecy of all men
and my unwords no less an acquaintanceship
That I am manifold
a man pursuing the big lies of gold

or a poet roaming in bright ashes
or that which I imagine myself to be
a shark-toothed sleep   a man-eater of dreams
I need not then be all-smart about bombs
Happily so   for if I felt bombs were caterpillars
I'd doubt not they'd become butterflies
There is a hell for bombs
They're there   I see them there
They sit in bits and sing songs
mostly German songs
and two very long American songs
and they wish there were more songs
especially Russian and Chinese songs
and some more very long American songs
Poor little Bomb that'll never be
an Eskimo song   I love thee
I want to put a lollipop
in thy furcal mouth
A wig of Goldilocks on thy baldy bean
and have you skip with me Hansel and Gretel
along the Hollywoodian screen
O Bomb in which all lovely things
moral and physical anxiously participate
O fairyflake plucked from the
grandest universe tree
O piece of heaven which gives
both mountain and anthill a sun
I am standing before your fantastic lily door
I bring you Midgardian roses   Arcadian musk
Reputed cosmetics from the girls of heaven
Welcome me   fear not thy opened door
nor thy cold ghost's grey memory
nor the pimps of indefinite weather
their cruel terrestrial thaw
Oppenheimer is seated
in the dark pocket of Light
Fermi is dry in Death's Mozambique
Einstein his mythmouth
a barnacled wreath on the moon-squid's head
Let me in   Bomb   rise from that pregnant-rat corner

nor fear the raised-broom nations of the world
O Bomb I love you
I want to kiss your clank   eat your boom
You are a paean   an acme of scream
a lyric hat of Mister Thunder
O resound thy tanky knees
BOOM   BOOM   BOOM   BOOM   BOOM
BOOM ye skies and BOOM ye suns
BOOM BOOM ye moons   ye stars BOOM
nights ye BOOM   ye days ye BOOM
BOOM BOOM ye winds   ye clouds ye rains
go BANG ye lakes   ye oceans BING
Barracuda BOOM and cougar BOOM
Ubangi BANG   orangoutang
BING BANG BONG BOOM   bee bear baboon
ye BANG ye BONG ye BING
the tail the fin the wing
Yes   Yes   into our midst a bomb will fall
Flowers will leap in joy their roots aching
Fields will kneel proud beneath the halleluyahs of the wind
Pinkbombs will blossom   Elkbombs will perk their ears
Ah many a bomb that day will awe the bird a gentle look
Yet   not enough to say a bomb will fall
or even contend celestial fire goes out
Know that the earth will madonna the Bomb
that in the hearts of men to come more bombs will be born
magisterial bombs wrapped in ermine   all beautiful
and they'll sit plunk on earth's grumpy empires
fierce with moustaches of gold
*
*   *

Peter Orlovsky

1933–

FRIST POEM

A rainbow comes pouring into my window, I am electrified.
Songs burst from my breast, all my crying stops, mistory fills
    the air.
I look for my shues under my bed.
A fat colored woman becomes my mother.
I have no false teeth yet. Suddenly ten children sit on my lap.
I grow a beard in one day.
I drink a hole bottle of wine with my eyes shut.
I draw on paper and I feel I am two again. I want everybody to
    talk to me.
I empty the garbage on the tabol.
I invite thousands of bottles into my room, June bugs I call them.
I use the typewritter as my pillow.
A spoon becomes a fork before my eyes.
Bums give all their money to me.
All I need is a mirror for the rest of my life.
My first five years I lived in chicken coups with not enough
    bacon.
My mother showed her witch face in the night and told stories of
    blue beards.
My dreams lifted me right out of my bed.
I dreamt I jumped into the nozzle of a gun to fight it out with a
    bullet.

I met Kafka and he jumped over a building to get away from me.
My body turned into sugar, poured into tea I found the meaning
    of life
All I needed was ink to be a black boy.
I walk on the street looking for eyes that will caress my face.
I sang in the elevators believing I was going to heaven.
I got off at the 86th floor, walked down the corridor looking for
    fresh butts.
My comes turns into a silver dollar on the bed.
I look out the window and see nobody, I go down to the street,
    look up at my window and see nobody.
So I talk to the fire hydrant, asking "Do you have bigger tears
    then I do?"
Nobody around, I piss anywhere.
My Gabriel horns, my Gabriel horns: unfold the cheerfulies,
    my gay jubilation.

24 November 1957, Paris

SECOND POEM

Morning again, nothing has to be done,
               maybe buy a piano or make fudge.
At least clean the room up for sure like my farther I've done flick
            the ashes & butts over the bed side on the floor.
But frist of all wipe my glasses and drink the water
          to clean the smelly mouth.
A nock on the door, a cat walks in, behind her the Zoo's baby
    elephant demanding fresh pancakes—I cant stand these
    hallucinations aney more.
Time for another cigerette and then let the curtains rise, then I
    knowtice the dirt makes a road to the garbage pan –
No ice box so a dried up grapefruit.
Is there any one saintly thing I can do to my room, paint it pink
    maybe or instal an elevator from the bed to the floor,
    maybe take a bath on the bed?
Whats the use of liveing if I cant make paradise in my own
    room-land?
For this drop of time upon my eyes
like the endurance of a red star on a cigerate

makes me feel life splits faster than sissors.
I know if I could shave myself the bugs around my face would
 disappear forever.
The holes in my shues are only temporary, I understand that.
My rug is dirty but whose that isent?
There comes a time in life when everybody must take a piss in
 the sink – here let me paint the window black for a minute.
Thro a plate & brake it out of naughtiness – or maybe just
 innocently accidentally drop it wile walking around the
 tabol.
Before the mirror I look like a sahara desert gost,
 or on the bed I resemble a crying mummey hollaring for air,
 or on the tabol I feel like Napoleon.
But now for the main task of the day – wash my underwear –
 two months abused – what would the ants say about that?
How can I wash my clothes – why I'd, I'd, I'd be a woman if I did
 that.
No, I'd rather polish my sneakers than that and as for the floor
 its more creative to paint it then clean it up.
As for the dishes I can do that for I am thinking of getting a job in
 a lunchenette.
My life and my room are like two huge bugs following me
 around the globe.
Thank god I have an innocent eye for nature.
I was born to remember a song about love – on a hill a butterfly
 makes a cup that I drink from, walking over a bridge of
 flowers.

27 December 1957, Paris

CREEDMOOR STATE MENTAL HOSPITAL NIGHT SHIFT LOOK & MOP

By now hes dead & burried
 in the corner of my eye –
He was an old italian in the mad house
ward – every day I would see him –
Half blind & a palsy hand
 dressed in grey state robe –
Almost morning I meet him

he would say come, Peter – take me to the subway –
　　give me a
nickle – we go to my old
　　Barber shop – come, lets go now
One day I said ok & led him down the hall
　letting him believe I was takeing him to Brooklyn
　　but when we reached the door –
　　I was only an attendant
　　　not a doctor –
Hes a dead man now & burried
in the corner of my eye
& he taught me two italian words
Pichada & mangia
Piss & food

1959 NYC

SIGNATURE CHANGED!

A guy who, me, has a Bank
accound & writes his frist
signatures for Bank man & then
after months of drawing
with checks on his account,
one day, changes his signature.
inch long Y & Box R with
one line, right comeing
down more then left line.
Bank refuses to accept his
new checks this is not Mr
Orlovsky we Know who his
old good Signature – Mr. O
now cant remember old good
signature & Bank man wont
show him – hopeless lost
monney – poor trouble –

1960 NYC

THE SAN FRANCISCO SCENE:
1954–57

GARY SNYDER
1930–

RIPRAP

Lay down these words
Before your mind like rocks.
          placed solid, by hands
In choice of place, set
Before the body of the mind
          in space and time:
Solidity of bark, leaf, or wall
          riprap of things:
Cobble of milky way,
          straying planets,
These poems, people,
          lost ponies with
Dragging saddles –
          and rocky sure-foot trails.
The worlds like an endless
          four-dimensional
Game of *Go*.
          ants and pebbles
In the thin loam, each rock a word
          a creek-washed stone
Granite; ingrained
          with torment of fire and weight

Crystal and sediment linked hot
       all change, in thoughts,
As well as things.

FOR A FAR-OUT FRIEND

Because I once beat you up
Drunk, stung with weeks of torment
And saw you no more,
And you had calm talk for me today
     I now suppose
I was less sane than you,
You hung on dago red,
     me hooked on books.
You once ran naked toward me
Knee deep in cold March surf
On a tricky beach between two
     pounding seastacks –
I saw you as a Hindu Deva-girl
Light legs dancing in the waves,
Breasts like dream breasts
Of sea, and child, and astral
     Venus-spurting milk.
And traded our salt lips.

Visions of your body
Kept me high for weeks, I even had
     a sort of trance for you
A day in a dentist's chair.
I found you again, gone stone,
In Zimmer's book of Indian Art:
Dancing in that life with
Grace and love, with rings and
A little golden belt, just above
     your naked snatch,
And I thought – more grace and love
In that wild Deva life where you belong,
Than in this dress-and-girdle life
You'll ever give
Or get.

(from MYTHS & TEXTS) 17: THE TEXT

Sourdough mountain called a fire in:
Up Thunder Creek, high on a ridge.
Hiked eighteen hours, finally found
A snag and a hundred feet around on fire:
All afternoon and into night
Digging the fire line
Falling the burning snag
It fanned sparks down like shooting stars
Over the dry woods, starting spot-fires
Flaring in wind up Skagit valley
From the Sound.
Toward morning it rained.
We slept in mud and ashes,
Woke at dawn, the fire was out,
The sky was clear, we saw
The last glimmer of the morning star.

the myth

Fire up Thunder Creek and the mountain –
                    troy's burning!
The cloud mutters

The mountains are your mind.
The woods bristle there,
Dogs barking and children shrieking
Rise from below.

Rain falls for centuries
Soaking the loose rocks in space
Sweet rain, the fire's out
The black snag glistens in the rain
& the last wisp of smoke floats up
Into the absolute cold
Into the spiral whorls of fire
The storms of the Milky Way
"Buddha incense in an empty world"
Black pit cold and light-year
Flame tongue of the dragon
Licks the sun

The sun is but a morning star

Crater Mt. L. O. 1952 – Marin-an 1956

PHILIP WHALEN
1923–2002

SOURDOUGH MOUNTAIN LOOKOUT

For Kenneth Rexroth

I always say I won't go back to the mountains
I am too old and fat there are bugs mean mules
And pancakes every morning of the world

Mr. Edward Wyman (63)
Steams along the trail ahead of us all
Moaning, "My poor old feet ache, my back
Is tired and I've got a stiff prick"
Uprooting alder shoots in the rain

Then I'm alone in a glass house on a ridge
Encircled by chiming mountains
With one sun roaring through the house all day
& the others crashing through the glass all night
Conscious even while sleeping

Morning fog in the southern gorge
Gleaming foam restoring the old sea-level
The lakes in two lights: green soap & indigo
The high cirque-lake black half-open eye.

Ptarmigan hunt for bugs in the snow
Bear peers through the wall at noon
Deer crowd up to see the lamp
A mouse nearly drowns in the honey
I see my bootprints mingle with deer-foot
Bear-paw mule-shoe in the dusty path to the privy

Much later I write down:
    "raging.   Viking sunrise
    The gorgeous death of summer in the east"
(Influence of a Byronic landscape
Bent pages exhibiting depravity of style.)

Outside the lookout I lay nude on the granite
Mountain hot September sun but inside my head
Calm dark night with all the other stars

HERACLITUS: "The waking have one common world
But the sleeping turn aside
Each into a world of his own."

I keep telling myself what I really like
Are music, books, certain land and sea-scapes
The way light falls across them, diffusion of
Light through agate, light itself . . . I suppose
I'm still afraid of the dark

      "Remember smart-guy there's something
      Bigger something smarter than you."
      Ireland's fear of unknown holies drives
      My father's voice (a country neither he
      Nor his great-grandfather ever saw)

      A sparkly tomb a plated grave
      A holy thumb beneath a wave

Everything else they hauled across Atlantic
Scattered and lost in the buffalo plains
Among these trees and mountains

From Duns Scotus to this page
A thousand years
   ("... a dog walking on his hind legs –
   not that he does it well but that he
   Does it at all.")

Virtually a blank except for the hypothesis
That there is more to a man
Than the contents of his jock-strap

EMPEDOCLES: "At one time all the limbs
Which are the body's portion are brought together
By love in blooming life's high season; at another
Severed by cruel Strife, they wander each alone
By the breakers of life's sea."

Fire and pressure from the sun bear down
Bear down centipede shadow of palm-frond
A limestone lithograph – oysters and clams of stone

Half a black rock bomb displaying brilliant crystals
Fire and pressure Love and Strife bear down
Brontosaurus, look away

My sweat runs down the rock

HERACLITUS: "The transformations of fire
are, first of all, sea; and half of the sea
is earth, half whirlwind. . . . .
It scatters and it gathers; it advances
and retires."

I move out of a sweaty pool
   (The sea!)
And sit up higher on the rock

Is anything burning?

The sun itself! Dying
Pooping out, exhausted

Having produced brontosaurus, Heraclitus
This rock, me,
To no purpose

I tell you anyway (as a kind of loving) . . .
Flies & other insects come from miles around
To listen
I also address the rock, the heather,
The alpine fir

BUDDHA: "All the constituents of being are
Transitory: Work out your salvation with diligence."

(And everything, as one eminent disciple of that master
Pointed out, has been tediously complex ever since.)

There was a bird
Lived in an egg
And by ingenious chemistry
Wrought molecules of albumen
To beak and eye
Gizzard and craw
Feather and claw

My grandmother said:
"Look at them poor *bed*-
raggled pigeons!"

And the sign in McAlister Street:

>   "IF YOU CAN'T COME IN
>   SMILE AS YOU GO BY
>
>   L♡VE
>   THE BUTCHER

I destroy myself, the universe (an egg)
And time – to get an answer:
There are a smiler, a sleeper and a dancer

We repeat our conversation in the glittering dark

Floating beside the sleeper.
The child remarks, "You knew it all the time."
I: "I keep forgetting that the smiler is
Sleeping; the sleeper, dancing."

From Sauk Lookout two years before
Some of the view was down the Skagit
To Puget Sound: From above the lower ranges,
Deep in forest—lighthouses on clear nights.

This year's rock is a spur from the main range
Cuts the valley in two and is broken
By the river;   Ross dam repairs the break,
Makes trolley buses run
Through the streets of dim Seattle far away.

I'm surrounded by mountains here
A circle of 108 beads, originally seeds
       of *ficus religiosa*
              BO-Tree
A circle, continuous, one odd bead
Larger than the rest and bearing
A tassel (hair-tuft) (the man who sat
       under the tree)
In the center of the circle,
A void, an empty figure containing
All that's multiplied;
Each bead a repetition, a world
Of ignorance and sleep.

Today is the day the goose gets cooked
Day of liberation for the crumbling flower
Knobcone pinecone in the flames
Brandy in the sun

Which, as I said, will disappear
Anyway it'll be invisible soon
Exchanging places with stars now in my head
To be growing rice in China through the night.
Magnetic storms across the solar plains

Make aurora borealis shimmy bright
Beyond the mountains to the north.

Closing the lookout in the morning
Thick ice on the shutters
Coyote almost whistling on a nearby ridge

The mountain is THERE (between two lakes)
I brought back a piece of its rock
Heavy dark-honey-color
With a seam of crystal, some of the quartz
Stained by its matrix
Practically indestructible
A shift from opacity to brilliance
(The zenbos say, "Lightning-flash & flint-spark")
Like the mountains where it was made

What we see of the world is the mind's
Invention and the mind
Though stained by it, becoming
Rivers, sun, mule-dung, flies –
Can shift instantly
A dirty bird in a square time
Gone   Gate
Gone   Gate
Really gone   Paragate
Into the cool.   Parasamgate
Oh Mama!   Svaha!

Like they say, "Four times up,
Three times down." I'm still on the mountain.

1955–56

FURTHER NOTICE

I can't live in this world
And I refuse to kill myself
Or let you kill me

The dill plant lives, the airplane

My alarm clock, this ink
I won't go away

I shall be myself—
Free, a genius, an embarrassment
Like the Indian, the buffalo

Like Yellowstone National Park.

22:ix:56

LEW WELCH

1926–1971

CHICAGO POEM

I lived here nearly 5 years before I could
      meet the middle western day with anything approaching
Dignity. It's a place that lets you
      understand why the Bible is the way it is:
Proud people cannot live here.

The land's too flat. Ugly sullen and big it
      pounds men down past humbleness. They
Stoop at 35 possibly cringing from the heavy and
      terrible sky. In country like this there
Can be no God but Jahweh.

In the mills and refineries of its south side Chicago
      passes its natural gas in flames
Bouncing like bunsens from stacks a hundred feet high.
      The stench stabs at your eyeballs.
The whole sky green and yellow backdrop for the skeleton
      steel of a bombed-out town.

Remember the movies in grammar school? The goggled men
    doing strong things in
Showers of steel-spark? The dark screen cracking light
    and the furnace door opening with a
Blast of orange like a sunset? Or an orange?

It was photographed by a fairy, thrilled as a girl, or
    a Nazi who wished there were people
Behind that door (hence the remote beauty), but Sievers,
    whose old man spent most of his life in there,
Remembers a "nigger in a red T-shirt pissing into the
    black sand."

It was 5 years until I could afford to recognize the ferocity.
    Friends helped me. Then I put some
Love into my house. Finally I found some quiet lakes
    and a farm where they let me shoot pheasant.
Standing in the boat one night I watched the lake go absolutely
    flat. Smaller than raindrops, and only
Here and there, the feeding rings of fish were visible 100 yards
    away – and the Blue Gill caught that afternoon
Lifted from its northern lake like a tropical! Jewel at its ear
    Belly gold so bright you'd swear he had a
Light in there. His color faded with his life. A small
    green fish. . .

All things considered, it's a gentle and undemanding
    planet, even here. Far gentler
Here than any of a dozen other places. The trouble is
    always and only with what we build on top of it.

There's nobody else to blame. You can't fix it and you
    can't make it go away. It does no good appealing
To some ill-invented Thunderer
    Brooding above some unimaginable crag . . .

It's ours. Right down to the last small hinge it
    all depends for its existence
Only and utterly upon our sufferance.

Driving back I saw Chicago rising in its gases and I
    knew again that never will the
Man be made to stand against this pitiless, unparalleled
    monstrocity. It
Snuffles on the beach of its Great Lake like a
    blind, red, rhinoceros.
It's already running us down.

You can't fix it. You can't make it go away.
    I don't know what you're going to do about it,
But I know what I'm going to do about it. I'm just
    going to walk away from it. Maybe
A small part of it will die if I'm not around

    feeding it anymore.

IN ANSWER TO A QUESTION FROM P. W.

In Mexico I'll finish the novel I'll write, rough, while
    fire-watching in Oregon.
The problem is, what kind of typewriter to pack in?

I ought to be able to live 6 months in Mexico on what I
    earn on the Mountain in 4.
They say you can buy dirty books down there.

Since they give you horses to pack things in, how would it
    be if I took in a big old typewriter and left it there?
They don't give you horses to pack things out.

Going to Mexico by motorcycle would be the coolest, but
    Thoreau warns against any undertaking that
    requires new clothes.
Walking is pure, but I haven't achieved simplicity yet.
I'll never willingly hitchhike again.

Next winter I can buy Snyder's Austin for $200, but how
    can I get the money together?
They repossessed my Oldsmobile.
I've never made the foreign-country scene.

Like the sign over the urinal: "You hold your future
     in your hand."
Or what the giant black whore once said, in the back of my cab:

> *"Man, you sure do love diggin' at my*
> *titties, now stop that. We get where*
> *we going you can milk me like a*
> *Holstein, but I gotta see your*
> *money first."*

[I SAW MYSELF]

I saw myself
a ring of bone
in the clear stream
of all of it

and vowed,
always to be open to it
that all of it
might flow through

and then heard
"ring of bone" where
ring is what a

bell does

WOBBLY ROCK

> *for Gary Snyder*
>
> *"I think I'll be the Buddha of this place"*
>
> *and sat himself*
> *down*

    1.
It's a real rock

     (believe this first)

Resting on actual sand at the surf's edge:
Muir Beach, California

    (like everything else I have
    somebody showed it to me and I found it by myself)

Hard common stone
Size of the largest haystack
It moves when hit by waves
Actually shudders

    (even a good gust of wind will do it
    if you sit real still and keep your mouth shut)

Notched to certain center it
Yields and then comes back to it:

Wobbly tons

TAXI SUITE

1. AFTER ANACREON

When I drive cab
    I am moved by strange whistles and wear a hat.

When I drive cab
    I am the hunter. My prey leaps out from where it
    hid, beguiling me with gestures.

When I drive cab
    all may command me, yet I am in command of all who do.

When I drive cab
    I am guided by voices descending from the naked air.

When I drive cab
    A revelation of movement comes to me. They wake now.

Now they want to work or look around. Now they want
drunkenness and heavy food. Now they contrive to love.

When I drive cab
    I bring the sailor home from the sea. In the back of
    my car he fingers the pelt of his maiden.

When I drive cab
    I watch for stragglers in the urban order of things.

When I drive cab
    I end the only lit and waitful thing in miles of
    darkened houses.

[I KNOW A MAN'S SUPPOSED TO HAVE HIS HAIR CUT SHORT]

I know a man's supposed to have his hair cut short,
but I have beautiful hair.
I like to let it grow into a long bronze mane.

In my boots. In my blue wool shirt.
With my rifle slung over my shoulder
among huge boulders in the dark ravine,

I'm the ghost roan stallion.
Leif Ericson.
The beautiful Golden Girl!

In summer I usually cut it all off.
I do it myself, with scissors and a
little Jim Beam.

How disappointed everybody is.

Months and months go by before they can
worry about my hairdo

and the breeze
is so cool

Michael McClure
1932—

FROM THE INTRODUCTION TO GHOST TANTRAS:

Poetry is a muscular principle and a revolution for the body-spirit
and intellect and ear. Making images and pictures, even when
speaking with melody, is not enough. There must be a poetry of
pure beauty and energy that does not mimic but joins and exhorts
reality and states the daily higher vision. To dim the senses and
listen to inner energies a-roar is sometimes called the religious experience. It does not matter what it is called. Laughter as well as love
is passion. The loveliness the nose snuffs in air may be translated to
sound by interior perceptive organs. The touch of velvet on the fingertips may become a cry when time is stopped. Speed like calmness
may become a pleasure or gentle muffled sound. A dahlia or fern
might become pure speech in meditation. A woman's body might
become the sound of worship. A goddess lies coiled at the base of
man's body, and pure tantric sound might awaken her. There are no
laws but living changing ones, and any system is a touch of death.

Read these poems as you would Lorca, or Mayakovsky, or
Lawrence but READ ALOUD AND SING THEM.

These are spontaneous stanzas published in the order and with the
natural sounds in which they were first written. If there is an
"OOOOOOOOOOOOOOH" simply say a long loud "oooh". If
there is a "gahr" simply say gar and put an h in.

Look at stanza 51. It begins in English and turns into beast language—star becomes stahr. Body becomes boody. Nose becomes noze. Everybody knows how to pronounce NOH or VOOR-NAH or GAHROOOOO ME.

Pronounce sounds as they are spelled and don't worry about details—let individual pronunciations and vibrations occur and don't look for secret meanings. Read them aloud and there will be more pleasure.

GHOST TANTRA 39

MARILYN MONROE, TODAY THOU HAST PASSED
THE DARK BARRIER
—diving in a swirl of golden hair.
I hope you have entered a sacred paradise for full
warm bodies, full lips, full hips, and laughing eyes!
AHH GHROOOR. ROOOHR. NOH THAT OHH!
OOOH...
Farewell perfect mammal.
Fare thee well from thy silken couch and dark day!
AHH GRHHROOOR! AHH ROOOOH. GARR
nah ooth eeze farewell. Moor droon fahra rahoor
rahoor, rahoor. Thee ahh-oh oh thahrr
noh grooh rahhr.

GHOST TANTRA 51

I LOVE TO THINK OF THE RED PURPLE ROSE
IN THE DARKNESS COOLED BY THE NIGHT.
We are served by machines making satins
of sounds.
Each blot of sound is a bud or a stahr.
Body eats bouquets of the ear's vista.
Gahhhrrr boody eers noze eyes deem thou.
NOH. NAH-OHH
hrooor. VOOOR-NAH! GAHROOOOO ME.
Nah droooooh seerch. NAH THEE!
The machines are too dull when we
are lion-poems that move & breathe.

WHAN WE GROOOOOOOOOOOOOOOOR
hann dree myketoth sharoo sreee thah noh deeeeeemed ez.
Whan eeeethoooze hrohh.

A GARLAND

OH LET LOVE OH ME LOVE OH LET LOVE YOUR SWEET
BONES AND BREASTS
sweet slim round arms and firm ass. Touch you
where you swell. Kiss your soft flesh. Make meat
of you and bite your pale lips. Push my finger
in you, BODY, warm where. Oh let me lick. I kiss
your slim fingers. Kiss you in your hair and bite
your waist. Feel the skin of you like lace moved and
torn by the touch of what I make to you. And press
your shoulder. Hug your back
to me. And slip my dry cock under your moist ass,
and bite you on the neck. Rub your
belly with my hand and finger your lips
and hole. OH LET LOVE OH ME.
I want it.

OH LIE OH LET LOVE DOWN BEFORE ME SPREAD YOUR
HAIR LONG
on the pillow. Black pantied, no nake! Open
your eyes and mouth wide. Your dark eyes and hair
over the pillow. Leave your long white-pink open
spread before me. With a picture of Jesus beside
on the bedstead. And mouth open smile, I
climb and hunch over your face. Fondle my cock
and lick my balls beneath your chin! No
I hurry. Open your mouth wide your
red mouth, your white teeth the pink roof
of your throat. Your long hair spread
on the pillow.

OH SMIRKING SMILE OH OH MURKY HOLE BE GONE BE
LOVE
invented. Be enormous as a fuck. Fucked arm,
fucked mouth and ass. Let me lick salty
water from your belly. Let me run my stiff
cock between your breasts, beneath your arm.
I suck your tits and ears. Tongue your
clitoris. Dream and lie upon your belly, push
my fingers in your hole and feel your ass,
and you lick and suck my
soft cock to make it hard again.
!THIS IS A CLASP!
Hold my balls in your mouth and breathe
upon my ass. Lick come from my fingers. Jack
me off. Smell yourself upon my hands
and prick. I bite the arm you slip beneath
my back.
I plunge within the hole you open
there before me. Feel your cunt pull open
wide.
OH SMIRKING SMILE OH OH MURKY HOLE BE GONE BE
LOVE

OH LET OH LIE LOVE SLIP DOWN ON YOUR KNEES AND
BLOW ME
See your mouth pushed open spread with the size
of the thing in it. See your lovely face misshapen
into new beauty. Feel the hard slick thing
in it. Feel the pink head of it
back in your throat! Down on your knees
before me. Hands held to your cheeks and ears,
your long soft legs folded under you. Only
warm damp wet moist mouth hot hot with my cock
in it. Working to make me come, eyes flashing
upward. Seeing the arms held to your cheeks to feel
the cock pushing inside them. Seeing
my face above. Hearing the groan. Catching
the shot splash of come on your tongue.

LIE OH HUNCH OH LOVE CLIMB OVER ME PUT YOUR ASS
                                              OVER
        my face put your mouth over my cock. I look up
    into your asshole and hole! I feel your lips and teeth
        on my cock. Tongue I put against your asshole,
      your sweet asscheeks I spread with my hands. Tip
        tongue I move over the crease circled hole, feel
        you relax and slip it inside. And feel your tense
      of shame. Sleek clean inner asshole. Put my tongue
      to your cunt and lick upward, the whole crease.
  Tongue over hole tongue over asshole. One hand kneading
              your breast. Feeling your hair
                  and breath on my toes.

MAD SONNET

THE PLUMES OF LOVE ARE BLACK! THE PLUMES OF LOVE
                                    ARE BLACK
            AND DELICATE! OH!
    and shine like moron-eyed plumes of a peacock
      with violetshine and yellow on shadowy black.
They spray SPRAY from the body of the Beloved. Vanes shaking
                                              in air!

AND I DO NOT WANT BLACK PLUMES OR AGONY. . .
                                    AND I DO
      NOT SURRENDER. And I ask for noble combat!!
              to give pure Love
              as best I can
              with opened heart
                  LOVE!!
        I have not seen you before and you're
            more beautiful than a plume!

      Stately, striding in Space and warm . . . (Your
            human breasts!)
LET ME MAKE YOUR SMILE AND HEARTSHAPED FACE
                                    IMMORTAL

YOUR GRAY EYES ARE WHAT I FINALLY COME TO
WITH MY BROWN!
AND YOUR HIGH CHEEKS, and your hair rough
for a woman's – like a lamb. And the walking Virtue
that you are!

LAWRENCE FERLINGHETTI
1919–

LOUD PRAYER

Our father whose art's in heaven
hollow be thy name
unless things change
Thy wigdom come and gone
thy will will be undone
on earth as it isn't heaven
Give us this day our daily bread
at least three times a day
and forgive us our trespasses
as we would forgive those lovelies
whom we wish would trespass against us
And lead us not into temptation
too often on weekdays
but deliver us from evil
whose presence remains unexplained
in thy kingdom of power and glory
oh man

UNDERWEAR

I didn't get much sleep last night
thinking about underwear
Have you ever stopped to consider
underwear in the abstract
When you really dig into it
some shocking problems are raised
Underwear is something
we all have to deal with
Everyone wears
some kind of underwear
Even Indians
wear underwear
Even Cubans
wear underwear
The Pope wears underwear I hope
Underwear is worn by Negroes
The Governor of Louisiana
wears underwear
I saw him on TV
He must have had tight underwear
He squirmed a lot
Underwear can really get you in a bind
Negroes often wear
white underwear
which may lead to trouble
You have seen the underwear ads
for men and women
so alike but so different
Women's underwear holds things up
Men's underwear holds things down
Underwear is one thing
men and women have in common
Underwear is all we have between us
You have seen the three-color pictures
with crotches encircled
to show the areas of extra strength
and three-way stretch
promising full freedom of action

Don't be deceived
It's all based on the two-party system
which doesn't allow much freedom of choice
the way things are set up
America in its Underwear
struggles thru the night
Underwear controls everything in the end
Take foundation garments for instance
They are really fascist forms
of underground government
making people believe
something but the truth
telling you what you can or can't do
Did you ever try to get around a girdle
Perhaps Non-Violent Action
is the only answer
Did Gandhi wear a girdle?
Did Lady Macbeth wear a girdle?
Was that why Macbeth murdered sleep?
And that spot she was always rubbing—
Was it really in her underwear?
Modern anglosaxon ladies
must have huge guilt complexes
always washing and washing and washing
Out damned spot—rub don't blot—
Underwear with spots very suspicious
Underwear with bulges very shocking
Underwear on clothesline a great flag of freedom
Someone has escaped his Underwear
May be naked somewhere
Help!
But don't worry
Everybody's still hung up in it
There won't be no real revolution
And poetry still the underwear of the soul
And underwear still covering
a multitude of faults
in the geological sense—
strange sedimentary stones, inscrutable cracks!
And that only the beginning

For does not the body stay alive
after death
and still need its underwear
or outgrow it
some organs said to reach full maturity
only after the head stops holding them back?
If I were you I'd keep aside
an oversize pair of winter underwear
Do not go naked into that good night
And in the meantime
keep calm and warm and dry
No use stirring ourselves up prematurely
'over Nothing'
Move forward with dignity
hand in vest
Don't get emotional
And death shall have no dominion
There's plenty of time my darling
Are we not still young and easy
Don't shout

SOMETIME DURING ETERNITY ...

      Sometime during eternity
                 some guys show up
and one of them
         who shows up real late
             is a kind of carpenter
    from some square-type place
           like Galilee
      and he starts wailing
         and claiming he is hip
     to who made heaven
         and earth
            and that the cat
      who really laid it on us
           is his Dad

And moreover
        he adds
                It's all writ down
                        on some scroll-type parchments
        which some henchmen
                leave lying around the Dead Sea somewheres
            a long time ago
                        and which you won't even find
    for a coupla thousand years or so
                        or at least for
        nineteen hundred and fortyseven
                            of them
            to be exact
                    and even then
        nobody really believes them
                    or me
                        for that matter

    You're hot
            they tell him

    And they cool him

    They stretch him on the Tree to cool
        And everybody after that
                        is always making models
            of this Tree
                    with Him hung up
    and always crooning His name
                        and calling Him to come down
            and sit in
                    on their combo
        as if he is *the* king cat
                    who's got to blow
        or they can't quite make it

    Only he don't come down
                    from His Tree

Him just hang there
    on His Tree
       looking real Petered out
    and real cool
      and also
   according to a roundup
       of late world news
  from the usual unreliable sources
       real dead

THEY WERE PUTTING UP THE STATUE . . .

They were putting up the statue
  of Saint Francis
 in front of the church
 of Saint Francis
   in the city of San Francisco
in a little side street
    just off the Avenue
       where no birds sang
  and the sun was coming up on time
       in its usual fashion
   and just beginning to shine
      on the statue of Saint Francis
   where no birds sang
  And a lot of old Italians
     were standing all around
  in the little side street
     just off the Avenue
   watching the wily workers
     who were hoisting up the statue
  with a chain and a crane
    and other implements
  And a lot of young reporters
     in button-down clothes
  were taking down the words
     of one young priest
  who was propping up the statue

                             with all his arguments
         And all the while
                  while no birds sang
                         any Saint Francis Passion
and while the lookers kept looking
                    up at Saint Francis
       with his arms outstretched
                     to the birds which weren't there
a very tall and very purely naked
                  young virgin
     with very long and very straight
                straw hair
       and wearing only a very small
                     bird's nest
      in a very existential place
                   kept passing thru the crowd
                         all the while
        and up and down the steps
                    in front of Saint Francis
     her eyes downcast all the while
                    and singing to herself

CONSTANTLY RISKING ABSURDITY . . .

      Constantly risking absurdity
                    and death
         whenever he performs
                above the heads
                    of his audience
  the poet like an acrobat
          climbs on rime
              to a high wire of his own making
and balancing on eyebeams
           above a sea of faces
      paces his way
           to the other side of day
    performing entrechats
             and sleight-of-foot tricks
  and other high theatrics

and all without mistaking
any thing
for what it may not be

For he's the super realist
who must perforce perceive
taut truth
before the taking of each stance or step
in his supposed advance
toward that still higher perch
where Beauty stands and waits
with gravity
to start her death-defying leap

And he
a little charleychaplin man
who may or may not catch
her fair eternal form
spreadeagled in the empty air
of existence

AUTOBIOGRAPHY

I am leading a quiet life
in Mike's Place every day
watching the champs
of the Dante Billiard Parlor
and the French pinball addicts.
I am leading a quiet life
on lower East Broadway.
I am an American.
I was an American boy.
I read the American Boy Magazine
and became a boy scout
in the suburbs.
I thought I was Tom Sawyer
catching crayfish in the Bronx River
and imagining the Mississippi.
I had a baseball mit

and an American Flyer bike.
I delivered the Woman's Home Companion
at five in the afternoon
or the Herald Trib
at five in the morning.
I still can hear the paper thump
on lost porches.
I had an unhappy childhood.
I saw Lindberg land.
I looked homeward
and saw no angel.
I got caught stealing pencils
from the Five and Ten Cent Store
the same month I made Eagle Scout.
I chopped trees for the CCC
and sat on them.
I landed in Normandy
in a rowboat that turned over.
I have seen the educated armies
on the beach at Dover.
I have seen Egyptian pilots in purple clouds
shopkeepers rolling up their blinds
at midday
potato salad and dandelions
at anarchist picnics.
I am reading 'Lorna Doone'
and a life of John Most
terror of the industrialist
a bomb on his desk at all times.
I have seen the garbagemen parade
in the Columbus Day Parade
behind the glib
farting trumpeters.
I have not been out to the Cloisters
in a long time
nor to the Tuileries
but I still keep thinking
of going.
I have seen the garbagemen parade
when it was snowing.

I have eaten hotdogs in ballparks.
I have heard the Gettysburg Address
and the Ginsberg Address.
I like it here
and I won't go back
where I came from.
I too have ridden boxcars boxcars boxcars.
I have travelled among unknown men.
I have been in Asia
with Noah in the Ark.
I was in India
when Rome was built.
I have been in the Manger
with an Ass.
I have seen the Eternal Distributor
from a White Hill
in South San Francisco
and the Laughing Woman at Loona Park
outside the Fun House
in a great rainstorm
still laughing.
I have heard the sound of revelry
by night.
I have wandered lonely
as a crowd.
I am leading a quiet life
outside of Mike's Place every day
watching the world walk by
in its curious shoes.
I once started out
to walk around the world
but ended up in Brooklyn.
That Bridge was too much for me.
I have engaged in silence
exile and cunning.
I flew too near the sun
and my wax wings fell off.
I am looking for my Old Man
whom I never knew.
I am looking for the Lost Leader

with whom I flew.
Young men should be explorers.
Home is where one starts from.
But Mother never told me
there'd be scenes like this.
Womb-weary
I rest
I have travelled.
I have seen goof city.
I have seen the mass mess.
I have heard Kid Ory cry.
I have heard a trombone preach.
I have heard Debussy
strained thru a sheet.
I have slept in a hundred islands
where books were trees.
I have heard the birds
that sound like bells.
I have worn grey flannel trousers
and walked upon the beach of hell.
I have dwelt in a hundred cities
where trees were books.
What subways what taxis what cafes!
What women with blind breasts
limbs lost among skyscrapers!
I have seen the statues of heroes
at carrefours.
Danton weeping at a metro entrance
Columbus in Barcelona
pointing Westward up the Ramblas
toward the American Express
Lincoln in his stony chair
And a great Stone Face
in North Dakota.
I know that Columbus
did not invent America.
I have heard a hundred housebroken Ezra Pounds.
They should all be freed.
It is long since I was a herdsman.
I am leading a quiet life

in Mike's Place every day
reading the Classified columns.
I have read the Reader's Digest
from cover to cover
and noted the close identification
of the United States and the Promised Land
where every coin is marked
In God We Trust
but the dollar bills do not have it
being gods unto themselves.
I read the Want Ads daily
looking for a stone a leaf
an unfound door.
I hear America singing
in the Yellow Pages.
One could never tell
the soul has its rages.
I read the papers every day
and hear humanity amiss
in the sad plethora of print.
I see where Walden Pond has been drained
to make an amusement park.
I see they're making Melville
eat his whale.
I see another war is coming
but I won't be there to fight it.
I have read the writing
on the outhouse wall.
I helped Kilroy write it.
I marched up Fifth Avenue
blowing on a bugle in a tight platoon
but hurried back to the Casbah
looking for my dog.
I see a similarity
between dogs and me.
Dogs are the true observers
walking up and down the world
thru the Molloy country.
I have walked down alleys
too narrow for Chryslers.

I have seen a hundred horseless milkwagons
in a vacant lot in Astoria.
Ben Shahn never painted them
but they're there
askew in Astoria.
I have heard the junkman's obbligato.
I have ridden superhighways
and believed the billboard's promises
Crossed the Jersey Flats
and seen the Cities of the Plain
And wallowed in the wilds of Westchester
with its roving bands of natives
in stationwagons.
I have seen them.
I am the man.
I was there.
I suffered
somewhat.
I am an American.
I have a passport.
I did not suffer in public.
And I'm too young to die.
I am a selfmade man.
And I have plans for the future.
I am in line
for a top job.
I may be moving on
to Detroit.
I am only temporarily
a tie salesman.
I am a good Joe.
I am an open book
to my boss.
I am a complete mystery
to my closest friends.
I am leading a quiet life
in Mike's Place every day
contemplating my navel.
I am a part
of the body's long madness.

I have wandered in various nightwoods.
I have leaned in drunken doorways.
I have written wild stories
without punctuation.
I am the man.
I was there.
I suffered
somewhat.
I have sat in an uneasy chair.
I am a tear of the sun.
I am a hill
where poets run.
I invented the alphabet
after watching the flight of cranes
who made letters with their legs.
I am a lake upon a plain.
I am a word
in a tree.
I am a hill of poetry.
I am a raid
on the inarticulate.
I have dreamt
that all my teeth fell out
but my tongue lived
to tell the tale.
For I am a still
of poetry.
I am a bank of song.
I am a playerpiano
in an abandoned casino
on a seaside esplanade
in a dense fog
still playing.
I see a similarity
between the Laughing Woman
and myself.
I have heard the sound of summer
in the rain.
I have seen girls on boardwalks
have complicated sensations.

I understand their hesitations.
I am a gatherer of fruit.
I have seen how kisses
cause euphoria.
I have risked enchantment.
I have seen the Virgin
in an appletree at Chartres
And Saint Joan burn
at the Bella Union.
I have seen giraffes in junglejims
their necks like love
wound around the iron circumstances
of the world.
I have seen the Venus Aphrodite
armless in her drafty corridor.
I have heard a siren sing
at One Fifth Avenue.
I have seen the White Goddess dancing
in the Rue des Beaux Arts
on the Fourteenth of July
and the Beautiful Dame Without Mercy
picking her nose in Chumley's.
She did not speak English.
She had yellow hair
and a hoarse voice
and no bird sang.
I am leading a quiet life
in Mike's Place every day
watching the pocket pool players
making the minestrone scene
wolfing the macaronis
and I have read somewhere
the Meaning of Existence
yet have forgotten
just exactly where.
But I am the man
And I'll be there.
And I may cause the lips
of those who are asleep
to speak.

And I may make my notebooks
into sheaves of grass.
And I may write my own
eponymous epitaph
instructing the horsemen
to pass.

DOG

The dog trots freely in the street
and sees reality
and the things he sees
are bigger than himself
and the things he sees
are his reality
Drunks in doorways
Moons on trees
The dog trots freely thru the street
and the things he sees
are smaller than himself
Fish on newsprint
Ants in holes
Chickens in Chinatown windows
their heads a block away
The dog trots freely in the street
and the things he smells
smell something like himself
The dog trots freely in the street
past puddles and babies
cats and cigars
poolrooms and policemen
He doesn't hate cops
He merely has no use for them
and he goes past them
and past the dead cows hung up whole
in front of the San Francisco Meat Market
He would rather eat a tender cow
than a tough policeman
though either might do

And he goes past the Romeo Ravioli Factory
and past Coit's Tower
and past Congressman Doyle
He's afraid of Coit's Tower
but he's not afraid of Congressman Doyle
although what he hears is very discouraging
very depressing
very absurd
to a sad young dog like himself
to a serious dog like himself
But he has his own free world to live in
His own fleas to eat
He will not be muzzled
Congressman Doyle is just another
fire hydrant
to him
The dog trots freely in the street
and has his own dog's life to live
and to think about
and to reflect upon
touching and tasting and testing everything
investigating everything
without benefit of perjury
a real realist
with a real tale to tell
and a real tail to tell it with
a real live
   barking
     democratic dog
engaged in real
    free enterprise
with something to say
     about ontology
something to say
    about reality
      and how to see it
       and how to hear it
with his head cocked sideways
     at streetcorners
as if he is just about to have

his picture taken
for Victor Records
listening for
His Master's Voice
and looking
like a living questionmark
into the
great gramaphone
of puzzling existence
with its wondrous hollow horn
which always seems
just about to spout forth
some Victorious answer
to everything

THE WORLD IS A BEAUTIFUL PLACE . . .

The world is a beautiful place
to be born into
if you don't mind happiness
not always being
so very much fun
if you don't mind a touch of hell
now and then
just when everything is fine
because even in heaven
they don't sing
all the time

The world is a beautiful place
to be born into
if you don't mind some people dying
all the time
or maybe only starving
some of the time
which isn't half so bad
if it isn't you

Oh the world is a beautiful place

                              to be born into
              if you don't much mind
                          a few dead minds
                in the higher places
                              or a bomb or two
                now and then
                              in your upturned faces
          or such other improprieties
                              as our Name Brand society
                is prey to
                          with its men of distinction
              and its men of extinction
                          and its priests
                  and other patrolmen
                          and its various segregations
          and congressional investigations
                              and other constipations
                that our fool flesh
                          is heir to

      Yes the world is the best place of all
                                  for a lot of such things as
              making the fun scene
                          and making the love scene
    and making the sad scene
                          and singing low songs and having inspirations
          and walking around
                          looking at everything
                                      and smelling flowers
          and goosing statues
                      and even thinking
                                  and kissing people and
              making babies and wearing pants
                                  and waving hats and
                      dancing
                              and going swimming in rivers
                  on picnics
                      in the middle of the summer
              and just generally
                          'living it up'

Yes
       but then right in the middle of it
                                    comes the smiling
               mortician

JOHN WIENERS

1934–2002

ACT #2

For Marlene Dietrich

I took love home with me,
we fixed in the night and
sank into a stinging flash.

¼ grain of love
        we had,
2 men on a cot, a silk
cover and a green cloth
over the lamp.
        The music was just right.
I blew him like a symphony,
    it floated and
        he took me
down the street and
        left me here.
3 AM. No sign.

    only a moving van
    up Van Ness Avenue.

Foster's was never like this.

I'll walk home, up the
    same hills we
      came down.
He'll never come back,
     there'll be no horse
     tomorrow nor pot
tonight to smoke till dawn.

He's gone and taken
my morphine with him
Oh Johnny. Women in
   the night moan yr. name

        6.19.59

A POEM FOR THE OLD MAN

God love you
  Dana my lover
lost in the horde
on this Friday night,
500 men are moving up
& down from the bath
room to the bar.
Remove this desire
from the man I love.
Who has opened
  the savagery
of the sea to me.

See to it that
his wants are filled
on California street
Bestow on him largesse
that allows him
peace in his loins.

Leave him not
to the moths.
Make him out a lion
so that all who see him
hero worship his
thick chest as I did
moving my mouth
over his back bringing
our hearts to heights
I never hike over
   anymore.
Let blond hair burn
on the back of his
neck, let no ache
screw his face
up in pain, his soul
   is so hooked.
Not heroin.
Rather fix these
hundred men as his

A POEM FOR COCKSUCKERS

Well we can go
in the queer bars w/
our long hair reaching
down to the ground and
we can sing our songs
of love like the black mama
on the juke box, after all
what have we got left.

   On our right the fairies
giggle in their lacquered
voices & blow
smoke in your eyes let them
it's a nigger's world
and we retain strength.
The gifts do not desert us,

fountains do not dry
up there are rivers running,
there are mountains
swelling for spring to cascade.

    It is all here between
the powdered legs &
painted eyes of the fairy
friends who do not fail us
   in our hour of
     despair. Take not
away from me the small fires
I burn in the memory of love.

6.20.58

A POEM FOR VIPERS

I sit in Lees. At 11:40 PM with
Jimmy the pusher. He teaches me
Ju Ju. Hot on the table before us
shrimp foo yong, rice and mushroom
chow yuke. Up the street under the wheels
of a strange car is his stash—The ritual.
We make it. And have made it.
For months now together after midnight.
Soon I know the fuzz will
interrupt, will arrest Jimmy and
I shall be placed on probation. The poem
does not lie to us. We lie under
its law, alive in the glamour of this hour
able to enter into the sacred places
of his dark people, who carry secrets
glassed in their eyes and hide words
under the coats of their tongue.

6.16.58

A POEM FOR RECORD PLAYERS

The scene changes

Five hours later and
I come into a room
where a clock ticks.
I find a pillow to
muffle the sounds I make.
I am engaged in taking away
from God his sound.
The pigeons somewhere
above me, the cough
a man makes down the hall,
the flap of wings
below me, the squeak
of sparrows in the alley.
The scratches I itch
on my scalp, the landing
of birds under the bay
window out my window.
All dull details
I can only describe to you,
but which are here and
I hear and shall never
give up again, shall carry
with me over the streets
of this seacoast city,
forever; oh clack your
metal wings, god, you are
mine now in the morning.
I have you by the ears
in the exhaust pipes of
a thousand cars gunning
their motors turning over
all over town.

6.15.58

Bob Kaufman
1925–1986

ABOMUNIST MANIFESTO

ABOMUNISTS JOIN NOTHING BUT THEIR HANDS OR
    LEGS, OR OTHER SAME.

ABOMUNISTS SPIT ANTI-POETRY FOR POETIC REASONS
    AND FRINK.

ABOMUNISTS DO NOT LOOK AT PICTURES PAINTED
    BY PRESIDENTS AND UNEMPLOYED PRIME
    MINISTERS.

IN TIMES OF NATIONAL PERIL, ABOMUNISTS, AS REALITY
    AMERICANS, STAND READY TO DRINK THEMSELVES
    TO DEATH FOR THEIR COUNTRY.

ABOMUNISTS DO NOT FEEL PAIN, NO MATTER HOW
    MUCH IT HURTS.

ABOMUNISTS DO NOT USE THE WORD SQUARE EXCEPT
    WHEN TALKING TO SQUARES.

ABOMUNISTS READ NEWSPAPERS ONLY TO ASCERTAIN
    THEIR ABOMINUBILITY.

ABOMUNISTS NEVER CARRY MORE THAN FIFTY
    DOLLARS IN DEBTS ON THEM.

ABOMUNISTS BELIEVE THAT THE SOLUTION OF
PROBLEMS OF RELIGIOUS BIGOTRY IS, TO HAVE A
CATHOLIC CANDIDATE FOR PRESIDENT AND A
PROTESTANT CANDIDATE FOR POPE.

ABOMUNISTS DO NOT WRITE FOR MONEY; THEY WRITE
THE MONEY ITSELF.

ABOMUNISTS BELIEVE ONLY WHAT THEY DREAM ONLY
AFTER IT COMES TRUE.

ABOMUNIST CHILDREN MUST BE REARED ABOMUNIBLY.

ABOMUNIST POETS, CONFIDENT THAT THE NEW
LITERARY FORM "FOOT-PRINTISM" HAS FREED THE
ARTIST OF OUTMODED RESTRICTIONS, SUCH AS:
THE ABILITY TO READ AND WRITE, OR THE DESIRE
TO COMMUNICATE, MUST BE PREPARED TO READ
THEIR WORK AT DENTAL COLLEGES, EMBALMING
SCHOOLS, HOMES FOR UNWED MOTHERS, HOMES
FOR WED MOTHERS, INSANE ASYLUMS, USO
CANTEENS, KINDERGARTENS, AND COUNTY JAILS.
ABOMUNISTS NEVER COMPROMISE THEIR
REJECTIONARY PHILOSOPHY.

ABOMUNISTS REJECT EVERYTHING EXCEPT SNOWMEN.

NOTES DIS- AND RE- GARDING ABOMUNISM

Abomunism was founded by Barabbas, inspired by his dying
words: "I wanted to be in the middle, but I went too
far out."
Abomunism's main function is to unite the soul with oatmeal
cookies.
Abomunists love love, hate hate, drink drinks, smoke smokes,
live lives, die deaths.
Abomunist writers write writing, or nothing at all.
Abomunist poetry, in order to be compleatly (Eng. sp.)
understood, should be eaten ... except on fast days,
slow days, and mornings of executions.
Abomunists, could they be a color, would be green,
and tell everyone to go.

Uncrazy Abomunists crazy unAbomunists by proxy kicky
    tricks, as follows:
  By telling psychometric poets two heads are better
    than none.
  By selling middle names to impotent personnel
    managers.
  By giving children brightly wrapped candy fathers.
  By biting their own hands after feeding themselves.
  By calling taxis dirty names, while ordering fifths
    of milk.
  By walking across hills, ignoring up and down.
  By giving telescopes to peeping Toms.
  By using real names at false hotels.
Abomunists who feel their faith weakening will have to
    spend two weeks in Los Angeles.
When attacked, Abomunists think positive, repeating over
    and under: "If I were a crime, I'd want to be
    committed...
        No! ... Wait!"

FURTHER NOTES

(*taken from* "Abomunismus und Religion" *by Tom Man*)

Krishnamurti can relax the muscles of your soul,
Free your aching jawbone from the chewinggum habit.
Ouspensky can churn your illusions into butter and
Give you circles to carry them in, around your head.
Subud can lock you in strange rooms with vocal balms
And make your ignorant clothing understand you.
Zen can cause changes in the texture of your hair,
Removing you from the clutches of sexy barbers.
Edgar Cayce can locate your gallstones, other organs,
On the anarchistic rockpiles of Sacramento.
Voodoo Marie can give you Loas, abstract horses,
Snorting guides to tar-baby black masses.
Billy can plug you into the Christ machine. Mail in your
Mind today. Hurry, bargain God week, lasts one week only.

$$ ABOMUNUS CRAXIOMS $$

Egyptian mummies are lousy dancers.
        Alcoholics cannot make it on root beer.
Jazz never made it back down the river.
        Licking postage stamps depletes the body fluids.
Fat automobiles laugh more than others, and frink.
        Men who die in wars become seagulls and fly.
Roaches have a rough time of it from birth.
        People who read are not happy.
People who do not read are not happy.
        People are not very happy.
These days people get sicker quicker.
        The sky is less crowded in the West.
Psychiatrists pretend not to know everything.
        Way out people know the way out.
Laughter sounds orange at night, because
                reality is unrealizable while it exists.
Abomunists knew it all along,
                but couldn't get the butterscotch down.

STILL FURTHER NOTES DIS- & RE- GARDING ABOMUNISM

The following translation is the first publication of the Live Sea Scrolls, found by an old Arab oilwell driller. He first saw them on the dead beds of the live sea. Thinking they were ancient bubblegum wrappers he took them to town to trade in for hashish coupons. As chance would have it, the hashish pipes were in the hands of a visiting American relief official, who reluctantly surrendered them in return for two villages and a canal. We developed the cunic script by smearing it with tanfastic sun lotion, after which we took it down to the laundromat and placed it in the dryer for two hours ($1.20). We then ate four pounds of garlic bread & frinked; then we translated this diary. We feel this is one of the oldest Abomunist documents yet discovered.

MONDAY—B.C.—minus 4–10 o'sun, a.m.

Nazareth getting too hot, fuzz broke up two of my poetry readings last night. Beat vagrancy charge by carrying my toolbox to court—carpenters O.K. Splitting to Jeru. as soon as I get wheels.
TUESDAY—B.C.—minus 3–8 o'sun, p.m.

Jeru. cool, Roman fuzz busy having a ball, never bother you unless someone complains. Had a ball this morning, eighty-sixed some square bankers from the Temple, read long poem on revolt. Noticed cats taking notes, maybe they are publisher's agents, hope so, it would be crazy to publish with one of those big Roman firms.

WEDNESDAY—B.C.—minus 2–11 o'sun, a.m.

Local poets and literary people throwing a big dinner for me tonight, which should be a gas. Most of the cats here real cool, writing real far out—only cat bugs me is this Judas, got shook up when I refused to loan him thirty pieces of silver, he seems to be hung on loot, must be a lush.

THURSDAY—B.C.—minus 1–10 o'sun, p.m.

I am writing this in my cell. I was framed. How can they give the death sentence on charges of disorderly conduct and having public readings without a permit? It's beyond me. Oh well, there's always hope. Maybe that lawyer Judas is getting me can swing it. If he can't, God help me.

FRIDAY—Neutral—5 o'sun, a.m.

Roman turnkey was around passing out crosses. The two thieves have good connections so they got first crack at them—I got stuck with the biggest one. One of the guards doesn't dig my beard and sandals—taunted me all night. I'm going to be cool now, but tomorrow I'll tell him to go to hell, and what's so groovy is: he will. . . . somebody coming. I feel sort of abomunable. Barabbas gets a suspended sentence and I make the hill. What a drag. Well, that's poetry, and I've got to split now.

[AS USUAL]

As usual
   the usual axe
      falls on the usual neck
         in the usual place
            at the usual time
as usual.

WAR MEMOIR:
JAZZ, DON'T LISTEN TO IT AT YOUR OWN RISK

In the beginning, in the wet
Warm dark place,
Straining to break out, clawing at strange cables
Hearing her screams, laughing
"Later we forgot ourselves, we didn't know"
Some secret jazz
Shouted, wait, don't go.
Impatient, we came running, innocent
Laughing blobs of blood and faith.
To this mother, father world
Where laughter seems out of place
So we learned to cry, pleased
They pronounced human.
The secret jazz blew a sigh
Some familiar sound shouted wait
Some are evil, some will hate.
"Just Jazz, blowing it's top again"
So we rushed and laughed.
As we pushed and grabbed
While Jazz blew in the night
Suddenly we were too busy to hear a sound
We were busy shoving mud in men's mouths,
Who were busy dying on living ground
Busy earning medals, for killing children on deserted
     streetcorners
Occupying their fathers, raping their mothers, busy humans
     were

Busy burning Japanese in atomicolorcinescope
With stereophonic screams,
What one-hundred-percent red-blooded savage would waste
    precious time
Listening to Jazz, with so many important things going on
But even the fittest murderers must rest
So we sat down on our blood-soaked garments,
And listened to Jazz
                  lost, steeped in all our dreams
We were shocked at the sound of life, long gone from our own
We were indignant at the whistling, thinking, singing, beating,
    swinging
Living sound, which mocked us, but let us feel sweet life again
We wept for it, hugged, kissed it, loved it, joined it, we
    drank it,
Smoked it, ate with it, slept with it
We made our girls wear it for lovemaking
Instead of silly lace gowns,
Now in those terrible moments, when the dark memories come
The secret moments to which we admit no one
When guiltily we crawl back in time, reaching away from
    ourselves
We hear a familiar sound,
Jazz, scratching, digging, bluing, swinging jazz,
And we listen
And we feel
And live.

JAZZ CHICK

Music from her breast vibrating
Soundseared into burnished velvet.
Silent hips deceiving fools.
Rivulets of trickling ecstasy
From the alabaster pools of Jazz
Where music cools hot souls.
Eyes more articulately silent
Than Medusa's thousand tongues.
A bridge of eyes, consenting smiles

Reveal her presence singing
Of cool remembrance, happy balls
Wrapped in swinging
Jazz
Her music. . .
Jazz.

CROOTEY SONGO

DERRAT SLEGELATIONS, FLO GOOF BABER,
SCRASH SHO DUBIES, WAGO WAILO WAILO.
GEED BOP NAVA GLIED, NAVA GLIED NAVA,
SPLEERIEDER, HUYEDIST, HEDACAZ, AX—, O, O.

DEEREDITION, BOOMEDITION, SQUOM, SQUOM, SQUOM.
DEE BEETSTRAWIST, WAPAGO, LOCOEST, LOCORO, LO.
VOOMETEYEREEPETIOP, BOP, BOP, BOP, WHIPOLAT.

DEGET, SKLOKO, KURRITIF, PLOG, MANGI, PLOG MANGI,
CLOPO JAGO BREE, BREE, ASLOOPERED, AKINGO LABY.
ENGPOP, ENGPOP, BOP, PLOLO, PLOLO, BOP, BOP.

WAITING

SOMEWHERE THERE WAITS, WAITING
A BOOK IS WAITING, WAITING,
TO BE WRITTEN.
COLD COLD PAGES, WAITING,
TO BE WRITTEN,
MAN SEEKS GOD.
IN A BOOK.

SOMEWHERE THERE WAITS, WAITING
A PICTURE WAITS, WAITING,
WAITING TO BE PAINTED
COLD COLD CANVAS, CANVAS.
WAITING TO BE PAINTED.
MAN SEEKS GOD IN A PICTURE.

SOMEWHERE THERE WAITS, WAITING
A WOMAN WAITING, WAITING,
TO BE LOVED, WAITING,
COLD COLD WOMAN,
WAITING TO BE LOVED,
MAN SEEKS GOD IN A WOMAN.

SOMEWHERE THERE WAITS, WAITING
A MAN IS WAITING, WAITING,
COLD COLD MAN, WAITING,
TO BE WANTED, WAITING,
MAN SEEKS GOD
IN MAN

SOMEWHERE THERE WAITS, WAITING
A BABY IS WAITING, WAITING.
WAITING, WAITING TO BE BORN,
COLD COLD BABY, WAITING,
TO BE BORN, BLOOD OF EARTH,
WAITING TO BE.
MAN SEEKS GOD.
IN A BABY.

WIND, SEA,
SKY, STARS,
SURROUND
US.

LENORE KANDEL
1932–

FIRST THEY SLAUGHTERED THE ANGELS

I.

First they slaughtered the angels
tying their thin white legs with wire cords
and
opening their silk throats with icy knives
They died fluttering their wings like chickens
and their immortal blood wet the burning earth

we watched from underground
from the gravestones, the crypts
chewing our bony fingers
and
shivering in our piss stained winding sheets
The seraphs and the cherubim are gone
they have eaten them and cracked their bones for marrow
they have wiped their asses on angel feathers
and now they walk the rubbled streets with
eyes like fire pits

II.

who finked on the angels?
who stole the holy grail and hocked it for a jug of wine?
who fucked up Gabriel's golden horn?
      was it an inside job?

who barbecued the lamb of god?
who flushed St. Peter's keys down the mouth of a
North Beach toilet?
who raped St. Mary with a plastic dildo stamped with the
Good Housekeeping seal of approval?
        was it an outside job?

where are our weapons?
where are our bludgeons, our flame throwers, our poison
gas, our hand grenades?
we fumble for our guns and our knees sprout credit cards,
we vomit canceled checks
standing spreadlegged with open sphincters weeping soap suds
from our radioactive eyes
and screaming
for the ultimate rifle
the messianic cannon
the paschal bomb

the bellies of women split open and children rip their
way out with bayonets
spitting blood in the eyes of blind midwives
before impaling themselves on their own swords

the penises of men are become blue steel machine guns,
they ejaculate bullets, they spread death as an orgasm

lovers roll in the bushes tearing at each other's genitals
with iron finger nails

fresh blood is served at health food bars in germ free
paper cups
gulped down by syphilitic club women

in paper mache masks
each one the same hand painted face of Hamlet's mother
at the age of ten

we watch from underground
our eyes like periscopes
flinging our fingers to the dogs for candy bars
in an effort to still their barking
in an effort to keep the peace
in an effort to make friends and influence people

III.

we have collapsed our collapsible bomb shelters
we have folded our folding life rafts
and at the count of twelve
they have all disintegrated into piles of rat shit
nourishing the growth of poison flowers
and venus pitcher plants

we huddle underground
hugging our porous chests with mildewed arms
listening to the slow blood drip from our severed veins
lifting the tops of our zippered skulls
to ventilate our brains
          they have murdered our angels

we have sold our bodies and our hours to the curious
we have paid off our childhood in dishwashers and miltown
and rubbed salt upon our bleeding nerves
in the course of searching
          and they have shit upon the open mouth of god
they have hung the saints in straitjackets and they have
tranquilized the prophets
they have denied both christ and cock
and diagnosed buddha as catatonic
emasculated the priests and the holy men and
censored even the words of love
          Lobotomy for every man!
and they have nominated a eunuch for president

Lobotomy for the housewife!
Lobotomy for the business man!
Lobotomy for the nursery schools!
and they have murdered the angels

IV.

now in the alleyways the androgynes gather swinging their
lepers' bells like censers as they prepare the ritual
rape of god
      the grease that shines their lips is the fat of angels
      the blood that cakes their claws is the blood of angels

they are gathering in the streets and playing dice with
angel eyes
they are casting the last lots of armaggedon

V.

now in the aftermath of morning
we are rolling away the stones from underground, from the
caves
we have widened our peyote-visioned eyes
and rinsed our mouths with last night's wine
we have caulked the holes in our arms with dust and flung
libations at each other's feet

and we shall enter into the streets and walk among them and
do battle
holding our lean and empty hands upraised
we shall pass among the strangers of the world like a
bitter wind
and our blood will melt iron
and our breath will melt steel
we shall stare face to face with naked eyes
and our tears will make earthquakes
and our wailing will cause mountains to rise and the sun to halt

THEY SHALL MURDER NO MORE ANGELS!

      not even us

THE SECOND WAVE: NEW YORK
1958–60

Diane DiPrima
1934—

THIRTEEN NIGHTMARES

NIGHTMARE 1

Well, I had gotten to a warmer place for starving and lived on
beaches, and it seemed to me that everything would swing if I had
some book or other. So I wrote my mother (found paper) and told
her General Delivery and then I went back to beach and waited.
Nights warm enough to sleep and fish ok and paper occasionally a
poem, and then it seemed like time enough and I went to the post
office.

A package I said a book my name is thus and they said
identification please. And I looked in all pockets but a lucky wave
had gotten the cards with my name.

Please I said, please please please. A book inside, Rimbaud, open
and look for gods sake please.

Sorry they said why not go home they said and get your i.d.

Sure I said I'll ask that wave next time I see it but now give me
package.

Sorry they said and put it on shelf
high
behind wire and screen. Rimbaud there and maybe food probably
tucked around. Salami and cans of things food you know.

Please I said please well good day.

Good day they said.

NIGHTMARE 2

Having a cleaner house than usual I did the dishes. Gathering
those long slime worms, dayold spaghetti, I dropped from the sink
into the garbage them whereupon one slithered to the floor and
lay there smirking.

Ugh I said but having a cleaner floor than usual I tried to pick it up,
whereupon it nudged limply over and again smirked. After ten
minutes of chase I with dirtier hands than usual gave up.

Oh well I said under the water faucet it will be hard as nails
tonight the bastard and I'll pick it up stiff as a board.

Whereupon looking down again I saw a line of sleek roaches was
marching the worm away and singing *Onward Christian Roaches*.

The din was unbearable and I remained horrored to the spot until
a slightly larger roach, obviously leader, nudged me to see if I too
could be carried off.

NIGHTMARE 3

Spent fascinated hours watching the uncool of a young moth
doing herself in at the flame of my nonessential bohemian candle.

Which was ok, till she sideways gave up and clicked to crisp end of
nothing curled with small smoke.

Which was ok till from across ceiling room leaped flew another,
raced, and screaming "Dido" followed her.

NIGHTMARE 4

Many days hungry laid out on table dish raw chopped questionable meat probably edible, hope so, and went for matches.

Returned with frying pan somehow washed found on the table no meat, cat, no meat. Motherfucking bitch I said and flattened her with the frying pan squashed her bones practically dead and left her for tears. On bug-jumping bed I cried screamed and then cried to eventually recover and heel-toe to kitchen to see just to look and make sure.

On the table, still flat now stiff lay cat all dead not hungry now, but trails of drying sometime blood to floor and back told how she'd gone to get the now beside her meal (she thought) for me, a mouse she killed and died.

NIGHTMARE 5

Knock knock

Who is it I said

The man he said to turn your meter off.

Sorry I said but I'm in bed and things and come back later please.

I'll wait he said.

Do that I said and gave him 57 hours 40 minutes to give up. Went out then to hall jon, eagerly.

Hello he said

Hello I said

Sorry he said to turn your meter off. I gotta make a buck he said I gotta family.

I know I said its what they always say and go ahead. When you go home I'll saw the damn lock off.

That wont work now he said they gotta alloy. Spent 30 million dollars making it. Cant saw it thru no matter what he said.

OK I said go to it and go home. I'm going to the jon.

I did, he did, he left, I found a chair. And tried saw hammer chisel tried slipped bruised nails tried tried saw tried. Soup to cook.

Twelve hours later went to druggist. Sam I said I have a charge account for bennies give me some hydrofluoric acid.

Mac he said I dont know. Bennies is one thing Mac he said this acid jazz is something else.

Sam I said I gotta cook they locked the meter soup you know food you know.

OK Mac he said but take it easy.

Drip

Hole also in table, floor, maybe downstairs dont know but hole in lock too soup open great. Wow.

But ha no matches jokes on me the gas on and no matches let it go. Plenty of gas guess I wont eat.

NIGHTMARE 6

Get your cut throat off my knife.

NIGHTMARE 7

One day I forgot my sleeve and my heart pinned to my arm was burning a hole there.

Discovered in pocket fifty cents no more; on 42nd looked for a pleasant movie.

Until the most beautiful god he was I think up to me hood walked and smiled knowing everything and then knowing.

Are you busy he said and I laughed because no busy would be busier than seeing him and he knew it.

And he laughed knowing all and acknowledging simply yes that is so there is garish and hurt but not us.

And walked all three him and me and our hands between and he had a room where the ceiling danced for me danced all night.

Till morning awakened and yawning with dirty teeth he said well babe now how much do you get?

NIGHTMARE 8

Then I was standing in line unemployment green institution green room green people slow shuffle. Then to the man ahead said clerk-behind-desk, folding papers bored & sticking on seals

Here are your twenty reasons for living sir.

NIGHTMARE 9

Keep moving said the cop. The park closes at nine keep moving dammit. God damn things you think you own the park.

Not talking huh not going noplace? We'll see. Send you up for observation a week of shock will do you good I bet.

And he blew his whistle.

Whereupon white car pulled up.
white attendants
who set about their job without emotion.
It wasnt the first time theyd seen a catatonic tree.

NIGHTMARE 10

I saw it man, I read it in one of their god damned trade journals:

"Open season on people over 21 in dungarees or ancient sneakers, men with lipstick,
women with crew cuts,
actors out of work,
poets of all descriptions. Bounty for heads ten dollars. Junkies and jazz musicians five dollars extra."

You can say I'm mad but that dont mean I'm crazy. Ask any cabdriver.

NIGHTMARE 11

I really must get a new vegetable brush. Everytime I forget and use it on my face the vegetables I scrub next day turn brown and kinda strange . . .

NIGHTMARE 12

I went to the clinic. I twisted my foot I said.

Whats your name they said and age and how much do you make and whos your family dentist.

I told them and they told me to wait and I waited and they said come inside and I did.

Open your eye said the doctor you have something in it.

I hurt my foot I said.

Open your eye he said and I did and he took out the eyeball and washed it in a basin.

There he said and put it back that feels better doesnt it.

I guess so I said. Its all black I dont know. I hurt my foot I said.

Would you mind blinking he said one of your eyelashes is loose.

I think I said theres something the matter with my foot.

Oh he said. Perhaps you're right. I'll cut it off.

NIGHTMARE 13

It hurts to be murdered.

LeRoi Jones/ Amiri Baraka

1934–

IN MEMORY OF RADIO

Who has ever stopped to think of the divinity of Lamont
    Cranston?
(Only Jack Kerouac, that I know of: & me.
The rest of you probably had on WCBS and Kate Smith,
Or something equally unattractive.)

What can I say?
It is better to have loved and lost
Than to put linoleum in your living rooms?

Am I a sage or something?
Mandrake's hypnotic gesture of the week?
(Remember, I do not have the healing powers of Oral
    Roberts. . .
I cannot, like F. J. Sheen, tell you how to get saved & *rich!*
I cannot even order you to gaschamber satori like Hitler or
    Goody Knight

& Love is an evil word.
Turn it backwards/see, see what I mean?
An evol word. & besides
who understands it?

I certainly wouldn't like to go out on that kind of limb

Saturday mornings we listened to *Red Lantern* & his undersea
    folk.
At 11, *Let's Pretend*/& we did/& I, the poet, still do, Thank
    God!

What was it he used to say (after the transformation, when he
    was safe
& invisible & the unbelievers couldn't throw stones?) "Heh,
    heh, heh,
Who knows what evil lurks in the hearts of men? The Shadow
    knows."

O, yes he does
O, yes he does.
An evil word it is,
This Love.

FOR HETTIE

My wife is left-handed.
Which implies a fierce de-
termination.
A complete other
worldliness. IT'S WEIRD BABY
The way some folks
are always trying to be different.
A sin & a shame.

But then, she's been a bohemian
all her life ... black stockings,
refusing to take orders. I sit
patiently, trying to tell her
what's right. TAKE THAT DAMM
PENCIL OUTTA THAT HAND. YOU'RE
RITING BACKWARDS. & such. But
to no avail. & it shows
in her work. Left-handed coffee,

left-handed eggs: when she comes
in at night ... it's her left hand
offered for me to kiss. DAMM.

& now her belly droops over the seat.
They say it's a child. But
I ain't quite so sure.

1958

PREFACE TO A TWENTY VOLUME SUICIDE NOTE

For Kellie Jones, born 16 May 1959

Lately, I've become accustomed to the way
The ground opens up and envelopes me
Each time I go out to walk the dog.
Or the broad edged silly music the wind
Makes when I run for a bus ...

Things have come to that.

And now, each night I count the stars,
And each night I get the same number.
And when they will not come to be counted,
I count the holes they leave.

Nobody sings anymore.

And then last night, I tiptoed up
To my daughter's room and heard her
Talking to someone, and when I opened
The door, there was no one there. . .
Only she on her knees, peeking into

Her own clasped hands.

BLACK DADA NIHILISMUS

.Against what light
is false what breath
sucked, for deadness.
                    Murder, the cleansed

purpose, frail, against
God, if they bring him
                    bleeding, I would not

forgive, or even call him
black dada nihilismus.

The protestant love, wide windows,
color blocked to Mondrian, and the
ugly silent deaths of jews under

the surgeon's knife. (To awake on
69th street with money and a hip
nose. Black dada nihilismus, for

the umbrella'd jesus. Trilby intrigue
movie house presidents sticky the floor.
B.D.N., for the secret men, Hermes, the

blacker art. Thievery (ahh, they return
those secret gold killers. Inquisitors
of the cocktail hour. Trismegistus, have

them, in their transmutation, from stone
to bleeding pearl, from lead to burning
looting, dead Moctezuma, find the West

a grey hideous space.

2. From Sartre, a white man, it gave
the last breath. And we beg him die,
before he is killed. Plastique, we

do not have, only thin heroic blades.
The razor. Our flail against them, why
you carry knives? Or brutaled lumps of

heart? Why you stay, where they can
reach? Why you sit, or stand, or walk
in this place, a window on a dark

warehouse. Where the minds packed in
straw. New homes, these towers, for those
lacking money or art. A cult of death,

need of the simple striking arm under
the streetlamp. The cutters, from under
their rented earth. Come up, black dada

nihilismus. Rape the white girls. Rape
their fathers. Cut the mothers' throats.
Black dada nihilismus, choke my friends

in their bedrooms with their drinks spilling
and restless for tilting hips or dark liver
lips sucking splinters from the master's thigh.

Black scream
and chant, scream,
and dull, un
earthly

hollering. Dada, bilious
what ugliness, learned
in the dome, colored holy
shit (i call them sinned
or lost
          burned masters
                    of the lost
                              nihil German killers
                                        all our learned

art,' member
what you said
money, God, power,
a moral code, so cruel
it destroyed Byzantium, Tenochtitlan, Commanch

                                      (got it, *Baby*!

For tambo, willie best, dubois, patrice, mantan, the
bronze buckaroos.

                For Jack Johnson, asbestos, tonto, buckwheat,
                billie holiday.

                For tom russ, l'overture, vesey, beau jack,

(may a lost god damballah, rest or save us
against the murders we intend
against his lost white children
black dada nihilismus

Frank O'Hara
1926–1966

A STEP AWAY FROM THEM

It's my lunch hour, so I go
for a walk among the hum-colored
cabs. First, down the sidewalk
where laborers feed their dirty
glistening torsos sandwiches
and Coca-Cola, with yellow helmets
on. They protect them from falling
bricks, I guess. Then onto the
avenue where skirts are flipping
above heels and blow up over
grates. The sun is hot, but the
cabs stir up the air. I look
at bargains in wristwatches. There
are cats playing in sawdust.
                    On
to Times Square, where the sign
blows smoke over my head, and higher
the waterfall pours lightly. A
Negro stands in a doorway with a
toothpick, languorously agitating.
A blonde chorus girl clicks: he
smiles and rubs his chin. Everything

suddenly honks: it is 12: 40 of
a Thursday.
         Neon in daylight is a
great pleasure, as Edwin Denby would
write, as are light bulbs in daylight.
I stop for a cheeseburger at JULIET'S
CORNER. Giulietta Masina, wife of
Federico Fellini, *è bell' attrice.*
And chocolate malted. A lady in
foxes on such a day puts her poodle
in a cab.
         There are several Puerto
Ricans on the avenue today, which
makes it beautiful and warm. First
Bunny died, then John Latouche,
then Jackson Pollock. But is the
earth as full as life was full, of them?
And one has eaten and one walks,
past the magazines with nudes
and the posters for BULLFIGHT and
the Manhattan Storage Warehouse,
which they'll soon tear down. I
used to think they had the Armory
Show there.
         A glass of papaya juice
and back to work. My heart is in my
pocket, it is Poems by Pierre Reverdy.

                     (1956)

THE DAY LADY DIED

It is 12: 20 in New York a Friday
three days after Bastille day, yes
it is 1959 and I go get a shoeshine
because I will get off the 4: 19 in Easthampton
at 7: 15 and then go straight to dinner
and I don't know the people who will feed me

I walk up the muggy street beginning to sun
and have a hamburger and a malted and buy
an ugly NEW WORLD WRITING to see what the poets
in Ghana are doing these days
                              I go on to the bank
and Miss Stillwagon (first name Linda I once heard)
doesn't even look up my balance for once in her life
and in the GOLDEN GRIFFIN I get a little Verlaine
for Patsy with drawings by Bonnard although I do
think of Hesiod, trans. Richmond Lattimore or
Brendan Behan's new play or *Le Balcon* or *Les Nègres*
of Genet, but I don't, I stick with Verlaine
after practically going to sleep with quandariness

and for Mike I just stroll into the PARK LANE
Liquor Store and ask for a bottle of Strega and
then I go back where I came from to 6th Avenue
and the tobacconist in the Ziegfeld Theatre and
casually ask for a carton of Gauloises and a carton
of Picayunes, and a NEW YORK POST with her face on it

and I am sweating a lot by now and thinking of
leaning on the john door in the 5 SPOT
while she whispered a song along the keyboard
to Mal Waldron and everyone and I stopped breathing

                                                    (1959)

POEM

Khrushchev is coming on the right day!
                              the cool graced light
is pushed off the enormous glass piers by hard wind
and everything is tossing, hurrying on up
                              this country
has everything but *politesse*, a Puerto Rican cab driver says
and five different girls I see
                        look like Piedie Gimbel

with her blonde hair tossing too,
                              as she looked when I pushed
her little daughter on the swing on the lawn it was also windy

last night we went to a movie and came out,
                              Ionesco is greater
than Beckett, Vincent said, that's what I think, blueberry blintzes
and Khrushchev was probably being carped at
                              in Washington, no
                                        politesse
Vincent tells me about his mother's trip to Sweden
                                        Hans tells us
about his father's life in Sweden, it sounds like Grace Hartigan's
painting *Sweden*
                    so I go home to bed and names drift through my
                                                            head
Purgatorio Merchado, Gerhard Schwartz and Gaspar Gonzales, all
          unknown figures of the early morning as I go to work

where does the evil of the year go
                              when September takes New York
and turns it into ozone stalagmites
                              deposits of light
                              so I get back up
make coffee, and read François Villon, his life, so dark
      New York seems blinding and my tie is blowing up the street
I wish it would blow off
                              though it is cold and somewhat warms
                                                            my neck
as the train bears Khrushchev on to Pennsylvania Station
      and the light seems to be eternal
      and joy seems to be inexorable
      I am foolish enough always to find it in wind

                                                  (1959)

PERSONAL POEM

Now when I walk around at lunchtime
I have only two charms in my pocket
an old Roman coin Mike Kanemitsu gave me
and a bolt-head that broke off a packing case
when I was in Madrid the others never
brought me too much luck though they did
help keep me in New York against coercion
but now I'm happy for a time and interested

I walk through the luminous humidity
passing the House of Seagram with its wet
and its loungers and the construction to
the left that closed the sidewalk if
I ever get to be a construction worker
I'd like to have a silver hat please
and get to Moriarty's where I wait for
LeRoi and hear who wants to be a mover and
shaker the last five years my batting average
is .016 that's that, and LeRoi comes in
and tells me Miles Davis was clubbed 12
times last night outside BIRDLAND by a cop
a lady asks us for a nickel for a terrible
disease but we don't give her one we
don't like terrible diseases, then
we go eat some fish and some ale it's
cool but crowded we don't like Lionel Trilling
we decide, we like Don Allen we don't like
Henry James so much we like Herman Melville
we don't want to be in the poets' walk in
San Francisco even we just want to be rich
and walk on girders in our silver hats
I wonder if one person out of the 8,000,000 is
thinking of me as I shake hands with LeRoi
and buy a strap for my wristwatch and go
back to work happy at the thought possibly so

(1959)

WHY I AM NOT A PAINTER

I am not a painter, I am a poet.
Why? I think I would rather be
a painter, but I am not. Well,

For instance, Mike Goldberg
is starting a painting. I drop in.
"Sit down and have a drink" he
says. I drink; we drink. I look
up. "You have SARDINES in it."
"Yes, it needed something there."
"Oh." I go and the days go by
and I drop in again. The painting
is going on, and I go, and the days
go by. I drop in. The painting is
finished. "Where's SARDINES?"
All that's left is just
letters, "It was too much," Mike says.

But me? One day I am thinking of
a color: orange. I write a line
about orange. Pretty soon it is a
whole page of words, not lines.
Then another page. There should be
so much more, not of orange, of
words, of how terrible orange is
and life. Days go by. It is even in
prose, I am a real poet. My poem
is finished and I haven't mentioned
orange yet. It's twelve poems, I call
it ORANGES. And one day in a gallery
I see Mike's painting, called SARDINES.

(1956)

ALEXANDER TROCCHI
1925–1984

(From) CAIN'S BOOK

My scow is tied up in the canal at Flushing, N.Y., alongside the landing stage of the Mac Asphalt and Construction Corporation. It is now just after five in the afternoon. Today at this time it is still afternoon, and the sun, striking the cinderblocks of the main building of the works, has turned them pink. The motor cranes and the decks of the other scows tied up round about are deserted.

Half an hour ago I gave myself a fix.

I stood the needle and the eye-dropper in a glass of cold water and lay down on the bunk. I felt giddy almost at once. It's good shit, not like some of the stuff we've been getting lately. I had to be careful. Two of the workmen in wide blue dungarees and wearing baseball caps were still hanging about. From time to time they crossed my catwalk. They were inquisitive. They had heard the noise of the typewriter during the afternoon and that was sufficient to arouse their curiosity. It's not usual for a scow captain to carry a typewriter. They lingered for a while, talking, just outside the cabin. Then, a few minutes before five, I heard them climb back on to the dock and walk away.

Lying on the bunk, alert to the sudden silence that has come over the canal, I hear the buzz of a fly and notice it is worrying the dry corpse of another fly which is half-gouged into the plank of the wall. I wonder about it and then my attention wanders. A few minutes have passed. I hear it buzz again and see that it is still at its work, whatever it is, settled on the rigid jutting legs of the corpse. The legs grow out of the black spot like a minute sprout of eyelashes. The live fly is busy. I wonder if it is blood it wants, if flies like wolves or rats will eat off their own kind.

—Cain at his orisons, Narcissus at his mirror.

The mind under heroin evades perception as it does ordinarily; one is aware only of contents. But that whole way of posing the question, of dividing the mind from what it's aware of, is fruitless. Nor is it that the objects of perception are intrusive in an electric way as they are under mescalin or lysergic acid, nor that things strike one with more intensity or in a more enchanted or detailed way as I have sometimes experienced under marijuana; it is that the perceiving turns inward, the eyelids droop, the blood is aware of itself, a slow phosphorescence in all the fabric of flesh and nerve and bone; it is that the organism has a sense of being intact and unbrittle, and, above all, *inviolable*. For the attitude born of this sense of inviolability some Americans have used the word "cool."

It is evening now, the temperature has fallen, objects are growing together in the dim light of the cabin. In a few moments I shall get up and light my kerosene lamps.

—*What the hell am I doing here?*

At certain moments I find myself looking on my whole life as leading up to the present moment, the present being all I have to affirm. It's somehow undignified to speak of the past or to think about the future. I don't seriously occupy myself with the question in the "here-and-now," lying on my bunk and, under the influence of heroin, inviolable. That is one of the virtues of the drug, that it empties such questions of all anguish, transports them to another region, a painless theoretical region, a play region, surprising, fertile, and unmoral. One is no longer grotesquely involved in the becoming. One simply is. I remember saying to Sebastian before he returned to Europe with his new wife that it was imperative to know what it was to be a vegetable, as well.

...the illusory sense of adequacy induced in a man by the drug. Illusory? Can a ... "datum" be false? Inadequate? In relation to what? The facts? What facts? Marxian facts? Freudian facts?

Mendelian facts? More and more I found it necessary to suspend such facts, to exist simply in abeyance, to give up (if you will), and come naked to apprehension.

It's not possible to come quite naked to apprehension and for the past year I have found it difficult to sustain even an approximate attitude without shit, horse, heroin. Details, impressionistic, lyrical. I became fascinated by the minute to minute sensations and when I reflected I did so repetitively and exhaustingly (often under marijuana) on the meaningless texture of the present moment, the cries of gulls, a floating spar, a shaft of sunlight, and it wasn't long before the sense of being alone overtook me and drained me of all hope of ever entering the city with its complicated relations, its plexus of outrageous purpose.

—The facts. Stick to the facts. A fine empirical principle, but below the level of language the facts slide away like a lava. Neither was there ever a simple act; in retrospect I couldn't isolate such a thing. Even while I lived in my act, at each phase, after the decidings, it unfolded spontaneously, and frighteningly, and dangerously, at times like a disease run riot, at times like the growing morning sunlight, and if I find it difficult to remember and express, and difficult to express and remember, if sometimes words leap up, sudden, unnatural, squint and jingling skeletons from the page, accusing me and amusing me with their obscene shakes and making the world mad, I suppose it is because they take a kind of ancestral revenge upon me who at each moment is ready to marshal them again for death or resurrection. No doubt I shall go on writing, stumbling across tundras of unmeaning, planting words like bloody flags in my wake. Loose ends, things unrelated, shifts, nightmare journeys, cities arrived at and left, meetings, desertions, betrayals, all manner of unions, adulteries, triumphs, defeats ... these are the facts. It's a fact that in the America I found nothing was ever in abeyance. Things moved or they were subversive. I suppose it was to escape this without going away, to retreat into abeyance, that I soon came to be on a river scow. (Alternatives: prison, madhouse, morgue.)

I get up off the bunk and return to the table where I light an oil-lamp. When I have adjusted the wick I find myself fumbling again amongst the pile of notes, extracting a certain page. I hold it close to the lamp and read:

—Time on the scows. . .
Day and night soon became for me merely light and dark, daylight or oil-lamp, and often the lamp became pale and
transparent in the long dawns. It was the warmth of the sun
that came on my cheek and on my hand through the window
which made me get up and go outside and find the sun already
far overhead and the skyscrapers of Manhattan suddenly and
impressively and irrelevantly there in a haze of heat. And as for
that irrelevance . . . I often wondered how far out a man could
go without being obliterated. It's an oblique way to look at
Manhattan, seeing it islanded there for days on end across the
buffering water like a little mirage in which one isn't involved,
for at times I knew it objectively and with anxiety as a nexus of
hard fact, as my very condition. Sometimes it was like trum-
pets, that architecture.

I find myself squirting a thin stream of water from the eye-dropper
through the number 26 needle into the air, cooking up another fix,
prodding the hardened cotton in the bubbling spoon . . . just a small
fix, I feel, would recreate the strewn ramparts of Jericho.

*Tout ce qu'on fait dans la vie, même l'amour, on le fait dans le train express
qui roule vers la mort. Fumer l'opium, c'est quitter le train en marche; c'est
s'occuper d'autre chose que de la vie, de la mort.*
—Cocteau

At 33rd Street is Pier 72. At the waterfront there are few buildings and they are low. The city is in the background. It has
diners at its edge, boxcars abandoned and stored, rails amongst
grass and gravel, vacant lots. The trucks of moving and storage
companies are parked and shunted under the tunnels of an area of
broad deserted shadows, useful for murder or rape. The wharves jut
forward into the Hudson River like the stunted uneven teeth of a
prehistoric jaw. The George Washington Bridge is in the north.
After eight, when the diners close, the dockside streets are fairly
deserted. In winter the lights under the elevated roadway shine as in
a vast and dingy shed, dimly reflecting its own emptiness. An occasional car moves in from the dark side of the crosstown streets,

turns into the feebly-lit dockyard area, travels ten or twenty blocks south, and then moves out, outwards again into the city. Walk three blocks east to Ninth Avenue and the lights get brighter. A woman bawls her husband's affairs to a neighbour in the street from the window in which she leans thirty feet above your head as you walk along.

Pier 72 is the one immediately north of the new heliport which lies in the southern end of the basin formed by Piers 72 and 71. The remainder of the basin is used to moor the scows of a stone corporation with quarries at Haverstraw, Tomkin's Cove, and Clinton Point on the Hudson River. Piers 72 and 73 are close together. Nine scows at most are moored there. Looking in from the river you see the gabled ends of two huge and dilapidated barns perched on foundations of stones and heavy beams, with a narrow walk round three sides of each. The gable-end of Pier 73 is a landmark from the river because it is painted with red, white, and blue stripes representing American Lines. At the end of Pier 72 there is a small landing-stage set with bollards and cleats of cast iron. A little wooden box painted green is nailed to the gable end of the shed. It houses lists from the dispatcher's office of the crushed stone corporation, lists which pertain to the movements of the scows.

An hour ago I smoked some marijuana which came from Chile. It was particularly good. But for me it is an ambiguous drug. It can induce control or hysteria, and sometimes a terrifying and enervating succession of moods, new beginnings, generated spontaneously in the unwatched part of oneself . . . slow, quick, switchback, tumbling away from oneself in a sickening fashion, and then, suddenly, being in control. This can be exhausting. Intense concentration on an external object suddenly shatters, and one has a fleeting, ambiguous glimpse of one's own pale face. The cause of what is to be shunned is the junction of the seer and the seen. The ordinary logic of association ceases to be operative. The problem, if one takes the trouble to pose it at all, is to find a new criterion of relevance. Understandably, at such times, the list in the box at the end of Pier 72, indicating as it does the hour at which a tug will arrive to take one's scow in tow, has a fatality about it. One had hoped to go into the Village on arrival at the pier but on reading the list one finds one's scow amongst those to be picked up immediately.

This particular night—it was in the middle of winter—I was not on the list. I went over it twice very carefully, running my finger down the column of scows, O'Brien, Macdougal, Campbell, O'Malley, Matteotti, Leonard, Marshall, Cook, Smith, Peterson: Red Star, on arrival; Coogan, Baxter, Haynes, Loveday: Colonial, with the tide. There were a few scowmen hanging around the end of the pier, mostly those who were going out at once.

I went back to the scow. In the cabin I stowed away some things that were lying about, my hashish pipe, a bottle of benzedrine, locked the cabin and climbed over four scows and on to the pier. I walked along the huge beam which provides the narrow footpath parallel to the shed as far as the dock. I walked slowly, using a flashlight to guide my feet. On my left the corrugated iron of the shed, on my right, about fourteen feet below me, the still dark water of the basin reflecting a few naked lights. Its surface was smeared with oil and dust. Finally I reached the dock and walked between some parked boxcars to the street under the elevated road. I cut diagonally across town and at 23rd Street on Eighth Avenue I took a taxi to Sheridan Square. I telephoned Moira from the drugstore that sells all the paperbacks. She told me to come over.

She was glad to see me. We hadn't seen one another for over two weeks.—Have you taken dope? Nope.—Our conversation was sometimes limited. She had smoked pot for some years but her attitude towards heroin was rigid. It made our relationship tense and hysterical. Sometimes I wondered why I bothered to go to see her, and that was the way it was with most of my friends who didn't use junk. "It's none of my business," Moira said. "I've got no sympathy for them."

It would make me very angry when she said that. I wanted to shake her. "*You* say that! Sometimes I think of all those ignorant cops, all those ignorant judges, all those ignorant bastard people committing bloody murder like they blow their noses! They think it so fucking easy they can stamp it out like syphokles, whatever it is, jewry, heroin-addiction, like some kind of streptococcus, and getting high an un-American rabies, Jesus, to a healthy paranoid like me who likes four walls and police-locks on all doors and a couple of good Frankensteins to draw off the mob with their flaming torches, it looks like anyone who depicts you, dear Saviour, with a beard will be dealt with cold turkey until they take him before a judge and then, because it can't stand, being bestial, scarcely human, the quivering, blubbering, vomiting mass is given half a grain of morphine ten minutes before he is arraigned so that they won't have to take him in on a stretcher and run the risk of having some irresponsible goon send for a doctor!"

"It's none of my business!" Moira screamed.

"Whose business is it? What are you going to do? Leave it to the experts? Tomorrow, the Age of the Doctors! They're already challenging the tax men and the F.B.I. for a profitable monopoly. Let's put it on prescription, eh? confine it to the laboratories for more tests. They're always talking about a lack of scientific evidence, about its being unsafe to make it public! They're scared the public will find out it ain't that fucking horse after all!"

"*They're* scared! Who's *they?*"

"You! Dammit to hell, Moira! You!"

"I don't want to discuss it! I won't argue with you!"

At that moment the telephone rang. She was grateful for the distraction. But it was Tom Tear. As welcome as a newborn Mongolian idiot. He had heard I was in town and wanted to know if I wanted to score. She held her hand over the mouthpiece of the receiver and her face became angry as she became aware of my hesitation. She spoke coldly into the telephone: "He's here now. You'd better speak to him yourself." As she handed me the telephone she said she didn't want him telephoning me there. She avoided my disbelieving eyes and her face became set and hard. I could see only the back of her head now, the long blonde hair in a smooth bell.—I remember the first time I smelled it; her cheek was cold; it was the middle of winter and in Glasgow there was snow in the streets. By the time I turned my attention to the telephone I knew I would score, that it was only a question of arranging the time and the place. The thought of an evening with her in her present mood was stifling. Tom's voice, because he had been sensitive to the tone of Moira's, was apologetic, almost wheedling. "Don't be so fucking sorry," I said to him, watching her overhear. "Where'll I meet you?" A place at Sheridan Square in half an hour's time. I put down the telephone. Moira was pouring coffee.

I had to say something. I said: "Look, Moira, I know what I'm doing."

"I don't want to talk about it," she said dully.

And we didn't. I wanted to explain and not to explain. At the same time I considered her attitude impertinent. I drank my coffee and left.

Fay was with Tom. Tom made the run alone and Fay and I walked over together to his place from Sheridan Square. We walked quickly so as to get there by the time he returned with the heroin.

"It's going to be good, baby," Fay said.

The room has a low sloping ceiling with two small windows on one side and a fireplace with a raised brick hearth in an opposite corner, at the far end of the adjacent side. Sometimes Tom Tear burned a few sticks in the grate and we sat with our knees at the level of the fire which cast shadows on the dirty ceiling and walls and on the bricks of the fireplace, the three of us on a small, backless couch spread over with a fawn blanket, looking into the fire, Fay in the centre, still wearing her moth-eaten fur coat, her arms folded, her head sunk on her chest, her slightly bulbous, yellowish eyes closed. We sat there after we had fixed and watched wood burn. The white boxwood burned quickly. Tom Tear leaned forward and added a few sticks to the blaze. He is a tall man in his late twenties, lean, with a beautiful, pale, lean face expressionless often as porcelain, the nose long, the eyes half-closed and heavily lidded under the drug.

I also am tall. I was wearing my heavy white seaman's jersey with a high polo neck, and I sensed that the angularity of my face—big nose, high cheekbones, sunken eyes —was softened by the shadows and smoothed—the effect of the drug—out of its habitual nervousness. My eyes were closed. My elbows rested on my thighs and my hands were clasped in front of me. Tom Tear is a negro who sometimes speaks dreamily of the West Indies.

At that moment I felt impelled to speak and I said: "My father had false teeth."

I was aware that I flashed a quick, intimate glance first at Tom, across Fay's line of vision, and then, turning my head slightly, I caught the glint of appraisal in her pale protruding eyes.

"Yes," I said, and my face grew radiant, encouraging them to listen, "he had yellow dentures."

Tom's teeth—they are long and yellowish and give his mouth a look of bone—were clenched in a tight smile, the pale lips falling away, exposing them. It was almost a mask of ecstasy, *part of the game*, I might have said in some contexts, in some rooms.

Fay's face was more reserved. Swinish? More like a pug than a pig. Her untidy dark hair tumbled into her big fur collar. A yellow female pigdog, her face in its warm nest beginning to stir with knowing.

"He was outside in the hall, spying on the lodgers," I said. "My father was a born quisling, and he had false teeth."

Tom Tear's face was patient and serene. The flicker of the fire stirred in the sparse black stubble on his lower face, making the hairs glint.

I went on for the friendly silence: "While he was in the hall his false teeth were squatting like an octopus in a glass of water on the kitchen dresser. The plates were a dark orange brick colour and the teeth were like discoloured piano keys. They seemed to breathe at the bottom of the glass. The water was cloudy and tiny bubbles clung to the teeth. That was the kitchen where we lived, and they sat there like a breathing eye, watching us."

Fay's bluish lips had fallen apart in a smile. She made a grunt of understanding through her decayed teeth. Fay is forty-two. She has lived all her life in this city.

Tom Tear leaned forward and threw more wood on the fire. Wood is plentiful. We gather it, when we can be bothered, on the streets.

"He went on tiptoe about the hall for nine years," I said, "in tennis shoes and without his teeth. The hall was No-man's Land."

Tom Tear nodded as he leaned back again away from the fire. His right cheek, which was all I saw from where I sat, was impassive, long and smooth.

"If someone came to the front door he came flying back into the kitchen for his teeth. He came in puffing and blowing with his hand on his paunch. He wore a collarless shirt with a stud in it and he went round in his shirt sleeves and this old grey, sleeveless pullover." I paused. A white stick darkened and burst into flame. "When he grew older he became less frantic about the teeth," I said, smiling. "He slipped them into his mouth furtively in front of the visitor as though he suddenly remembered and didn't want to give offence. Perhaps he no longer needed defences."

"He'd given up by that time," Fay said. She looked straight into the fire.

We were all silent for a moment. I felt I had to go on. I said: "I'll tell you a story. . ."

The others smiled. Fay touched the back of my hand with her fingertips. I remember noticing she had prominent eye-teeth.

"It's not really a story," I said. "It's something I read somewhere, about a river bushman. This man wanted to track down some bushmen and he went to a place called Serongo in the swamps. One day he caught sight of a bushman paddling alone in a boat and he asked his head bearer if he would speak to him and get him to lead them to his tribe. The bearer told him he had known the bushman for thirty years, that he lived alone on a termite mound in the middle of the swamps, and he was deaf and dumb as well."

The others looked at me. I moved my clasped hands forward and stared at the thumbs. They were dirty at the knuckles and at the nails.

We were all silent.

"It's necessary to give up first," I began tentatively, "but it should be a beginning. . ." I sensed an ambiguity, something not quite authentic, and stopped speaking.

"Go on," Tom said after a moment.

But the inauthenticity was in the words, clinging to them like barnacles to a ship's hull, a growing impediment. I shook my head, closed my eyes.

Again we were all silent. The smoke from the burning wood wound its way towards the chimney, some of it spilling outwards into the room where it clung to the low ceiling.

"Does anyone want to go out?" Fay said.

When neither of us answered she made the motion of snuggling inside her warm fur coat. "It's cold outside, too cold," she said.

I was sitting hunched forward with my eyes closed, my chin deep in the high woollen collar. The phrase *"ex nihil nihil fit"* had just come to me. It seemed to me that nothing would be beginning, ever.

Tom Tear, who a moment before had moved to a stool at the side of the fireplace, was leaning backwards against the wall and his soft black eyelashes stirred like a clot of moving insects at his eyes. His face had the look of smoke and ashes, like a bombed city. It was at rest, outwardly.

There is a bed in the room, a low double bed on which three dirty grey army blankets are stretched. On the wall between the two square windows—they are uncurtained and at night the four panes of glass in each are black and glossy—is a faded engraving, unframed. It curls away from the wall at one corner where the scotch tape has come away. There are two similar engravings on two other walls, both of them warped and one of them with a tear at the corner. On the fourth wall there is an unskilful pencil sketch of some trees and a water colour of a woman's face, vague and pink, and painted on flimsy paper. This is the work of Tom Tear's girlfriend. A self-portrait. He talks of her now and again, always vaguely. She is kicking her habit in some clinic out of town. The last piece of furniture apart from the backless couch and the stool on which Tom Tear sat is a draughtsman's table which tilts on a ratchet to any required angle. This is the table on which Tom Tear will work if ever he becomes an architect. At that moment the table was horizontal and there was a clock on it, and an electric lamp which didn't work, and a burning candle, and a radio with a plastic cabinet in which another clock was inlaid. Both clocks said twenty-five past nine. That was all there was on the table, apart from the spike, and the glass of water, and the spoon.

We had fixed over an hour ago. We had used all the heroin.

Each of us was conscious of the well-being of the others. The blaze of wood in the fireplace made our cheeks glow. Our faces were smooth, and serene.

"I can't do with it and I can't do without it," Fay had said earlier as she prodded the back of her left hand—the flesh was thin there and waxy—in search of a possible vein. At the third attempt she found a vein and the blood rose up through the needle into the eye-dropper and appeared as a dark red tongue in the colourless solution. "Hit," she said softly, with a slow smile. When she put the eye-dropper with the needle attached back into the glass of water and dabbed the back of her bluish hand with tissue paper there was no longer any fear in her eyes, only certainty, and in their yellowish depths ecstasy. I knew at that moment she was impregnable. I laughed softly at her and touched the slack flesh of her cheek lightly with my fingers. At that moment I was happy for her and I knew that she, when she watched me fix a moment later, would be happy for me.

Each of us was conscious of the well-being of the others. The sense of well-being in each of us was reinforced by that consciousness.

I said suddenly that the wheel hadn't been invented yet.

"What's a wheel?" Tom Tear said.

We were sitting, three absent faces towards the fire, a crude fire, and gloom beyond our shoulders. Fay's motheaten fur coat was gathered under her chin like an old animal skin. "Outside," Fay said, her protruding yellow eyes glinting dully in the firelight, "there is the jungle." She laughed huskily and laid her friendly blue hand on my knee.

Tom's face, tilted towards the ceiling, was idyllic, inviolable.

"And it's raining outside," she said softly.

A moment later, she said: "You said your father was a spy, Joe. You mean he was inquisitive?"

I said: "The job he had before he became unemployable was a spy's job. He was a musician to begin with but he became a spy. His job was to snoop round clubs and concert halls to see that no one infringed copyrights. He was the fuzz, the executioner, the Man. He was always closing curtains ..." I leaned across and whispered loudly in Fay's ear, "Don't you know that people can see in?"

I said: "In the end he identified himself so completely with Authority that he became unemployable, he took too much upon himself, he felt himself free to make executive decisions, even if he was only the doorman. When he was summoned during the war for selling confectionery at black market rates without coupons—he sold it by the quarter pound to anyone who expressed conservative sentiments—he ranted against Socialism and red tape. When he was arrested for soliciting on the street he pleaded with tears in his eyes that he was only trying to control a queue."

Fay was poking at the fire with a stick, smiling like a yellow idol.

"I'll go and break some more wood," I said. I got up and moved over to the door. As I opened it Tom's dog bounded in. "That damn dog again," I heard Fay say as I crossed the large, low studio, now brimming over with lumber and other materials, into which the door led. I selected a flimsy box and began breaking it into pieces.

TED JOANS
1928–2003

THE TRUTH

If you should see

a man walking

down a crowded street

talking aloud

to himself

don't run

in the opposite direction

but run toward him

for he is a POET!

You have NOTHING to fear

from the poet

but the TRUTH

UH HUH

THERE IT IS
UH HUH
YEP
THAT'S IT
UH HUH
THERE IS NO DOUBT ABOUT IT
UH HUH
THAT'S IT!!
UH HUH!
YES SIREE
UH HUH
MAN, THIS IS IT!
UH HUH
THE REAL THING
UH HUH
NO SHIT
HERE
UH HUH
THE REAL BIT!!
UH HUH
HERE IT IS
UH HUH
A FACT
UH HUH
RIGHT BEFORE THE EYES
UH HUH
THIS IS REALLY IT
UH HUH
YEP YEP
A TRUTH
UH HUH
REALITY!
UH HUH
WELL I'LL BE DAMNED
UH HUH
HERE NOW
UH HUH   THIS   UH HUH   NOW   UH HUH   THERE
  UH HUH   UH HUH UH HUH UH HUH!!
THE   COLORED   WAITING   ROOM!!!!!

WHITEYES ON BLACKTHIGHS

I KNOW YOU DIG DARK ME
I KNOW YOU WANT A TASTE
BUT IF YOU LAY A HAND
ON   ME
I'LL RUN
A RAZOR BLADE
SEVEN TIMES
A CROSS
YOUR PALE
CRACKER
FACE

THEY FORGET TO FAST

THE STATUE OF CHARLIE PARKER   TEN FEET TALL
                    THREE TONS OF CONCRETE/BRONZE/
AND MARBLE BASE/   STANDS AT   SHERIDAN SQUARE
                                        FACING ME
FROM WHERE I SIT   HERE IN TIMBUCTOO   STONED AS
                                    THE STATUE!
THE STATUE OF CHARLIE PARKER   WITH ALTO SAX
                    ACROSS THE CHEST   MAKES ME
RECALL   NUMBER FOUR BARROW STREET   (REPLACED
                    NOW BY PARKER TOWERS,PITY!)
FOR IT WAS THERE   WHERE WE SHARED: POT/PAINT/
                    POEMS/MUSIC/FOOD & PLENTY PUSSY
FROM OVER-ANXIOUS OFAY BITCHES
NOW LATE EVENING WHITE BIRDS   EAT CRUMBS
                    SPRINKLED AT THE FEET
OF THE STATUE OF   CHARLIE PARKER   AND THESE
                    LATE EVENING   WHITE 'BIRDS' EAT
AND THEY COPY AND THEY CHEAT AND THEY EAT AND
            THEY COPY AND THEY CHEAT AND THEY EAT
AND FINALLY   WITH OVER STUFFED GUTS   THEY FLY
                    JUST HIGH ENOUGH TO
ALIGHT ON THE   STATUE OF   CHARLIE PARKER   AND
                    THEY SIT AND THEY SHIT!
THEY   FORGET   TOO   FAST

OPEN MINDED

She opened her eyes   and she saw me
She opened her ears   and she heard my words
She opened her nose   and smelled the truth
She opened her dress   and revealed body and soul
She opened her arms   and I knew her need
She laid back/opened her legs, opened her heart,   and separated her
lonely knees   Yes indeed   Yes Indeed   Yeeessss INDEED!

DUKE'S ADVICE

I live Uptown in Harlem   I took Duke's advice
and took the "A" Train   Now I'm surrounded by my tribe again
in Harlem
I sleep in bed between two dream queens black   naked women
in Harlem
I dream this same dream every night Uptown "A" Trainland
in Harlem
What I'm trying to not say   is Uptown I have erotic dreams
it seems about
Bessie Smith   and Billie Holiday   When I close my eyes they
stay and we lay
Uptown   in "A" Trainland   in a big black bed   in Harlem

WATERMELON

Its got   a good shape/the outside color is green/its one of them
foods from Africa
its got stripes sometimes like a zebra   or Florida prison pants
Its bright red inside/the black eyes are flat and shiney/it wont
make you fat
Its got heavy liquid weight/the sweet taste is unique/some people
are shamed of it/
I aint afraid to eat it/indoors or out/its soul food thing/Watermelon
is what I'm
talking about   Yeah watermelon is what I'm talking about
Watermelon

MY BAG

MY BAG   IS HERE   IT IS JUST MY SIZE
MY BAG IS DEEP   AND DARK   SO DONT
BE TOO SMART   I   HAVE MY BAG
IT IS ALL MY OWN   AND I   AND I ALONE
KNOWS WHAT IS HAPPENING IN MY BAG
MY BAG IS WARM   SOMETIMES HOT BUT HIP
MY BAG IS   NOTHING MORE THAN MY BAG
THUS IT MAY JUST BE TOO DAMN HEAVY
FOR YOU TO WORRY OR TRY TO CARRY   BUT
DONT GET UPSET AND SCARY   ITS MY BAG
I KNOW MY BAG   CAUSE IT IS MY BAG
I KNOW EXACTLY WHERE ITS AT   MY BAG

NATURAL

thick lips/ natural
wide nose/ natural
kinky hair/ natural
brown eyes / natural
wide   smile / natural
black skin/natural
& if you're proud/of what you
naturally got
then your soul/is beautiful/thus
naturally hot   so be natural
stay natural   swing natural   think natural
and for black god's sake   act natural

JAZZ IS MY RELIGION

JAZZ is my religion   and it alone do I dig   the jazz clubs are
my houses of worship   and sometimes the concert halls   but some
holy places are too commercial (like churches)   so I dont dig the
sermons there   I buy jazz sides to dig in solitude   Like man/Harlem,
Harlem U.S.A. used to be a jazz heaven where most of the jazz
sermons were preached   but now-a-days due to chacha cha and

rotten rock'n'roll alotta good jazzmen have sold their souls   but jazz
is still my religion   because I know and feel the message it brings
like Reverend Dizzy Gillespie/Brother   Bird and Basie/Uncle
Armstrong/Minster Monk/Deacon Miles Davis/Rector Rollins/
Priest Ellington/His Funkness Horace Silver/and the great Pope
John, John COLTRANE   and Cecil Taylor   They Preach A
    Sermon
That Always Swings!! Yeah jazz is MY religion   Jazz is my story
it was my mom's and pop's   and their moms and pops from the
days of Buddy Bolden who swung them blues to Charlie Parker and
Ornette Coleman's extension of Bebop   Yeah jazz is my religion
Jazz is a unique musical religion   the sermons spread happiness
    and
joy   to be able to dig and swing inside   what a wonderful feeling
jazz is/YEAH BOY!!   JAZZ is my religion and dig this: it wasnt for
us to choose because they created it for a damn good reason   as   a
weapon to battle our blues! JAZZ is my religion   and its
international   all the   way   JAZZ is just an Afroamerican music
and like us its here to stay   So remember that JAZZ is my religion
but it can be your religion too but JAZZ is a truth that   is always
black and blue   Hallelujah I love JAZZ so   Hallelujah I dig JAZZ
    so
Yeah JAZZ   IS   MY   RELIGION

NO MORE

I love her black butt
the way it moves   when she walks
I dig her natural lips   unpainted/full/ & soft
I adore her dark eyes
they way they flash   when she lets go
I dig sister soul   but she dont want me   no more

THE NICE COLORED MAN

Nice Nigger Educated Nigger Never Nigger Southern Nigger
Clever Nigger Northern Nigger Nasty Nigger Unforgivable Nigger

Unforgettable Nigger Unspeakable Nigger Rude & Uncouth
    Nigger
Mean & Vicious Nigger Smart Black Nigger Smart Black Nigger
Smart Black Nigger Smart Black Nigger Smart Black Nigger Smart
Black Nigger   Smart Black Nigger   Smart Black Nigger Knife
Carrying Nigger Gun Toting Nigger Military Nigger Clock
    Watching
Nigger Food Poisoning Nigger Disgusting Nigger Black Ass Nigger
Black Ass Nigger Black Ass Nigger Black Ass Nigger Half White
Nigger Big Stupid Nigger Big Dick Nigger Jive Ass Nigger Wrong
Nigger Naughty Nigger Uppity Nigger Middleclass Nigger
Government Nigger Sneaky Nigger Houndog Nigger Grease Head
Nigger Nappy Head Nigger Cut Throat Nigger Dangerous Nigger
Sharp Nigger Rich Nigger Poor Nigger Begging Nigger Hustling
Nigger Whoring Nigger Pimping Nigger No Good Nigger Dirty
Nigger Unhappy Nigger Explosive Nigger Godamn Nigger
Godamnigger Godamnigger Godamnigger Godamnigger
Godamnigger Godamn Nigger Godamnigger Godamnigger
Godamnigger Godamnigger Godamnigger

                                    Neat Nigger Progressive
Nigger Nextdoor Nigger Classmate Nigger Roomate Nigger
    Laymate
Nigger Weekend Date Nigger Dancing Nigger Smiling Nigger
    Ageless
Nigger Old Tired Nigger Silly Nigger Hippy Nigger White Folks
Nigger Integrated Nigger Non-Violent Nigger Demonstrating
    Nigger
Cooperative Nigger Peaceful Nigger American Nigger
Uneducated Nigger Under Rated Nigger Bad Nigger Sad Nigger
Slum Nigger Jailhouse Nigger Stealing Nigger Robbing Nigger
Raping Nigger
                Lonely Nigger Blues Singing Nigger Dues
Paying Nigger Unemployed Nigger Unwanted Nigger
Impossible Nigger Cunning Nigger Running Nigger Cruel Nigger
Well Known Nigger Individual Nigger Purple Nigger Beige
Nigger Bronze Nigger Brown Nigger Red Nigger Bed Nigger
Yellow Nigger Tan Nigger Mulatto Nigger Creole Nigger
Inevitable Nigger Mixed Up Nigger Slave Nigger Unfree Nigger
Savage Nigger Jazz Nigger Musical Nigger Godamnigger
Godamnigger Godamnigger Godamnigger Godamnigger

Godamnigger Jesus Loves Us Nigger Preaching Nigger We Shall
Overcome Nigger Someday Nigger Militant Nigger Real Nigger
Brave Nigger Real Nigger Violent Nigger Real Nigger Intelligent
Nigger Real Nigger Active Nigger Real Nigger Wise Nigger Real
Nigger Deceitful Nigger Real Nigger Courageous Nigger Real
Nigger Cool Nigger Real Nigger Hip Nigger Real Nigger Hot
Nigger Real Nigger Funky Nigger Real Nigger (I Cant Figger
This Nigger He's Too Much This Nigger! He's All Over Us This
Nigger I Dont Trust This Nigger He's Far Too Much He's
Everywhere . . . . . This Nigger!)

Eeny Meeny Minee Mo
Catch Whitey By His Throat
If He Says—Nigger CUT IT!!

RAY BREMSER

1934–1998

BACKYARDS & DEVIATIONS

1.

my sister used to dress me up (I think)
some kind of giddy kiddie anagram or
entertainment game
of bobbiesox & implethoric girlie girlie
plum breast applica!
but I was nervous, hungry,
ate a plum & did the bit with
half a laughed at chest of bubbling
sans gruesome awesome plausible
cupbola-boola breast!

thus the brilliant sabotage was done
& sometime later (meanwhile)
I began to feel an Escadrillian hot wild
for silken drawers & wonder wished
that god or sister Arlie
would anoint me with all panacea
mountainous high girl come
good to shine the teeth
& blend the skin all feminine

—or rub it on your chest
& murder pachyderm
& cowardice
& acne
& perfunctorily one's own cachet of personality!

whereat the fall's commodious bright tears
ack acked the heart with lobar requiems
so that, in fact,
the sudden terror tumbled mastodon
had aardvarked into graceful pirouette
—the ballerina's unscalpel & cut unsurgery—
Pavlovial apt sap, my ample thighs
& Arlie's dumb plasticity
made half a Ballet Russe Nijinsky out of me!
(& all we did was dress me up in fruit tits
raucous operatic mime & supercilious soft snatch
—the latch & wretchedness of queerdom, meanwhile,
giggling abrosial cocksuckeries at me!
I ate a plum whose reconnoitering myth-pit
concealed this misfit halfass bastard poetry!)

2.

so sister did me in & wouldn't hump!
not that I pitched a line or anything
except when I was ten
I snuck around like a secret movie spy
& copped the key to Arlie's room
where all my disarrangement every midnight
locked her in!
the room was a greyhound terminal for moonmad
cosmic ostriches!
wild light came in through vents & opulence
had snugged all snuggie into clefts
& haloed all the craggy swag her melting belly button drew
—all navel puffball dapplings of sheer
come-on-you-damn-insatiable-awkward-fool-of-a-boob-for-
    brother!

so sister slept while I imbibed
& touched the cloth she slept upon
& touched the sleeper on the cloth
& cupped her breast with crazy hand
& cooled it, quiet, stealing stealthily
down boulevards of Appalachian hot want—
& put my thickness tongue in cheek
& put my thankful tongue on her cheek,
put my thirsty tongue in sleek-maneuvered
oval navel—dug the cotton balls
& christened all the waistband of her drawers,
my nose gone digging foxholes of get-evener
& payback, old revenge, vendetta, crucifix & damn the whole
   thing,
fell, without revenge & fallow to the floor in fear
& simple dreadful drudgerous kind of love
with one's own pretty impossible hyacinth for a sister!

(meanwhile) next thing I knew
my fourteen year old sister awoke
& accused & accused & other bright bouquets
of maledict, the witch!
(computer hiccoughed haughty mother
fuckers to the wind!)

lesson in marriage:
           never comptometer opp
           what your chances might be
           without whiskey in brain
           without muscle in arm
           without husky pudendum in ritual stick
           & all HARD if you're soft!

3.

finally at 25 I get the gonest notions
of reconnaissance or retrosex
or something very inadaptable
come Thursday!
the scrawling, violent

unborn broken poet in my head
waylays my youth
& irises my eyes
with baby puke
& leotard andante epicures
whose molecules embowel me
with great aplomb,
surprise,
& freckles, topaz, roses,
endocrine!

out of the fall the knuckled Tamerlane
keeps coming–& dollop-chargers
reindeer my small sled gone erewhon nowhere
like lake Placid into bed!
the bed's own stately baggage weight of Arlie,
sister Arlie, sleighbell glistening & birthday high,
benights this gray Jurassic of a brother
who knows? diggerpoetfiend!
bred like the great old Guernsey dam,
ensconcing artificiality & semen she bears a breed
of eunoch-mutants,
vague diminuendos & symposiums
all goofballed
incest-fighting for Canace
which batter down my head
with no respite . . .

JACK MICHELINE
1929–1998

LETS SING A SONG

The night came quickly and the bells of churches rang.

The crowds poured out of the subway entrances
$\qquad\qquad$ to their homes.

A million hearts drawn like a magnet
$\qquad\qquad$ to the roar of time.

  Which one is his master?

    Which one smiled amidst the crucifixion?

    Which one bared the pain of pent up prisons?

I saw their faces walking down the street.

I enjoyed looking at
  swivelhipped young women
    with paint on their faces
      sorrowful eyes
        blank stares
          of emptiness
        their insides
        waiting to jump
      and their voices
  to sing a song.

It was a cold sight
   in a big city
      where love is the roar
        and death is the beat
          the beat.

And I yelled like a
   madman
      at the top of my voice
        Everybody sing
        Everybody sing
       I started to sing a song
      about pretty flowers
     then the men with white coats
   came with their jackets
and I told them to sing also
   and they took me away.
      Let's sing a song
        Let's sing a song
          and they took me away
        away
          away
            from the roar
           and the beat
          the beat
           the beat.

RIVER OF RED WINE

Golden haze
  morning sun
    alabaster city
      tenement street
       iron bed night
         of rooftop summers
       along the cobbled streets
         rummies mumble jig saw puzzles
     ghostlike invisible men
       inhabit fringe cities
         of darkness
      in vacant lots
        they sit on old crates
          talking to rusty beer cans
           window screens and loose tobacco
           voices soft and loud
           wine of universe
             quench their thirst
               fire charged they will live
                 in new worlds of madness
               Gimp Leg, One Eye, Wildman
           lost memories of youth
          covered in the glories
        of scream filled nights
     you've played games
       with bed bugs
     musicians blew trumpets
       down back alleys
    corn is gold in the Iowa sun
      get close to the earth
        and smell it
          your green fields are waving
           in the wind
          memory lane, I cannot understand
        memory lane

speak up Wildman speak up
Nelly why'd ya do it Nelly
why'd ya do it?
Father Ago don't use the whip
I love ya I'm buyin tonight
got to show my brothers old lady
I'm a millionaire
gimmee another whimple, Sagamore
takin a vacation
sandy zoo of pebble lakes
uzz head, muzz head
Doc Beans my beast friend
buddy buddy son of a
copper, copper
leave me alone
Christ Saves
you call that music
rubber tourniquet
tomato juiced arm
here pussy here pussy
I'm a scarfaced hero
ha ha ha ha ha ha ha
O'Shannessy more wine
icebox stone blue
vacation jinx
Scotty gimmee
two bits
two bits
shirts made of alpaca
Frenchy everybody's beautiful
who stole my comb
gonna sleep tonight
down memory lane
in a trailer by the river
with the I won blues
leave me alone
too many salesmen
cemetery battlefield
belief in man buried
in potato sacked graveyards

standin on corners
by silent gutters
wobbly legged, tobacco juiced
flophouse of dreamers
get close to the earth
only close to the earth
near stone steps of marble hallways
freight train and loco weed
in winters freezing cold
corn is gold in the Iowa sun
your green fields are wavin
in the wind
cosmos fed the hungry eyes
potters field had no stone
monuments of falseness
forest of lilacs
grass of feathers
gently I kiss my enemy
in tears
hand shackled, gun straped
river soaked, dungeon borne
route of death
in a railroad graveyard
in solitary
near skys of purple
I felt your warmth
in sweetness
pussywillows
in boxcars
on main streets
mountain red near open desert
Butte, Montana
Seattle dockyards
New Orleans foghorns
Miami sun in cocanut groves
L.A. to San Frans golden gate
to bowery jive
hamburger dinners
factory belched black smoke
heartbeat of subways

big city of small town gossipers
heat ripped, mind shattered
fear winded to hate
morning haze
of rainbow sunrise
Johnny pumped music
of morning glories
pigeon of flight
pigeon cooped
concrete covered
five bucks a pint
for a river of red wine
wire wagon, cage of lions
straw grows stronger
in the wind
we are bleeding in the
deserts of your world
and drops of our freedom
is birth.

JENNY LEE

you never had a chance
standing on a corner
in the belly of Harlem
and the horns were blowing crazy   jenny lee

shaking as a monkey has his way
your veins bulged like rivers
mad dogs are always biting
the needle hard as iron   jenny lee

you had to make a dollar
hustling in the street
always voices in the rooms
voices in your brain   jenny lee

you were fifteen when you started
   just earth and dogs and saliva cum
      hard rock
         black cat
            red bird   jenny lee

you never had a chance jenny lee
   scream and shake and vomit green
      the horns are always blowing

your guts cut out at twenty
   no black Jesus on a cross of neon
      preachers still wailing
         blue balls on the corner   jenny lee

you're born and you die
   no sweet ride for you baby
      the monkeys always jumpin
         all the faces of the angels

no more walking easter sunday
   no more turkey trimmings baby
      no more five star, rot gut sour whiskey   jenny lee

a sky full of flowers
   a yellow moon for you
      jenny died on the corner
         where all the voices were
            the horns were blowing crazy
            a siren wailed that night
               your body wrapped in flowers
                  in the gutters of the sky
                     out in the open
                        out in the street
                           heaven in your eyes   jenny lee

NIGHT CITY

Above the sounds
dark cities
lie in shadows
foghorns blast in silence
prayers of lost children
by light of mountains
darkness to light
light to darkness
I stand looking
down at the city
steeples rise in magic shapes
arcs of bridges
cover the river
steam white crosses
illuminate the eye
black tar of loneliness
billboards neon red
buildings stand and fall
but man remains
like dying timbers
in a forest
man remains
on a warehouse stairway
to the moon
three empty wine bottles stand

Nuns

Vipers

Holy Mary Face

that is not yours

but you are all

madness of cities

King majesty

drunk with awe

quiet, tired, restless city

Black tar in the night

Black tar in the night

> 1957
> Rooftop on Crosby Street
> New York City

SOUTH STREET PIER

The bridge had risen

above the stone and lights of Manhattan

the river weaves with wrinkles of Christs head

the red brick warehouse stands

the stevedores haul the rigs to the masts

the Kids fight in the streets

Mechanics Alley where the Rabbis sat and prayed

O chaos and pain of our youth

I am drunk with the moon

and the Mexican line swims in my mouth

There is love in my eyes

the Statue of Liberty is always in the water

Staten Island waits

the cleaning girls are scrubbing Maiden Lane

the smoke pours stacks from the Brooklyn shore

the fog horn tickles my belly

I hear the Drums beating

throw my ashes from this pier when I die.

POET OF THE STREETS

I walk east of Bleecker
the sky is blue
on this Sunday evening

there is something deeper than the earth
there is something deeper than the stone cities
there is something deeper than our existence
than all the robes of power

power and the night bleeding gutters with crutches
power and the night and the neon vibrating
the night and thirty moons and sharpies
the night and the railroad yards gleaming
the night and the sky
the night and billboards and darkness

across a nation skeletons and machinery
jaundice, joints and lips of connivers
burnt Christmas trees
jazz horns and drummers

above concrete
above whimpering voices
above calculators
riders with tokens in their hands
riders to the sea

a nation of cowards
cowards wrapped in academic cloth

over all in darkness
over all who live in deserts
over all shells covering
over all that are wasted
burying all in nothingness
burying all that is soul
burying all with layers of armour
burying herds with still voices
burying all in the nowhere of silence

herring and fish in cans
turkey and chicken in cans
humans in cells of unknowing
there is more to life than the lights of savage civilizations
there is more to life than all the words spoken
there is more to life than the eye can see

I see the sun of angels
hemp and sugar and wheat
blood and sinew within the flesh
ticker tapes, grey hair, jowls on faces
dollars and gods and people sold and traded

people dying for nothing
people selling their minds and bodies
people without courage
people with no teeth in drug stores

death loaded with goods
givers of death and more death
cranes and deep hookers
cutting shears for the young
newspapers stunting the mind
dollars the spoiler of ships of bananas

I see your faces as I stroll through the cities
the wind touching the faces of whores

the vision of poets encompassing all
songs of children outside the brick houses
there is nothing deeper than life and the livers of life
mankind raped in the bank vaults of steel
dead soldiers, battlefields surrounded by iron and ironies

a million lost sunsets
a poet unconquered with the legacy of Whitman and Lorca
a poet unconquered by stone, by glass, by greed, by madness

the lights blaze on in the night
lights and the cold wind
visions above all death
cows milked dry, golden crosses
the sky blazing with miracles

a poet walks in the cold wind
his head raised humble and unafraid
death around him filled with waste and banners
death all around him
walking alone with birds above the canoe shaped moons
sounds are heard and the sky glows in darkness
I am not afraid.

> January 31, 1960
> East Bleecker
> New York City
>
> This poem turned the tide of my death,
> written on First Avenue off the Bowery
> in an alley of great souls.

BIOGRAPHICAL NOTES ON WRITERS

Ray Bremser

Bremser has a jazz rhythm to his lines, like a long saxophone solo made from unlikely rhymes, repeats and choruses, making him one of the most beat of the Beats. Born in Jersey City, New Jersey, 22 February 1934, and died in Utica, New York, 3 November 1998. Bremser did six years in Bordentown Reformatory for an armed robbery committed at the age of eighteen and it was in jail that he began writing poetry. In 1957 he made contact with Allen Ginsberg and Gregory Corso who were then living at the Beat Hotel in Paris and they suggested he send his poems to LeRoi Jones in New York, who was editing *Yugen*, one of the key Beat literary magazines. When he got out of jail, Jones held a party for him and introduced him to Kerouac and the other Beat writers. After more jail time and a spell in Mexico, during which he prostituted his wife Bonnie on the streets to get money for drugs, Bremser returned to the States destitute and lived for a while on Ginsberg's poetry farm in Cherry Valley, NY; set up specifically to 'dry out' poets.

Cat Digging Walls. Los Angeles, 1959. Semina.
Poems of Madness. New York, 1965. Paperbook Gallery.
Angel. New York, 1967. Tompkins Square Press.
Black Is Black Blues. Buffalo, NY, 1971. Intrepid.
Blowing Mouth. Cherry Valley, NY, 1978. Cherry Valley Editions.
Born Again. Philo, CA, 1985. Am Here Books.
The Conquerors. Sudbury, MA, 1998. Water Row Press.
The Dying of Children. Sudbury, MA, 1999. Water Row Press.

William S. Burroughs

Burroughs' grandfather invented the adding machine, but the family sold most of their shares in the Burroughs Corporation during the Depression. He was born in St. Louis, Missouri, 5 February 1914, and grew up in a wealthy middle-class environment receiving a $200 a month income from his parents on graduation from Harvard which continued until the mid-sixties. He began writing in 1935 at Harvard and 'Twilight's Last Gleamings' dates from that time, co-written with his room-mate Kells Elvins. He studied medicine in Vienna but returned to the USA with the rise of the Nazis after first marrying an Austrian Jewess in order to get her a US entry visa and very likely saving her life. After working as an exterminator in Chicago, he moved to New York City where in 1944 he met Allen Ginsberg and Jack Kerouac through his friend Lucien Carr, whom he knew from St. Louis. They were impressed by the older man who introduced them to the work of Céline, Spengler, Hart Crane, Cocteau and Blake. Kerouac, Burroughs and Ginsberg were room-mates at Joan Vollmer's communal apartment on West 115th Street and it was here that Burroughs first developed his 'routines' – ideas pushed to their outer, most bizarre limits – to entertain his friends. He also used this form in letters, particularly those to Allen Ginsberg written first from Mexico City, where he and Joan Vollmer lived, and later from Tangier. These became the source material for *The Naked Lunch*, a novel he completed at the Beat Hotel in Paris in 1959. This same year he began his experiments with cut-ups, a project which was to dominate his work for the next decade. The pieces here are taken from his early work when he was most associated with the Beat movement. Burroughs died in Lawrence, Kansas, 2 August 1997.

Junkie (as William Lee). New York, 1953. Ace.
The Naked Lunch. Paris, 1959. Olympia.
Minutes To Go (with Brion Gysin, Sinclair Beiles and Gregory Corso). Paris, 1960. Two Cities.
Exterminator (with Brion Gysin). San Francisco 1960. Auerhahn.
The Soft Machine. Paris, 1961. Olympia.
The Ticket that Exploded. Paris, 1962. Olympia.
Dead Fingers Talk. London, 1963. Calder.
The Yage Letters (with Allen Ginsberg). San Francisco, 1963. City Lights.

Nova Express. New York, 1964. Grove.

Roosevelt After Inauguration. New York, 1965. Fuck You.

Time. New York, 1965. C-Press.

APO-33. New York, 1965. Fuck You. Reprinted Beach Books, San Francisco, 1966.

The Soft Machine (first revision). New York, 1966. Grove.

The Ticket that Exploded (revised). New York, 1967. Grove.

The Soft Machine (second revision). London, 1968. Calder.

The Job. New York, 1970. Grove.

The Last Words of Dutch Schultz. London, 1970. Cape Goliard.

Ali's Smile. Brighton, 1971. Unicorn.

The Wild Boys. New York, 1971. Grove.

Electronic Revolution. Cambridge, 1971. Blackmoor Head.

Exterminator! New York, 1973. Viking.

White Subway. London, 1973. Aloes seolA.

Port of Saints. London, 1973 (1975) Covent Garden.

The Book of Breathing. Ingatestone, Essex, 1974. Ou. (reprinted in *Ah Pook is Here*).

The Job (revised edition, paperback only) New York, 1974. Grove.

The Last Words of Dutch Schultz (revised edition). New York, 1975. Viking.

Cobble Stone Gardens. Cherry Valley, New York, 1976. Cherry Valley Editions.

The Retreat Diaries. New York, 1976. City Moon.

Junky (unexpurgated). New York, 1977. Penguin.

The Third Mind (with Brion Gysin). New York, 1978. Viking.

Letters to Allen Ginsberg. Geneva, 1976. Givaudon/Am Here (reprinted by Full Court Press, New York, 1982).

Naked Scientology (with *Ali's Smile*), (bilingual edition). Bonn, 1978. Expanded Media.

Blade Runner, A Movie. Berkeley, 1979. Blue Wind.

Ah Pook is Here. London, 1979. Calder.

Port of Saints (revised edition). Berkeley, 1980. Blue Wind.

Early Routines. Santa Barbara, 1981. Cadmus.

Cities of the Red Night. New York, 1981. Holt Rinehart.

A William Burroughs Reader. London, 1982. Picador.

The Place of Dead Roads. New York, 1983. Holt Rinehart.

The Burroughs File. San Francisco, 1984. City Lights.

The Adding Machine. London, 1985. Calder.

Queer. New York, 1985. Viking.

The Cat Inside (with Brion Gysin). New York, 1986. Greenville.

The Western Lands. New York, 1987. Viking.

Apocalypse (with Keith Haring). New York, 1988. Mulder Fine Arts.

Interzone. New York, 1987. Viking.

Tornado Alley. Cherry Valley, New York, 1989. Cherry Valley Editions.

Ghost of Chance. New York, 1991. Whitney Museum.

Seven Deadly Sins. Los Angeles, 1992. Lococo-Mulder Fine Arts.

The Letters of William S. Burroughs: 1945–1959. New York, 1993.
   Viking.

Ghost of Chance. New York, 1995. High Risk/Serpent's Tail.

My Education: A Book of Dreams. New York, 1995. Viking.

Word Virus. New York, 1998. Grove.

Conversations With William S. Burroughs. Jackson, 1999. U of
   Mississippi.

*Burroughs Live. The Collected Interviews of William S. Burroughs
   1960–1997*. Los Angeles, 2001. Semiotext(e).

Naked Lunch, the Restored Text. New York, 2001. Grove.

Junky, (definitive text edition). New York, 2003. Penguin.

Neal Cassady

Born in Salt Lake City, Utah, 8 February 1926, and raised by his
wino father in a series of flophouses in Denver's skid row, young
Cassady somehow got himself to school each day but most of his
education was on the streets. He stole his first car at the age of fourteen and estimated that by the age of 21 he had stolen more than
500; never to sell, just for the thrill of driving them. He became a
superb driver, able to predict openings in traffic and negotiate slip-
pery surfaces with the skill of a getaway driver. Allen Ginsberg fell
in love with him and he is the subject of many of Ginsberg's early
poems. He also became Jack Kerouac's muse and many of his
books, including *On The Road*, feature Cassady as the hero.
Cassady was famous for his – usually amphetamine induced –
monologues, in which he attempted a simultaneous description of
many levels of awareness of what was going on at that time.
Kerouac maintained that Cassady's letters were a strong influence
on his own work, which is likely because Cassady's writing is more
like a recording of his actual speech than constructed prose, as the
short texts included here show. In the sixties, after serving time in
jail, Cassady took on a new role, this time as the driver of Ken

Kesey's famous bus. Cassady died of exposure on the railroad tracks outside San Miguel de Allende, Mexico, on 4 February 1968, walking home from a Mexican wedding party.

The First Third. San Francisco, 1971, (revised ed. 1981) City Lights.
Grace Beats Karma, Letters From Prison 1958–1960. New York, 1993. Blast.
Neal Cassady Collected Letters, 1944–1967. New York, 2004. Penguin.

Gregory Corso

Born in Greenwich Village, New York City on 26 March 1930 to a sixteen year old mother and a seventeen year old father. A year later his mother returned to Italy and Gregory entered a series of orphanages and foster homes. His unhappy childhood culminated in three months in Bellevue at the age of thirteen for breaking into a hostel to sleep. At the age of seventeen, he organised a robbery using walkie-talkies and was sent to Clinton Prison for a three year stretch. Here he discovered literature and read his way through a turn-of-the-century dictionary and the classics. He came out age twenty in love with Shelley, Keats, Chatterton and Marlowe. He met Allen Ginsberg in a lesbian bar in Greenwich Village in 1950 and through him got to know Kerouac, Burroughs and the other Beats. In 1954 he spent two years living in Cambridge, Massachusetts, and in 1956 more than 50 students from Harvard and Radcliffe contributed money for the publication of his first book of poems, *The Vestal Lady On Brattle.* Most of the poems printed here were written while living at the Beat Hotel in Paris with Allen Ginsberg and William Burroughs when he was at the height of his powers. His later years were marred by heroin addiction but Allen Ginsberg remained convinced of his genius and helped to support him throughout his lifetime. Corso died at his daughter's home in Robbinsdale, Minnesota, on 17 January 2000.

The Vestal Lady On Brattle and Other Poems. Cambridge, MA. 1955. Richard Brukenfeld.
Gasoline. San Francisco, 1958. City Lights.
Bomb (broadside). San Francisco, 1958. City Lights.
Happy Birthday of Death. New York, 1960. New Directions.
American Express. Paris, 1961. Olympia.

Selected Poems. London, 1962. Eyre and Spottiswoode.
Long Live Man. New York, 1962. New Directions.
The Mutation of the Spirit. San Francisco [np] 1964.
Ten Times a Poem. New York, 1967. Poet's Press.
Elegiac Feelings American. New York, 1970. New Directions.
Herald of the Autochthonic Spirit. New York, 1981. New Directions.
The Riverside Interviews. 3: Gregory Corso. London 1982. Binnacle.
Mindfield. New York, 1989. Thunder's Mouth.

Diane DiPrima

Born in New York City on 6 August 1934 into an Italian American family. DiPrima attended Swarthmore college between 1951 and 1953 before moving to Greenwich Village to concentrate on her poetry. Her first book, *This Kind Of Bird Flies Backward* was published by LeRoi Jones' Totem Press in 1958 and she later worked with him as co-editor of the *Floating Bear* poetry newsletter and in 1961 set up the New York Poets Theatre with Jones and others. In 1969 she wrote an amusing erotic autobiography for Maurice Girodias's Olympia Press called *Memoirs of a Beatnik* in which she described the orgy involving herself, Jack Kerouac, Allen Ginsberg and several others that occurred on the very first day she met them in 1957. As one of the few women involved on a creative level – rather than a domestic level – in the Beat Generation, she had to fight hard to be taken seriously by her contemporaries. Even then she faced discrimination; she was left out of Donald Allen's *The New American Poetry 1945–1960* for purely political reasons. She is best known for her *Revolutionary Letters*, published throughout the sixties. The selection printed here comes from her first book of prose, *Dinners and Nightmares*, published in 1960.

This Kind of Bird Flies Backward. New York, 1958. Totem.
Dinners and Nightmares. New York, 1961. Corinth.
The New Handbook of Heaven. San Francisco, 1963. Auerhahn.
Poets Vaudeville. New York, 1964. Feed Folly.
Earthsong: Poems 1957–59. New York, 1968. Poets Press.
Hotel Albert: Poems. New York, 1968. Poets Press.
L.A. Odyssey. San Francisco, 1969. Poets Press.
Memoirs of a Beatnik. New York, 1969. Olympia.
Revolutionary Letters. San Francisco, 1971. City Lights.

Kerhonkson Journal, 1966. Berkeley, 1971. Oyez.

Loba, Part 1. Santa Barbara, 1973. Capra.

Freddie Poems. Point Reyes, CA, 1974. Eidolon.

Selected Poems 1956–1976. Plainfield, VT, 1977. North Atlantic.

Loba: Parts I–VII. Berkeley, 1978. Wingbow.

Pieces of a Song. San Francisco, 1990. City Lights.

Seminary Poems. 1991. Floating Island.

Recollections of My Life as a Woman. New York, 2001. Viking-Penguin.

Allen Ginsberg

The son of a high school English teacher, Ginsberg was born in Newark, New Jersey, 3 June 1926, and grew up in Paterson, New Jersey. At Columbia University he quickly became part of the circle of friends that included Jack Kerouac, William Burroughs, Herbert Huncke and Lucien Carr. Huncke, a professional thief and hustler moved in on him and used his apartment to store stolen goods. When the police closed in, Ginsberg's father, lawyer and his professors at Columbia University saw to it that he went to the Columbia Psychiatric Institute instead of jail and it was there he met Carl Solomon, one of the 'best minds of my generation' that Ginsberg saw as damaged or destroyed by the system. 'Howl' was dedicated to Solomon. After travels in the Mexican jungle, Ginsberg arrived in California, hoping to re-establish his sexual relationship with Neal Cassady but it was not a success. However, it was in San Francisco that Ginsberg finally found his poetic voice, and 'Howl' was written, and first read in public there. It was also in San Francisco that he met his life-time on-and-off companion Peter Orlovsky. Ginsberg was a central figure in the Beat Generation, and some say it was all his invention. He was convinced that all his friends were geniuses and played a major role in getting them all published. After the success of 'Howl' he went with Kerouac and Orlovsky to work with William Burroughs in Tangier to organise the manuscript of *The Naked Lunch*. After exploring France and Italy, Ginsberg and Orlovsky finished up in Paris where they took a room at the Beat Hotel. They were joined there by Gregory Corso and Burroughs. It was in Paris that Ginsberg began work on 'Kaddish', his great tribute to his mother, Naomi, who died in the mental hospital. The poem tell the story of her illness in harrowing detail. Throughout the sixties, Ginsberg became something of a spokesman for the hippies and the anti-war movement, devoting much of his time to non-poetry causes. In the seventies he became a Tibetan Buddhist and taught at the Naropa Institute, a Buddhist college in Boulder, Colorado. He died in his loft in New York City on 5 April 1997.

Howl And Other Poems. San Francisco, 1956. City Lights.

Empty Mirror. New York, 1961. Totem/Corinth.

Kaddish And Other Poems. San Francisco, 1961. City Lights.

Reality Sandwiches. San Francisco, 1963. City Lights.

The Change. London, 1963. Writers' Forum.

Prose Contribution To Cuban Revolution. Detroit, 1966. Artists'
    Workshop.

Wichita Vortex Sutra. London, 1966. Peace News.

TV Baby Poems. London, 1967. Cape-Goliard.

Planet News. San Francisco, 1968. City Lights.

Ankor Wat. London, 1968. Fulcrum.

Airplane Dreams: Compositions From Journals, Toronto, 1968. Anansi.

Wales, A Visitation. London, 1968. Cape Goliard.

Indian Journals. San Francisco, 1970. City Lights.

Improvised Poetics. San Francisco, 1972. Anonym.

Iron Horse. Toronto, 1972. Coach House.

Bixby Canyon Ocean Path Word Breeze. New York, 1972. Gotham
    Book Mart.

The Fall Of America. Poems On These States 1965–1971. San Francisco,
    1972. City Lights.

The Gates Of Wrath. Bolinas, 1972. Grey Fox.

Allen Verbatum, Lectures On Poetry, Politics, Consciousness. New York,
    1974. McGraw-Hill.

The Visions Of The Great Rememberer. Amherst, MA. 1974. Mulch.

Gay Sunshine Interview With Allen Young. Bolinas, CA. 1974. Grey Fox.

First Blues, Rags, Ballads & Harmonium Songs 1971–74. New York
    1975. Full Court.

Sad Dust Glories. Berkeley, 1975. Workingman's Press.

Chicago Trial Testimony. San Francisco, 1975. City Lights.

To Eberhart From Ginsberg. Lincoln, MA. 1976. Penmaen.

Poems All Over The Place, Mostly 'Seventies. Cherry Valley, NY, 1978.
    Cherry Valley.

[With Cassady, Neal]: *As Ever, The Collected Correspondence*. Berkeley,
    1977. Creative Arts.

Journals, Early Fifties, Early Sixties. New York, 1977. Grove.
Take Care of My Ghost, Ghost. N.p. 1977. Ghost.
Mind Breaths. (San Francisco, 1978. City Lights.)
Mostly Sitting Haiku. Paterson, NJ, 1978. From Here.
Composed On The Tongue. Bolinas, CA. 1980. Grey Fox.
The Riverside Interviews 1: Allen Ginsberg. London, 1980. Binnacle.
[With Orlovsky, Peter]: *Straight Heart's Delight, Love Poems & Selected
    Letters.* San Francisco, 1980. Gay Sunshine.
Plutonian Ode. San Francisco, 1982. City Lights.
Many Loves. New York, 1984. Pequod.
Collected Poems 1947–1980. New York, 1985. Harper & Row.
Howl, Original Draft Facsimile. New York, 1986. Harper & Row, 1986.
White Shroud, Poems 1980–1985. New York, 1986. Harper & Row.
Old Love Story. New York, 1986. Lospecchio.
Your Reason and Blake's System. Madras, 1988. Hanuman.
Allen Ginsberg: Photographs. Altadena, CA, 1991. Twelvetrees.
Thieves Stole This Poem. Hull, 1993. Carnivorous.
Visiting Father & Friends. Louisville, 1993. Thinker Review.
Snapshot Poetics. San Francisco, 1993. Chronicle.
Journals Mid-Fifties: 1954–1958. New York, 1994. HarperCollins.
Mind Writing Slogans. Boise, ID, 1994. Limberlost.
Cosmopolitan Greetings. New York, 1994. Harper & Row.
Selected Poems 1947–1995. New York, 1996. HarperCollins.
Luminous Dreams. Gran Canaria, 1997. Zasterle.
Death & Fame, Last Poems 1993–1997. New York, 1999.
    HarperFlamingo.
Family Business: Two Lives In Letters and Poetry. (with Louis Ginsberg)
    New York, 2001. Bloomsbury.

Lawrence Ferlinghetti

Born in Yonkers, New York City, 24 March 1919, the fifth son of
Clemence Monsanto who was committed to a mental asylum
shortly after his birth, having been driven mad with grief by the
death of Ferlinghetti's father. His aunt, Emily Monsanto, took the
baby to France. They returned to the US when he was five and he
was placed in an orphanage but he lived with her whenever circumstances permitted. Emily worked as a French governess for the
wealthy Lawrence family, founders of Sarah Lawrence College, who
took Lawrence in after she mysteriously disappeared. He attended

the University of North Carolina at Chapel Hill where he began writing. He joined the navy and became a Lieutenant Commander in charge of a sub chaser during the war. Afterwards he studied poetry at the Sorbonne on the G.I. Bill. In 1952 he started the City Lights Bookshop in San Francisco which rapidly became the headquarters for the city's literary scene. He began publishing the Pocket Poets series, the fourth of which was Allen Ginsberg's first book, *Howl and Other Poems*. Because of *Howl* Ferlinghetti and his shop manager were arrested for selling obscene publications and the resulting trial, which they won, established City Lights as a major poetry publishing house and Ginsberg's reputation as a poet. Ferlinghetti's own poetry was mostly published by New Directions and his 1958 collection *A Coney Island of the Mind* is one of the biggest selling poetry books in America with close on a million copies in print. Ferlinghetti's genius is to have what he calls an 'Unblinking Eye': to clearly see the reality of everyday events, and sometimes add a little surreal twist.

Pictures of the Gone World. San Francisco, 1955. City Lights.

A Coney Island of the Mind. New York, 1958. New Directions.

Tentative Description of a Dinner Given to Promote the Impeachment of President Eisenhower. San Francisco, 1958. Golden Mountain.

Her. New York, 1960. New Directions.

One Thousand Fearful Words for Fidel Castro. San Francisco, 1961. City Lights.

Starting From San Francisco. New York, 1961 (revised paperback ed, 1967). New Directions.

Unfair Arguments With Existence. New York, 1963. New Directions.

Routines. New York, 1964. New Directions.

Where Is Vietnam? San Francisco, 1965. City Lights.

An Eye On the World: Selected Poems. London, 1967. MacGibbon & Kee.

After the Cries of the Birds. San Francisco, 1967. Dave Haselwood.

The Secret Meaning Of Things. New York, 1969. New Directions.

Tyrannus Nix? New York, 1969. New Directions.

The Mexican Night, a Travel Journal. New York, 1970. New Directions.

The Illustrated Wilfred Funk. San Francisco, 1971. City Lights.

Back Roads To Far Places. New York, 1971. New Directions.

Open Eye, Open Heart. New York, 1973. New Directions.

Who Are We Now? New York, 1976. New Directions.

Northwest Ecolog. San Francisco, 1978. City Lights.
Landscapes of Living and Dying. New York, 1979. New Directions.
The Sea and Ourselves at Cape Ann. Madison, 1979. Red Ozier.
Mule Mountain Dreams. Bisbee, AZ, 1980. Bisbee.
Literary San Francisco (with Nancy Peters). New York, 1980. Harper &
    Row/City Lights.
Endless Life: The Selected Poems. New York, 1981. New Directions.
The Populist Manifestos. San Francisco, 1981. Grey Fox.
A Trip To Italy and France. New York, 1981. New Directions.
Leaves of Life (First Series) Fifty Drawings From the Model. San
    Francisco, 1983. City Lights.
Seven Days In Nicaragua Libre (photographs by Chris Felver). San
    Francisco, 1984. City Lights.
Over All the Obscene Boundaries: European Poems & Translations.
    New York, 1984. New Directions.
Love In the Days of Rage. New York, 1988. E. P. Dutton.
Inside the Trojan Horse. San Francisco, 1988. Don't Call It Frisco.
When I Look At Pictures. Salt Lake City, 1990. Peregrine Smith.
Wild Dreams Of a New Beginning. New York, 1988. New Directions
The Canticle of Jack Kerouac. Boise, IO, 1993. Limberlost.
Triumph of the Post Modern. Hull, 1993. Carnivorous Arpeggio.
These Are My Rivers: Selected Poems 1955–1993. New York, 1993.
    New Directions.
A Far Rockaway of the Heart. New York, 1997. New Directions.
The Hopper House at Truro. New York, 1997. Lospecchio.

John Clellon Holmes

Born in Holyoke, Massachusetts, 12 March 1926, Holmes first met
Ginsberg and Kerouac at Columbia University in 1948. He was a
key figure in the early days of the Beat Generation and remained
close to Kerouac until his death. However, he saw himself as an
intellectual and academic and disapproved of the wild side of the
Beats: the drugs, the excess, the crazy pointless travelling. He used
his experiences as a youth member of the group to write *Go*, published in 1952. Like Kerouac's work, it was a *roman-à-clef*. It
featured Kerouac as Gene Pasternak, Ginsberg as David Stofsky,
Cassady as Hart Kennedy and Holmes himself as Paul Hobbes.
Kerouac was jealous when Holmes received a $20,000 advance for
the paperback version of the book, a huge amount at the time,

money Holmes used to buy himself the house in Old Saybrook, Connecticut where he died on 2 March 1988.

Go. New York, 1952. Charles Scribners.

The Horn. New York, 1953. Random House.

Get Home Free. New York, 1964. E. P. Dutton.

Nothing More To Declare. New York, 1967. E. P. Dutton.

The Bowling Green Poems. California, PA, 1977. The Unspeakable Visions of the Individual.

Death Drag: Selected Poems 1948–1979. Pocatello, ID, 1979. Limberlost.

Visitor: Jack Kerouac In Old Saybrook. California, PA, 1981. Knight.

Gone In October. Pocatello, ID, 1985. Limberlost.

Displaced Person, Selected Essays, Volume One. Fayetteville, 1987. U of Arkansas.

Representative Man, Selected Essays, Volume Two. Fayetteville, 1987. U of Arkansas.

Passionate Opinions, Selected Essays, Volume Three. Fayetteville, 1988. U of Arkansas.

Dire Coasts. Boise, ID, 1988. Limberlost.

Night Music: Selected Poems. Fayetteville, 1989. U of Arkansas.

Herbert Huncke

Huncke was born in Greenfield, Massachusetts, on 9 January 1915. His father manufactured machine tools first in Detroit and then Chicago and Huncke grew up in upper middle-class luxury. His parents divorced when he was twelve and he ran away from home, getting as far as Geneva, New York, before being picked up by the police. He began staying out all night, taking drugs and, from the age of fourteen, picking up men. He arrived in New York City in 1939 and headed straight for Times Square. Here he survived as a male prostitute, as a con man and thief. No matter how desperate someone's circumstances, Huncke would still steal their last dime. The Times Square cops thought he was the most despicable of their many low-life citizens and called him 'The Creep' but to the Beats he was a romantic character. Burroughs described him as 'a character, a rarity, a real picaresque antihero in the classical tradition. Huncke was a great storyteller, usually about his misfortunes.' It was because Huncke used Allen Ginsberg's apartment to store stolen goods that Ginsberg almost went to jail, and spent time in the Columbia Psychiatric Institute instead. Huncke himself spent long periods in jail, including most of the 1970s. Huncke's wealthy background gave him a precision and eloquence of speech that he never lost. He had a large vocabulary and knew how to construct a story. Though he produced very little in the way of writing, he was a central figure in Beat mythology; he featured in books by Burroughs, Kerouac and Holmes as well as in Ginsberg's 'Howl'. Huncke died in New York City, 8 August 1996.

Huncke's Journal. New York, 1965. Poet's Press.
The Evening Sun Turned Crimson. Cherry Valley, NY, 1980. Cherry Valley.
Guilty of Everything (single story). Madras, 1987. Hanuman.
Guilty of Everything. New York, 1990. Paragon.
The Herbert Huncke Reader. New York, 1997. William Morrow.

Ted Joans

Known as the 'jazz poet of the beat generation' Ted was a regular reader at the Café Bizarre, Café Wha and the Café Rafio in Greenwich Village:

> I had developed a method of reading my poems that was similar to the way I blew trumpet. Each time I took a solo on my horn, on any of the standard songs, that solo would inevitably be different ... I would soar off into spontaneous creativity that would sometimes surprise me as well as my fellow musicians. This is my method of creating jazz poetry which is totally different from most of the so-called self-styled 'jazz poets'.

Ted brought energy and humour to the sometimes overly serious beat scene; for instance he was one of the tongue-in-cheek organisers of Rent-a-Beatnik, a company that provided bongo-playing, bearded bohemians to attend straight society parties and entertain the guests with 'Beat' poetry. Jones was born on a riverboat in Cairo, Illinois, on 4 July 1928 and died in Vancouver, British Columbia on 25 April 2003 but his body was not discovered until 7 May. Though never as famous as the other Black Beat poets,

Ted got right to the heart of beatdom. He travelled widely, spreading the message, spending much of his time in Timbuktu and in Paris.

All Of Ted Joans and No More. New York, 1961. Excelsior Press.
The Hipsters. New York, 1961. Corinth.
Black Pow-Wow Jazz Poems. New York, 1969. Hill and Wang.
Afrodisia. New York, 1971. Hill and Wang.
A Black Manifesto In Jazz Poetry and Prose. London, 1971. Calder & Boyars.
Spetrophilia Poems and Collages. Amsterdam, 1973. Amsterdam Literary Café.
Flying Piranha (with Joyce Mansour). New York, 1978. Bola Press.
Honey Spoon. Paris, 1991. Handshake.
Double Trouble (with Hart Leroy Bibbs). Paris, 1992. Editions Bleu Outremer.
Okapi Passion. Berkeley, 1994. Ishmael Reed Publishing Co.
Teducation. Minneapolis, 1999. Coffee House Press.
Wow. Mukilteo, WA, 1999. Quicksilver/Quartermoon.
Select One or More. Berkeley, 2000. Bancroft Library Press.
Lost & Found: "In Thursday Sane". Davis, CA, 2001. Swan Scythe Press.
Our Thang. Victoria, BC, 2001. Ekstasis Editions.

LeRoi Jones/ Amiri Baraka

Born LeRoi Jones in Newark, New Jersey, on 7 October 1934. After attending Rutgers, Howard and Columbia Universities he took an MA in German Literature at the New School for Social Research. He moved to Greenwich Village at the age of 25 to make a life as a poet. He married Hettie Cohen and in 1958 they published *Yugen* magazine, one of the most influential of all Beat generation literary periodicals. They also started the Totem Press, publishing books by Gary Snyder, Diane DiPrima, Jack Kerouac and his own *Preface To a Twenty-Volume Suicide Note*. In 1961, Jones and Diane DiPrima began publishing the *Floating Bear*, a free mimeograph poetry newsletter, keeping everyone on the scene up to date with each other's new work. After the assassination of Malcolm X in 1965, Jones questioned his involvement with the white, essentially middle-class, Beat scene and he left his white wife and moved to Harlem to found the Black Arts Repertory Theater. In 1966 he became a Muslim and adopted the religious name Amiri Baraka. He made the final break and returned to Newark, to become a Marxist-Leninist Third World Socialist (his description) at a time when the black communities were under tremendous police and establishment persecution. His plays and jazz writing are still well received, and he often lectures on drama and music.

Preface To a Twenty Volume Suicide Note. New York, 1961. Totem/Corinth.

Blues People: Negro Music In White America. New York, 1963. Morrow.

The Dutchman and The Slave. New York, 1964. Morrow.

The Dead Lecturer. New York, 1964. Grove.

The System of Dante's Hell. New York, 1965. Grove.

Home: Social Essays. New York, 1966. Morrow.

Black Art. Newark, 1966. Jihad.

The Baptism and The Toilet. New York, 1967. Grove.

Tales. New York, 1967. Grove.

Arm Yrself or Harm Yrself. Newark, 1967. Jihad.

Black Music. New York, 1967. Morrow.

Black Magic: Poetry 1961–1967. Indianapolis, 1969. Bobbs-Merrill.

Slave Ship. Newark, 1969. Jihad.

Four Black Revolutionary Plays. Indianapolis, 1969. Bobbs-Merrill.

It's Nation Time. Chicago, 1970. Third World.

In Our Terribleness (with Fundi). Indianapolis, 1970. Bobbs-Merrill.

A Black Value System. Newark, 1970. Jihad.

Jello. Chicago, 1970. Third World.

Raise Race Rays Raze. Essays Since 1965. New York, 1971. Random.

Kawaida Studies, the New Nationalism. Chicago, 1972. Third World.

Spirit Reach. Newark, 1972. Jihad.

Afrikan Revolution. Newark, 1973. Jihad.

Hard Facts. Newark, 1976. Jihad.

The Motion of History. New York, 1978. Morrow.

What Was The Relationship of the Lone Ranger To the Means of Production? New York, 1978. AICU.

AM/TRAK. New York, 1979. Phoenix.

The Sydney Poet Heroical. Berkeley, 1979. Reed & Cannon.

Selected Poems of Amiri Baraka-LeRoi Jones. New York, 1979. Morrow.

Selected Plays and Prose. New York, 1979. Morrow.

The Autobiography of LeRoi Jones/Amiri Baraka. New York, 1984.
  Freundlich Books.
The LeRoi Jones/Amiri Baraka Reader. New York, 1991. Thunder's
  Mouth.
Transbluesency: Selected Poems 1961–1995. New York, 1995. Marsilio.

Lenore Kandel

Born in New York City in 1932 of Turkish and Russian ancestry,
her parents moved within a year to Los Angeles where her father
was a screenwriter. She first met the Beats when she went to San
Francisco for a weekend, met Lew Welch and ended up going to Big
Sur with Jack Kerouac. He named her Ramona Schwartz in *Big Sur*
and wrote that she was 'intelligent, well read, writes poetry, is a Zen
student, knows everything . . .' She remained in San Francisco,
living for a time with Lew Welch and continuing her Zen studies.
The poem included here comes from her Beat period rather than her
later, more psychedelic material. She is best known for *The Love
Book*, published in 1965 and the subject of a court case for obscenity. She defended her erotic poems before the judge, saying they
expressed her 'belief that sexual acts between loving persons are
religious acts.'

An Exquisite Navel. San Francisco, 1959. Three Penny.
A Passing Dragon. San Francisco, 1959. Three Penny.
A Passing Dragon Seen Again. San Francisco, 1959. Three Penny.
The Love Book. San Francisco, 1966. Stolen Paper Editions.
Word Alchemy. New York, 1967. Grove.

Bob Kaufman

Born of a Catholic mother from Martinique and a German
Orthodox Jew in New Orleans, Louisiana, on 18 April 1925,
Kaufman was one of thirteen children. At the age of thirteen he
joined the US Merchant Marines and served for twenty years at sea
before arriving in San Francisco just as the Beat Generation was
beginning to happen in North Beach. The coffee shop poetry readings were very much to his taste and he became a fixture at the
Co-existence Bagel Shop and other North Beach hangouts. In May
1959, Kaufman, his wife Eileen, Allen Ginsberg, John Kelly and

others began *Beatitude* magazine in Cassandra's Coffee Shop; a magazine that became the West Coast mouthpiece for the movement. Meanwhile City Lights Books published his *Abomunist Manifesto* and other 'vituperative visionary broadsides'. At the assassination of John F. Kennedy in 1963 he took a vow of silence which he upheld for twelve years, and three years later spent a further four years in silence. These are his great humorous howls and cackles of rage that very much represent the energy, the humour and intensity of San Francisco's North Beach scene in the late fifties. Bob Kaufman died in San Francisco on 12 January 1986.

Abomunist Manifesto. San Francisco, 1959. City Lights.
Second April. San Francisco, 1959. City Lights.
Solitudes Crowded With Loneliness. New York, 1965. New Directions.
Golden Sardine. San Francisco, 1967. City Lights.
Watch My Tracks. New York, 1971. Knopf.
The Ancient Rain: Poems 1956–1978. New York, 1981. New Directions.
Selected Poems. Minneapolis, 1995. Coffee House.

Jack Kerouac

Sometimes referred to as 'The King of the Beats' after he jokingly once called himself that, Kerouac was certainly the most famous of the Beats and, oddly, the one who lived the least Beat life; preferring to live in the suburbs or in small towns with his mother who worked in a shoe factory to provide for him. Born in Lowell, Massachusetts, 12 March 1922 to a French Canadian Catholic family, Kerouac only ventured out into the Beat world of Cassady, Ginsberg, Burroughs, Corso and the others to have adventures that he could then go home and write about. His prolific note taking, his photographic memory and his all-seeing eye meant that he could write entire books about the events of just a few weeks. His books were not novels; they were very thinly disguised chronicles of actual events, but they were literature. He developed the theory of spontaneous prose, reprinted here, thinking that the first thought was sacred and should not be changed, though he often made small changes to his work. (Truman Capote condemned it as 'just typewriting') The energy and vitality that he brought to his writing set him apart from the other writers of his day and the huge success of *On The Road* not only popularised the ideas of the Beat

Generation, but made celebrities of his characters, in particular Neal Cassady who, under the name of Dean Moriarty, was the hero of his book. Kerouac took enormous risks in his writing, and *Visions of Cody*, another huge account of Neal Cassady and his life, incorporated near abstract 'spontaneous bebop prosody' as well as a literal transcript of a tape recorded conversation with Cassady which prefigured Andy Warhol's *a* by many years. The extract from *On The Road* called 'Jazz of the Beat Generation' was first published as a separate piece in *New World Writing 7*, in April 1955 under the pseudonym of Jean-Louis (this was in case his wife saw it and claimed child-support for their daughter). The piece shows the strong influence of jazz on his work, as well as his huge energy and enthusiasm, and the enormous scale and scope of his writing as if he were attempting to explain and describe the whole of North America in his prose. He died of alcoholism in Saint Petersburg, Florida, 21 October 1969.

The Town and the City. New York, 1950. Harcourt Brace and Co.

On The Road. New York, 1957. Viking.

The Subterraneans. New York, 1958. Grove.

The Dharma Bums. New York, 1958. Viking.

Doctor Sax. New York, 1959. Grove.

Maggie Cassidy. New York, 1959. Avon.

Visions of Cody (selections). New York, 1959. New Directions.

Mexico City Blues. New York, 1959. Grove.

The Scripture of the Golden Eternity. New York, 1960. Corinth.

Tristessa. New York, 1960. Avon.

Lonesome Traveler. New York, 1960. McGraw-Hill.

Book Of Dreams. San Francisco, 1961. City Lights.

Pull My Daisy. New York, 1961. Grove.

Big Sur. New York, 1962. Farrar, Straus & Cudahy.

Visions of Gerard. New York, 1963. Farrar, Straus & Cudahy.

Desolation Angels. New York, 1965. Coward-McCann.

Satori In Paris. New York, 1966. Grove.

Vanity of Duluoz. New York, 1968. Coward-McCann.

Scattered Poems. San Francisco, 1971. City Lights.

Pic. New York, 1971. Grove.

Visions of Cody. New York, 1973. McGraw-Hill.

Heaven & Other Poems. Berkeley, 1977. Grey Fox.

Pomes All Sizes. San Francisco, 1992. City Lights.

Good Blonde & Others. San Francisco, 1993. Grey Fox.
Old Angel Midnight. San Francisco, 1993. Grey Fox.
The Portable Jack Kerouac. New York, 1995. Viking.
Selected Letters: 1940–1956. New York, 1995. Viking Penguin.
Book Of Blues. New York, 1995. Penguin.
Some of the Dharma. New York, 1997. Viking Penguin.
Selected Letters: 1957–1969. New York, 1999. Viking Penguin.
Atop an Underwood. New York, 1999. Viking.
Orpheus Emerged. New York, 2002. I-Books.
Book of Haikus. New York, 2003. Penguin Poets.

Michael McClure

Born in Marysville, Kansas, on 20 October 1932, McClure grew up in Seattle. He spent his adolescent years in Wichita, Kansas, and moved to San Francisco after a year at the University of Arizona at Tucson. McClure was a core member of the Beat Generation, San Francisco chapter, and was one of the poets at the legendary Six Gallery reading where Ginsberg first read 'Howl'; it was his first public reading. He evolved his own unique 'beat language' as a way of articulating the otherwise inexpressible. He tested his lion poetry by going to the San Francisco zoo and roaring at the lions there. They roared back. McClure later wrote successful plays and a novel but the groundbreaking poetry from the late fifties was what established his distinctive voice.

Passage. Big Sur, 1956. Jonathan Williams.
Peyote Poem. San Francisco, 1958. Semina.
For Artaud. New York, 1959. Totem.
Hymns To St. Geryon and Other Poems. San Francisco, 1959. Auerhahn.
The New Book/A Book of Torture. New York City, 1961. Grove.
Pillow. New York, 1961. New York Poets Theatre.
Dark Brown. San Francisco, 1961. Auerhahn.
Meat Science Essays. San Francisco, 1963. City Lights. (expanded edition, 1966)
Ghost Tantras. San Francisco, 1964. Privately published.
13 Mad Sonnets. Milano, 1964. East 128.
The Beard. San Francisco, 1965. Privately printed.
Poisoned Wheat. San Francisco, 1965. Privately printed.
Dream Table. San Francisco, 1965. Dave Haselwood.

Unto Caesar. San Francisco, 1965. Dave Haselwood.

Mandalas (with Bruce Connor). San Francisco, 1965. Dave Haselwood.

Love Lion Book. San Francisco, 1966. Four Seasons.

The Blossom; or, Billy the Kid. Milwaukee, 1967. Great Lakes Books.

Freewheelin Frank, Secretary of the Hells Angels, by Frank Reynolds, as told to Michael McClure. New York, 1967. Grove.

Hail Thee Who Play. Los Angeles, 1968. Black Sparrow.

The Sermons of Jean Harlow and the Curses of Billy the Kid. San Francisco, 1968. Four Seasons/Dave Haselwood.

Muscled Apple Swift. Los Angeles, 1968. Love.

The Surge. Columbus, OH, 1969. Frontier.

Little Odes & The Raptors. Los Angeles, 1969. Black Sparrow.

Star. New York, 1970. Grove.

The Cherub. Los Angeles, 1970. Black Sparrow.

The Mad Cub. New York, 1970. Bantam.

The Adept. New York, 1971. Delacorte.

Gargoyle Cartoons. New York, 1971. Delacorte.

The Mammals. San Francisco, 1972. Cranium.

The Book of Joanna. Berkeley, 1973. Sand Dollar.

Solstice Blossom. Berkeley, 1973. Arif.

Fleas 189–195. New York, 1974. Aloe.

On Organism. Canton, NY, 1974. Institute of Further Studies.

Rare Angel. Los Angeles, 1974. Black Sparrow.

September Blackberries. New York, 1974. New Directions.

A Fist Full (1956–1957). Los Angeles, 1974. Black Sparrow.

Jaguar Skies. New York, 1975. New Directions.

Man of Moderation. New York, 1975. Frank Hallman.

Gorf, or Gorf and the Blind Dyke. New York, 1976. New Directions.

The Grabbing of the Fairy. St. Paul, MN, 1978. Truck.

Antechamber and Other Poems. New York, 1978. New Directions.

Fragments of Perseus. New York, 1978. Jordan Davies.

Josephine: The Mouse Singer. New York, 1980. New Directions.

Seasons (with Joanna McClure and Wesley Tanner). Berkeley, 1981. Arif.

Scratching the Beat Surface. San Francisco, 1982. North Point.

The Book of Benjamin (with Wesley Tanner). Berkeley, 1982. Arif.

General Gorgeous. New York, 1982. Dramatists Play Service.

Fragments of Perseus. New York, 1983. New Directions.

The Beard & Vktms. New York, 1985. Grove.

Specks. Vancouver, 1985. Talonbooks.

Selected Poems. New York, 1986. New Directions.

The Stitching. Santa Barbara, 1986. Table Top.
Rebel Lions. New York, 1991. New Directions.
Adventures of a Novel in Four Chapters (with Bruce Connor). San
    Francisco, 1991. Limestone.
Simple Eyes. New York, 1992. New Directions.
Red Cages. San Francisco, 1992. Blue Beetle.
Lighting the Corners. Albuquerque, NM, 1993. U of NM.
What Crevices. Berkeley, 1993. Tangram.
Rain Mirror. New York, 1999. New Directions.
Touching the Edge: Dharma Devotions From the Hummingbird Sutra.
    Boston, 1999. Shambala.
Plum Stones: Cartoons of No Heaven. Oakland, 2002. O Books.

Jack Micheline

Born Harold Silver, in the East Bronx, New York City, on 6
November 1929 and died in San Francisco on 27 February 1998,
Micheline was one of the old time hard-drinking Beats who never
attempted to infiltrate the academic life but stayed out on the streets
and nighttime bars. He pushed a handcart in the New York garment
district, worked as a farmer, dishwasher, actor, union organiser,
messenger boy, street singer and panhandler. All through the '50s he
was writing poetry and in 1957 won a poetry reading contest at the
Half Note Café on Hudson Street judged by Charles Mingus, Nat
Hentoff and Jean Shepard. Shortly afterwards, LeRoi Jones published his poem 'Steps' in the first issue of *Yugen* magazine alongside
work by Allen Ginsberg and Philip Whalen; it was his first time in
print. Also in 1958, his first book, *River of Red Wine*, was published with an introduction by his friend Jack Kerouac. He chose the
name 'Jack' after Jack London, and Micheline was his mother's
maiden name with an 'e' added to it. He distanced himself from the
Beats, saying they were too commercial, and preferred to see himself
as more of an old style bohemian, but the term Beat is wide ranging,
and he had the genuine Beat spirit; more so than most.

River of Red Wine and Other Poems. New York, 1958. Troubadour.
I Kiss Angels. New York, 1962. Interim.
In The Bronx and Other Stories. New York, 1965. Sam Hooker.
Tell Your Mama You Want To Be Free. Los Angeles, 1969. Dead Sea
    Fleet.

Yellow Horn and Other Poemsongs. N.p. 1969. Dead Sea Fleet.

Angel Baby. N.p. 1971. Midnight Special.

Pussy Poems. N.p. 1972. Midnight Special.

Low Class. New York, 1972. Midnight Special.

Monkey Meat Farm Poems. San Francisco, 1973. Privately published.

Poems of Dr. Innisfree. San Francisco, 1975. Beatitude.

Street of Lost Fools. Mastic, NY, 1975. Street Press.

Yellow Horn. San Francisco, 1975. Golden Mountain.

Last House In America. San Francisco, 1976. Second Coming.

North of Manhattan: Collected Poems, Ballads, and Songs: 1954–1975. South San Francisco, 1976. ManRoot.

Purple Submarine. San Francisco, 1976. Greenlight.

Skinny Dynamite. San Francisco, 1980. Second Coming.

Dreamers, Hustlers, Touts, Sharpies, Greed & the Big Kill. San Francisco, 1981. Second Coming.

Acappella Rabbi: A Jack Micheline Sampler. Pueblo, CO, 1986. Quick Books.

Imaginary Conversation With Jack Kerouac. Oakland, 1989. Zeitgeist.

Outlaw of the Lowest Planet. Oakland, 1993. Zeitgeist.

A Man Obsessed Who Does Not Sleep Who Wanders About At Night Mumbling To Himself Counting Empty Beer Cans. San Francisco, 1994. Road Kill.

Souls. San Francisco, 1997. Express Poem.

A Dagger At Your Heart. San Francisco, 1997. Midnight Special Editions.

Sixty-seven Poems For Downtrodden Saints. San Francisco, 1997. FMSBW.

Frank O'Hara

Born in Baltimore, Maryland, on 27 June 1926, educated at Harvard, O'Hara was an associate curator at the Museum of Modern Art, New York. His gay sophisticated midtown life mixed poetry with the moneyed art crowd, making the midtown glass towers seem intimate living spaces for his musings on everyday trivialities. Though more closely allied to the so-called New York School of Kenneth Koch, John Ashbery and himself, his friendship group included Allen Ginsberg, who was one of his lovers, and he lived in the Lower East Side, by Tompkins Square, the heart of Beat territory. If anything he was the go-between, connecting the wealthy art and culture crowd with the starving poets. His poetry was deceptively simple: diary listings, musings, everyday events, making the mundane into the universal. He died in Fire Island, New York, on 25 July 1966, run over by a beach buggy in a bizarre accident.

A City Winter and Other Poems. New York, 1952. Tibor de Nagy.
Oranges. New York, 1953. Tibor de Nagy.
Meditations In an Emergency. New York, 1957. Grove.
Jackson Pollock. New York, 1959. Braziller.
New Spanish Painting and Sculpture. New York, 1960. Museum of Modern Art.
Second Avenue. New York, 1960. Totem/Corinth.
Odes. New York, 1960. Tiber.
Lunch Poems. San Francisco, 1964. City Lights.
Love Poems (Tentative Title). New York, 1965. Tibor de Nagy.
Robert Motherwell. New York, 1965. Museum of Modern Art.
Nakian. New York, 1966. Museum of Modern Art.
In Memory of My Feelings. New York, 1967. Museum of Modern Art.
Two Pieces. London, 1969. Long Hair Books.
The Collected Poems of Frank O'Hara. New York, 1971. Knopf.
Belgrade, November 19, 1963. New York, 1973. Adventures In Poetry.
The Selected Poems of Frank O'Hara. New York, 1974. Knopf.
Hymns of St. Bridget (with Bill Berkson) New York, 1974. Adventures In Poetry.
Art Chronicles 1954–1966. New York, 1975. Braziller.
Standing Still and Walking in New York. Bolinas, CA, 1975. Grey Fox.
Early Writing. Bolinas, CA, 1977. Grey Fox.
Poems Retrieved. Bolinas, CA, 1977. Grey Fox.
Selected Plays. New York, 1978. Full Court.

Peter Orlovsky

Born in the Lower East Side of New York City on 8 July 1933 and grew up in Queens, where the family lived in a converted chicken coop. Orlovsky dropped out of high school and went to work in a mental hospital tending to senile patients. In 1953 he was drafted and sent to boot camp in West Virginia where a lieutenant discovered him reading and asked if he was a Communist. 'An army is an army against love,' Peter told him. He was sent to work as a medic in the army hospital in San Francisco for his remaining service. He met Allen Ginsberg in 1954 and though Orlovsky was primarily attracted to women, they formed a relationship that continued until Ginsberg's death in 1997. In 1957 they travelled to Tangier and Europe, settling in the Beat Hotel in Paris at the end of the year, and it was here that Orlovsky began to write. He never did learn to spell properly and his eccentric spelling contributes to the gentle surrealism and charm of his work.

Dear Allen: Ship Will Land Jan 23, 58. Buffalo, NY, 1971. Intrepid
    Press.
Leper's Cry. New York, 1972. Phoenix Bookshop.
Clean Asshole Poems & Smiling Vegetable Songs. San Francisco, 1978.
    City Lights.

Gary Snyder

Born in San Francisco on 8 May 1930 and grew up in Washington State and Oregon, where he grew to love the mountains and the outdoor life. He studied at Reed College where he met Lew Welch and Philip Whalen. All three moved to San Francisco in the mid-fifties to become poets. Snyder is an example of the great diversity among the Beats: his studies of mountain peaks and laying riprap (stones used to repair mountain tracks) could not be further from the jazz poems of Bremser or Kaufman, or the utterly urban concerns of William Burroughs, and yet the same sensibility – a search for the unadorned truth – permeates them all. Snyder studied in the Asian Language programme of the University of California at Berkeley, working quietly in his cottage, taking time out only for orgies with Kerouac and Ginsberg and occasional marathon drunken revels. He was Japhy Ryder in Kerouac's *The Dharma Bums*, providing another angle on the Beat character; that of the Zen bum. He was one of the Six Gallery poets, present when Ginsberg first read 'Howl' and would have played a larger role in the San Francisco Beat scene had he not moved to Japan to study Zen just as the public discovered what they were all doing. He was an early ecology activist and did a lot to increase the American public's awareness of ecological issues.

Riprap. Ashland, MA, 1959. Origin Press.
Myths and Texts. New York, 1960. Totem/Corinth.

Riprap and Cold Mountain Poems. San Francisco, 1965. Four Seasons.
Six Sections From Mountains and Rivers Without End. San Francisco, 1965. Four Seasons.
A Range of Poems. London, 1966. Fulcrum.
The Back Country. London, 1967. Fulcrum.
The Blue Sky. New York, 1969. Phoenix.
Earth House Hold. New York, 1969. New Directions.
Regarding Wave. New York, 1970. New Directions.
Manzanita. Bolinas, CA, 1972. Four Seasons.
The Fudo Trilogy. Berkeley, 1973. Shaman Drum.
Turtle Island. New York, 1974. New Directions.
The Old Ways: Six Essays. San Francisco, 1977. City Lights.
On Bread and Poetry (with Philip Whalen and Lew Welch). Bolinas, CA, 1977. Grey Fox.
He Who Hunted Birds In His Father's Village. Bolinas, CA, 1979. Grey Fox.
The Real Work: Interviews & Tales 1964–1979. New York, 1980. New Directions.
Axe Handles. New York, 1982. Farrar, Straus & Giroux.
Passage Through India. San Francisco, 1984. Grey Fox.
Left Out In the Rain. Berkeley, 1986. North Point.
The Practice of the Wild. San Francisco, 1990. North Point.
No Nature: New and Selected Poems. New York, 1992. Pantheon.
A Place In Space. San Francisco, 1995. North Point.
The Gary Snyder Reader. Washington, DC, 1999. Counterpoint.

Carl Solomon

Born in the Bronx, New York City, on 30 March 1928, Solomon was a gifted child and graduated at the age of fifteen. Depressed at the death of his father in 1939, he eventually dropped out of City College and in 1943 enrolled in the Merchant Marine which enabled him to explore Europe. In Paris he discovered Surrealism and Dada, attending an exhibition organised by André Breton, seeing one of Genet's plays and, in 1947, watching Antonin Artaud give a terrifying performance of his poetry. He smuggled books by Genet and the Surrealists back to the USA and read everything he could find on the subject. After reading Kafka, he decided that he must be insane and presented himself on the steps of the Columbia

Psychiatric Institute, demanding to be lobotomised. There he met a fellow patient, Allen Ginsberg, who dedicated his most famous poem, 'Howl', to him. His 'Report From the Asylum' first appeared in *Neurotica* magazine, the same issue that saw Ginsberg's first appearance in print in the spring of 1950. In 1953, while working as an editor for his uncle A. A. Wyn, Solomon published William Burroughs' first book, *Junky* but when Kerouac submitted his *On The Road* on one continuous roll of paper, Solomon rejected it despite having already paid a small advance. Carl Solomon died in the Bronx in 1993.

Mishaps, Perhaps. San Francisco, 1966. City Lights.
More Mishaps. San Francisco, 1968. City Lights.

Alexander Trocchi

Born in Glasgow, 30 July 1925, Trocchi was the founder-editor of *Merlin* (1952–1955) the Paris-based, avant-garde literary periodical that first introduced Samuel Beckett to the post-war generation. He was closely involved with the Olympia Press and wrote many erotic books for them under the name of Frances Lengel. He is best known for his novels *Young Adam* and *Cain's Book*, the latter about his experiences as a junky in New York during the '50s, working as the captain of a scow on the Hudson River and spending all his free time in the Beat Generation 'pads' of Greenwich Village. His heroin addiction consumed him and he wrote very little from 1960 until his death in London on 15 April 1984.

Helen and Desire (as Frances Lengel). Paris, 1953. Olympia.
The Carnal Days of Helen Seferis (as Frances Lengel). Paris, 1954.
   Olympia.
Young Adam (as Frances Lengel). Paris, 1954. Olympia.
School For Sin (as Frances Lengel). Paris, 1954. Olympia.
Frank Harris – My Life and Loves, Volume 5. Paris, 1954. Olympia.
Thongs (as Frances Lengel). Paris, 1955. Olympia.
White Thighs (as Frances Lengel). Paris, 1955. Olympia.
Sappho of Lesbos. New York, 1960. Castle.
Cain's Book. New York, 1961. Grove.
Man At Leisure. London, 1972. Calder & Boyars.

Lew Welch

Born in Phoenix, Arizona, on 16 August 1926, Lew Welch studied at Reed College where he wrote one of the first college studies on the work of Gertrude Stein. At Reed his room-mates were Gary Snyder and Philip Whalen and he shared many of their interests, including a love of mountains and an interest in Zen Buddhism. After working in advertising in Chicago, he joined them in San Francisco in 1958, working on odd jobs and periodically disappearing into the woods. He suffered from depression and on 23 May 1971, while staying at Gary Snyder's ranch in the Sierra Nevada mountains in Northern California where he was planning on building a cabin in the woods, he left a brief farewell note to his friends and disappeared into the forest north of Nevada City, carrying a 30–30 rifle.

Wobbly Rock. San Francisco, 1960. Auerhahn.
Hermit Poems. San Francisco, 1965. Four Seasons.
On Out. Berkeley, 1965. Oyez.
Courses. San Francisco, 1968. Dave Haselwood.
The Song Mt. Tamalpais Sings. San Francisco, 1969. Maya.
Redwood Haiku and Other Poems. San Francisco, 1972. Cranium.
Ring Of Bone: Collected Poems 1950–1971. Bolinas, CA, 1973. Grey Fox.
How I Work As a Poet. Bolinas, CA, 1973. Grey Fox.
Selected Poems. San Francisco, 1976. Grey Fox.
I, Leo: an Unfinished Novel. Bolinas, CA, 1977. Grey Fox.
I Remain: The Letters of Lew Welch. Bolinas, CA, 1980. Grey Fox.

Philip Whalen

Born in Portland, Oregon on 20 October 1923, Whalen served in the US Army Air Force from 1943 until 1946 before attending Reed College where he studied Literature and Languages. Together with Lew Welch and Gary Snyder he moved to San Francisco and became a central figure in the San Francisco end of the Beat Generation movement, appearing as Warren Coughlin in Kerouac's *The Dharma Bums*. Whalen published several novels and numerous volumes of poetry, but his abiding interest was Zen Buddhism and after studying in Japan for a number of years in 1973 he was ordained as a Buddhist monk under the religious name of Zenshin Ryufu. He served as head monk at the Tassajara retreat centre in Big Sur and in 1991 was made abbot of the Hartford Street Zen Centre in San Francisco. He died in San Francisco on 26 June 2002.

Self Portrait, From Another Direction. San Francisco, 1969. Auerhahn.
Like I Say. New York, 1960. Totem/Corinth.
Memoirs of an Interglacial Age. San Francisco, 1960. Auerhahn.
Every Day. Eugene, OR, 1965. Coyote.
Highgrade: Doodles, Poems. San Francisco, 1966. Coyote.
T/O. San Francisco, 1967. Dave Haselwood.
You Didn't Even Try. San Francisco, 1967. Coyote.
The Invention of the Letter: a Beastly Morality. New York, 1967. Carp & Whitefish.
On Bear's Head. New York, 1969. Harcourt Brace.
Severance Pay: Poems 1967–1969. San Francisco, 1970. Four Seasons.
Scenes of Life at the Capital. Bolinas, CA, 1971. Grey Fox.
Imaginary Speeches For a Brazen Head. Los Angeles, 1972. Black Sparrow.
The Kindness of Strangers: Poems 1969–74. Bolinas, CA, 1976. Four Seasons.
Decompressions: Selected Poems. Bolinas, CA, 1977. Grey Fox.
Off The Wall: Interviews. Bolinas, CA, 1978. Four Seasons.
Enough Said: Poems 1974–79. San Francisco, 1980. Grey Fox.
The Diamond Noodle. Berkeley, 1980. Poltroon.
Heavy Breathing: Poems 1967–1983. San Francisco, 1980. Four Seasons.
For C. San Francisco, 1984. Arion.
Two Novels. Somerville, MA, 1985. Zephyr.
Canoeing Up Carbarga Creek. Buddhist Poems 1955–1986. Berkeley, 1996. Parallax.
Mark Other Place. Pacifica, CA, 1997. Big Bridge.
Overtime: Selected Poems. New York, 1999. Penguin.
Goofbook For Jack Kerouac. Pacifica, CA, 2001. Big Bridge.

John Wieners

Born in Milton, Massachusetts, on 6 January 1934 and studied at the famous Black Mountain College under Charles Olson and Robert Duncan from 1955 to 1956. He lived in San Francisco from 1958 until 1960 where he was a major force in the North Beach poetry scene, writing uncompromising poetry about his life as a drug user and as a homosexual. His first book, *The Hotel Wentley Poems*, published in 1958 was banned for the use of the word 'cock'. Wieners died in Boston, Massachusetts on 1 March 2002.

The Hotel Wentley Poems. San Francisco, 1958. Auerhahn.

Ace of Pentacles. New York, 1964. James F. Carr and Robert A. Wilson.

Chinoiserie. San Francisco, 1965. Dave Haselwood.

Pressed Wafer. Buffalo, NY, 1967. Gallery Upstairs.

Asylum Poems. New York, 1969. Angel Hair.

Nerves. London, 1970. Cape-Goliard.

Selected Poems. London, 1972. Jonathan Cape.

Playboy. Boston, 1972. Good Gay Poets.

Hotels. New York, 1974. Angel Hair.

Behind the State Capitol; or, Cincinnati Pike. Boston, 1975. Good Gay Poets.

Selected Poems 1958–1984. Santa Barbara, 1986. Black Sparrow.

Cultural Affairs In Boston. Santa Rosa, 1988. Black Sparrow.

ACKNOWLEDGEMENTS AND COPYRIGHTS